UNDERWORLD

UNDERWORLD

PETER CONRAD

Chatto & Windus
London

Published in 1992 by
Chatto & Windus Ltd
20 Vauxhall Bridge Road
London SW1V 2SA

A CIP catalague record for this book is
available from the British Library.

ISBN 0 7011 3895 5

Phototypeset by Intype, London
Printed in Great Britain by
Mackays of Chatham PLC
Chatham, Kent

1

Last week, in another part of the city, a human head turned up. It no longer owned a body. Sealed in a plastic bag and swaddled tightly in cloth, it was being used by some boys for a football. 'LOCAL RESIDENTS SHOCKED' said the newspapers in megaphonic capitals. 'This is getting out of hand,' said one of the local residents about the pummelled head, which police retrieved from a gutter.

We were spared photographs of the head. We had to imagine it. I was not quite sure how I should picture it. The pigmy heads in the ethnological museum, severed then shrunken, had the right leathery complexion, but they were too small for footballs. They were more like grinning, wizened golf balls. I needed to know for how long the head had existed independently, and the police were coy about that. Was it rock-hard or still all bruising, squelchy flesh? Had it been softened for a while in the water? Was its hair still growing? – a sign, now the eyes were extinguished, that life of a kind was continuing within, until the message at last got through. I pictured the dry strands, still unreeling from inside that dented globe. It seemed important to know about the hair. I had often thought, watching mine turn grey, that we grow our own premature shroud.

At least I knew about the part of the city where it happened. To be accurate, it was a valley where the city briefly gave up, to resume half a mile away on the other side. The valley baffled the city because it could not be built on. It was a fold of sliding, unstable land; its sides were catacombed cliffs and its bottom was a marsh. Once it had been an inlet of the river. Then the earth must have shaken itself and turned over in its sleep. The river ran away, though the floods in the valley each year remembered it.

The valley had become a shadowy replica of the city around it. Side roads led into it from the highways which sped by on both sides. Down those roads the homeless slouched or criminals scurried. People like that found refuge in the valley. And the industrious poor, confined to the upper floors of apartment blocks, sometimes made forays in at the weekend, to tend vegetables on patches of squashy ground they had claimed as their own. One of the side roads was bordered with impromptu huts, a way station for recent immigrants to the city. Here they waited until the city made room for them; if it declined to do so, they retreated into the valley. It was in one of the alleys between these huts that the boys were playing with the bagged, bandaged football.

The valley was on the far side of the city, on none of my usual tracks. I thought about going over there to poke around. I just wanted to see where it had happened. But what, I cautioned myself, would I be looking for, and why should the incident interest me so much? I began to feel ashamed of my curiosity. Still I could not stop thinking about it. It wasn't that I wanted to know, as the police did, whose head it was. I knew it could have been anyone's; why shouldn't it have been my own? I found myself checking, when I woke up in the middle of the night, that the join still held, that the neck was still there.

With an errand to do one day in the suburbs, I let myself drive past that vent which led into the valley. Three lanes of howling traffic protected me from it; the most I could manage was a quick glance sideways. Like brambles, the huts on either side of the track converged in the middle. Between them you would have to squeeze or wriggle to get into the valley. Behind them a cliff stood guard. The cliff was, I remember thinking, a terminus, an end to speculation, a wall of brick – in fact of limestone and shifting sands – against which you banged your head . . . perhaps until it came off in your hands. Here, the cliff announced, reality ran out. On the other side there were dreams.

2

The boy idly swung his stick as he debated the matter. What if he destroyed this little world he was looking at?

He was standing in a field among a raggle-taggle formation of cabbages. He had been walking down a track between the cabbages when he noticed the tower. It had not been there when he was last in the field. They must have built it overnight; it had grown faster than the cabbages with their knobbly stems and flopping leaves. His fingers fastened on his stick as he considered destroying it. One swipe would topple the thing. He stood there, the stick dangling as he weighed his power. What if?

He was on his way somewhere else when he saw that the tower had happened – erupted from earth to haul itself hand over fist up the sky. The track led from the hut he lived in across the vegetable patch to a stone wall which was his vantage point. The wall, a hasty assemblage of stones, declined after a few yards into a hillside; the hillside skidded into a valley. Having reached a seeping bottom, the valley shinned up another hill. There the city began again, along a rampart of flashing glass and skeletal steel.

He often spent afternoons astride the wall, watching events in the valley below. Someone hoeing the earth, or bent over scratching for potatoes. A scooter spluttering, or a donkey cart which wobbled over the cobbles. A water-logged field in which a car had stalled. Trousers, their legs fat with wind, flapping on a line. The systematic advance of a goat across the yard it was eating.

Late each afternoon the air down in the valley moistened into visibility. Then the fence of tall glass on the opposite hill began to burn. The row of buildings which marked the border between the valley and the city looked back towards the setting sun. Ignited planets flamed in the windows, and glared at the boy like eyes which scorched and seared. Though the sun was behind him, he could feel it, in their reflected fury, on his face. If he watched for long enough, the eyes blinked or were blinded. When the light in them went out, it was time for him to go. Back in the hut his grandfather would be eating. The dogs had already begun to wail.

That particular afternoon he did not even reach the wall, because while crossing the field he came upon the tower. It was a puzzle at first: a tilting chimney of grey dust, enveloping weeds and thistles into the structure it was raising. Each hairy leaf or thick frond was taken over as the platform for another storey. The plants became girders. But the thistle which anchored the thing was crooked. Whiskery and twisted, it reminded the boy of his grandfather. Its touch stung. Since it grew at a hobbling, arthritic angle, the tower whose spine it was wavered diagonally in the air. The workers, seething inside, were still adding floors. Didn't they know that after a few more inches the thing would over-reach and fall apart? The thistle would shake it off, like his grandfather shrugging to express indifference. Already, alive within, it seemed to shudder in the unsupporting air. He would not even need to bang it hard, as his grandfather did when slamming his mug on the table or kicking a dog which had got in the way. A nudge, a tap would do it.

The ants, he realised, had built it. He knew about their nests underground, the habitable mines they dug beneath the cabbages. A trap-door would open in the soil, through which they filed to forage, to which they returned with the grains or atoms they collected, rolling molecules of food along in teams as if they were boulders. If he sat down to watch, they would soon link black expeditionary columns around his feet and legs like rope with which they were tying him up. However many he killed, exterminating families and decimating societies by rubbing his hand on his legs, there were always more. What if they were able to tighten their black threads round him and truss him up? What if, intent on food, they invaded the soft, edible inside of him – down the ears, up the nose, through the mouth? Could they hollow out your head like the earth in which they burrowed?

He asked his grandfather once whether they could do this to you. 'Don't be bloody silly', his grandfather said. So he was still not sure. But since he had later seen his grandfather pour the steaming contents of a kettle through the trap-door, the skylight of the ants' domain under the cabbages, he thought it might be possible.

This time, defying his grandfather, the ants had taken a greater risk. This hill they had built above ground. The leaves of the plants were plaited into galleries, concreted together with earth they had aerated, reducing clods to grey, fine grains. He knelt on the path to inspect this small world, while he thought over how he should deal with it. The tower silently buzzed. He could see nothing, but it gave off a charge, like one of the wires which his grandfather, working on a stolen car, had told him once was live. This meant that the wire was able to kill you. His grandfather later chased him with it, alleging that it could bite.

He had learned about killing things from his grandfather, whose main pleasure it was. Sometimes the killings were in order to eat: a scrawny hen which he had to position across the block while his grandfather swung the axe; in the case of a rabbit, a slap of the palm on a twitching neck. Or the killings could be to safeguard their property: his grandfather, prising snails off the cabbage leaves, demonstrated how you ground them under your boot, heard their shells crackle like shattered glass and felt your heel slither on their unprotected innards. Other deaths were for enjoyment's sake: a stray cat might be served a treat of poisoned fish bones. If there were no animals handy, his grandfather damaged plants, grabbing blooms or bushes as he passed and discarding the flowers or leaves at once, content with the thought of ruptured wood and bleeding greenery. He was determined to make his mark. 'Bloody pests,' he would say of the birds whose nests he raided in the spring. 'It got in me way' was his verdict on a branch he had lopped off or a flower he decapitated without altering his pace.

The stick was his grandfather's gift to him. It was a trophy of war: his grandfather had brained a dog with it once. Not one of their own dogs, but a mongrel which scavenged from the shanties over near the highway. It disliked his grandfather. One

5

day it took up a position on the cobbled lane which ran down from the shanties through sterile fields to the bottom of the valley; when it saw him coming, it began to growl. 'Talk about the hound of hell,' said his grandfather, working up the encounter into a story. He collected a lump of stone and a spar of wood from the ditch, and dared the dog to combat. The wood, which had a rusted nail in it, crunched against the side of the dog's head. 'I landed him one all right,' said his grandfather, aglow with the memory.

Having brought the stick home to show off the stripe of blood and black hair around the nail, his grandfather decided to whittle it. He had a gadget, stolen from one of the cars, which unfolded into a cutlery cabinet of knife blades, together with a cork-screw, a pair of pincers for chopping the ends off your nails with and a file for smoothing their edges. He thought of this as his survival kit. Opening it up so that all the blades glinted maliciously in the sun, he would say, 'I could get by with this in the wild. This is all I'd need. Anyway,' he would add – glancing round at the tumbledown sheds and bankrupt farms and potholed, puddled tracks between them – 'we're in the wild already, to all intents.' He illustrated: with this blade he could kill the beast, with that one skin it, with the other have its guts out. Should a bottle turn up in the wilderness (as it often did here, stolen too), he had the means of uncapping or uncorking it.

Meanwhile, it served to whittle the club he had used on that surly dog. But he didn't carve it into any shape. He hacked at it, digging knots out with the prong of the corkscrew, pulling it apart by hand when the grain gave way. The boy – who was not more than five years old then, it was a while ago – sat watching him, and wondered what the knives were about to create from the timber or disclose within it. His grandfather sliced and sawed, with the tip of his tongue stuck lizard-like between his teeth, angry enough to bite that off too.

'What are you making?' the boy asked him.

'A pile of sawdust,' said his grandfather. 'Here, take the flaming thing.' He tossed it away, half hoping that it might crackle into fire and char itself in obedience to his curse. Instead it thudded, obtuse and uncombustible, into the dust.

6

The boy gathered it up and spent an hour on the ledge of rock above the valley looking at it: its sinews and fibres, its navel-like whorls, and the brutal evidence of amputation. He had been looking at it ever since. They were inseparable; it counted as another limb. He used to sleep with it, though now it waited for him all night in the corner of the room. He never took a knife to it, and did not need to. He could picture its transformations without having to punish it into some form other than its own, which was blunt and block-like, but to him as malleable as Adam's rib.

Sometimes it was an animal, warm and somnolent beside him on the lumpy mattress, curled despite its angularity into the empty crook of his body. Or it could be a buoyant plank, a straw to clutch at to save him from foundering in bad dreams on nights when the dogs yelped in fury or moaned in despair while the moon turned the valley to a ghost of itself. For a while it was a stick person, and a companion he could talk to. It had no arms or legs and only a stubborn knot where a head might once have been, but the boy found it easy to invent the accidents which did away with these appendages. Imitating the planes which shrieked low over the valley on their way in to land, he often wished wings on the piece of wood. He would throw it, hoping that one day it would veer off on a course of its own and roar like the planes towards the vanishing-point of his world. But it always plopped down to ground. Finally he accepted the fact that it would probably never fly.

Once he gave up the belief that it was alive, it acquired another use for him. As a wand it had failed him, but it might serve as a tool. It could prod and poke, dig holes and discover things, thought not at the cost of killing them, like his grandfather's pocket-sized scalpels and cutlasses. With it he could lever up the stones between which the lizards flicked and trace the crevices where they pretended not to exist. He could scratch away the soil of the vegetable patch and identify the white filaments of root unravelling in quest of food. He could operate on a weed whose stem, if crushed, bled milk, which his grandfather rubbed into his warts. He could scrape the moss from rocks, though he wasn't able to understand how this fuzzy green hair grew from an unnourishing, unbreakable skull of stone. He also used the stick to draw with. Near the cave which the dogs guarded, the earth was as smooth and fickle as sand. He sometimes spent the morning scribbling on the slate of dust. His grandfather erased the drawings with his boots.

Now the stick hovered in judgment over the ant-hill. He raised it, and rehearsed a downward chop like that used by his grandfather on the necks of rabbits. Then he stopped the stick before it descended. He admired the tapering funnel of refined soil held in place by the weeds: why knock it down? But he needed to know. What were those shuttling chores and urgent deliveries which went on in there, so that the grey pillar shivered with the flurry of a million motions and motives inside it? I could, he thought, just give it a push – elbow it, help it along.

The stick, however, dragged his hand along with it and, cleaving the air like a scythe, battered the tower of powder near its base.

The thistle shook, the pillar came apart in a rain of specks. Its piled-up hierarchy tumbled around his feet. Before he could look down, still numb with the shock of what he or the stick had done, the desert which used to be a city had begun to move. The granules of soil boiled with black pellets. If you knocked a head off, if you sliced one open, this is how it would look. The ant-hill was a sectioned brain; it teemed with frantic, expiring thoughts. And now the black creatures like desperate seeds with a mission to discharge were hunting through the soft fall-out of their levelled building. They raked and sifted until each of them found the white capsule it had to save. Within minutes, the exodus had begun. Lining up, the ants made a detour around the boy and carried their eggs away. They were off to begin the world over again somewhere else.

'Wilf!'

It was his grandfather's voice, calling him from the hut. The dogs understood his rasp of annoyance, and began to call the boy names of their own.

'Wilf! Get over here!' By the time he looked around his grandfather was lurching down the trail between the cabbages. He had put his hat on, and dragged it down tight over his temples, so that its brim obliterated his eyes; he wore his jacket, and he had done up the top button of a dirty shirt which had no collar. He meant business. 'Come on,' he said, 'what are you playing at? Can't you see what the time is?' The eyes, Wilf noticed, were ablaze along the glass parapet of the valley. The last evacuees were quitting the demolished city at his feet; those which had left first were laying foundation stones on the other side of the field. As if shaken awake, he resumed his own life and remembered what he had to do.

'Get your coat on,' said his grandfather, throwing it at him. 'Forget about having to work, did you?' From the pocket of his own jacket he pulled a green bat with its underside painted red. As Wilf wriggled into his coat and stowed his stick in a safe place beneath the wall, his grandfather urged him on with a shove of the bat, harder than the blow which had brought down the ant-hill. On they went, the boy taking care to keep ahead of the lumbering old man, towards the wall overlooking the valley.

The fire had gone out of the eyes on the opposite ridge. They were bleary now, as if it were already next morning and they had suffered through a bad night.

3

'ONE OF THESE days I'll put your lights out,' muttered his grandfather as he lunged along the ridge beside the wall. He was addressing the buildings on the opposite ridge, whose rooms – now that the sun no longer scorched them – had winked into visibility. A hundred boxes of possessions already hung there, suspended in the sky; soon there would be hundreds more. The sight enraged his grandfather, who remembered a time before the city had pushed its border that close and raised a wall with a spine of broken glass on purpose, he felt, to keep him out. He devised revenges during afternoons in the vegetable patch. He dreamed of arson or inundation, or of the buildings detonated and crumbling to their knees in a flurry of dust. But every evening the rooms were switched on all the same. To their owners, he was a lame, elderly insect going about its trivial business on the other side of the valley.

'I'll teach you,' he mumbled, 'to look down on me.' Then he belched.

He had eaten a piece of meat and some pickled onions before setting out. He admitted that the pickled onions didn't agree with him. Aware of the violence they always did to his insides, he disliked the very look of them: bottled in brine on the shelf, they looked as malevolent as the ulcer his mother had once had cut out of her, which she brought home for a souvenir and kept in a jar on a table beside her bed – a brown, wizened bud of flesh. His mother would often stare at the thing in the jar, wondering at the contents of her body. Still, the memory of that ulcer did not warn him off the bottle of vinegary pickles. 'A man's got to eat,' he would say, crunching the onions. Within ten minutes they would be resolving themselves into acid and suffocating fumes. For a while it would feel as if he had swallowed a grenade. At last he was able to belch.

The sound was not a satisfied after-effect. It roared and rumbled from inside him, like a dyspeptic volcano. Arriving in the open air, it unrolled a long, rattling croak, like a machine gun working through a round of cartridges. It was useful to him as a means of expression. He aimed it now at the buildings, and hurled the sound across the valley like a thunderbolt. For a moment he thought that the lighted walls had repulsed the missile and bounced it back to him as an echo, but it was only the noise of a klaxon from the highway. One of the rooms switched itself off at that instant: perhaps his cannon-ball of gas had made its mark.

Despite his satisfaction, he felt obliged to complain to Wilf. His ailments were his prerogative, his privilege, which the boy was supposed to respect; they were also a warning of what life turned out to be like when you gave up playing with sticks. 'My stomach's acting up again,' he said. 'You'll have to go and get me some of that mixture.' Every month Wilf was sent out of the valley to a chemist in a side street beyond the highway to replace his grandfather's supply of a chalky, chocolate-coloured medicine with soothed the upsets inside him. The old man would swill from it, and abuse it as he did so: 'Filthy stuff. Is that chemist trying to do me in, or what?' After which he would belch, this time with gently melodious relish. 'Wait and see,' he said to Wilf, who backed away from the belches as if from blows, 'you'll have a stomach like this yourself one day. Then you'll know.' It seemed to Wilf an argument in favour of never growing up. Meanwhile he regarded the pickled onions as a vinegary collection of evil eyes.

Another belch ricocheted from his grandfather as he advanced down the rough path. One of his legs, stiffened by arthritis, was shorter than the other; the disparity did not slow him down but accelerated his pace. He used the shorter, stiffer leg for propulsion. It struck the ground at an angle, and he swerved the good leg and the rest of his body behind it in an arc. The bulk of him swivelled and tilted above the unequal pins, which he used as nimbly as crutches. His jaw was white with the bristles of whiskers like shoots piercing dry cracked soil. The rest of his face receded beneath the brow of his hat.

He removed the hat only to sleep. It lent him authority, he thought. It also, since he had rolled the brim at a rakish angle over his eyes, gave him a useful air of menace. 'A man can't be without his hat,' he often said. He had started Wilf off already with a cap, which was in the pocket of the jacket he handed him. Wilf did not get the point of it, and in any case it was a poor fit – too large by several years, so that it slipped from side to side of his head and in gusts of wind was liable to blow off. 'You're a pin-head,' said his grandfather whenever this happened. 'That's what's wrong with you. Can't even keep your hat on. Your head'll come loose one of these days.'

His grandfather had already rotated round a corner, where a pack of dogs began to yap, yelp, bay and wail, clattering their chains like a dungeon of felons. Wilf ran to catch up. They had always had a dog. They usually had several dogs: there were eight at present. They were all called Dog. His grandfather, when the second arrived, forbade anything so foolish as individual names for them. That created attachments, and the dogs were not pets. Even the occasional bitch was called Dog, though his grandfather was opposed to bitches on principle, because they distracted the dogs from their job.

The interchangeable Dogs could still be distinguished by breed. The pack contained an Alsatian and a German shepherd, and a pit bull with the chilling eyes and snout of a white devil. These were stolen from the gardens of the richer suburbs, after being quietened with lumps of doped meat. The others were mongrels, recruited from the lanes which led off the highway, cast out from the back doors of the apartment buildings as offenders against the racial rules. They came and went, discharged from duty on the chain gang if they fell ill or happened to be injured by their colleagues in the competition for food. They were tethered to tree stumps or fence posts or spikes in the ground, positioned far enough apart so they could snap at one another. There were feuds between them, though their chains were shortened if they seemed liable to rip each other to pieces. That would have been uneconomical. No one could pass through their barricade of teeth. If he got them when they were young enough, Wilf's grandfather teased and tormented them to warp their tempers. Often he told Wilf, 'Go and aggravate the dogs for me. Give them a clout with that lump of wood, then it might be good for something.'

His grandfather fed them irregularly, just to worsen their dispositions. They were, after all, the guardians of the loot. Sometimes they howled all night long, calling each other names or sobbing for the home they had lost. In the thick darkness outside the cave, they rehearsed carnage whenever a twig snapped or a tree creaked. You couldn't see them unless the maddening moon was full or, down at the bottom end of the valley, the gasworks flared; but you could always hear their growls of grievance and spasms of fury, and the perpetual rattling of chains.

Today was one of the days when Wilf's grandfather had chosen to feed them. He had a bag of scraps, with a few skinny rabbits and some slippery offal. The bag was soaked with blood: he did not believe in cooking for them. 'In the wild,' he said, 'they like it raw. They're wolves, that's what.'

He scattered the mess at intervals along the line of chained sentries. The Dogs snarled, more concerned to steal from adjoining piles that to eat their own portions. The Alsatian at the end of the row looked on dolefully. Wilf's grandfather noted at once the loss of appetite: a first sign of weakness; first of the terminal symptoms. 'That one's had it,' he said to Wilf. 'Fallen by the wayside. You can let him go.' As Wilf advanced, the Dogs crouched like gunners behind the weapons in their mouths. He reached across and unchained the Alsatian.

The Dogs, understanding, went back to their food. The Alsatian also understood. It drooled foam and shivered; it glanced blankly in Wilf's direction. Then, with its tail depressed, it limped away towards the bushes. The ground sloped upwards beside the cave. The Alsatian thought it over, discounted the climb, and shouldered its way into the bushes.

'That's the thing about animals,' Wilf's grandfather said. 'They don't kick up a fuss. No weeping and carrying on. Just off into the bushes to croak on the quiet. I'll have to talk to the lads about a replacement for him.'

Wilf looked back as they turned another corner away from the guzzling, quarrelling Dogs. The bushes did not move. In its crypt of thorns and brambles, the Alsatian patiently waited.

Around the corner, other dogs (not called Dog, not tethered, existing merely to enjoy themselves) raced to greet them. They belonged to the lads, as Wilf's grandfather called them. The lads were a family of thieves who dispersed throughout the city at night and brought back cars, wallets, passports, jewels, electrical appliances and occasionally dogs. They lived in the outbuildings of an abandoned farm, around a paved yard. A meal was being cooked in the farm's kitchen.

The men, the lads themselves, were gathered in the draughty barn, drinking around a brazier. As the fire sparked, faces came and went in the darkness: three masks leered out of the dark then vanished into it, reappearing an instant later with different expressions. The fire lashed their cheeks with strips of red and orange, like daubed-on war paint; it deepened the wrinkles round their eyes to trenches. They were deciding on their shopping list for the night. 'Ern,' called one of them to Wilf's grandfather, 'come over here.'

The old man swung himself round on the axis of his inflexible leg, and made towards the fire. They could surely pick up a new Dog for him on their rounds. One of the lads thrust a stick into the brazier; the fire hissed at them. 'We was wondering when you'd turn up,' said another lad. 'What's your fancy tonight, then?'

This, Wilf knew, would take time. At the door of the barn, a dog which was not a Dog deciphered the traces of all the Dogs on his legs and hands. Across the yard in the kitchen, something sizzled angrily and someone swore. Deep in the barn, away from the brazier where the men grumbled and chortled, he heard another sound: the patter of a single voice chasing itself, swooping into shrillness, arrested for a moment by a groan, punctuated by the muffled cheers of an unseen mob. Wilf blinked his way through the darkness.

Sprawled on a seat which had been ripped from a car, its

leather punctured and its stuffing tugged out by the handful, a boy of his own age had his ear pressed to a box. Wilf knew the boy: Horry was his name, the son of one of the lads. 'What's that then?' asked Wilf.

'Football,' said the boy. 'My Dad nicked me a transistor. It's the Robins and the Magpies. I'm for the Magpies. What's your team?'

'I don't know, I don't have one. What's the difference?'

'The Robins are red,' said Horry, heaving a sigh, 'and the Magpies are black and white. You can tell from their jerseys.'

'No, I mean how do you know which one is yours?'

'My Dad told me. We've always been for the Robins here. Anyway, the Magpies can't kick the ball. They'd be the team for you.' The commentator inside the radio hooted in glee: the Magpies had just scored a goal. Never mind, thought Horry. Wilf would not know the difference.

'Have you ever seen them? You know, gone to a match?'

'Of course not. My Dad says this is better. And you don't have to pay.' The stadium was on the far side of the city, an oval of concrete tiers with floodlights turning the night sky into glaring noon.

Horry turned up the volume and began to interpret. 'See,' he said to Wilf as the transistor spat distracted sound like the crackling brazier with its sparks, 'he's got him down, he's booting him in the head, now he's going for the kidneys. Come on the Robins!' The commentator was having hysterics.

'Turn that thing down,' yelled Horry's father from the other end of the barn, 'or I'll have it off you.'

Horry thumbed the dial back as far as it would go and pressed the box to his ear. Wilf could hear nothing but a tinny rattling. Miles away, the stadium like a concrete trumpet expelled noise into the air; the box picked up its vibrations and breathed them back into the trumpet-shaped cavity of Horry's ear. He squirmed on the car seat as he followed the movements of the invisible game, and vaulted along with a player who leapt for the ball.

Watching him twitch and gibber, Wilf wondered if he had taken a fit. 'Are you all right?' he said. But there was no room

15

in Horry's head for Wilf's voice. And he heard his grandfather whistling for him from the open door of the barn.

'What was going on over there?' asked his grandfather.

'He was listening to the football. He told me who his team was.'

'Bloody silly,' grunted his grandfather, and belched as an exclamation mark. The lads had given him some spirits to drink; the alcohol was already gnawing at his stomach. 'Waste of time,' he added. Games annoyed him. Any kind of play made him grumble. He disliked the idea of boys or grown men running round in circles or kicking balls for no better reason than to burn energy and enjoy motion. It was all an evasion of the truth. Life for him meant to grub a living, and also to suffer stomach pains. There was no surplus to expend in befriending dumb sticks or chasing stupid balls.

From the kitchen a woman's voice called the lads to their food. They drifted out of the barn, careful not to answer the summons too quickly. Their power expressed itself in their dawdling leisure. Now they lingered to say goodbye to Ern, while the woman's voice offered to bash Horry. 'We'll see you later then, Ern,' said Horry's father, and strolled off across the yard.

'Are we coming back here?' Wilf asked his grandfather. 'After, I mean?'

He knew by now that when people said they would see you later, it was not necessarily a promise. But it might be a guarantee of something to look forward to; he never gave up hope. Whenever the phrase turned out not to mean what it said, he could not help feeling disappointed.

Tonight, the alternative was the usual routine in the hut. He would watch his grandfather doze in front of the fire, his mouth sagging open like a trap, his arms jerking up as if yanked by unseen strings. The head tumbling sideways and resting on the chest seemed about to roll off, as if only fraying tendons attached it to his shoulders. The body meanwhile, no longer commanded from the top, rumbled and quaked independently. His leg was liable to strike out sideways with a wakefully accurate aim. Then he would shudder, reposition his head squarely on his shoulders, and say, 'Don't you think I was asleep. I was watching you. I saw you eat that biscuit' or 'I saw you playing with yourself' or 'I saw you poke your tongue out at me. One of these days I'll have that stick of yours for kindling. Can't you go to bed without me telling you?' But soon his neck would slacken again, his head would slump, and the body with its four unquiet crab-like feelers would start into life. His grandfather seemed to hover between this world and another, and often sat up with a start and a whinny, eyes wide with the terror of something foreseen across the border between sleep and waking.

Would all this be postponed tonight? Would they see the lads later?

'No,' his grandfather said, 'we're not coming back here. But they might come down and see us. There's one or two things they need.'

Wilf did not ask for more details. It was enough that this night would be slightly different from all the others.

Before they climbed down to the tunnel, there was one last pause, a final station on the journey they made most days of their lives: the fountain. Wilf heard it drooling and splashing ahead of them, spilling into its trough of stones and seeping back into the spring; from there it would find its way up again through layers of rock into the mouth of tarnished copper. Its liquid tongue burbled about arcane channels beneath the parched clods and compressed boulders – perhaps about the slowly stirring, heaving lake on which it all rested. The water had a reputation. From all over the valley people trudged with bottles or buckets, and waited in respectful queues as if at a shrine. It was always cool, and it tasted sweet. There were rumours of its having cured the sick, at which Wilf's grandfather hooted. 'It might be able to cure your thirst,' he said, 'but that's about all. And I wouldn't drink it meself unless there was nothing stronger going.'

The fountain thrust itself accidentally through a wall of rock, but over the years a home had been built for it, to make its emergence seem less arbitrary and to save it from wasting itself on the hungry dust of the path. First the spout of copper, with a sink below; against the rough wall, an alcove of tiles with a carved face cemented into it.

The tube of brass, like a protruding gullet, stuck through the lips of a faun. Its eyes were wild, its hair tousled (or else twined, where its ears should have been, into horns); its mouth gaped to make way for the rivulet of spittle or prophecy. Among all the valley's livestock there was no creature like it. The horns which prodded through the hair belonged to a goat, but the look of cunning in its narrowed eyes was nothing like the undiscriminating stare of a goat, which only wondered if you were edible or not; a wolf would have been closer, though the creature from within whose body the fountain rose was sleeker, less shaggy than a wolf; maybe a fox, kin to those which ate their way through the hen coops and rabbit hutches of the valley. It was a hybrid beast, a joking idea of bestiality, crossbreeding all the animals which had ever been kneaded together from clay and stiffened with shavings of rock in the valley. It was the image of every terror which scratches at the door or claws its way into the head.

Wilf himself once felt it fastening on his chest, sniffing and salivating before it bit, and woke up in a sweat. Afterwards he searched for it in the room. It wasn't there, but then it reared into form again when his eyes were shut. That night he went to sleep with his fist gripping the stick. Horry used to report sightings of the actual beast in the hills behind the cave of contraband, describing eyes like hot coals, teeth like sabres, and a tail which ended in a prong. Wilf passed on the story to his grandfather, who scoffed at it. For him, there was nothing unknown in the valley, no animal he had not at one time or another killed. 'You'd believe anything,' he said. 'You don't know the difference.' The difference between what, Wilf wanted to ask, but thought better of it.

The fountain gargled in the grey air. Wilf, who knew what his grandfather thought of him for believing in things he hadn't seen, decided not to ask about the white shape backing away from the water spout. But his grandfather also saw it: a cloud, except that it pulsed like a protesting heart. 'What in hell is *that*?' he asked.

Wilf would not know the answer; the fact that he addressed

the question to himself out loud hinted at doubt, even dread. Wilf wished he had not left the stick behind.

Now the shape gathered itself together and became a woman. The cloud she had floated on consisted of her hair, unravelling around her head like a sticky cobweb, and a white smock, over which she had pulled a cardigan with its buttons hastily stuck in the wrong holes. She was old, and she looked loony – or was it just that one eye was awry in its socket, and conducted its own separate scrutiny of a world out of sight around the corner? Though she had come to the fountain, she brought no bucket or bottle with her.

'Hello, missis,' Ern said to her. Wilf had not heard this tone of cautious courtesy in his voice before.

'You gave the boy a fright,' he added, to apologise to himself for his deference. She still did not speak.

'You're out late,' he went on, hoping this would extort some explanation from her. It did not.

'Are you lost, or what?' He could think of nothing else. Shouldn't she have been afraid of him?

Angry at her and nervous, he belched. 'Pardon me,' he said, and then was angry at himself for such cowardly good manners.

'Yairs,' she said, stringing out the syllable pensively, as if she had thought it over before deciding to pardon him.

Wilf meanwhile was looking her up and down. The hair was a thicket, a white forest. The dislocated eye swivelled sideways. But the good one fixed his grandfather and held him at a distance, as if down the length of a gun barrel. The smock had a dirty hem. The muddled cardigan's pockets drooped: a foliage of papers and handkerchiefs poked out of one; lettuce leaves grew from the other. She was unlike any woman he had ever seen before. The assorted wives of the lads for instance, who were forever stirring pots or wringing clothes or beating children with their capable hands. He could not imagine them wandering like this one, or staring like her, or maintaining such a baleful, jittery silence. And then there was his mother, whom he must have seen but could not remember. When she deposited him with his grandfather, she became an absence, a vacant place filled up with his grandfather's stories – she ran off with a sailor who jumped ship; she's a barmaid in town somewhere; no, someone saw her patrolling the avenue in high heels last week; she was always good-for-nothing; it was her who ate the apple – and with Wilf's vague efforts to imagine the opposite of whatever his grandfather told him, as difficult as dressing his splintery stick in flesh.

Either way, this was not her. A mother was an idea of sustenance and comfort. This woman was stringy, raddled, absorbed in herself. Her body contained no folds or yielding valleys to nestle in. Her good eye had travelled over him, but merely to be sure that there was nothing here to delay her. It passed on, obliterating him.

His grandfather hesitated between annoyance and intimidation. 'Are you all right then?' The question concealed a plea for the usual answer.

'Yes, of course I am.' That was not the usual answer, at least not when said with such disdainful gruffness.

Then she changed her mind. 'No, I'm not all right.' That, as an answer, was even less usual. She said it crossly, crankily. It was not a request for sympathy; it implied that he might be to blame.

He did not ask for particulars. She gave them anyway, blurting them out. 'I've got a splitting headache. I can't see for it. I can't find what I came out for. I might just as well be blind. Are you looking for it too?'

Wilf wished that his grandfather would ask what she meant. The old man was too bewildered; in any case he did not need to.

'First I watch the sun go down from up on top. And then I wait for the fires to start, the fires in the sky. I've got a place I can see from over there. Then tonight I lost my way. My head feels like it's had a cleaver through it. I shouldn't have looked for so long when the sun was going down. It all started because I came out early to pick these greens. After it went down, everything was yellow, even though I knew it was already dark. All I could see was sunflowers, but I know they don't grow round here. I always take that same path – where's it gone to? And I've missed the fires tonight.'

She overcame her annoyance in the telling. She explained it as carefully and patiently as if it were someone else's problem. She seemed to be accustomed to the practical jokes planned on her by time and space: the unpunctual fires, the path which had been rolled up like a carpet and unrolled somewhere else. Neither was she expecting assistance. Sooner or later the wound in her head would heal and her eyes would be able to sort out black from white; the spinning earth would slow down, the path settle back under her feet, and the fires flare up again, feeding on air.

Wilf's grandfather said 'What fire are you talking about? Do you need some kindling?' He must be alarmed, Wilf thought, if he humoured her like this.

'The fires down that way,' she said, pointing across an uncertain arc. 'You can see them all night long. They're blue, there are these pipes they come out of. Don't say you haven't seen them. Though it could be I'm the only one that can.' She shook her head, saddened by the effort of explanation.

The old man smirked in recognition, and also in contempt. She must be off her head. 'It's the gas works you're after, is it? You missed your turning to the lookout. You've come down too far.'

They were close to the bottom of the valley, where a road followed a backbone of bumpy rock between pits of sand and squelching marshes. The barricade of lighted apartments had dropped behind the ridge above them, as if collapsing into a sudden crevice of earth. They had only to scramble down a last slope of footloose clods and they would be at the tunnel. But further up, half way along another track which inched between piles of rubble from the apartment buildings to the tunnel, there was a view down the length of the valley as far as the gas works.

The valley narrowed before it reached the river, which had withdrawn when the land cracked and rearranged itself. There on waste ground they had built a city of drums, pipes, chimneys and silver scaffolding. When the sun shone, no one noticed it. The apparatus of metal disappeared in the reflected glare of the river. Flames breathed from chimneys, as if a match had been struck to ignite the old man's belches, but the daylight erased them. You heard a brief hiss of evacuation, and saw a simmering

21

agitation in the air: it might have been a patch of sky boiling. After dark, however, the blue fires had no competition from the sun. They gushed out in a panic, expelled by explosions, and opened into a garden of poisonous blooms whose petals fluttered for a moment before they fell; the flowers whitened round the edges, curled in the heat and were consumed.

Wilf's grandfather took an elaborate pleasure in showing the woman how far she had strayed. 'You go back up there until you get onto the gravel, then along the top of that hill. When you get to where the two paths meet up, you take the left hand one. Follow that and you'll be back where you belong. Want me to go through it again?' She shook her head indignantly. He could not resist a final challenge. 'What's the gas works to you, anyway? Are you on the night shift?'

She had started up the hill, but she turned back and glared at him, bringing her good eye to bear. 'I'm watching,' she said, 'that's all.'

'What for?' he called after her.

Striding off, she muttered an answer. By now he was out of earshot: she had managed to have the last word.

The old man, who disliked being outwitted, gave Wilf a shove to cheer himself up. 'What are you dawdling for? Mad old bat. Silly as a snake.' There were said to be snakes in the valley – not necessarily silly ones, but silly was the most wounding word the old man knew. 'One of these nights she'll run into the lads. They'll knock the gas works out of her.' He grinned at the thought of it, then grimaced: she had aggravated his indigestion.

He pushed Wilf towards the slope which led to the road. The boy glanced over his shoulder at the path, but the dusk had rubbed her out. 'Watch where you're going,' said his grandfather. 'I'll give you a clip on the ear.' He grabbed Wilf's arm, to use him as a walking stick on this last untrustworthy stretch of ground. The boy bent under his weight, edging down sideways. There were cars on the road below, sounding their horns at both sides of the tunnel. 'She's made us late', grumbled his grandfather.

Wilf – remembering the frazzled hair and the needling eye, the paper and the greenery spilling out of her pockets, the urgent marching pace with which she had mounted the hill – wondered who she was and what she was for. She was the kind of figure who invaded his dreams, mouthing words he did not understand, telling him things which would make him cry out and wake up, glad he had already forgotten them.

Dislodging pebbles and kicking lumps of earth to dust, he scrambled onto the road, his grandfather's fingers digging into his shoulder. They were at the bottom of the valley. Half way up, the woman had found her lookout, and stared towards the aperture where the valley tipped into the river and the gas works rehearsed the end of it all.

4

MY GUESS IS that he was taking a short cut through the valley. The man whose head it was, I mean. They say that it could not have belonged to anyone who lived in the valley: his expensive root canal work proved that. (Only his dental repairs vouched for whoever it was he had once been.)

Everyone knew about the short cut, and the risks you ran in exchange for the time you saved. It was popular in the mornings and evenings, when the avenues on either side of the valley were choked with cars. I remember taking it once myself. You swung into an alley between some shanties, then caught up with the paved lane which once linked the defunct farms. You had to tolerate abuse from mange-ridden moulting dogs and grubby children.

Further on you had to beware of bandits, who held up cars and then went to earth untraceably with their pickings – car radios, car stereos, portable phones and the wallets of the drivers, who were allowed to proceed after their appliances and their identity cards had been removed from them; once in a while, a car would be confiscated, driven into hiding somewhere across the fields to have its identity altered with a coat of paint, while its owner hiked back to the highway.

The lane curled down a hill to the floor of the valley. There it thrust itself into a tunnel, which jerked round an abrupt bend. The bend was forced on it by the whim of a creek embedded in the valley, which slopped over its banks whenever it rained and made the road a bog; the tunnel happened because a railway line once branched through the valley to connect the rusty industrial outpost of tanners and metal-beaters and furniture-makers near the northern edge with the city which had fed it workers and fed on their work; the disused trestles still roofed over the road.

Here there was a problem. The road as it burrowed beneath the railway line crashed headlong into darkness, uncertainty. It might have gone underground. And because of the bend, you could never be sure that there was not another car rushing towards you. Two cars could not pass in there: the road had been meant for wagons drawn by donkeys or (if the farms were affluent) by horses reprieved from the glue factory further up the valley.

After the first collisions, the valley evolved a system for determining right of way. During the hours when the short cut was most in use, two signallers manned posts at either end of the tunnel. They could not see each other, but communicated by shouts and whistles or by counting the numbers of cars they allowed through; they communicated with the drivers who were their customers by holding up little bats, green and red, with which someone else (not the signallers themselves surely) had once played ping-pong. They expected a tip from their regulars. At Christmas they expected a bonus. With some of the proceeds they built themselves sentry boxes – a few upright planks with a ceiling of tin – at both entries to the tunnel, so they could wave you through with the green bat or keep you waiting with the red one even when the rain churned up the road and made the creek boil over.

There were two of them, a boy and an old man. If you crossed the valley from east to west, you got the boy first and the old man at the other end of the tunnel; west to east, you travelled through the ages backwards. They must have been related. The tunnel, linking them down its echoing length, was the defile of time which had produced them both and would produce an indefinite number of others when they deserted their posts. For the few seconds it took to get through the tunnel, time ran both ways at once. They allowed you, by reversing their ping-pong bats, to speed forward from youth to age and then to back-track from age to youth. Perhaps, during those few seconds, the boy sprinted ahead of the car to reappear at the exit as a grim and whiskered caricature of himself, having revved through six decades in as many instants; then, when you drove in from the west, the old man could just as well have decomposed into ash

25

and air the moment you passed him, only to be reconstituted on the other side as the boy.

All the same, it was only supposition which related them. Their customers, travelling through at speed, did not pause to ask questions, or even to look. Valley-dwellers were notoriously oblique about personal identity and family relationships. And any likeness between this pair would have to be imaginary, because (as I remember from my one glimpse) the boy's face was still unwritten – open-eyed in amazement, with nothing as yet concealed behind those eyes – while the old man's was so scrawled and scribbled on, cross-hatched and coloured-in, revised a dozen times and then written on diagonally once the horizontal lines were full, that it could not longer be read.

The old man's flesh had creased or puckered over his bones. All expressions were lurking somewhere between the droopy curtains of skin. He could make his face leer or threaten or beam or, with a lax jaw and watery eyes, appeal for pity. But the expressions got mixed up and sent out contradictory signals, as if he were brandishing the green and red bats at once. When he meant to be genial he looked malign, with eyebrows like barbed wire and jagged uneven teeth. Drivers giving him money never knew whether he was pleased with the sum, or furious.

The boy, however, never checked the value of the coins – to him they were interchangeable, since what could he spend them on in the valley? – and he stared at all the drivers with the same mystified respect. They might have been in transit from outer space, with their dark glasses and their percussive music and the gadgets they could talk into except when they were going through the tunnel: for those tense moments, they were alone, bereft, sealed off from radio waves and the satellites which made their telephones work. What world was it (the boy must have asked himself) that contained such people? The old man, however, could tell the difference between these glistening, briefly grounded strangers. He briskly catalogued each car and driver as he flagged them past. They had all been through here before. It was the straight gate and the narrow way.

Everyone left the tunnel with a rush of grateful acceleration. Still, if you were travelling across the valley like the sun from east to west, the trickiest sectors lay ahead. After the tunnel, the road had to skirt the marsh into which all the valley's effluents and sluices seeped. In the winter, the marsh sometimes extended across the road. A car would have to feel for firmness as it crept along. The road became notional, a tightrope stretched across a stagnant lake of mud. The old man and the boy would only vouch for your passage through the tunnel; they accepted no responsibility for flooding further on.

Once you survived the marsh, there was another hill to climb, steeper than the one which had eased you down towards the tunnel. The road zigzagged between the rough stone walls which once divided the fields and separated the farms.

This is where hold-ups were likeliest to occur. The gangs could hide behind the walls, and across the fields there were tracks – as spidery and as teasingly interrupted as the lines on your hand – which they used when scampering off with whatever they had relieved you of. After a while, the fields tumbled over the edge of a precipice, sliding down a chute to perdition. The earliest slippages had happened here, and left the cliffs riddled with caves, like a chest of drawers chiselled from limestone. Here the bandits stored their merchandise. They were even said to have a cave with room enough for stolen cars. You could go shopping there, according to the rumour, if you knew your way over the fields and through the weedy dunes into which the cliff sifted, and if they decided to trust you. Apparently a supermarket of discount wares was stowed in the cliff, and they would guide you around its various departments by torchlight. They stocked it from their raids on cars, and from their expeditions into the suburbs. In case you thought of stealing back something they had stolen from you, they had guard dogs tethered everywhere: slavering, snapping, starved.

On the top of the hill, the slum resumed. A warren of amateurish home-made homes clustered here: half-way houses for those who lived between the valley and the city – immigrants who dreaded the valley and waited for the city to find a place for them, emigrants who had been refused a place by the city or had forfeited one and were drifting by apathetic degrees into the

27

valley. Then came the barrage of towers, less glassy than those on the eastern edge, with washing strung from their balconies.

Here you rejoined the highway, and were re-admitted to the city with its rules and regulations and its filing systems for people and cars. Instead of the two-faced ping-pong bats wielded by the boy and the old man, who also might have been the two faces of a single creature, there were now batteries of green and red lights which flashed above the lanes of traffic, triggered at intervals by some computerised control miles away; instead of the inconclusive paths over fields or the bewildering cruxes where trails diverged in the valley, there were signboards reasserting all points of the compass, Westwood and East End, North Beach and South Side. Arrows steered you to any destination you could imagine, closing in successively on the spot of world which was tagged with your name and number, where your key found the one lock it could fit, like two hands earnestly clasping to reach a final agreement. Inside the door would be the hoard of bits and pieces which were your ballast, the photographs of those with whom (holding hands again) you made up a family, the mirror which showed you who you still were.

All these assurances the valley discounted, or rudely snatched away. You could lose anything or everything while crossing it – an appliance or an appendage, your headphones or your head. To enter it was to vanish from the radar. It was on the flight path into and out of the airport, officially because no one lived there so there would be no damage to anyone on the ground if a plane ploughed into it, actually (if you ask me) because it was already a limbo, a non-place which was bound for nowhere, just like a plane.

So far no pilot had mistaken the valley's infirm or uneven landscapes for the steam-rollered landing strip to the north-west, where little trucks had labels saying FOLLOW ME painted on their rears and men with semaphoring ping-pong bats guided you home. But one day it would have to happen. And when it did, it would not be a navigational error but a correct mental calculation: the choice of these facts – the crumbling, fractured crust of the earth – rather than that improbable flat and regular fiction of tarmac a few miles to the north-west. The valley would have no difficulty in consuming a crashed plane and recycling its contents: scrap metal for the roofs of huts, suitcases like Christmas hampers thudding down from the sky to be rifled. Of course there would also be samples of bodies: arms flapping like scarecrows in the scorched trees, a head or two pretending to be vegetables in the blood-irrigated furrows. The pickings would be rich.

Society assumed that you were lost as soon as you followed one of those beguiling side roads into the valley. Here there were no maps, so how – in the absence of streets with names and houses with numbers – could you be located? It was a place of oblivion, either cruel or merciful depending on your particular case. The refugees and illegal aliens society preferred to forget were stowed there, but those who wanted to forget themselves also sought it out, and passed over into it with a shudder of gratitude, shedding whatever history they had accumulated outside. They had arrived in a place where no questions were asked. Nothing could be traced back to its previous incarnation outside. Cars were equipped with new number plates and appliances with new serial numbers. People acquired aliases, and identity cards (for use when they ventured out of the valley) with the names of strangers.

Occasionally, half-heartedly, the police nosed in, trying to forge again the link which had broken in the valley between a body and its identity, a car and its owner, the present and an accusing past. They never got very far. A patrol car, its blue light flashing just in case, would be parked on a lane as straggly as a rigmarole. A man in uniform who had started out to quiz some barefoot children would find that they helped him to excess: each child told him something different.

Meanwhile, the donkey carts and scooters and repainted motor cycles with transplanted number plates brayed or honked in the tangled lane, unable to pass the car with the plaintive blue light. The policeman eventually drove off to write a report which he would first have to invent.

5

WHO WAS HE?
It was a joke, really, that once his head was off nobody knew his name, because his name was an obsession with him. He had made it omnipresent in the city. It had a reputation for working wonders. It was a synonym for skill in making deals: with a conjurer's dexterity he could cause profits to materialise on a computer screen, and send elastic rows of noughts bouncing around the globe as if on pogo sticks.

His name had other uses. It secured him tables at restaurants which were full, it guaranteed him a supply of women to take to the restaurants. Almost the only thing it could not do was unblock the afternoon traffic on the avenues out of the city, which is why he had decided to turn off and go through the valley.

He was not accustomed to being kept waiting. What mobs and herds and litters of people the world contained. The noughts on the screens were uncountable too, but they did not occupy space, and never needed to be converted into quantities, obstructive objects: piles of notes greasy with thumb prints, blocks of gold hacked out of the earth. They skipped in an instant from New York to Tokyo whenever a button was pressed, holidayed permanently in the Seychelles and an archipelago of other offshore havens, fleet-footedly kept ahead of the tax inspectors in several territories at once. People, though, were not so easily managed or mobilised. They answered back; they insisted on their own wants and wishes. Right now they all wanted to travel down the same coagulated avenue, and one of their rattling cars had died in the process. So he made a deftly illegal manoeuvre across the lawn in the middle of the avenue and drove back towards the short cut across the valley.

His initials were on everything, applied as relentlessly as a cattle brand. They were on his shirt pocket in fine stitching, and on his cuff links in entwined metal; on the brass tag clamped to the handle of his briefcase – the combination for undoing the lock consisted of his birth date – and, printed on a strip of thick plastic tape, on the telephone beside him on the car seat. The number plate of the car contained the initials too, with an extra vowel as a make-weight.

The company's name was the same as his own: it incorporated him. There were other insignias: the scrawl of his pen on a letter, imitating informality by pretending to render his name illegible; a stamp with the chunky initials sculpted in rubber; another automatic pen which required no hand to hold it, and had been trained to produce a legible signature purporting to be his. At the switchboard, women with wire cages looped through their hair whispered his name a dozen times a minute all day long into little furry buds which jutted out from the cages in front of their mouths. If you passed through the room, you overheard a mumbled melodious litany, eternally praising that name. He sometimes called the switchboard himself, just to check that they were not gabbling it, pronouncing it with a lower-class whine, or omitting it altogether. Anyone who took that name in vain was asked for her own name, and promptly sacked over the telephone. He felt vaguely resentful when he met others with the same name (it was a common one), and thought of them as imposters. Even the members of his family, less successful than him, seemed to be trading on it, using it as a letter of credit. Should he have it copyrighted?

That afternoon – or evening, for by the time he got back to the side road the western sky beyond the valley was crimson, then purple like a black eye – he was late. He was on his way to the airport. Every few months he had to follow his agile digits around the world. His passport was in his pocket, a fortnight's supply of suits and initialled shirts were packed in the back seat. With a minute of empty air between them, planes swooped and screeched over the valley, lowering the talons with which they would grip the runway. The sunset glanced off their scything wings. Away in the north-west, other planes took off, aimed like spears at the sun.

He enjoyed all the sensations of flight: the first shuddering rush towards the point where the runway converged in a dot; the reprieve when, just in time, the great projectile launched itself into the sky; the mental adjustment you had to make soon after that, when you felt your armchair riding the gusts, kept aloft by nothing but your imagination; the battles through turbulence, the sudden plunges into chasms of vapour. For as long as it lasted, he felt like a prince of the air.

Now, however, he was condemned to crawl down the side road, negotiating pot holes and piles of garbage. There was the usual abuse to endure from the children who lived in those leaking, rickety hovels. The windows were up already; he turned the music on to insulate himself. A black voice chanted bluesily from the speakers behind him, while the faces outside the windows silently opened and shut, unable to hurt him.

Once or twice he had arrived home, rewound the tape to hear his phone messages, and found that the room was suddenly filled with ravings of such strangers. A man with a booze-slurred voice against a clatter of glasses and a subdued roar of conviviality would offer to come round sometime and break his legs – except that he addressed him as Vic, which was not his name. Another time it had been a trio of school girls crammed into a booth, spending the money they had been given for sweets by randomly terrorising the owners of answering machines. They took turns to invent obscenities. 'We're going to shove your head up your mother's crack,' one of them promised. Difficult, he thought, since he didn't live with his mother. In fact she was dead. 'We can see you now,' hissed the girls, having fed another coin into the box and needing to devise three new minutes of flesh-crawling filth. 'We're looking at you.' He lived on the eighteenth floor; no one could see him.

He heard the sorority of small murderers out, then wiped them. They don't even know who I am, he thought. It wasn't me they wanted to frighten. That number was not listed. They could only have reached it by accident.

People, he remembered thinking. People: an alien race. From

his balcony he looked across the city. The lights were on in the empty towers, for the benefit of cleaners. The streets below clanged and howled. There must be a fire somewhere, a car crash somewhere else. By day his city consisted of acrobatic, exponentiating numbers which blinked on the screens like batting eyelids; it was a gigantic gadget with brain cells of silicon and a network of fibre-optic nerves. At night, after its electronic head had been switched off, the rest of it became restive. Perhaps he should have been worried by the giggling voices, so causelessly avid for revenge. Something thumped the back of his car as it trundled around the last pot hole. One of the children had kicked it.

He gained speed on the road which wriggled down the hill. He was through the alley with its border of hovels and out into the shelving, rubbly fields. Each month more of the land was annexed as new arrivals huddled against the walls of the settlement and extended planks of their own from the tilted roof beams; the improvised community grew like a reef. Some men were mixing cement in a bucket and pasting bricks together. Within hours there would be a room for another family to sleep in. He caught a glimpse of the waiting occupants, camped in the field: a swarthy woman boiling water over a fire, the above-average number of brats, who by next year would have learned enough swear words to join in the game of name-calling and car-bashing up in the alley.

The contrast with his own case had occurred to him – his sprawl of six rooms plus balcony plus technological magic: the microwave which cooked food in seconds by a bombardment of rays, the telephone extension in the bathroom, the concealed speakers which relayed music into every corner. Not to mention the bed which (as he liked to tell whoever was currently sharing it) could accommodate three, the aquarium where polka-dot fish lolled and bubbled at leisure in a flooded forest, and of course the city with its lights winking at him from every window.

The people who lived in these fields sold their labour, mortgaged their bodies – that is, if they worked. The men dug the roads, the women lounged for inspection on the street corners (and later genteelly graduated to cleaning the houses of the rich).

33

Those who did not work subscribed to the theory of property as theft, and made it their duty, like itchy-fingered bailiffs, to recover as much of it as possible. Gangs of children were trained as muggers: one ten-year-old is harmless, but half a dozen can immobilise you and strip you of all you own in minutes. With adolescence, they were promoted to house-breaking. The city's commodities circulated, as if on some eternal carousel, in and out of the valley, bought with profits from the toil of the valley-dwellers, grabbed back by their guile and stored in those limestone warehouses to await resale. And if property was theft from other people, who had to make do with less so you could have more, then wealth was a theft from nature: we grub out minerals, bake them into ingots, and derive an artificial value from them.

In neither way did he consider himself guilty. From whom had he stolen? He employed none of these people; he robbed nothing from the earth, since the riches he created for himself and others were the pure result of speculative daring, aided by the abracadabra of the screens.

'You may think this is business,' he would often say. 'I see it more as an art.' He would often say this to the women he took to the restaurants where the mention of his name caused a table to materialise from nowhere. The women, who learned about art from their beauticians, appreciated the point. 'Besides,' he would go on, 'I did it all myself. No inherited advantages. All I inherited was disadvantages.' Not quite — his family was suburban, happy with what they had and reluctant to imagine anything more — but he knew how good it sounded. 'You are looking at a self-made man,' he would conclude, and sit back to allow whoever it was to look.

He leaned across to look appraisingly at the slice of himself on exhibition in the rear-vision mirror: eyes alert for the main chance, and a brow uncreased by cares. The eyes had learned to be expressionless when he was making bargains or nudging those juggernauts of zeros near to the edge; the brow knew better than to betray tension, and was as wrinkle-free as one of the synthetic shirts he no longer wore, on the grounds that clothes should announce not only their expense but the difficulty of their upkeep. There was also the mouth, sealed as tight as an envelope except when allowing dangerous glimpses of teeth.

This, he thought, is all the equipment I need, the oblong visage or visor hanging there back to front against the dark windscreen. The rest was robotic: arms to drive cars with, feet to kick balls with, a pelvic hinge in the middle to make love with. Reduced to that stripe between the unblinking eyes and the sealed mouth, he could still function, so long as the calculator continued to tick behind. The extensions were inconveniently needy. Not satisfied with the dance of numbers, they demanded feeding, exercise, sexual relief. Even sex became anti-climactic when transferred downstairs; the intensest excitement happened behind the eyes. The head knew how to fly. The body was a plodder, all its motions predictable. The head could outwit it any time.

He prided himself, for that reason, on doing without lunches. 'My stomach doesn't *dare* get hungry', he told his employees as they produced furtive sandwiches from their desk drawers. They regarded him as a mystic being. So far as they were concerned, he subsisted on air and amphetamines. And, he could have added, on the incense of power, inhaled not ingested. He liked to prophesy that in the next century all this chomping and gnashing would be done away with, replaced by colour-coded nutritive pills. Or perhaps you'd inject yourself, getting the chemicals instantly into the blood and off to the brain. Though blood, come to think of it, was a squalid and messy means of communication, and even the brain was a pulp of soft wet vulnerability. The human body could learn a lot from electronics. Software at least was never soft.

He was reconciled to living behind the features he could see in the mirror. They were as near to armoured as flesh would ever get; they advertised an inability to be hurt. But then the slice of face, just as he was reflecting that he did rather like the look of it, caught fire. It melted in a white heat and was blotted out: the headlights of a car behind him exploded into the mirror like sun spots. He blinked as the lights changed their angle, and checked that he still existed. He did. However, the imperturbable eyes were wide with shock. He had to steady his hands on the steering wheel. The car was bucking. The jolting track tried to throw it off, rearing like an unbroken horse.

He swung the car left. He had reached the ridge where the valley opened up, with the gas works visible for a minute – before the crease in the hills folded tight again – at the far end. The chimneys exhaled blue flames.

On the ridge, like a sentinel on a parapet, a woman stared towards those seething exhausts. A smock billowed as his headlights raked across her; she had wild hair. Her back was stiff, as if she was standing to attention. Just one more valley-dweller: it was not only the dispossessed who drifted in here; the deranged too, who gibbered and sobbed in the streets now there were no institutions to hold them, discovered a place where they were free to devote themselves to their private missions – scratching their sores, inventing private languages, paying homage to the gas works, God only knew what. He shrugged and passed on.

For his part, he disliked the gas works. They stank, perfuming that area of the city with a suspicion of rot; they made you smell a rat. They were a reminder of the strained huffing and puffing with which society manufactured energy to keep itself going. Electricity sang down the lines into power points in his walls, but the conversion of water into light or heat or motion had happened a hundred miles away, out of sight and mind; who ever thought about frenzied rivers jumping off cliffs or turbines mashing their froth and striking sparks from it?

At the gas works, the whole operation was scandalously visible, and audible too as gusts hissed from the chimneys before bursting into fire. He could have been looking at a heaving body, stripped bare of all its protective outer layers: wheezing bellows, a pump which sometimes jumped beats, a furnace clamorous for fuel. Already, while still in operation, it reeked of decay. He understood why there were such pickings to be made (he had made them himself) from sprays to squirt in your mouth and gummy sticks to rub under your arms and in all your other suppurating hollows. The body fights a daily rearguard action against its reduction to a whiff of gas and a sprinkle of powdered bone; its only weapons are toiletries. Forget the notion of the autonomous brain, its electronic abacus ticking away as it moved numbers around. It was in hock to a ramshackle organism, which like the car he was driving could stall or run out of juice or otherwise refuse service whenever it chose.

The gas works had recently made another contribution to the city's stock of anxieties. The pipes beneath the streets were old and corroding. Gas stealing through pin holes gathered in brimming lakes under the pavement and awaited its chance. There had been geysers of hurled bricks, smashed windows, crushed cars and fragmented passers-by throughout the city. The pipes would take years to replace. Meanwhile he remembered to tread carefully. Tiptoes, he would think. It could blow at any moment. I will be safer in the air. No need for an infrastructure up there.

Before the sensations which he looked forward to – the roller-coaster ride without a track – there were the rituals, which he also relished. They were all renunciations, a series of abandonments without regret. The car to be left in the long-term lot, waiting for the day when he would choose to return. The suits and the shirts in that hanging bag: it looked like the zip-fastened envelopes where they stowed the corpses collected every night from the city's tenements and tips or trawled from the river. Everything else he needed had been filed away in a satchel which he could push under the seat in front of him when he was on board. Papers were in the brief-case with the combination lock. He winnowed possessions before these trips, making harsh decisions about what he needed and marvelling finally at how minimal a man's needs were. He could pick up extras along the way, and discard them too. Lastly the summary of himself in the little stitched book with its grinning photograph and its smudged, over-written pages, forty of them: a short story. Still, there had been occasions when the man in the booth had recognised his name in the book. That name was the one thing he could not do without. So long as he had that, he was ready to fly.

But he shivered when he remembered how slippery his grip on it could sometimes seem. He had made love the night before. He always did before leaving. It almost counted, like the rituals ahead of him at the airport, as a farewell, an act of departure.

There was always some association to terminate: relationships could not be expected to outlast his absence.

Except that yesterday it had not seemed that way. The woman had already withdrawn herself during their dinner. She intended to co-operate to the last – he employed her, after all – but without desire and without illusions. He caught her looking at him when, in the restaurant, he glanced up from the menu. She might have been looking through him. Her face betrayed no distaste, only a contemplative reckoning. Her eyes accorded him no special value. He refused to feel diminished by her indifferent, out-of-focus look. In any case she re-focused her eyes on him as if adjusting a lens, and required her mouth to smile. He took it as a challenge. He promised himself a reconquest. Later, in the bed whose size she was no longer impressed by, he performed with his usual expertise, but with an additional anger. Sex had the rhythm of a beating, pounding against a door which stayed resolutely shut. He knew he had pleased her. Yet in doing so his fury had obliterated her. She was not there, she need not have existed, she was merely a convenient emptiness where he laboured at his own annihilation.

Having achieved that, he was numb. He seemed to have ejected himself from a body which once answered to his name. No one could bear that state of stark eviction for long. He must have been grateful to fall asleep, though he could not remember. He awoke alone.

At the office he cleared his desk, and marvelled at his efficiency in bringing all the long-drawn-out, circuitous stories strewn across it to a simultaneous conclusion. To be continued, he thought as he surveyed the empty expanse of wood, when I get back.

No one was sure when that would be. He enjoyed the idea of surprising them all, swooping down from the air unannounced like a god in a play and striding in to discover who was taking a late lunch or receiving a personal telephone call. He relished the alarm of their faces when the door opened. Once there was a construction crane next to the office; he had persuaded the builders to let him ride up on it and peer in at his own windows. That way, no message could be sent up from the panic station in the lobby to announce his return. The crane suspended him in mid-air outside the floor of winking screens and muffled telephones. People looked out in his direction, but did not recognise him: he had been made to wear a hard hat and a dust coat, and his identity was forfeit to the borrowed clothes. He had thought of waving, then decided against it. He was not up here to greet them, after all. On the crane, he felt like a ghost who had failed to haunt anyone.

It was not only his employees he wanted to startle. He was also keeping the time of his return, and the place he would return from, a secret from himself. Airports were to him a crossroads of multiple possibility. He would decide on an impulse to go here rather than here, to travel east or west, to detour or double back on himself. Whenever he grazed the ground there was business to be done, and once he had been catapulted aloft again he was a happy nomad, free-associating along paths which were written on air. Always, he told himself, keep your options open.

Around a last bend, he was near to the bottom of the valley. He looked at his watch as he steered the car across a notorious pot-hole. He felt a momentary twinge of fright, which stuck in his stomach and prodded his bowels: had his watch stopped? He stared at it, willing it to resume. The thin hand, which clucked its tongue all day and night and never needed rewinding, had paused for an eternity on the speck of a second. It sat there, like a fly fastening to a grain of food. With his eyes fixed on it, he felt himself paralysing: the car continued to move, shunting unsteadily down the slope towards the tunnel, but it no longer owed its motion to him, it might have been running out of control while he gripped the wheel helplessly, rigid with dread. Why had the watch stopped?

Then he laughed at himself in relief. It had not stopped; he had been staring at it for a second, the time it took his eyes to blink, and somehow the instant had lengthened inside his head. Now he could hear the motor running again, and sense the blood rushing through its channels inside him, his pulses tapping like impatient fingers on a table. He held the watch to his ear, just to make sure: the hand discounted seconds with a click. He was alive; he was still in business.

Ahead of him, the lights of the car suddenly found a face in the black gulf at the bottom of the valley. It was a white face, and a round one, as blankly unmarked as a full moon or as one of those satellite dishes which eavesdropped on the sky from the tops of buildings. Its eyes were wide but, blinded by his lights, they could not see him. He was a midnight sun, plummeting into the valley with its engine growling. The face covered its eyes and backed away.

It belonged, he knew, to the boy with the ping-pong bat who would signal him through the tunnel. Every so often he gave the boy some coins, never bothering to look at him. Now his face, dazed by the lights of the car, was pinned to the darkness behind it, as if held there to undergo examination. He looked at the boy, seeing him for the first time.

The lights of the car seemed to make a transparency of him: he could conceal nothing. No one could hide behind that defenceless face, or inside those clothes which drooped from him, denying his ownership of them. The lights might have been a firing squad, and he offered himself without question to the drilling beams. I have all my defences, thought the driver; the house, the car, the music inside the car, the passport in the pocket, the wallet and of course the face which knows how to feign: all my insulations. And there he is, too trusting to run and too simple to take refuge behind a mask. Who decides which of us is to be which? And is the decision final? Perhaps that is why people – other people – have children. Not to bequeath their possessions, but to experiment with beginning their lives once again. Does each of us contain the potentiality to be any or all of the others? This kid might grow up into me, while I. . . .

The boy looked back into the glare, from which music reverberated. At the core of the nocturnal sun, a voice was singing. It seemed to be in pain. He recognised the lamenting arcs it made: the cordoned Dogs sometimes howled like that, unable to translate their misery into words. Locked inside the car, locked inside that inside a box resembling Horry's transistor, the voice still seeped out and threatened to fill the valley like water when the creek flooded.

He could not imagine what this lilting grief was all about. His job was to pass it on as quickly as he could. So he checked that the way ahead was clear, and held up the green side of the bat.

The car drew level with him, its lights forcing him to retreat as if a wave were about to break over him, the bottled song inside it battering at the windows. The wave avoided him and spilled on to the road ahead, drowning the music. The car drove into the tunnel.

I suppose it must have been planned. Except that it did not go according to plan. It never does. Plots are – the world is – a compromise between destiny and accident, choice and chance. What actually happened was not supposed to happen. Though how can you be sure? Some need or compulsion, some logic which transports lines towards revelation or undoing, must have been at work. The thing that was not meant to take place was the thing most fraught with meaning. It had to happen; it had no alternative; it happens for everyone. Chaos is what we call an order too refined for our understanding.

Certainly it began chaotically enough. An hour before, Wilf and his grandfather scrambled down the bank on to the road and took up their positions on either side of the tunnel. They agreed to let the cars through half a dozen at a time: six one way, then six the other. But Ern and his stomach were still grumbling because the woman with the vigil to keep had managed to steal the last word from him, and had left him guessing about what she might be up to. So he amused himself by setting up one or two near-misses in the tunnel. He started sending cars through from his side when only five had emerged from Wilf's end. There were no crashes, more's the pity, but much exchanging of insults inside the tunnel, followed by humiliating climbdowns and crawling reversals.

Bustling about to supervise blockages, ordering all the cars on his side to back up, he enjoyed disbursing sympathy as he collected tips from the drivers whose journey home he had playfully ruined. 'I don't know,' he would fuss, brandishing the red side of the bat with one hand while the other, cupped, was passed around for contributions. 'I really don't. These drivers today.

41

They won't obey the rules of the road. I ask you.' There was more pleasure in store for him: he was already rehearsing the tirade in which he would blame Wilf for the mix-up. 'Six at a time, I told you, six. Can't you even count? Some of my best customers got pranged in there. Scratched their paint, and all on account of you. I'll tan your hide for that.' He belched in the sweetness of anticipation, and apologised to the drivers for his manners. 'It's the traffic does it to me. I can't digest my meal in peace.'

Within half an hour his fun was over. Only a dribble of cars crossed the valley, not enough to be worth making mischief with. His griping mood returned, and he promised himself that Wilf would pay. The boy after all was a whipping boy. What other use did he have? 'I'll warm you up when I get you home,' he muttered. 'You won't need no fire tonight.'

'Talking to yourself, Ern?' whispered a voice behind him, so close he could feel its laughing burst of breath. The fright jolted him; his teeth clattered. It was the lads, who had – as pre-arranged – slunk down the hill. Gliding over the ground, merging with shadows and then materialising from them: these were their particular skills. Occupied with his self-righteous rage at Wilf, he had forgotten they were coming down.

'To tell the truth,' he lied, 'I was just wondering where you were. A bit behind time, aren't you?' From the look of annoyance which passed between the lads, he could tell that he was right, even though he had been bluffing; he gloated quietly.

'Yes,' said one of the lads, 'we had an incident on the way.'

This was Athol, who was Horry's father and who counted – sly, tricksy, quick with figures – as the leader of the lads. Then there was Jacko, Athol's brother, shaggier and slower, mainly employed to lurk in hedges and watch out for patrol cars, though valuable for heavy chores like unloading fridges and freezers from the backs of waylaid lorries. The third of the lads was their nephew Clem, recruited from a branch of the family which had turned respectable and gone to live in the suburbs. Clem, a throwback, had returned to the valley after a spell in prison. He tended to be violent: they used him in moderation. He was their last resort. Clem had the gnawing, indifferently destructive look of a ferret. They huddled together under a tree on the side of the road.

Ern enquired about the incident.

'Clem had a run-in with some hag up the hill,' said Athol. Jacko grunted, and Clem kicked a rock to express contempt.

'The one in the nightie? Who is she anyway?'

'They closed the asylum down, so the loonies are in here with us. All this one bothers about is looking at the gas works. She thinks that if she stops looking, the flames will go out. She hangs about our yard sometimes and talks religion; the wife feeds her. She was minding her own business, but Clem wolf-whistled her. She didn't take any notice, so he threw a stone. And she flew at us. You should have heard her shriek. She called Clem everything under the sun. Come on Clem, tell Ern what she called you.'

Clem sulked, and kicked another rock, wishing his shoe was a sledgehammer.

Athol numbered the epithets on his fingers, and enjoyed watching his nephew squirm. 'He's too bashful. But she called him a sod and a mongrel and a half-wit. She said he was scum, she told him he was lower than a snake, and she said she'd eat his eyes for breakfast, she threatened to shrivel his prick up . . .'

'I don't remember her saying that,' said Jacko unhelpfully.

Clem kicked another rock, and stubbed his toe. 'Let's get on with it,' he said.

'You're right,' said Athol, and Jacko nodded. 'We've got to do our shopping. We need some stereos tonight. Have they been keeping you busy, Ern?'

'Average I'd say,' said Ern. 'You might have left it a bit late.' He was eager to add to the case against Clem, who glanced at him with casual scorn.

Jacko, who would sooner have been drinking in the barn, proposed that they come back tomorrow. Clem growled that they should stop debating and go to work. So they forgot their differences and returned to the shadows; darkness folded over them, rustling and snapping as they retreated into it.

Alone on the road, Ern suddenly felt cold. He waved the cars through dismissively. Three more, he told himself, and then I'll turn in. During the pauses between cars, he unreeled in his head the lecture he planned for Wilf on their way home, just to check that the phrases were all in their right places – will be the death of me; always said you was simple; whatever do they teach in them schools. He even forgot to raise his hat in the usual gesture of fawning gratitude when one of the drivers threw a coin at his feet.

He was still fumbling on his knees, groping for the coin and then reading its value with his fingers like a blind man's book, when the second car puttered through. Not a car at all, this one: a scooter with a shelf attached to it, which the valley-dwellers with vegetable patches used for ferrying their produce. He recognised the heartbeat of the motor while it was still in the tunnel. The driver, his helmeted head unrecognisable, laughed at the old man grubbing in the dust.

He straightened himself in time for the third car.

It sped out of the tunnel without caution. A pity there was nothing coming the other way: he fancied a head-on, after all the evening's tribulations. Nor had the car dimmed its lights. They veered towards him and pushed him back, like a body flung upwards by rifle-fire. He felt himself dangling there, his arms grabbing at air as he tried to cover his face (he had dropped the bat when the lights assaulted him), his legs dancing as if they too were skipping to avoid bullets. The lights seemed to rip the clothes from him, and after that they peeled off the dessicated skin. They left only the pinched nerves and limbs which complained as they jerked in their sockets, operated for the time being by a thumping, irregular engine. He wanted to shout, but could not – anywhere in his scarecrow of flayed flesh – locate a voice. So the beams bored through him and passed on.

Only when they were gone and he had found his footing again did he hear the music. The car keened with it as it drove further into the night. Ah well, he thought, that's that then. This is where you get off.

They were waiting for him in a culvert further up the road. The music made their choice for them.

It happened in such a rush that it did not seem to be happening to him. He was the spectator of it, watching the faces framed in the windscreen which were mouthing words not synchronised with the chanting of the voice inside the car. Like all physical shocks, it left him unable to feel; the danger and the damage would only be apparent afterwards.

Later too there would be time (would there?) to wonder why, when the pastily flood-lit faces blocked the road and then advanced through the lights to peer in at his windows, he did not simply speed up and run them over. Or why he had left the car doors unlocked, enabling them to reach in and pull him out? The sensations lagged behind the events: can it be *me* they are doing this to? he asked himself. It was like a film, comically speeded up and given the wrong sound track.

Then one of them turned off the music. At first there was silence, like his first shock a stunning absence. Then he heard a sound of drumming, which he realised came from inside himself. His mouth was parched and prickly, as if stuffed with hot sand. He gulped, and tried to swallow; the sides of his throat, strangling, were gripped together.

Back it up a bit, he thought. Make it unhappen. This can't be right. It can't have been meant.

He looked at them, not having registered yet how many they were and what differences there were between them. First they had been a barrier of bodies, then a screen of grimacing faces, after that an invasion force consisting only of hands. Now he separated them from each other.

One was thin, wry, detached, grinning at the ironic upsets of the situation: the brains. Another was thicker, thick all over, with a neck like an elephant's foot and fists like hams. Those were the hands which had hauled him from the car, though the first one had unbuckled his seat belt. The third, his own age, was the one to watch out for: this one looked at him with dislike, whereas on the faces of the other two he saw only amusement or incomprehension; this one had a twitchy energy, placed in the service of an unreasonable hatred.

If he had seen the three of them by the side of the road, he would have relegated them to a category, a species he need never encounter: muggers, car thieves or kidnappers perhaps, operating just across the border where people tumbled out of society and into the valley. You could generalise about them, and speculate on what made them do it. Everyone had an opinion about them. They had no work, they had no homes, and they had to live. 'Do they?' he once demanded, impatient with this argument. Evidently – it now seemed – they did. Standing obstructively between him and the use of his legs, his car, his will, they insisted on it.

All right, he thought, now can I go? Minus my wallet, of course, I grant you that.

He was about to propose this aloud when the young one produced a knife. It sprung open in the palm of his hand, its blade poking out like a sixth finger. Its appearance altered the state of affairs.

They were disagreeing about what they wanted from him. Athol was prepared to settle for the stereo at the top of his shopping list, and of course the wallet. Clem fancied taking the car as well. Athol said Clem should do as he was told, which was what provoked Clem to introduce the knife into the discussion. Jacko's contribution was 'Steady on.' Clem, aware of the difference the knife made, then arrived at a grander idea: 'We'll take him as well. Someone might pay to get the bastard back.'

A car went past. Did they look as if they were having a companionable chat, the four of them, in the ditch at the side of the road? Athol called his nephew a mad dog. Jacko grunted his assent. Clem ripped open a seam of air with the knife, cutting across a semi-circle which included the other three.

Shock is briefly merciful: it bereaves you of feeling, but not indefinitely. Now the anaesthetic was weakening. It could no longer be denied that someone, something had chosen him for this to happen to. This, a megaphonic voice announced, is *your* life. No one else is prepared to live this bit of it for you. Just try to bargain or buy your way out, or get back to who you were three minutes before. The plane will leave without you.

Though his wallet, passport and the accordion of plastic cards were still in his pocket, he began to compute what he had already lost. They had taken him out of the car, which was a worse insult than taking the car from him: they're welcome to it, he thought. Because they had demonstrated, by that gruff laying on of hands, how feeble a support it actually was, like childish armour made from tin. Buckled into it, urging it along, deriving its power from your own body (even though all you do is insert a key and turn the wheel), you enjoy the illusion of control. The road ahead, like a screen in a video arcade, throws up jesting menaces and obstacles made of coagulated dots: you torpedo the lot. The perspective unrolls ahead of you, free and limitless. What's to stop you becoming airborne at the point where all lines converge and the road turns to a mattress of transparent foam?

What stops you is this: the screen fills with three faces, which cannot be wished away by fiddling with the dial. You can also be brought to a halt abruptly by an undeniable icicle of sharpened steel six inches long.

His legs felt tottery. Just as the car which was his shield and fortification had been removed from him, now the muscles which held him upright were turning to water, and the bones, brittle as straw, could not do it alone. A quake of fear made its way through him, travelling along the fault line it had found: from his shuddering flanks to his bowels, which it left boiling and sulphurous; from there to the pit of his stomach, which it struck with a single punch; up to his syncopating heart, and out into his mouth. He tasted it, gasping, on his tongue. It made him retch, but all he could expel was air, not even a coughing flame like the pipes at the gas works.

The effort rocked him, and knocked his feet from under him. He was kneeling, he noticed, on the ground, his hands gripping the stones in the road.

'Begging for mercy, are you?' said Athol. 'Or drunk?'

'Up you get,' said Jacko encouragingly.

Clem prodded him with the knife, a playful nudge – using the handle – in the back of his bent neck.

But despite their mockery and their threats, he could not do it. Crouched there, he realised he had lost power over his body. It was like a stalled car. His hands grabbed the stones for anchorage; he had forgotten the message you sent down the length of unresponding arms to dislodge them. He had forgotten everything. What *was* my name? Who did I ever imagine myself to be? To whom did the self-advertising signatures belong? Whose was the face in the passport photograph, smiling at the idea of mobility?

They had to lift him to his feet. It took two of them to do it. Yanking him from the car had been easy; now he seemed to be adhering to the ground. It was a tug of war with gravity.

Having levered him up, they removed him from the road and leaned him against a tumbling wall which had once marked off someone's field. Jacko kept an eye on him while the other two conferred. Jacko watched him in amazement, almost in fear. His chest heaved with swallowed sobs. Were those tears on his face? He was not behaving in the way their victims usually did – as gallant good losers, or else weary cynics, sighing 'Not again' and wanting to get it over with as quickly as possible. There was an etiquette, which this one had flouted. He seemed to be crumpling, like a solid object warped and laughably deformed by heat. Only his suit held him together.

Jacko did not know where to look or what to think. It was a sight you should not see: a woman giving birth; a mystery. He fumbled for a phrase which might jolly it back to normality. Be a man? But a man was too difficult a thing to have to be. Blow your nose, perhaps? – or whatever else you said to children wailing at their life sentence. This convulsion was like the shrill, red-faced crying of a child: not a protest at spilled milk, a withdrawn nipple or a shattered toy; rather an objection to existence itself.

Jacko awkwardly stepped forward, and sensed the man's body stiffening against the wall. He could no longer hear him breathing. He was waiting for a blow. Instead Jacko softly thumped him on the shoulder in a matey imitation of fisticuffs.

He recoiled from the touch, and wondered why it had not hurt. His body had no other purpose than to feel pain. They had not actually done him any physical harm yet, unless he counted the grip which tugged him from the car or the insinuation of the knife handle against the cloth on his back. But emotional distress, the collapse of morale, should count as pain. Like a disease, it upset all the body's routines. It was a cold night; he was tropically slick with sweat. Like a humidifier in a room which demonstrates that the air is sodden, a swamp of droplets, this fear was turning him to water. His skin, soaking, sucked at his clothes, while his mouth and throat were a valley of ashes.

Behind the wall, they were negotiating over him. 'Give him to me,' said Clem. He had put the knife away, but Athol did not need reminding of the advantage it signified. So long as he got the stereo one of his clients had ordered, along with the telephone he had found in the car, Athol was ready to compromise. Still, this insistence on stealing something that could not necessarily be resold, something with so low a market value as a human body, puzzled him.

'What are you going to do with him?'

'I'll think of something,' said Clem. 'And you can have the car.'

'I don't need it. There's no demand for flash cars like that.'

'I'll throw in his wallet as well.'

'Where are you going to take him?'

'Just up the hill.'

'Then keep him away from us. We don't want to know.'

'I'll send Jacko back to you.'

'And the wallet.'

Clem slid through a gap in the wall. The driver was staring into the dark. He did seem drunk, as Athol had said, suffering through some ecstasy of alteration within himself. He came to briefly when Clem reached into the pockets of his suit, and stiffened: was he expecting his heart to be torn out? Clem removed the wallet with a surgeon's deftness and patted the cloth on his chest as if sealing a wound. He threw the wallet at Jacko, and said 'Off you go. I'll take him the rest of the way.'

Jacko trotted back to the road. Doors slammed. The car drove on.

'So now,' said Clem, 'it's just the two of us.'

He said it more or less to himself; saying it was part of the game and, unless he said it, play could not properly begin. He reached out to grab the man's chin and twisted the lolling head.

He wanted to make those eyes – sunstruck, unseeing – confront his own. The valley for him was any kind of battle zone, an arena floored with gorey sand or a trench of infested mud or simply a back-alley of clattering rubbish tins: the wasted place where he and the enemy fought it out. But first he had to eyeball his opponent, his victim. There had to be some exchange between them, like boxers clumsily joining their gloved hands before a bout. And this one would not or could not look at him: he refused to confirm Clem's existence by being afraid of him. He certainly was afraid. He was moist with it, he stank of it. But the fear came from losing his car, his wallet, his freedom. It was not a specific tribute to Clem. He had not appreciated what a difference it made that the other two – small-minded thieves in Clem's opinion, collectors of electronic gadgets – had handed him over. Released him, thought Clem, into my custody.

The knife perhaps would concentrate his mind. Clem scraped it across his jaw. 'Feel that?' he said. It nipped the flesh, almost playfully. The man's eyes finally met his.

'Let me go,' he said. 'I can pay. You can have all I've got.'

'But you don't have nothing,' said Clem. 'You're cleaned out. And we don't use money, here in the valley. We live off the land. It's back to basics here. You've got a lot to learn. Come on, I'll show you.' He pulled him from the wall, swivelled him, and aimed him into the field. 'Quick march,' he said. 'I'll be right behind you.' He poked the knife at the man's back as if switching on a motor, and gashed the cloth of his jacket.

His legs propelled him involuntarily. He stumbled over dry clods and through unplanted furrows; like an infant whose feet have not yet learned to decipher the terrain, he toddled, his arms flailing for balance when his legs miscalculated. Like an infant too, he had no conception of a straight line: Clem corrected his course, steering him with the knife. He could see nothing, though the furrows felt like the corrugations of a thick, unstirring ocean across which, seasick but somehow weightless, he lurched. Why don't I go under? he wondered. Why doesn't it let me sink? Back there when he fell over, his body had been like a boulder, inertly crashing, tugged underground. Now he was not heavy enough to fall or sink. His legs seemed skittish, past caring where they took him. Or were they anxious to reach the end?

Long grass rose around him at the edge of the field. Thorns

clung, then tore at him when they could not make him stay. Twigs lashed his face, springing back to swat him. His feet now could not find earth: they rebounded from knotty vines and wriggling roots, a cushioning undergrowth as dense and tangled as the veins and fibrous tubes inside his body.

He forgot to feel pain when the twigs slapped his face or a thistle bit his fingers; he felt as little as the twigs did when he jerked them out of joint or the thistles when he crushed them. This was how it was, here in the valley. This was one of the things Clem had promised to show him. The prick of the knife in the small of his back, directing him, pointed it out. In the valley you did not ask in advance where you were headed, or pause to catch your breath and inquire how far it was. You struggled on regardless, and kept moving because you were afraid to look behind. Now he was trudging through spongy soil, splashing in puddles. It was the ancestral journey in reverse, wading into the swamp not out of it. The knife had peeled away centuries.

Having paddled through the creek, his shoes crunching broken bottles and his ankles snared by weeds, he stumbled against another wall – no, a hill, which the knife ordered him to climb. He scrambled up it on all fours, grabbing at bushes which seemed, when he found time to think about it, to rend his hands. Clem, who knew where there were footholds, hopped up the slope behind him, and encouraged him by reaching down to slash his clothes. He felt his jacket disintegrate into strips of flapping cloth. The blade knew how to avoid his skin; it was satisfied with reducing the outer man to tatters. It even managed to scratch slits in his trouser legs: vents which ripped open as he climbed, like the mouths of beached, expiring fish.

The hill flattened. He was sprawled on a track along the top. He forced himself upright in painfully tentative stages: his hands on his bent knees raised the torso above them as if hoisting a load of bricks; then the hands, digging into his flesh, scaled a ladder as far as his waist, and from there straightened his back; after that he could think about convincing the knees to unkink themselves. This was the most arduous climb of all, up his own body. Yet when he looked down, surveying it as though from a cliff he had scaled with sweating, bleeding fingers, what he saw was a digest of the landscape he had struggled through. His shoes were boggy, like prehistoric paws. His clothes, scarred by the knife, hung from him in strips: the foliage of a dejected tree. Furry grasses adhered to his knees, and a snail was mounting his leg along a pearly thread of slime. The palms of his hands were clumps of thorns, like the bristles which once – when all men lived in the valley – had sprouted there from under the skin.

'You look like shit,' said Clem. 'Didn't I tell you I'd show you a thing or two? Go and get a drink. Feel free.' He executed a jesting flourish with the knife, and pointed out the fountain where the faun still dribbled.

The man turned to look for it in the darkness. He could not see it, but he stumbled towards the sound, and thrust his head under the spout. The water numbed him with its cold; it poured into his throat and choked him. Coughing, he thought: Is this it? is it over? did he mean I was free from him, or something else?

He opened his eyes, saw the faun leering at him, and realised that it was not over yet. The eyes of the faun rolled backwards into its skull, retracting to watch the shadowy chases and snuffling captures which happened within; its mouth stretched wide, grinning; it spat in his face. It had no intention of letting him go.

He turned away from it. Clem was pondering him, amused by the wet flaps of listless cloth and the pool he now stood in after drenching himself; amused most of all by the sight of a person coming apart at the seams.

And now there were two others watching him. Judge and jury? But what have I done? He recognised them: the old man and the boy from the tunnel, who half an hour ago had motioned him on towards this encounter. They were not visitors from the recent past. They had wandered back from some unattainable future which he would never see, a time when there would be roads, rights of way, a language of colours agreed by everyone which symbolically said STOP or GO, and a city standing outside the valley. Citizens of another century, migrants in time, they would not regard him as their responsibility.

All the same, he thought, I must try. It was after their tunnel that it happened. Perhaps I am still in their tunnel.

'Help me!' he said to them. If you only knew how many kinds of help you could give me. He repeated it: 'Help me?' They did nothing.

'Go on,' Clem said, taunting them all, 'help him if you want to. He looks like he could do with it.'

The old man studied him diagnostically. The expression on his face was that of a specialist who tells you that your case is inoperable. The boy was wide-eyed with puzzlement. Did this scene, like sex, belong to some complicated adult game which looked joyless and even desperate until you learned how to play it? They fidgeted, but still did nothing.

Ern was thinking about the Alsatian they had untethered earlier that night; about the difference between dying and being killed. When you die, you renounce things gradually. It takes time, but time is what it is about: it has its stages, and though you have no practice at it, you seem to know what they are, and can make yourself ready to pass from one to the next. His own mother had narrated her death to him bit by bit as it advanced inside her. 'I'm just not meself today,' she first announced; a month after that, she took to her bed; a week later, 'It won't be long now' she assured him, and it was not: it was punctual. But when you were killed, you had no time and no grace for these successive surrenders. It came as a surprise. Or you did not know it was happening, and you missed it altogether. Which was maybe why Clem was so particular about dragging it out.

Wilf was thinking about the ant-hill he had toppled that afternoon, and the evacuation of the eggs. A knife, not indicating any of them in particular, dangled from Clem's hand. Clem's knife and Wilf's stick were instruments of knowledge: they knew where the line was drawn between being alive and being dead. Strange that the man appealed to them for help. Didn't he know that he was helping Clem mapping the border for him?

His grandfather gave him a push, then a shove. 'We'll be leaving you to it,' he said to Clem. His hand forced the boy along the path up the hill; he rotated behind on his uneven legs.

He could not stop Wilf from looking back. By the fountain

he could still see the man's drained face, and the man could see his face too, pale and wavering like a moon behind clouds, as it twisted for a glimpse over his shoulder. Then the clouds muffled and dimmed it. The face at the fountain shone for another moment before the darkness gathered it in.

'Get a move on,' said his grandfather, with more urgency than irritation. Feeling a belch on the way, he stifled it. Out of respect, he told himself.

Clem let them get ahead, then gave an order with the knife. The man picked himself up, pulled himself together. The knife pointed him towards the hill.

Before he set off, he glanced around him: the trickling pipe and the plughole which swallowed the stream again; a crop of weeds, fed by the spilled water, growing up so that soon the faun would be able to hide in them. Soon. He sensed that he was taking stock, counting the sum of persistent, unkillable things which the world would always contain. The path skirted a farmyard, distantly noisy with the rumour of life. A woman railing at unruly children, the shrilling of a radio.

It made him feel suddenly resentful. There were so many people going about their business, to whom this had not happened. Yet he was dismayed to realise that his resentment was not personal outrage: it was disinterested, puzzled by the arbitrariness of destinies. Who or what determined the draw? Perhaps stories should be told back to front; perhaps a life should be chronicled from end to beginning. You may begin accidentally, but you choose your ending, you write your own last page. I am here because I was going to the airport, because I was in a hurry and took the short cut, because I had a flash car with music playing in it – because I am who I am, or who I was, the self-made man with the self-sculpted face. Those who imagine they have invented themselves defy life to prove them wrong by destroying them, and there is always a volunteer prepared to take up the challenge. Clem was his intended. The match was made wherever they programme the coincidences. Like an angel or a demon, like an auditor or a detective, Clem had been assigned to his case.

He wanted to look back. Clem, rather than leading, followed him. Who was leading whom?

He turned, holding out his hands to show he had no intention of, no belief in resistance or escape. What he saw startled him. Clem was caught unawares, unprotected by the customary sneer, like an animal which has not had time to run for cover. His eyes told the truth: he was frightened. He got his courage from the knife, he took his orders from a compulsion which dragged him along behind it.

'What do you want?' he said, without his usual contemptuous drawl.

The only possible answer was: Nothing. But before he could say it, the darkness ahead turned audible.

'Those bloody hounds,' said Clem, which silenced them.

Clem took him by the shoulder and led him through the cordon of Dogs. Some of them tugged at the flaps of his slashed jacket, others lapped his hands. One of them jumped at him and clasped his legs; he felt its nose wetly nuzzling his groin. With Clem to vouch for him, they welcomed him through.

Beyond their chain of mouths, another mouth yawned: a gap in the earth, like the tunnel below the valley; a cave. He walked towards it, or rather was drawn in by its thickening shadows. Clem had to grab his shoulder again and pull him away, as if dragging him out of an advancing tide. He pushed him towards another cliff. 'Up,' he said.

They mounted on a crumbling ledge. He tripped once, stumbling on a clump of grass and teetering over the drop; Clem steadied him, and kept him from falling. He had to stop himself from saying thanks, then had to stop himself from laughing at the incongruity of it.

At the top, Clem said 'Not much longer to go.' Did he mean not much further?

The cliff top was abrupt, an unexpected ending. The land divided there like a tired cloth, like his own clothes when the knife bit them. They crossed another field, oddly flat underfoot, as if its hectic jungle of stalks had once been a garden. After the field he saw a house, or the remains of one: a rib cage of beams. The roof creaked. At one end it still had its cladding of shingles

– except that the shingles suddenly separated, took to the air, whirled in a noisy circle, and settled again on another section of the roof, scraping and abrading as they slotted into place: crows, their sleep disturbed. Was Clem shivering? And before the roof had quietened, while its charcoal-coloured shingles were still complaining, a grey fog gathered inside the house, drifted towards a hole which used to be a door, and condensed there into a person. It was the woman he had seen on his drive down into the valley, staring at the chimneys of blue fire.

Save me, he thought he said. He was not sure that he had said it aloud. But he must have done, because it alerted Clem, who saw her too and yelped. The fog evaporated; Clem could not chase it.

Beyond the house, trees closed around them. The branches pressed and prodded as the knife had done, urging them along together. Then the trees cleared, retreating from a pile of stones. A shed, or a chapel, or a crypt? Wherever it was, they were there. Clem prised open the door.

He went inside, without waiting to be told. The dank stones sighed: it was his own breath they were giving back to him. He felt a small eruption far down in his body, as automatic and absurd as hiccups. So this is the whimper with which a life ends. You are just a coiling, entangled tract with a web of nerves wrapped round it; your terror translates into a flurry of escaped gas.

Sorry, he said. He didn't say it aloud, because he was saying it to himself.

The door closed. He could no longer see. Clem had become the darkness. But he heard him say, with that leisurely and humorous drawl, 'Before we start, there's something you forgot. You didn't introduce yourself. Come on, don't be shy. So what's your name?'

6

THERE WERE MANY ways of describing the valley.
All the sciences of explanation, and the pseudo-sciences too, had their ways of accounting for it.

I suppose that geology should be allowed first place in the sequence: its time, computed in millennia, precedes the punctilious time of history.

One day, eternities ago, the earth must have opened. A line of low uneventful hills tore apart. Suddenly the land lost its assurance of firmness and fixity: it became an emptiness into which things toppled – houses, horses, carts, people who were walking along a dusty path which triggered a trap-door beneath their feet. The land cleaved all the way to the river, like a body in groaning parturition. Except that this was a birth in reverse. Nothing was brought forth; everything was re-absorbed, secreted below to crumble, disperse and germinate again as something else.

When the ground stopped crying out and the atomic anarchy of dust cleared, the survivors crept to the edge of what was now a valley and looked down into the gulf. What they saw – the exposed flanks of limestone, as soft and porous as human flesh; a squashy marsh into which the river oozed – made them realise the error of their ways. They had made a mistake about their patch of arable earth: they had trusted it, treated it as a bed for their crops and a floor for themselves. The crater, like a mouth split in half by laughter, put them right.

Only the surface of the world is tough, briefly hardening into a scab. Underneath, all is pathetically soft. The upper few inches consent to be fertile, and are gripped in place by the roots of our plants, as desperate in their tenacity as we who plant them. Below, the crushed tiers and compressed cities of rock have their own ideas and their own timetable, waiting for however many centuries it takes until they decide to demolish themselves, overturning the irrelevant garden of tendrils at the top and scattering them like a madwoman tugging out her own hair. When the hills cracked open, they gave the lie to the notions of settlement and security. The ledges and indentations of limestone were like rope ladders let down precariously from the ripped, ragged surface. Beneath them was the marsh, a sump of forgetful water. That was what their shelters were built on, their names inscribed on.

Even now, whenever there is a season of rain, the valley becomes a gullet. All the streams in the hills decant into it. Mashing the ground and carving gutters through the rock, they suck at the foundations of the huts, guzzle the fields, sometimes wear down a wall of piled stones like a carious tooth and swill it away. As the valley narrows, the water churns to a torrent. You can see uprooted bushes, drowned dogs, scraps of buoyant machinery bobbing on it in bewildered merriment. At the bottom of the valley it all swirls away down some universal plug-hole, faintly chortling under cover of concrete and tar before the drains release it into the river. The valley, like the human body, is a sluice.

That's why the sight and the throttled sound of it are so terrifying when it floods. What percentage of water are our bodies composed of? Seventy? Ninety? The quotient, whatever it is, is shocking, because we imagine ourselves as durable bone or at least stiffened muscle. Sure, we produce water – though, preferably, between the perpetual miseries of childhood and the drooling laxity of age, from only one of our apertures, and then fugitively, behind locked doors in closets designed for the purpose. But to think that the whole apparatus, apparently home and dry, is a leaky bag of fluid! The valley in a flood is a reminder that the solid (ourselves included) is soluble, and easily disposed of.

Geology demonstrated for certain that the time of the earth and the time of the dwellers on it and delvers in it are not synchronised. Human beings toil in industrious, reassuring circles, confident that whatever happens will happen again, as repetitiously as agriculture or the seasons; the ground beneath their plodding feet is meanwhile brewing explosions and preparing to rearrange itself into a crevasse. None of the cities we pile on the crust, none of the roads we seal it with, none of the memories we dig holes for six feet below – none of them is final. An impromptu, unforeseen valley, lazily yawning open one day, can consume the lot.

Nevertheless, history cannot let itself be demoralised by geology. It has its own version of the valley – or rather the area before the valley arrived in it, since once the valley ate up the hills there was no more history there: no human purposes, no constructive energies, no confidence that one thing led to another; only the dim-witted tropisms of animals. Why did a goat chew its way across a field in that direction rather than this one? Why did they choose to stop this car instead of another? Why did Clem . . . ? Where there are no motives, there can be no motion. Time stops, or never really starts. It cannot exist without time-keepers, without someone to tell time like the story it is. And, as a wise fool once almost remarked, there are no clocks in the valley.

But there were clocks until a few decades ago. They stopped during the afternoon when the hills split, like a closed book whose pages part to disclose some of the secrets written in it. This latest quake was not pre-historic. It was reported in the newspapers. Still, it brought local history to an end.

Before that afternoon, the hills west of the city were a region where nature was redesigned by humans: not land but a land-scape. What are now meaningless pits of rubble used to be smooth humps and cocooning folds of terrain. When the sun set behind the hills, they looked like bodies lolling along the horizon as if on a divan, asleep in a haze of stupefied purple air. The hills were divided into estates where the city's rich men played at being farmers when miasmal summers drove them out of town.

Actually they employed other people to grow their crops and gather them in, while they and their families concentrated on a charade of rural life, gliding down honey-coloured steps onto lawns which imitated the bouncy consistency of carpets. They were fond of exotica, species expensively imported to transform the estates into fantasies of tropical luxury: scrawny palm trees from which they strung paper lanterns; peacocks to preen and screech on the lawns; swans for which ponds had to be installed. Out of sight, menials tugged milk from the cows or plodded behind the ploughs or stooped over the harvest.

It all failed because of the perspective. The city advanced towards the dozing, hazily purple hills. Each year it redefined its boundary, like a fat man surreptitiously loosening his belt a notch or two. The market gardens were annexed as factories; country roads became suburban streets. Now the city was not far enough off for there to be enchantment in the view. The eastern sky thickened with fumes and dust. If the fiction was to be sustained, it would have to make a cautionary retreat. Besides, there were developers coming to call, with schemes to slice up the fields and build houses.

The amateurish absentee farmers moved to the coast and took up their last stand there, pretending this time to be beach-combers. Their employees were hired by the factories, or worked in the gangs which laid railway tracks across the fields. Some of the cottages were built: cartons for packaging people in, deposited on the lawns. The houses which the would-be farmers had abandoned were stranded now in the hinterland of pine-board boxes, fragrant with newness. They terrorised the cottages like sanctuaries which, even though disgraced and derelict, might still contain a mystery. The children peeped through shutters at standing shrouds, sometimes ruffled by a draught: dust sheets spectrally muffling the useless furniture. Then one of the children would be sure that a floorboard had complained inside, and they would scatter like the flustered bats.

The houses were already rickety when the hills, disturbed by a bad dream, turned over in their sleep. The tremor rattled them. They had been weakened by damp, nibbled at by fire. Their roofs were shedding slates, the balustrades of their verandahs had been knocked away like ten pins. Shaken by a tantrum deep in the rock, they were shovelled like food into the vacuum which opened around them. The cottages crumpled too. In the evening, people picked through the leavings of their lives and moved on, like ants evacuating their eggs.

Avoiding the valley, the city reoriented itself towards the north. After a while, making a mental leap across the crevasse and taking care not to look down, it continued on the other side of the valley behind a palisade of apartments. But the road east to west made a circumlocutory loop to the north.

The valley could not be altered or mended: the cracked halves of limestone would never grow together again. Nor could it be concealed, since its sodden, shifting floor was too untrustworthy to be built on. It could only be ignored, and so it studiously was. No one spoke of it; the maps gave it no name, and were ambiguous about its colour, muddying it somewhere between park and scrub. It was the city's obscure secret, its embarrassing nether region. It served as a site where you disposed of things; it was good only for riddance. People who lived around the edges dumped rubbish from the cliffs. The southern end was ideal for the gasworks, since who was there to complain of the sweet reek of poison or the chimneys which regurgitated fire all night long?

A few teachers with advanced views led their pupils in on foraging expeditions: the cliffs were a library of fossils, and the marshy floor was a display case of shells, trapped here when the sea drained and left the river stranded. From the comma-shaped skeletons and grounded sea creatures stored in the rock to the gutted mansions and bankrupt factories spared by the landslip, the valley recited the saga of life on earth. It was a history book in bone, stone, sand and rusty metal.

Because it was the city's blind spot, it became the refuge of people the city overlooked. Roads encircled the valley, with alleys between the buildings enticing you in; it was a simple matter to saunter down one of them, turn a corner and vanish. You erased yourself from the electoral roll and from the taxation files. You left only your police record behind you, and an unsolved row of typographic dots like footprints sifting gradually away in the sand.

History had no more knowledge of you, though sociology made earnest efforts to trace you: each emigrant from the city to the valley constituted a problem, and could be worked up –

if the social workers were allowed to get close enough – into a case study.

Ern cantankerously refused to be categorised. No upsets in the city had made him seek out the valley. He scorned the idea. 'I'm one of the original settlers,' he would say, 'I'm a native.' He despised the fly-by-nights who hid in the valley until their angry wives or cheated partners got over their grievances or the police could not bother to investigate further, then crept gratefully back to the world of appliances, amenities, traffic lights.

'We've always lived in here,' said Ern, the plural referring to his forefathers not to his grandson. Ern's grandfather had worked on one of the farms, his father in one of the factories which replaced them. Ern was born in the hut where he still lived. 'We date right back' was his boast. He sent out to the city for his medicine; whatever else he needed he grew, or got by exchange with his neighbours. The coins donated by the drivers at the tunnel were practically useless. He hoarded them for emergencies, and once in a while treated himself to a new hat.

After Ern, the line was disrupted. When he married his wife, he promised her that they were bound for the suburbs. Later, after the child was born, she reminded him of his promise. 'I never said no such thing,' he declared. 'You were talking to yourself.' His wife moved to the suburbs on her own, and took the girl with her. She acquired an address; claiming to be a widow, she married a grocer, and served behind the counter. The girl, despite the grocer's nurturing, went to the bad. Once she got her first pair of high heels, she was off. She even wore them – the spikes spattered by mud as she jolted up the track – when she came to call on Ern, at the end of her abbreviated childhood. Her face reminded him of someone.

'Is that you, Thel?' he asked. They had called her Thelma.

'I go by Shirley now,' she answered, with a city-slicker's condescension.

She had a child in tow. The grocer, it transpired, had locked the door on her. She was alleged to have given the shop a bad name with what the grocer called 'her goings-on'. Those goings-on were embodied in the child. She had a favour to ask. 'You wouldn't look after the kid for a while, would you? I've got some things to do. And I wanted him to meet his grandpa.' The boy howled. There was a car waiting for her, she explained, down on the road, just by the tunnel.

Off she wiggled on her pronged heels, and never came back. It was a long time – longer than it took Ern to admit to himself that she had not been delayed – before the boy stopped crying.

Some days later, Ern realised that she had not paused long enough to tell him his grandson's name. The boy himself did not seem to know it. So he was christened Wilf, without benefit of clergy. Since he was born outside the valley, his grandfather considered him a feeble specimen. 'He takes after the other side of the family,' he would defensively explain when it became known that the boy was inseparable from a block of wood. 'I was landed with him.'

In the valley, the family had been redefined: here it was a team, an alliance of complementary skills. Its members belonged only if they could earn their keep, and when they dropped out – like the sick Dog in the line of carnivorous sentinels – no one mourned. It was not love which bound them together. Love would have lamented the loss of an individual, of some combination of qualities which was unrepeatable. In the valley, as in the state of nature, that was a sentimental folly, since everyone was replaceable. Ern kept Wilf on because he had his uses. He ran errands, he helped with the signalling, he washed up; he was someone to complain to, and to throw things at.

The lads, another only too typical case for the social workers, were just such a consortium. They began as a gang, then became a tribe. They had their mutually reinforcing specialities. Athol did the research, and consulted his contacts to discover what needed to be nicked – which model of car, the brand of video recorder with exactly which features. Jacko lugged the heavier items, and was an impressive prop: the lumbering sight of him convinced people to surrender their goods graciously. For anything grievous and bodily, however, Clem was called upon; Jacko did not really have the stomach (or the head). Jacko need not even have been Athol's brother, since Athol – keen on exhibitions of respect from the young – required Horry and the other kids to call all grown-ups uncle. Their fraternity was a professional matter.

For them, moving to the valley had been a business-like calculation, not a counsel of despair.

They were not like the men you saw pacing querulously along the verges of the highways at the valley's edge. Often one of these would sit at a bus stop for days at a time, looking back at the escarpment of towers and the shabby suburbs which had expelled him. Hunched there, he would consider the inevitable next move, as if on a window ledge awaiting a propitious moment for the jump. Then, taking himself by surprise, he would get up and do it: slouch down the nearest track into the valley. The traffic would go on hurtling by; no one in the bus queue would notice. The valley for him was the last stop, the depot where the vehicle went out of service.

But not for the lads. Their move, achieved overnight in a fleet of purloined vans and lorries which they ditched at daybreak, took place because they needed larger, safer premises. In the suburbs, they had to secrete their stock in backyard garages and attics, and there was always the danger of a raid by the police. In the valley, they had a cave as a torchlit store, with their canine security patrol outside, and any number of abandoned farms to camp in. If the police came to call – which they seldom did, having quietly decided that the valley was outside their jurisdiction – Athol had their story ready. They were up from the country, down on their luck, all they asked for was a chance, as soon as they found an opening in the city they would be gone.

Until then, it was business as usual: sorties after dark all over the city; the occasional hold-up on the road through the valley; days spent repainting stolen cars, redistributing registration plates, filing serial numbers off stolen appliances; easing commodities out of the cave and back into the cycle of ownership and forfeiture – that grand, rotating design which Athol loved to contemplate, because it imitated the motion of life itself. Those who presumed to own things and held them so jealously would have to let go in the end until, as Athol made the wheel spin faster, there were no more grasping people but only the orbiting, unanchored property they had lost. He loved it when cars came back to him, almost as if homesick. One low-slung sports job had passed through the valley and through his hands three times, though its colours and its number plates were different on each occasion. Disposing of the car after the last overhaul, he patted its bonnet affectionately as its temporary tenant drove it off and muttered to himself 'See you later, my lovely.'

Athol was in the business of circulation, like the farm workers he had supplanted in the valley, who spent their lives waiting for the earth to lumber through the rota of seasons so their seeds would sprout. It was husbandry, just as much as Ern's patch of cabbages. Athol's customers, besieging him with want lists, swore by him; so did his victims (who overlapped with the customers), since they knew they were likelier to retrieve whatever they had, well, mislaid by applying to him than by reporting the incident to the police. There was a fine to pay of course, but Athol in extracting it from them reminded them that wisdom came dear these days. 'You should have been more careful,' he would chide.

He operated a black economy, the nocturnal side of the city's daytime race for gain. His only problem was the profits: what to do with them, that is. Clem spent his share on weapons and women. Jacko sent his to their mother, who wondered crabbily how he had come by it but kept it all the same. Athol, deciding he would postpone thinking about what it was good for, had taken to burying it around the valley in spots known only to himself. He visited the interred boxes of loot every so often. Having checked that the damp or the rats had not got to them, he replaced the rocks or the charred floorboards and would think, Safe as houses – though houses, as he reflected with a shrug, were not safe at all.

It was a versatile place, the valley: everyone who entered it could reconstruct its dishevelled wreckage as they chose. Thus it came to contain home-made versions of all those institutions which the society outside had spent centuries devising as its means of enforcing order and perpetuating power.

For Ern, the valley was the family estate, his patrimony. For his daughter, it certainly was not that. She must have seen it as a boarding school, which conveniently kept its charges forever.

For Athol it was a bank vault, sealed tight because only he knew the right territorial combination. And for the old woman with the deranged hair it was an open-air cathedral, with an altar flame of blue and yellow sulphurous gas.

Her name was Mona, and she was a witness – a Joe's Witness as they called it in the suburbs, where the church she used to attend was a shed of planks with a lid of tin and a tapering pole above the padlocked front door (it was a bad area for vandals) in homage to the idea of a spire. She had begun witnessing Jehovah in this shed, which the congregation bought on the cheap from a local timberyard, where it had been an office. But Jehovah had not confined himself to the shed. He visited her at home, and once made an appearance in the street, while she was out shopping, provoking her to shriek his praises and later causing her to be hustled off to the hospital for examination.

Ecstasy like hers the suburbs could not contain. Her neighbours peered through slits in their blinds at her transports. She had let the back garden riot out of control, and galumphed through the knee-high weeds and stalks caterwauling a hymn. She stood at the fence every afternoon to watch the sun set. She insisted on staring at it as it burned a hole in the sky: it too needed witnessing. Then she staggered back into the house, blindly reeling in a hail of bronze and purple spots. The only relative anyone knew of was a sister who had lived with her, Eileen by name and also (according to the neighbours) 'a bit touched'; in any case, she was dead.

The social workers paid a call. 'And how are you in yourself?' they carefully asked Mona.

'All right,' said Mona, mildly affronted by the query. 'Except that my head's on fire.' She continued making a pot of tea.

The social workers, who came in pairs like nuns, exchanged a glance, which Mona saw them exchanging. Within days she had gone, leaving the taps to drip and the dust to thicken in the house and the brambles to interbreed in the yard; she found her way to the valley, and was sure she had been guided because there, even when the sun let her down, the gas works were her flagrant unfailing tabernacle.

And – who knows? – she may have been right. There were

still more ways of describing the valley; mythology must be allowed its say.

Like everyone else, Mona had a private notion of paradise, and was searching for the route which led back to it. She was always on the lookout for signals. But eventually she realised that the surest way to get there was to close her eyes.

First she watched the sun until the world blazed and she could see nothing but sparks and cinders. Setting off, she asked no directions, despite the headache which blackened her vision. She packed some street plans, and maps which (though she didn't notice) unriddled the labyrinth of the wrong cities; they stayed in her sagging pockets, never unfolded. She did her navigating with the eye which, twisted sideways in its socket, could see round corners. When she got to the valley, she overlooked the hillocks of rot outside the shanties, the barracking of the children who played in that compost, the corroded metal and arrested fly-wheels of the factories. She did not require it to be beautiful, so long as the chimneys fulminated on the horizon.

The religions would like to keep paradise to themselves, and award it only to their adherents. They make it a synonym for virtues we will never possess; they situate it irretrievably behind us, or project it into outer space and consign it to the after-life, since while on earth and alive, we will never qualify for admission. But why not reach up and pull the idea down? Paradise can be regained by being imagined. The valley could impersonate any kind of Eden. Wilf saw it as a wonderland of newborn oddities like the ant-hill. To the lads it symbolised liberty, a wide-open idyll where no laws applied. And for Mona it was the radiant site of a kingdom about to come.

Cosmology, the grandest of mind-bending sciences or the most outlandish of fictions, also had a theory about the valley.

Looking down on it after dark from the terraced apartments above, the valley was as imponderable as the night sky. Its tract of blackness, dizzily deep, could not be measured. There were no co-ordinates, no points of comfortingly human reference. Was this the formlessness of a world unawakened as yet by light, or the insentience of a world which had died? Odd particles of brightness sometimes glinted there, but there was no identifying

67

them without a way to gauge distance: they might have been fireflies in front of your eyes or a house burning a mile away or a meteor a few years off.

Daybreak demystified these interstellar spaces, assuring you that the valley was made of stone and soil and water, not of black air and absence. But then there were other puzzles to worry over. The valley, for instance, was relativity in action. The trudging and scavenging of its inhabitants, as they dug sustenance from the ground or dabbled in mud pies which they stacked up into dwellings, happened alongside the city's high-speed circuitry and its electronic ping-pong of signals, yet they belonged in difference epochs. Past and future unfolded simultaneously, though at different paces; the fourth dimension was next door.

The city impatiently transformed itself, destroying sections it considered old and replacing them with buildings which had outwitted nature: waterfalls splashed and spilled indoors, forests grew under glass, and no birds nested on the outside walls because the tingling cables frightened them away. Still, people continued to drop out into the valley, like tired swimmers resigning themselves to an undertow; suicidally relaxing, they sank through the centuries and adjusted themselves to the valley's inertia. Here the rule was not transformation but degeneration. Everything wasted, mouldered, until the decaying end restored the beginning. Then there would be another muffled bang from underground, and the whole process could start all over again. The gas works were a testament to the muddlingly wilful force which plotted the universe. Gas after all means chaos; consult the etymology.

And the tunnel? The valley had its own two-way perforation in space, the annihilating pocket into which all things vanished, which ate them up, even if they were as solid and indigestible as cars, and then perhaps – once they had learned in the darkness that the way forward and the way back are identical, that the two lanes overlap and the universe while seeming to speed ahead is actually rewinding – disgorged them, blinking at the unaccustomed glare and remembering nothing of the trauma inside; the same but different.

7

ALWAYS, RETURNING HOME at dawn, dropping out of the sky as the plane flung itself at the earth and tried to choke its headlong energy, he had the same dream.

Sometimes he had it before, sometimes during, sometimes after – nodding upright, while the sky above the clouds was still black; or stumbling half-awake through the routine for re-admission to life in the neon-lit airport; or later in the afternoon, when fatigue overtook him and he fell asleep again sitting at his desk and the day whirred into reverse.

It began so plausibly that it merged with reality. He was returning home at dawn. The plane tipped sideways to slice through clouds; where they were torn, like thready fabric, he could see a city. It might have been any city, any place where people huddle together. Its lights were still on: all cities are the same at night. The orange stripes of highways, the spouting blue pipes of a gas works, the plantations of boxes stirring reluctantly awake. Then the thud onto land, the screech and scorch of the tyres, the engines thrusting back to front. They were in the world again. But where in it?

The next part was believable because automatic. This, he thought, I could do in my sleep anyway. You follow the crowd, do what everyone else is doing. That is how you learn to live. They prised the doors off the capsule, and shovelled everyone out. There was a shock of cold grey air, a slap in the face to restore consciousness. But he could feel himself nodding off again at once. Just fumble along behind the others. There is a photograph for them to identify you by; no need to know or say your name. They wave you out into more of that cold air.

Then the dream went off the rails. The driver of the taxi asked where he wanted to be taken, and nodded in recognition of the address. But he had not heard himself say anything. He sat back, waiting to see whose life this would turn out to be.

They arrived. The taxi departed. It seemed that there was no question of payment. He knew the house, but also knew that it was not his. The sky was brightening. Birds sang in the garden. Having no key, he rang the bell. He held his breath, then had to release it: no one answered, no one came. A dog moped sleepily around the corner of the house and growled, then wandered off. He rang again, with his head pressed to the door. The bell shrilled in the empty rooms. Are they out? Will they ever return? Or will they squint through the peep-hole and, seeing a stranger, refuse to open? He waited, and at last admitted the truth. So what to do? Aching with weariness, he lay down under a tree in the garden. There was no point in weeping: to cry was to summon someone, and he knew that no one would come. In the dream, he fell asleep and hoped as he did so, desperately, that he would wake up and find . . .

And find that he belonged after all, that a cleaner in the lobby called him by a name he recognised. There was no tree in the frosty garden and no sniffy, unwelcoming dog; no garden in fact, unless you counted the view from the back windows of the apartment across the rot and rubble of the valley. Inside the lift, he pressed the number which corresponded to his slice of space, his life. He relied on blind-fold instinct to do it for him. Would he have been able to recall the number if someone had asked? The door of the lift slid open; he found the key in his case and opened the door of the apartment.

Inside it was still thick with sleep. Sleep hung in the hall like cobwebs in the castle with its enchanted sleeper. The mirror inside the door had its eyes closed and, when he stared at it in the gloom, would not show him his face. A coat hung listlessly from a hook, as if asleep on its feet. The front door faintly creaked as he shut it, grumbling as its timbers slumped back to rest. He pressed down the hall through the veils, the entangling vines, the sticky clinging webs of so much sleep.

In the bedroom there was a head on the dented pillow. The head lay inside a nest of hair, its face lurking somewhere behind the strands. The body, muffled under sheets, seemed to stir – a shuddering arm, a leg which quivered, the oceanic swell and the collapse likes waves on the shore when it breathed – but the head was still, concentrating on its own incommunicable dreams.

Then an eye looked at him, just one, through the tousled hair, not sure whether what it saw was in the room or flickering instead on the screen inside its lid. 'Paul,' she said, with the hint of a question suspended in the heavy, sighing atmosphere of the room.

Yes, Paul, he answered (though not aloud). It's me: you remembered.

He tugged at his clothes, exhausted and impatient. So many ropes we tie around ourselves, nooses at our necks, waists, feet, like bits of string around our fingers so we won't forget – whatever it was. So many buttons we lock ourselves inside. So much help we need, now limply discarded on the floor.

He tumbled into the bed as weightlessly as if someone had knocked him on the head so that the body, relaxed and not fearing the fall, could float to the ground and settle there like grains of dust rearranging themselves in another formation. He fumbled for a pair of arms under the covers, and wrapped them around him. He parted the hair and uncovered her face. She smelled of sleep: a room with the windows closed and thick furry velvet curtains pulled across them on a summer day. He clung to her, and slept. Sleep lunged down on him like the blade of a guillotine.

Which is when, this time, he had the dream.

He woke from it panting, his face slick with sweat, his fists clenched. The room was drowning in sun. She was not there.

He stumbled to the window and looked down over the valley, halved by shadow along a line which an axe might have incised: the sun had cleared the cliff of buildings but still had to clarify the far edge of the valley with its bluff of eroded limestone, its caves of contraband, its impromptu huts and shattered houses. The valley had not yet rubbed the sleep out of its eyes.

Down below a man was bent double in a field where some vegetables had been wheedled from the ground. He seemed to be attached the earth, his arms and legs fastened to the furrows;

this must be happening before people had learned how to be upright.

He found her in the kitchen, making coffee for herself. She explained that she thought she would let him sleep. She could tell that, to him, it counted as a desertion.

'Kate,' he said, 'I had the same dream. It woke me up. What time is it?'

He knew from the shadow across the valley exactly what the time was: the line of buildings they lived in marked the land beneath like a sun dial. He really wanted to know what day it was. It seemed to be tomorrow; he had lost a day somewhere, overnight above the ocean, or in the looped repetitions of that dream.

'Nine o'clock,' she said. 'When did you get here? Six?'

So it was still today: or rather, today was about to begin. The short night did not give the mind time to digest yesterday's dose of aggravations. It resisted having to cope with more. Soon the dream would invade his unguarded head whether he had been travelling or not. It summarised all his anxieties, as succinctly as a telegram.

She gave him the coffee she had made for herself. It's the least I can do, she thought. Perhaps it is all I can do. 'Greater love,' she said with a smile as she handed him the cup, and left him to complete the quotation. She then suggested, as she had done before, that he was afraid of flying.

He had considered that already, and rejected it. He had no fear while in the air. He got through the slow-motion hours in a state of affectless calm.

Often the analogy with death occurred to him. Not with dying – though he had once or twice imagined how that would be: bodies turning inside out as the plane, shrieking, corkscrewed down; the collating of jumbled limbs, which might not match each other; the identification parade, as on judgment day.

But no, the analogy was with what came after: with being dead. The numbness, the forfeiture of will, the centuries of hopeless expectancy. You sat there in noisy, propulsive limbo while they fed you, sedated you with films, told you more or less believable lies about what lay beneath the clouds and made vague promises about when you would arrive somewhere. But time had stopped. The plane did not feel as if it was moving ahead; all that energy was expended to keep it in the same indeterminate spot. You were ordered to make your watch go backwards, so the same inert hours had to be suffered through over and over again. Space had folded in on itself. That blinking light outside – a signal on the wing, feet away, or some cold and fathomlessly distant star? He felt no fear, just tired acquiescence, like the man who walks to the scaffold or to the chamber containing the chair, without needing to be frogmarched by guards or enticed by priests: it's not that he is brave, but that he no longer cares.

He poured the coffee into himself, and was grateful for its heat, its acids, its cargo of drugs. It persuaded him that he was alive – again? He could manage now without her sympathy.

But he refused to concede the argument to her. 'You're wrong,' he said. 'The dream isn't about the trip. It's about coming home.'

She let that pass. The coffee grinder testily chewed up his words. 'So how was it?' she asked. 'I mean, how did it go?'

He looked at her dubiously, not wanting to show that he was dubious. If only a human face could be be hidden behind. He yawned in self-protection and massaged his cheeks and forehead, skulking behind his hands, obliterated by the empty oval of the yawn. But it was not the dream she was asking about. She was not taunting him with a request for a replay. She meant the week away, the job he had been there to do.

He was an architect; he had been away to check on the progress of a building of his. It was the first design of his about which he had felt, Here is my monument: this one has my name on it.

It was an office block, though he did not concern himself much with the business to be transacted in it. Others in the firm had devised the innards. His contribution was the outside: a skin of glass, gripping the spindly pyramid of the structure. Twisting out of the scurf and scrub of tenements, in a part of the foreign city marked for aggressive redevelopment, it was to be a spar of shining ice, a glacial mountain, its summit squeezing into a polar sign-post which announced the top or the end of the world. The summit – people had already started metaphor-mongering about it – might also be an ice-pick: the building stabbed the sky, rather than scraping it.

Yet when the glass was on, the building intended to confound all metaphors by performing its last and most dazzling trick. It would simply vanish. Its reflectors would show the sky its own face. The triangular panels would trap clouds, slice them into sections and make it seem that they had been squeezed inside the building. When it rained, the building would look like a grey deluge, spilled from that suddenly unfrozen ice-cap. And on sunny days, when the sky was clear, it would efface itself like the deceptively smiling Cheshire cat. The loftiest tribute, he had once said, would be if a plane were to crash into it, unaware that it was there.

He hadn't told her this particular fancy. He knew what she was likely to make of it. 'It's going well,' he said. 'They've got the glass on almost half way up. You should see it, in among those old slum streets. It looks as if it just touched down. A visitor from another planet.'

'And what do the locals think of the visitor?'

'There aren't many of them around to notice. They're all being resettled in the suburbs, and very happy about it too. What's more, I talked to the developers about this other scheme of mine. The one for the valley. They're keen. We're going to talk again. They're definitely interested.'

'So we'll have a visitor from outer space in our back yard too?'

'Oh no we won't. Because we won't be here either. We'll be over there on the top floor with the best view of the city, if they let me go ahead.'

Paul had a vision for the valley. For it, not of it: his vision superseded the view of the valley which he blinked at every morning when he got out of bed. The valley, already the despair of the police, had also been given up as a hopeless case by the planners and developers. In the middle of the city, which had extended to its edge since the cave-in, it was waste land, wasted land, because who dared build on those unsound bluffs and that sodden marsh? But Paul had a project.

In California, a skyscraper straddled the rift running down

the coast, where shelves of rock grated and abraded and were bound (like incompatible couples, he thought) to split apart one day. The skyscraper, steely-nerved, was prepared for that. Its weight rested on two pediments, one on either side of the fault. Like a strong man with his legs spread to show off his calf muscles, it would not budge when the earth groaned open between its feet. The upper floors might shudder and shed glass, but the feet were safely buried in stable ground away from the fault.

That gave Paul the idea. Why not build a platform above the valley, braced and sustained where the cliffs could be trusted? It would be like floorboards laid at last over the quaking soil, or the lid of a coffin nailed down definitively on the valley's compost of bricks and bones, turds and fossils, its dross of criminals, derelicts and anachronistic rustics. The space beneath the platform, sloping down to the river, could serve as a drain-pipe for the city and a tunnel for traffic; and above the platform – loftily ignorant of its roots and of the catacomb in its basement – he could build a city in miniature, a digest of all the cities there had ever been, with a skyline of spires, domes, minarets, pagodas unfurling around its eaves.

He had been doodling versions of it for years. Scribbles on a pad, licensed to be extravagant because he thought the idea was impossible, proposed the different facets it might have as you walked around it: the Parthenon put together again, snow-white and fresh from the quarry; a range of crotchety Gothic pinnacles, like a huddle of sooty dwarfed cathedrals; maybe a frieze of orange tiles, with Chinese dragons guarding them; a boxy vista of old-time skyscrapers, filing cabinets in vertiginous stacks with a playful sideways tilt to them. With its pillars drilled into the ridges, its floor of reinforced concrete burying the carious ravines and gulping quagmires of the valley, his imaginary city marched step by step into the sky, unhindered by practical realities. But now there was an offer to pay for research, so the engineers and geologists could decide whether his fantasy would stand or not.

Kate encouraged him so long as it remained a fantasy, and had once or twice added extravagances of her own to his doodling: a balustrade of bronze pineapples; a colonnade of pencil pines

75

(trees he liked because they were so tidy and designed) to hide the gas works. She was a painter, practising wiles for her assault on the art of the past. Currently she was engaged in some thefts from the city's museum. She would identify a character in a painting at the museum, copy it, then translate it to a setting in the city outside. Rembrandt's 'Polish Rider' turned to stone on a monumental plinth in the middle of a square, unheeded by the passing buses and taxis. Gauguin's Polynesian girls as migrant housemaids, gossiping about home and exchanging nostalgic snapshots in the park on their day off. Caravaggio's Bacchus squeezed into torn jeans, attitudinising under a street lamp. Some Breughel peasants, valiantly attempting to rollick or roister among blighted crops and bankrupt factories in the valley she looked down on from her windows. She liked Paul's city when it was imaginary; her favourite buildings were the unbuilt ones. But if the scheme were ever to advance beyond the sketching pads, he knew she would be hostile. She did not like the idea of abolishing the valley.

They had been through this particular dispute before. He would observe that the valley was a rubbish dump. She would point out that it once was and still could be a landscape, with its quilted fields and stone-walled terraces. He would characterise its inhabitants as the city's rejects: authority tolerated the valley, he argued, because it was an open prison, to which the inmates – tramps, car thieves, illegal immigrants, bag ladies with cosmic hang-ups – had obligingly sent themselves. Once they were evicted from the valley, they could be cared for: jail for the villains, sedative cells for the bag ladies, resettlement in the suburbs for the industrious poor. She would then tell him that he was wrong to think that the city had rejected these people. Perhaps it was they who had rejected the city. She granted him the car thieves. Her own car had once, years ago, walked away from the place where she always parked it, and no doubt went to ground in the valley. But the other valley-dwellers were living much as people had always lived – and as they/we might have to do again. You can't just corral them and consign them to lock-ups or hovels with mod cons on the other side of the river. In the valley, they have a culture.

A culture! he would say, with comical incredulity.

Yes, a culture, would be the reply; it didn't only mean books and buildings, it meant a relationship to the land.

In the valley – he would then insist, with the hope of reaching a full stop – they don't even have an agriculture.

The front rooms of their apartment framed the official view of the city: a trellis of steel, stretching between the masts and dishes which interpreted signals from the sky and the whining, smoking track along the earth far below their balcony. The valley was the prohibited view from the back, blurred by the pebbly glass of the bathroom, shut out by the curtains in their bedroom or by blinds in the kitchen. These windows were a convenience for letting light in; you weren't supposed to look out of them. But they were Kate's favourite point of vantage.

From the front, you saw only other windows. From the back, you saw land which the city had not yet been able to obliterate. Like rear-vision mirrors, the windows showed our unravelling past. A man chopping holes in the ground for seeds. A woman stirring a pot. A child playing in a ditch.

'Come over here,' she said. She was at the window, holding her steaming cup in both hands. 'Look down there.'

Moving close to look, he nestled his head against hers. She flinched, then let her head loll beside his. Her hair, as bitter and aromatic as crushed leaves, made him gasp.

She was pointing at signs of life in the valley: the man in the shiny suit walking up the hill, off to work or off in search of work; the woman outside a hut scrubbing clothes in a trough of suds; the child on the bicycle with the crooked wheel, trying to ride across dunes of rubbish.

'Can I tell you something?' he said, disentangling himself from her hair. 'He probably has a pocket full of stolen credit cards, she's a highway hooker, and why isn't that kid at school? Oh, and the bicycle's stolen too.'

She swallowed some coffee and sat down. Then very softly – as if to mitigate the pain her words would cause, or perhaps merely, like a muffler on a gun, to avoid an uproar – she said 'Paul, think about it. You charge about ripping people up by the roots so you can build your follies on the bit of land where they lived. You say it doesn't bother you, that you're doing them a good turn. But then you come back and cry in your sleep because you can't find your home, or think you don't have one. Just listen to that dream of yours. You should have that dream seen to – you should take it in to be mended. Or mend it yourself.'

He went off to the bathroom, hoping that the reproachful look he gave her would cover his retreat. But he admitted to himself, as the needles of water pricked his face, that she was right, that she had wounded him with the truth.

Drenched, bedraggled, he scraped at his face and tried not to return his own glance in the bathroom mirror. Even if he avoided his eyes, the stubble, white before its time, accused him: the growth of death. How it crept up on you, wearing soft-soled shoes like a house-breaker; how it waited, consulting its own timetable, within. He jerked the razor down his cheek and nicked the skin. Blood leaked out, a single misplaced tear.

He thought, as he watched it slow to a halt and harden, She sees what I can only see when my eyes are shut: that there is no eternal city, that I am building illusions which will all the same – fictitious as they are – outlive me.

In the valley, he knew, people died without the sort of reassurance he sold. Anything would serve as a shelter – a cave, a barn, a box, a tarpaulin – and no one assumed that it would last longer than a night. Perhaps it would not even see the night out. Animals, more honestly, slept in the open. They were not afraid of dying, so did not need houses to defend them against an enemy who was in any case already on the premises. Breezily (when the wind blew) or torrentially (when the creek over-flowed), the valley dispensed with culture, structure, all fantasies of permanence. Which was why he hated it.

Once, while still at school, he had come upon a photograph in a book. It changed his life, he often thought; it decided for him what he wanted to be. Yet he was not sure he understood what it meant to him, and why it had both alarmed and excited him.

It was a photograph of a city in ruins: arches with their backs broken, towers with their heads knocked off. But there was no grandeur in its decay. It was shabby, paltry, its façades peeling like shed skin, its plaster flaking into powder like pounded bones. Weeds had taken possession.

Among the bushes sat some elephants. Not real elephants, not even stone ones, but elephants of papier-mâché, left in the rain to perish though still sitting upright on their rumps as if posing at the circus and flourishing their trunks like a brass band which has run out of breath. The city was Babylon, or some film-maker's notion of it, abandoned to the sceptical daylight when there were no cameras left to believe in it.

Around it, abridging millennia, another city had grown up, as incorrigible as the weeds. The decrepit palaces and disgraced temples and the arcades of elephants reared above a parallelo-gram of bungalows with picket fences and saplings which would one day cast shade. People came out to read newspapers on the porch or to water a sapling which wilted in that sandy soil and looked up at the mouldy monuments. They were not surprised at the sight: their own city was just as improbable, scratching like those trees for a foothold in an earth which disowned them. They had not yet memorised their new addresses. Sooner or later, the place would seem real.

He could not be sure whether he remembered parts of the scene, or had invented them. Were there really derricks in the backyards, nodding as they punctured the shallow dirt and searched for oil? And to one side, wasn't there another city-shaped organism of twining pipes, plump gullets and fire-breath-ing mouths: a gas works?

The photograph haunted him. He had gone for walks in it. He kicked up small cyclones in the unpaved streets, he heard the derricks creak, he could see the scaffolding (concealed in the photograph) which propped up Babylon. He even chose a room for himself to live in, at the back of one of those bungalows. He dreamed that he was able to make the wells spout oil or the elephants roar.

He also dreamed of knocking Babylon down. Sometimes he did so with a fusillade of pebbles, sometimes a kick was all it took. The city sank to its knees with slow, unprotesting grace; he had to take a stick to one of the elephants, which seemed reluctant to come apart.

79

Though the photograph had always been with him, imprinted inside his head, he was aware that its meaning had changed. When he was a boy, the gimcrack city would tumble and then, like film rewinding, re-erect itself at once, its bricks flying back together, the elephants glueing on their sundered trunks. It all happened in obedience to him: he must have known a spell. And it happened silently. No crash of masonry, no shriek from the expiring beasts. Later, growing up, he began to hear the sounds it made as it came apart. It roared; every atom felt is particular pain. He tasted the dust in his mouth and throat, stifling him.

Now too, when he thought of it, he would step away from himself in a shock as he saw that boy stamping on the clumps of stone or battering them with a cudgel. Was that ever me? Yes, it still is. Then when he had stacked the remnants up again into other shapes, the boy would sidle down the street between the bungalows, whistling fecklessly, and wait for a chance to nudge or shove his fancy pinnacles to the ground. His boot was as efficient as a bulldozer.

Why? he would ask the boy. He knew he could not stop him; he was merely curious to know the reason.

Because, shrugged the boy. Because I felt like it. Because I wanted to know how it felt. Because there's no room for me with all this in the way. But all the explanations had a questioning lilt to them, as if the boy were trying them out, aware that they explained nothing. He could see the boy looking at him with the deadly severity of childhood. You tell me, the boy seemed about to say.

He collected the bits of his current self from the bedroom floor where he had scattered them, threw some away, replaced others, pieced himself together, prepared a face. Kate was still in the kitchen, still tousled, drowsy-eyed. As he left, she said, 'I'm glad you're back.'

He hugged her, but he thought as he did so, No, I'm not back. That makes it sound as if time has stopped. One foot has grazed the floor, that's all; I have my arms around you, and now I have to disengage them – I need one of them to carry my briefcase. I have to return to the business of being myself, at least for another day.

Opening the door, he paused. It suddenly felt irreversible: a leap from a height. What could he say, to thank her or to plead with her? All he could think of was to ask how she was going to spend the day.

'I'll be out sketching,' she said. 'I'm looking for faces. Actually, for heads. See you.'

8

'HELL'S BELLS!' SAID Horry, and whistled.
But the story needed more by way of an introduction.
It required a proper oath, bleeding and blasphemous. 'Jeezus,'
he said, elongating the word like a slowly solemn roll on the
drums. And he added 'You can say that again' for good measure,
though Wilf – to whom he was reciting the events of the night
before – had so far said nothing.

Wilf's mouth was open, but only to gasp for air. What Horry
had already told him seemed to have knocked the breath from
him. His hand tightened on his stick, as if it were still a tree or
at least a fence post, against which he could steady himself.

'There was a hell of a row about it at our place,' said Horry.
'That's how I found out. They woke me up with their shouting.
My dad called Clem everything. He said he was a disgrace to
the family, that he'd ruin the business, that we didn't go in for
that kind of thing and he wouldn't help him out. And then my
mum started screaming.

'So I got up to have a look for myself. Jacko was asleep
through the whole thing. Anyway they were over in the barn,
and my dad looked as if his lid was about to blow and my mum
– when she stopped screaming, my dad told her to shut up –
looked like she was about to keel over. And there was Clem,
with all this red mud on him. He just stood there, sort of
grinning.

'I think that was what drove my dad so wild. He asked him
why he did it, and first of all Clem said "I don't know". "What
do you mean you don't know?" my dad yelled, and my mum
started moaning again. "You killed him without knowing why?
All we wanted was the car, and what he had on him. Where's
the profit in *killing* the poor bugger?" So then Clem said "There's

no profit in it at all, I didn't do it for profit. I did it because I felt like it. And by the end, he felt like it too. One thing I can tell you: it's hard work. No, doing it. I mean afterwards". Then he asked my mum to get him a drink.

'Well, she just stared at him. My dad abused him some more, and Clem said "Come off it, you got your car, didn't you? Don't be such a spoilsport. He's all disposed of. No one will find him. Or at least not all of it in the one place. And if they do, they'll have trouble sticking him back together. As for the mess, the rain will take care of that. Now how about my drink?"

'All my mum did was say "Look at you". It was splashed over his face. He had it in his hair. "Yeah, I know," Clem said, "amazing, isn't it? But what do you expect? Just think how many buckets of it we're lugging around inside us. It's a wonder the skin holds it all in."

'My dad asked Clem who he was – the other one, I mean. Clem said he couldn't care less. "Don't get me wrong, Athol. It wasn't nothing personal. More an experiment, really. As a matter of fact, I asked him what his name was. You know what he said? That it didn't matter. You could always look in his wallet, if you're that interested. Whoever he was, he wouldn't recognise himself now." How about that?'

Horry's eyes gleamed. The excitement of it tickled his spine and made him shiver; on the back of his neck, hair stiffened like quills.

Wilf dug his fingers into the stick. They might have been gouging holes in the wood. He felt himself clinging to the thing for dear life – except that life, it seemed, was not dear, and no matter how you tightened your grip you could not secure it. Can this happen? he thought. Is this what it will be like?

A long perspective cleared, and he looked straight ahead: he could see as far as the end. Squinting as if into a glare, he saw that the vista was empty. Of course there was the mess afterwards, but a soaking from the rain would take care of it. Clem guaranteed that. The valley would guzzle the spilled liquids, and gulp down the solid left-overs too. The executioner was not even a bogey. Wilf remembered the look on Clem's face last night at the fountain: the expression of someone who knew what would happen but was still coolly curious about whether it would happen differently this time. Years like miles unrolled in front of Wilf. Yet having crawled, stumbled, run, walked, limped and at last hobbled through them all, he was bound to arrive at the same place, where the man with the professional smile would be waiting to take him to pieces. The stick was not going to serve him as a weapon after all. It swung from his hand as stupidly as a body from the gallows.

'What then?' he asked Horry, ashamed that his voice sounded so weak.

Horry was eager to tell the rest, since this was where he became part of the story.

'Clem came out of the barn and seen me behind the door, where I was listening. He sent me back to the house to get a towel for him and some clothes. He said he needed them up by the tap. Clem was washing himself when I got there, scrubbing himself. He had his head under the spout: you know that animal you're so scared of. He dried himself and got dressed. Then he gave me the old clothes to get rid of. We've got that tin drum in the back of the barn to burn the rubbish in. My mum lit it up this morning, and I stuck the bundle in there. I suppose I'm his accomplice, don't you think? He couldn't have got away without me.'

'He got away? Where to?'

'I dunno, wherever he wanted to. He went back up the hill. That's where he did it. I heard the Dogs yapping later on. Maybe he gave them a feed?'

At which Horry, who had at last succeeded in alarming himself, fell silent.

Wilf thought back to the scene he and his grandfather had trespassed on last night: the man on his knees, croakily pleading for help; Clem standing over him, with the superior smirk of an animal trainer; the water dribbling into the dust from that gullet of brass. At the time, he had known better than to ask for an explanation. Adults were like foreigners. They conducted their business in a dialect of gestures he could not translate. Apparently you learned the language in time to become one of them.

His grandfather spent the rest of the evening cursing Clem

84

and pickled onions; this morning he sent Wilf out of the valley for more of the brown medicine, blaming Clem and the vinegary brine for his attack. On the way, Wilf met Horry, also bound for the city where he had to buy paint for his father's latest catch of cars. Horry, usually standoffish, ran to catch up with Wilf.

The story poured from him, after he had made Wilf swear (on pain of a visit from Clem, when he returned to circulation) that it would go no further. So now Wilf knew, well ahead of his time, what the tableau meant; how lives were short stories – abruptly curtailed, and for no good reason. As for passing the knowledge on, he realised that he was bound to secrecy by something other than his promise, solemnly enforced by crossing his heart and spitting into the dirt: there was no one he could tell. His grandfather would rant, rage and take it all out on Wilf. He would have to suffer the consciousness on his own.

Worst of all was the fact that Horry had not been able to tell him enough. He had his own glimpse of before; Horry supplied the details of afterwards. But what happened in between he was left to imagine. He had to reconstruct the events of the night before in some shadowed alcove inside his head. And he found it was only too easy: you made it up by turning it into a story about yourself. You volunteered to be the victim. Though who did the killing? That was also your responsibility. You had to do it to yourself.

Horry skidded ahead, yelping in relief at having passed on his burden. Wilf, straggling up the hill with the stick seeming limp and rubbery in his hand, rehearsed what must have happened.

He knew Clem had a knife. How had it felt when it made its entry? Flesh could not resist; it cleaved like butter. The sliver the knife made turned slowly red. Pain came later, as an afterthought. You would have to check to make sure what had been done to you. Oh, I've been killed – so that's it. Now everything will gush out, through that narrow slit: blood, breath, being. And while the contents slowly spilled, what was Clem feeling? Nothing much, apparently. He forgot that he too lived inside a skin like the one he was piercing. As if in a cartoon, the blade would silently exclaim ZAP! or POW! or SLASH! A face would contort in an absurd grimace, then drop out of the frame and

85

out of mind. Except that there was the mess. Clem admitted that. The puddle. The steaks, the chops, the slippery organs. Wilf could not stop himself speculating about the utensils. Clem said the man had been disposed of. Did that mean an axe, a saw, a meat cleaver? And it did not end there. Each bit would have to be dealt with separately. Ern, tossing to the Dogs some unplucked hens which had died of heat exhaustion, once said, 'They'll eat anything. It's all food to them.' Perhaps Clem had put them to the test. Wilf had seen the Dogs mashing bones in their mouths and gulping them down. But a head?

And why go to all the trouble? It had been hard work, Clem said. Yet worth it, if what he wanted was to see how a man came apart. Wilf felt an ache in every one of his joints. Of course, it was already happening there at the water spout. The man on his knees was falling to pieces. If his grandfather had not hurried him away, they might have witnessed it. The head could no longer make the rest of him see reason. The limbs flapped uselessly, the bowels boiled, the heart banged against the ribs like a head battering itself against the bars of a cage. This was an after-life already.

Wilf remembered another hen, this time one which had lived long enough to be killed by his grandfather. After its head was off, the rest of it danced in a jubilant circle around the yard. It seemed to be excited; Wilf could have sworn it was cackling. Then it flopped down exhausted, its brief flutter of independence over. His grandfather made him pick up the head and throw it away before the flies found it. He gripped its velvety comb between two fingers, and wondered at its weightlessness. The beak terrified him. He looked it in the eye: its eyes had retired behind a white film. The membrane of white erased in an instant every image which had flickered across the eyes.

Like the head, the eyes were empty. They had never been otherwise; they could not store thoughts and sights like the appliances which the lads stowed in the cave. A life was just a misunderstanding. The fowl's lap of honour told him that. How long would it take for the word to be passed along to the twitching feet and agitated wings? When did you realise you were dead? You looked forward to it all your life, but when it came you missed out on experiencing it. Unless you had Clem to talk you through it.

Wilf had played games like this with Horry and some of the others – the tribal kids who came and went among the huts beside the highway, and never stayed long enough for you to attach names to them. The game was played with ghostly weapons: invisible ack-ack guns which spat their bullets from your mouth; imaginary grenades; once or twice, when you got the enemy down, a flick knife whose blade was your index finger, endowed with the power to slit throats. The rules outlawed Wilf's stick, because it happened to be real and could do actual damage.

Disarmed, the boys rehearsed warfare in cratered fields and behind wrecked walls, in a landscape where matter had reverted to chaos without the aid of bombs. It was the noises they made which were lethal. Horry's throat coughed up stuttering rounds of ammunition; he shrilled as he lobbed shells through the air. He killed Wilf several times whenever they played.

Then one day Wilf refused to die. Horry, lurking behind a tree, fired directly into him and could see the bullets unzipping Wilf's chest. He waited for Wilf to tumble over and roll about clutching himself. But Wilf, looking back at Horry, thought: What if this time I didn't? Why should I?

'Go on,' said Horry, seeing him hesitate, 'get down. Die.' And sprayed him with another round.

Wilf blinked, immune, bullet-proof because unbelieving. He thought, I don't know how to do it: to die.

He knew the groaning sounds he was required to make, and the convulsive motions. But no one could tell him what to feel while it was happening. The Dogs, patient and abject, indulging in no amateur dramatics, could not help him. Nor could the chicken, batting its wings in a last attempt to leave the ground. The cats his grandfather poisoned, stretched in a stiff sleep, also kept the secret.

'I've forgotten how to' was all he said to Horry.

'I'll show you,' said Horry, and smartly kicked him in the stomach.

The blow felled Wilf, like a tree giving in to the axe. He

crumpled, too hurt to cry out. He tumbled into the pain. It was a shaft with no bottom, as if the tunnel through the base of the valley had been upended.

'Now you know,' Horry said and, crooking a finger into the shape of a trigger, finished him off with a bullet in the back of the head as he lay there.

Then, despite the black cavity of pain Horry's kick had opened in him, Wilf still did not know. Now he did.

He reviewed the world in the light of this knowledge. They were walking up the lane towards the highway. A bare tree scraped its branches together. The surface of a puddle faltered and shook as they passed. He looked up. A plane swivelled above them and flung itself at a strip of tarmac to the north. It must have left a gash in the clouds as its wings carved a way ahead. That scream: the engine or the ruptured air? Up there, the vacated sky; down here, dead wood and quaking mud and that shuddering puddle. The valley had consumed the bits of the body – swilled them down, or made a nourishing meal of them, absorbed them into itself. The sky, grinning blandly, insisted that it had seen nothing.

By now they were at the top of the hill, where shanties huddled on both sides of the lane. Ahead was the highway: a river of urgent metal, its currents flooding in both directions at once. After the highway came the city, which would separate them.

Horry, having shed the load of his story, kicked rocks for sheer joy. Wilf lagged behind: what reason could there be for putting one foot ahead of the other and hauling himself through the day? Horry took this as a tribute to his recitation.

And then he realised that he should not have told the story at all. He had made Wilf swear, but no oath could prevent the story from spreading. It whispered its way from one person to another like a germ. It escaped from you in each infected breath, it seeped out of you as sweat. Horry made the same promise to Clem, and had already broken it. Death was a secret you had to share.

Horry waited beside the highway for Wilf. He trailed the stick along the ground behind him, like a refractory animal. He was afraid to catch up, in case there was more he had to hear. Horry shouted 'Get a move on', which made Wilf consider bolting in the opposite direction. But in the opposite direction was the valley, with its cemetery of swamps and caverns, and Clem wearing shadows as camouflage. Though he dragged his feet, plodding as if through wet sand, he reached the highway.

'Remember what I told you,' Horry said. For the first time he was shifty; he was made afraid by Wilf's fear. 'Well, you better forget it. And don't tell no one. They'd only laugh at you. Anyway, I made it all up. Just to see how much you'd swallow.'

Wilf gaped at Horry. He longed to believe it. He would have given anything — if he had anything to give except his stick, which was no defence against the dark — to revoke the nightmare. He was about to thank Horry for having tricked him. Then he realised it was true after all. He had seen Clem and the man at the fountain. Horry, who had not let him say anything, did not know that. He looked back at Horry, who pretended to study the traffic.

'Horry,' said Wilf.

'What?' Horry's voice quavered like the pool of water in the lane.

Wilf raised his stick and aimed the whittled point of it at Horry. 'Drop dead,' he said.

Before Horry could hit him or think of a name to call him, Wilf had dodged into the traffic and fled to the other side of the highway. Horry tried to follow, but was forced back by a volley of car horns. By the time he got across, Wilf had vanished in the thronging street. The city, bloated with numbers, found space for one more, or for the mere fraction which was all Wilf represented; like the valley, where a disassembled body could be scattered and left to rot in peace, the city had a greedy appetite for people. Horry stomped off, defeated, to buy the paint which would alter a car's identity and begin its life over again.

Wilf meanwhile was buying his grandfather's medicine. The pharmacy smelled oddly sweet. Its aroma always worried Wilf. He knew the smells of the valley, which signalled digestion and decay. The way the soil turned suddenly fragrant after rain, the warm damp odour of mould, the curdled wind which the old man evacuated, the insinuating poison which hung in the air

89

around the gas works. In the shop he was baffled by scents he could not identify, meant to lure him away from the track which led to the man kneeling in the dust, Clem dabbling in red mud, the Dogs gulping their dinner.

He had stepped into a world of improbable perfection. Glossy red mouths smiled on placards, and revealed rows of teeth like luminous immaculate tombstones. The mouths belonged to no faces. They swam there independently, high up on the wall; they were crimson clouds containing heavenly cities. Elsewhere floated a single eye, too beautiful ever to find a partner for itself. Into it a nozzle was dropping a tear no emotion had generated. The eye dilated like an ice-blue sun. And there was an ear, also divorced from its face and detached from all other organs. It jutted in three dimensions, shaped from plastic. A thread wriggled out of its dark recess, and connected with a tiny cell behind the lobe: a transistor had taken over the business of hearing.

A man in a stiff starched jacket bagged the brown mixture and handed it down to Wilf. His face contained none of the ideal, impeccable organs distributed around his shop. Tufts of hair like twitch grass sprouted from his ears, and his eyes were assailed by bolts of red lightning. He opened his mouth on a yellow irregular fence of tilted palings. He said something to Wilf, which Wilf did not understand. The head bent lower. The mouth split further apart, the eyes — as those darts snaked across a discoloured sky — seemed set to explode.

He was asking about the stick. 'You don't look old enough to need that to walk with,' he was saying.

Wilf pushed the bottle into his pocket; his grip tightened on the stick.

'Oh,' said the man, 'so that's it — a hold up!' He raised both hands in a flustered parody of terror. 'Don't shoot,' he said, and made his teeth chatter.

Wilf was pinned by intersecting glances. The man behind the partition smirked at him, a woman in another white coat peeped round the corner to share the joke, a customer pursed a mocking mouth. Words blurted from Wilf as inadvertently as vomit.

'It wasn't me,' he heard himself saying. 'I didn't do it.'

His face scorched; he wished he could tear it off, like a scab from wounded skin. And now he felt the sting of tears. He pulled himself free of the eyes which held him there and ran out of the shop backwards. He banged into a shelf as he went. Laughter spilled through the door of the shop, as from an open mouth.

The crowd in the street closed around him and sheltered him. He drifted on: the city was a place where anything might happen, so perhaps something would happen to rescue him from his fear, or relieve him of his knowledge.

The city seen from the valley was different from the city when you were in it. From the valley it was a mountain range of gleaming slippery glass. From across the highway, with its brimming avenues of shuttling machines and rattling viaducts, it made sense as a machine, a vast apparatus for maintaining mobility. But once he was in it, it became a chaos of unknown faces and unreadable signs.

The signs jabbered at him, advertising things he had not learned to covet. The faces usually whirled past Wilf interchangeably, like blown leaves: these were people whose lives would never collide with his. Today he studied the faces as they passed, sifting them to make sure that none of them belonged to Clem, with that lazy lethal wolfish smile. Or to Horry, whom he thought he saw waiting to cross the street: it was someone else.

Heads hurried past him, and he gaped at their strangeness. What was it inside them that made them grow so unalike? A man whose face was divided down the middle by a purple patch, like a shadow which would not move or a stain which could not be scrubbed out. He seemed unaware of it. Did he know it had happened? A girl who had paused at the kerb, her mouth twisted round almost to her ear as her eyes occupied themselves with some internal calculation. Wilf shuddered. Had her face been melted down and rearranged? Then she moved her mouth back to where it should have been. He breathed again. She had only been thinking.

A fat woman, whose features had retired into puffy crevasses of flesh. She rotated her body along, swivelling it since her legs could not shift it ahead. Wilf remembered what Horry said Clem said about the red rivers and gushing creeks we all contained. Added to which, in her case, there was that bulk of stuffing.

91

Was it her insulation? Did it mean she could not be hurt? No, she could be carved as easily as lard.

A man who had his own stick: a tentative white cane. His eyes were milky, and circled vacantly. His face was terrifyingly innocent, without defences. He had never looked out from behind it, so had not trained it as a mask, to baffle those who looked back at him. He was old, but his skin still had the softness of putty. He groped serenely through a twilight of noises; people edged away from him. Wilf, staring at the useless eyes, forgot to move aside. The cane struck his leg, and fumbled upwards. It scratched Wilf's stick, then fidgeted on towards his waist. Sensing something that yielded, it crept higher and suddenly, like an index finger of accusation, prodded Wilf in the chest. He yelped. The blind face grinned, and the cane tapped on through the space Wilf emptied. The boy hurtled down a side street.

The street ended in a square, where there were benches under trees. He sat down, still feeling the jab of the cane as it touched his chest. Even a blind man had been able to see him. He tried not to gulp the air so desperately; he sat there longing not to exist, quietly shamming absence. Which was when he noticed what was happening in the window of the shop across the street in front of him: another killing.

It was a clothes shop, though the only clothes on view were worn by the two men engaged in the killing. Their victims were naked, though they had been wrapped in sheets of thick transparent plastic, which the men tore open. From these shrouds they dragged two reluctant, unsteady figures, whom they propped against a wall.

The bodies were not quite human yet. No hair pushed its way through their pink, infantile skin. No organs were pressed into the hollows of their heads: they saw and heard and spoke no evil. Where the legs of one of them met, a thick square wedge had been carved. The chest of the other one was raised in two triangles. But sex had not surfaced yet. They had not woken to the shock of consciousness, the awareness – which provokes our first cry – that this is me and everything else is not.

Or perhaps they were human once, and had outgrown their intermediate state. To Wilf, they resembled angels, their perfection unavailable to anyone outside the white nursery of the window: the man with the blotch, the woman who had misplaced her mouth. Until he saw what was wrong with their arms. The first figure had an arm lopped off at the elbow; the stump lay on the floor. The second figure held one arm upright, paralysed in a salute, while the other drooped by its side, like the empty sleeve of an amputee. Wilf wondered at the lack of blood, and the submissive silence. But the figures had no mouths to scream with, and the men who were handling them expected no spillage, since they had taken their shoes off and padded about in their socks.

Now the men set to work. At first Wilf thought they were going to repair the abused figures: one man plugged the stump back into place, the other lowered the saluting arm and fitted its twin into a socket, flexing it like a physiotherapist. This did not satisfy them. They worked the arms through a cranking sequence of dislocations. Wilf winced, remembering how Horry had once tugged an arm of his behind his back and held it there, promising that it would snap unless Wilf did something or other – beg for mercy, or buy his release, or tell a lie to cover Horry's truancy when it was inquired about at school. The men consulted each other, but could not agree on the most excruciating position for the arms. One of them made the male figure's wrist rotate through a complete arch, and laughed. The other retaliated by gripping the female figure around the waist, as if about to wheel her off across the white floor in a dance.

She wobbled in expectation. But the man's hands had found the fault line, the secret seam where she could be undone. With a slight heave, in imitation of an upbeat dance step, he removed her torso and spun away with it, while the deserted lower half of her reeled in shock. A quick loop of the cramped window proved his point, then he snapped the two parts of her back together. She was still shuddering; he grasped her shoulder and told her to forget it.

His friend in charge of the male figure was not to be outdone. His fingers stretched wide around the back of the figure's skull. With a magician's flourish, he plucked the head off. It came away cleanly: all that held it there was a prong of wood in the neck, the conduit where the cables were tangled which sent orders to the outlying limbs and received their relayed reports of pleasure or pain. The man held the head up in triumph, then jauntily tossed it from one hand to another.

But as he did so, demonstrating how easy it was to unplug all the body's circuits, the other man performed a swift repair job. He pulled the female's head from its neck and stuck it onto the male mannequin. The man who was bouncing the head in the air turned round to replace it and saw it had been unseated. With a shrug, he let it drop; it rolled heavily along the floor. He picked it up and checked it for damage, but wood neither bruised nor bled, and its paint had not chipped. He juggled it briefly, then decided to go along with the transplant of identities. He set it down where the female's head had been, hoping that the mismatched parts would get on with each other.

Now someone else arrived in the window with a bale of clothes, and the men began to invent personalities for the dummies. They fitted hats on their heads and draped scarves round their necks to conceal the sliver where body and head parted company. Now the figures knew who they were meant to be – or to impersonate – this time around; they were ready for the new lives which had been allotted to them. Wilf watched his bad dream acted out before his eyes. This was how people were torn apart, randomly put back together, then dressed up for the next incarnation.

A small crowd had gathered to watch the show. Someone yelped in sympathy when the arms of the figures were twisted, someone else gurgled terminally when a head came off. 'Fancy a swap?' said a boy to a girl as the heads changed places. She smiled and he kissed her: tongues twining, heads glued together, threatened flesh making common cause.

Everyone laughed. Wilf whirled around, sure they were mocking his amazement, his terror as the dream overlapped into daylight. Watching the laughter, he saw faces stretched out of shape like rubber, or sliced in half by gaping mouths as if concave valleys had opened there. Noise rumbled and shrilled from them like gunfire out of trenches. Dodging bullets, leaping over gulfs, he ran.

He was half way down the street before he realised that there was no point in running, because the dream ran with him. He stopped on the pavement. Where to go? How to live with the scene which went on enacting itself in his head?

Then he saw that after all he would have to run. For he was being followed.

9

THE DOOR SLAMMED behind Paul when he left that morning, after her remark about the quest for heads. A draught in the corridor, or his judgment on her? Perhaps his misunderstanding of what she meant? After all, she had wanted him to misunderstand. She merely needed a face to put in a painting; she was going out to trawl the streets for a suitable head. But by saying what she did, she issued a challenge and a threat. I am looking for faces which are not yours. Though maybe the head I have in mind belongs to you.

She looked at the door, still hearing the noise it made: the dull thud of a severing blade. The room was suddenly empty, containing only the aftershock of abandonment. She glanced at the signs of a life interrupted. His mug, not yet cold. A parcel, which he must have brought back for her but had no chance to hand over. Foreign coins, scattered from his pocket. Something stirred inside her. Not anger any longer, which had thrilled through her legs like voltage and made her skin singe. It tightened in her chest, as if a hand had closed round her heart. The name this contraction went by was remorse.

Even so, she felt indignant at her weakness. He relied on it, he derived strength from it. She had lain in bed awake and aching, cramped inside his tense arms. Only his hold on her saved him from submerging in dreams. Before she could get up, she had to prise herself free, bend the iron bars. She left him curled round a hollow in the mattress, clutching air.

Once, as a child, she was taken to visit an elderly relative, an old woman who smelled of lavender bags and used to buy Kate's affection with underhand donations of toffee. It was to be the last visit, though everyone knew that but Kate. When they were leaving, the old woman propelled herself towards Kate, and just before falling fastened her arms around her. Kate shivered inside the cold embrace: the old woman's flesh was frosty. The arms locked, as if a key had turned. Under papery white skin, Kate felt the constriction of bones. She tried to squirm, but could not. Then she was kissed. The mouth attached itself to her cheek. The chilling lips had no moisture in them; they adhered by suction. All of the sick body's will was concentrated on this one spot, where the mouth made a vacuum which plugged it to Kate's cheek. She felt tears on her face, without knowing if they were her own. She screamed.

Her parents came to her rescue. Her mother pulled open the rigid arms, her father led Kate away. They told her later that her sympathy for the old woman did her credit. As they said it, Kate realised that the imprint of the mouth was still there on her cheek. Nerves have long memories. Twenty years after, the wounded place remained tender.

She accepted the logic of it. When you are young, you feed on your mother; you must expect to be fed upon in your turn. She would have known now how to cope with the elderly relative. She would be able to disengage herself. Paul's demands on her were harder to tolerate. He was supposed to be a partner, not a dependant. He seemed to be caving in: a case of subsidence, like the valley.

She blamed his buildings. They were hostages to a future he would never see; they were investments in immortality, like all things that men made, but to prove their own permanence the buildings first had to engineer his demise. The more loftily extravagant they became, the more he mistrusted and resented them. He knew they were telling a lie, boasting of their resistance to time even though each of them was planted in the grave of another structure which had been felled, and the other structure was mouldering into the remains of some earlier tower or fortress or lair or midden.

He had said to her, 'I've got this far – half way – and it turns out that it's all been a mistake. Such an obsession to make something that lasts, when nothing does. They now say that buildings in the city have a life-span of a generation. Just twenty-

97

five years. So they're even more temporary than we are. What's the point?'

She could see that she was supposed to have an answer: that was her function, her vocation.

'Go with it,' she said. 'How about the first honest skyscraper? A building that bio-degrades. Like an ice palace, or a mud hut. Or the gingerbread house in the fairy tale.'

He laughed, then groaned because it was no answer.

'Paul, listen. I've told you before. If it really bothers you, there are two things to do. The only two things that don't quarrel with the facts of life in the way you're doing. You can plant a garden, or you can have kids – I can have them for you, that is, if I have a mind to. And of course to do the garden, you'd need to move back down to the ground floor. Otherwise, it's simple.'

She risked advancing these options because she knew he would dismiss them. He would say that cultivating your shrubbery or raising a family was the poor man's version of creativity. He had no intention of retreating to that lower floor she spoke of. And what child could compare with a building, which never spurned you or let you down or answered you back? 'I don't see the point,' he said. 'Why start another life when it only repeats your own? All the same confusions and miseries, all ending up in the same place. I know it's instinct, but instincts aren't rational. Why should I do nature's work for it? I don't have much of an opinion of nature anyway.'

Kate granted him all that, since she had quietly reached the same conclusion for her own different reasons. She refused to sacrifice herself to the future. She had no patience for the months spent waiting to see if seeds would grow. She wanted to be alive in the present, not to think of herself as some instalment to be completed later. She knew about what happened later. The visit to the elderly relative was her initiation into that. She dreaded the body's betrayal of us, inevitable as all other infidelities: that long living death which concluded with the old woman's lethal kiss. Meanwhile, before it began to happen, she refused to accept its inevitability. She luxuriated in her life. Each moment was an immersion. That was why she disliked these arguments with Paul. They involved appraisal, considerations of value. Couldn't she just *be*? That was the imperative; only a man would have gone on to ponder not being.

Paul was liable, however, to call her bluff about pot plants, progeny and edible architecture. 'Art can't be all bad. What about your paintings?'

'They're different,' she said quickly, while she wondered just how they differed from Paul's high-rise vanities.

That was his next question. 'So what's the difference?'

'Well, for a start I do them for myself. Nobody sees them but you. Oh, and friends. I don't show them off, I don't sell them.'

'That doesn't matter. The motive is the same.'

'Not really. Those buildings of yours won't let anyone ignore them. Writing and painting and music are all locked away inside libraries and galleries and concert halls. You have to go looking for them. They're private. All pleasures are. You can share them, but who's to know if the other person feels the same thing you do? Architecture is so loud, it takes up so much space. It wants to change *things*, not just the way we think about them or see them. But nothing much changes really. You can see that by looking out the window at those people in the valley. So the builders get angrier; they revenge themselves by destroying.'

'I know your paintings don't make a noise and that they never get out of the spare bedroom, but you still haven't said why that makes them so holy. A building starts life as a drawing, you know. Before that, it's a dream.'

'But it doesn't stay a dream. It's your challenge to the real world. You get yourself into a fight you can't possibly win. Those pictures of mine aren't so ambitious. I paint things I can't see, that I don't expect to see – really that I don't *want* to see, except when I close my eyes.'

Of course (and this she admitted only to herself) art was bad for you. You became an addict of perfection, a frequenter of artificial paradises. It spoiled you for life, made reality look like a poor, washed-out reproduction. No flowers were ever so yellow, showering the air with pollen like grains of gold. No stars ever burned that way in a navy blue midnight sky. It was as if you could get back to the instant when nature was created, when the first eyes opened on its gaudy strangeness, before everything got tarnished and faded. Her paintings remained in the spare room because she was afraid of the discontent they might encourage in her. She kept the curtains drawn to protect them from scrutiny by the sun: the room was a cave of fantasy, like the inside of our heads. She claimed in self-defence that she was not much of a painter, but felt ashamed when she realised how good she actually was. Not great; just good enough to be distracted and dictated to by a gift of vision which she had not asked to have bestowed on her.

Paul knew his way round her evasive modesty. 'They're not so ineffectual as all that. What about those quotes of yours? You shouldn't accuse me of demolishing ancient slums. You do the same thing. You're competing with the pictures you copy at the museum.'

One of her sly recent robberies was of Caspar David Friedrich's wanderer, improbably frock-coated for a hike through the mountains. She had taken him out of his own world and transposed him to hers. At his feet, mist was clearing – but not from the rippling recession of a mountain range which he still had to toil over. He was on top of an apartment tower, standing among the pampered shrubbery of a roof garden, and the thinning mist disclosed the city: their city, with its sky of florid neon, its crevasses of traffic, the distant incendiary chimneys of gas. Did he linger there in rapture, or was he aghast at the roaring ugliness of it? Might he have been some black-garbed ministering angel, who kept watch from this perch? No, he was probably intending to jump.

His back was turned, yet she had imagined a face for him. It belonged to Paul, and it had that look of puzzled terror which always reported on what he saw behind his eyes when the darkness crawled and rustled and congealed into substance. The man in black was not surveying the city. He was shuddering on the edge, tense with fright, too stiff to keep his balance. The wisps of ragged mist plucked at his ankles.

She thought of the picture, which she had not let him see, as she answered him. 'I don't consider I'm competing. I just want to peacefully coexist. The way they say that married people do. You only have to go for a walk in the city to see how the past and the present can get along together. All the times there ever were are happening side by side, like the rooms in the museum. There are so many ghosts in the streets. Really the city is like your own head. Only a lump of bone and tissue to look it. But inside there's the whole world – yours and everyone else's.'

She kept the rest of the thought to herself. For she went on to wonder where the valley figured in this. The city was an apparatus for retention and retrieval. Like the museum, it served as a collective memory: incomplete time with all its loose ends was here neatly organised into space. So the valley? It was whatever the city chose not to remember, whatever it preferred to keep obscure. It was boggy matter before the mind rolled it flat and drew straight lines of streets across it. If the city was a brain, then its jurisdiction ended at the neck. That was the border. Beyond it, beneath it, the body entered into its own: a gullet-shaped valley where signals were confused by the dark and shouted down by the roar of blood.

She could understand why Paul hated the place. It was our internal, personal abyss. The man she had painted on the ledge would be reconciled to it only if he could use it to put an end to himself. The valley was a long way down; merely consign the body to gravity and it will take care of the timid, shivering mind. The problem, for the man on the parapet, was not fear of heights. Quite the contrary. He loved heights, he was an inventor of them. He suffered from something she did not have a word for: fear of depths. Yet sooner or later the mind would give the body a push. Or the body would haul the mind along with it. He would jump so as to put a stop to the argument inside himself.

However, she thought, in my own case. . . . In my own case, there won't be a prolonged bargaining session on the edge. Why not leap as confidently as if you were diving into the sea? Why not leave the body to its own wise amphibious devices? The valley from the back window was a tract of green water, sleepily heaving. She felt it licking at her, slithering over her. You survived by not resisting. The body remembered a time before it was upright. It took to the water, to the valley, as to a bed. Love, sleep, swimming: they were all horizontal talents. She was happy to leave the vertical to Paul.

So why did she announce that she was going out in search of a face, a head?

She had been spending days in the Renaissance rooms at the museum, studying the loves of the gods. All those elaborate abductions and versatile disguises. A nymph carried off by an amorous bull, another folded in the feathers of a swan; the deity converting himself into cash as a tinkling pillar of gold coins, spinning through the air to land in the targeted lap. Those girls who lolled about, like starlets beside a pool, lacquering their nails or touching up their tan while they waited to have immortality thrust upon them, or into them. The rapacious gods, determined to copulate their way through the whole of creation.

The painted stories first amused her, then attracted her, though she could not be certain why. She did not disapprove of the prostrate girls, but nor did she share their foolish daydreams. She went back again and again to look, and to question her own motives for looking. It was the idea, she decided, of a time when the world had not settled into form, when it was still runny and volatile. Energy pulsed and seethed, spirits migrated between the species, gods and humans were mixed together in the same seed-bed. Nature's purpose was to perpetuate itself; even the promiscuous gods were enslaved to that. There were no people then, only organisms. And organisms did not waste time wondering why they existed. They were bodies which had not indulged in the luxury of a head. Their business was procreation. Art, that sad second-best bet, had yet to be thought of.

Kate had her suspicions about the painters who were so fond of these primeval matings. Of course they were peeping toms, who claimed to be illustrating myths when their real interest was in pink, flagrant flesh. But more than that, they were making up for something their own art lacked. Paint spurted onto their canvases like blood; it spread like the secretion from a gland. You could see where they had dabbled in it, pressed it into blushing skin or the soft surface of dishevelled velvet with their sticky fingers. All to no avail: the fluids could not survive outside the body. From close up, the paint was as sterile as the moon, pockmarked with craters of coloured dust. It only knew how to depict dry orgies, the impotent riots of imagination.

The stories began to seem tawdry. They were fables about looking, as opposed to living. But all the same, she wanted to tell one in a picture of her own, and to tell the truth about it.

She had chosen her subject, or singled out her victim: Persephone, carried off to the underworld by Hades while she was gathering flowers. Persephone picked a narcissus. As she did so, the earth opened; Hades rode from the crevice in his chariot to kidnap her. Kate could see that happening. It was a view she might have had from her back window, if she had been there on the day when the hills were pulled apart to make the valley. She could see the sequel too: the blighted land, the diseased crops, ordained by Demeter the goddess of the harvest to punish Zeus for allowing the capture of her daughter. What curse ravaged the starveling gardens of the valley? Then came the mission of Hermes, sent by Zeus to reclaim the girl and to reprieve the afflicted earth. But by now Persephone had eaten the pomegranate fed to her by Hades. The passionfruit stained her mouth, and thus bound her to return to the underworld. Like the sun, she was obliged to divide her favours, alternating between her mother's wholesome fields and the nocturnal realm below with its vivid, soiling delicacies.

A double life, thought Kate – a season of respectability in some Olympian tower like ours, followed by the compulsory descent to the valley and the disappearance through an aperture like that tunnel which ducked beneath the disused railway line. Did she walk down the hill slowly, with backward glances of regret at the skyline of glass above, then start to run in unashamed eagerness once the tunnel hid her? Why did no one in the story think to ask her which existence she preferred?

Kate knew exactly the scene she wanted to paint. The fissure in the ground, which had not healed. In the story she knew that the earth slid back to cover the retreating chariot, but she had imagined a gash, like the widened lids of a staring eye, unlatched to reveal the interior. The walls of moist clay and glinting minerals showed her an unformed world, like the paints which she squeezed from tubes and mixed in muddy pools while deciding what she would make them represent. At the bottom of the cliff would be Persephone, also smeared with paint, marked by the incriminating juice which dribbled from the pomegranate.

She knew whose head she would give to the woman: it would be her own. But she needed another face for the scene. At the top of the cliff she saw another figure, kneeling on the edge and looking down at the woman with the wet, bright mouth. The second figure was indistinct. She glimpsed it through mist; she could not identify it, though she was sure it must be male. An artist perhaps, squinting at the captive below, glad (in all probability) that she was out of his reach? Or perhaps just a passer-by, someone who lived in those fields, who on his way home stumbled upon the opening in earth and realised in a seizure of vertigo that the clods and stones he had always trusted as his life's foundation were a trampoline stretched across the underworld? He had sunk to his knees to grab the lumpy soil and the scattered rocks, imploring them to be solid. No, that was not it. Instead she thought of having the artist set up his easel and call down to the woman, ordering her not to move. Then she erased that.

As if inhabiting the picture she had not even begun to paint, she looked up at the face poking over the edge of the gulf. It had no features, like a bandit who pulls a stocking over his head and turns himself back into a smooth-skinned, sightless embryo. She wanted to see the expression on that blurred face. Its eyes would tell her who she was, why she was there, why she had chosen to eat the fruit. After all, the truth about the story was not so easy to discover. She would trust it only if she heard it from someone else — or read it, silently and without the intercession of words, in the other person's face. That was the face she went out to search for in the streets.

The streets could always be relied on. They spilled incidents, anecdotes, unimaginable people at her feet like tribute; they gave her alms, which she repaid by dropping coins in the hats or tins or hands of the beggars and buskers and snoring drunks who occupied the doorways. She paid her debts inconspicuously, depositing money while looking the other way. She did not want to be thanked, or even noticed. If she could be seen, then her own seeing would be marred, jammed.

As she walked along, submerged in the flux of numbers, she could feel herself becoming invisible. That was her state of grace. She had a costume which, like a nun's neutering habit, helped her to attain it: an old raincoat, a head scarf to crush her hair. She had once tried dark glasses, but discarded them because they invoked a mystery and hinted at an incognito. In place of them, she wore what she thought of as a blank look – dull-eyed, slack-skinned – and when it worked she could feel the blankness mercifully overtaking her. More than once she had paused at a shop window to study the reflection of someone standing on the pavement and noticed an anonymous person in a crumpled raincoat, the sort of figure bound to remain forever on the fringes of vision. A moment later she would realise, rapidly rejoining the drab body, that it was her, and would smile with joy and pride at the success of her self-deception, or her self-obliteration.

Though she told Paul she was going out to sketch, she carried no pad, and seldom took her hands out of the raincoat pockets. She did her sketching with her eyes only. The faces were incised inside her, as if by a scalpel; they were drawn – as she studied them and set herself to remember them on the walk home – by time itself, the sole designer of faces.

She forgot none of these faces, the flotsam of the streets. She stored them, saved them up like ancient unborn children. Once in a while she looked in on them, to make sure they all were still there, patiently awaiting their turns. Or she reshuffled them, introduced them to each other and speculated about how they would get on. She also speculated about why they had presented themselves to her in the street, like heads proffered on a plate.

The man she had once seen emerging from the valley, his gait as purposeful as an animal following a trail of clues through the air. She had wondered if the scent which lured him out of the valley would retain its power in the city. He blinked slightly at the bombardment of light and noise from across the highway. A night worker, she thought. She glanced sideways while they waited for the traffic to pause, wanting to check on his clothes. He wore a leather jacket with a collar of red pelt raised around his ears; he hunched inside the jacket as if inside his own skin. She should not have looked. He had an animal's wariness, and he sensed her curiosity. Before she could look away, he turned to face her. She could see a brief tremor of unease in that white face, which peered at her over its hedge of fur and hide. Then, realising he had nothing to fear from her, he grinned. Not a smile, which is a flowering of the face, a sunburst – he was too shadowy a man for that – but an insolent twisting of the mouth. His upper lip peeled back slowly. His mouth was about to shape itself into a soundless, suggestive phrase, while his eyes fixed her as roughly as hands grasping her shoulders. She bolted, not bothering to notice if the traffic lights had changed. As she ran, she imagined that she heard him laughing.

The woman seen another time in a park in the city, walking slowly, luxuriantly between ponds of sunlight under the trees. She was pregnant. The details of what that did to you fascinated Kate: this stranger swelling inside, demanding to be fed before being born, kicking crankily, giving orders for its immediate release in an onset of agony. The phantom lives Kate carried around inside her were no less troublesome. But the woman in the park evidently found creation easy. She leaned backwards to equilibrate herself, hands supporting her bulk by holding her hips; she had retired behind her body. Looking at her, Kate shivered. The woman was nurturing something which would crawl away from her, rebel against her, sentence her to death. Yet a sweet contentment was apparently your reward if you resigned yourself to being nature's employee. Perhaps the mind and its conviction of individuality were errors of evolution. The woman walked on into the sun and, as Kate squinted through the haze, her glowing body dissolved into the summer air, thick with spores, pollen, feathers and the precious dust which rained onto Danae. Kate felt like an empty house.

Then again, further into the city, the boy on the roller-skates, negotiating the tides of traffic while mouthing words to a song which his ear-phones piped into his head. Boy? Not really, he must have been twenty; she thought of him as a boy, she realised, to prohibit herself from feeling interested in him. Not a boy but some improbable young god who had skidded to ground in the middle of the street, who sped between the fuming cars and chanted his song above the grumble of the engines. A tawdry god, she had to admit, with his purple shorts and his jokey T-shirt and his streaming head band; no doubt an idiot, his brain pounded to mush by that percussive music; all the same, a spirit of aerodynamic motion who did not belong in the trudging, footsore city with its stalled traffic and blocked pavements. He was probably a messenger, a courier who skated between addresses. He had a cloth bag strung round his neck. Imagine, Kate told herself, all the dreary documents it contains. That will take the shine off him.

This morning she crossed the highway where the man from the valley smirked at her, made a detour through the park where the pregnant woman had been walking, elbowed her way down the block where she saw the skater. She thought of each of them as she passed. Did she already have her cast of characters for the painting: leering, lethal Hades, plentiful Demeter, Hermes with wheels not wings on his feet? But none of these were the face she was looking for.

The best way to find what you wanted in the city was to trust to accident. The city existed to arrange accidents, which – once they had occurred – you saw were not accidental at all. Her meeting with Paul, for instance, at a party ten years before. They had arrived with other people, and they both exchanged partners in the course of the night. That was how things were at that age, in that age: an amiable nuzzling and intersection of atoms, which resumed their courses in the morning. She dimly recalled listening to Paul expound a plan to dynamite half the city so he could construct some futuristic folly. It was the age of geodesic domes, as well as of sexual freedom. If he got his way, he intended to abolish streets. His new city would be all indoors. He's a weakling, she thought. Hence all the dynamite. Now who will I go home with?

He told her much later about his first impression of her: a girl convinced of her superiority just because she was young. What gave her the right to be so unimpressed by him? He especially disliked the way she toyed with a length of curly black hair, winding it round her finger, unwinding it and repeating the gesture. It was her demonstration of how bored she was. The rankling memory each had of the other was enough, the next time they met, to draw them together. They agreed, years after that, on a definition of love. It meant giving someone permission to wound you. Each held the other as a hostage. The accident of their encounter turned into an augury.

So, in the hope of another revelation, she walked through the streets. The secret was not to meddle with the city's arrangement of accidents by making any rational choice. She let herself float, borne along in the current of bodies. She did not even consciously look. The city showered her with images at random, twirling down like ticker tape: a visual litter, for the city existed to produce waste, to proclaim excess. Boys from the outer suburbs (or perhaps from the valley), disguised in top hats, tail coats and gloves, whistling for taxis outside the hotels. Banners flaunting above the portico of a department store; the reek of warm, perfumed air which breathed from its door. A man beside a shaft which led directly to the smoky, rumbling centre of the earth – you could hear the trains shrill and rattle under the streets – who wailed the same hoarse phrase over and over, like a priest, like a witch doctor, intoning some obscure digest of the sins or woes of the world: he was selling newspapers.

Shredded conversations, as if the piles of newspapers had begun all at once to chatter aloud, fluttered past her. Someone complained about the prices, someone else about the weather, and another voice castigated the traffic. Two girls deliciously conspired in giggles. The street like the newspapers being hawked on its corners was a babble of disjected phrases, sentences in which subjects never managed to arrive at their objects, paragraphs with twisted logic and broken backs. But all the newspaper's aborted, abbreviated stories added up into a choral dirge, and so did the street's overheard voices, underscored by the throb of motors, the screech of subterranean rails, and the whistles of the top-hatted porters.

Paul's fantasies about a city cooled and muted inside a bubble or redistributed on the glass tiers of a skyscraper seemed laughable as Kate gave herself up to the street, going wherever the jostling bodies collectively decided to take her. Architecture had no power over this swarm, this stream. It pretended that things were upright, sorted into hierarchies, when the truth on the ground was a relay race of jostling seeds, scattered by wind or swilled by water.

Kate experimented in living without the aid of signs, without interpretation. She kept her eyes down, so as not to recognise landmarks or read street names. Let me see, she thought, where I'll be deposited this time; whose life it will turn out to be; which hat, or head, I'll be wearing. An existential adventure, like those parties in the days when she first met Paul: you arrived not knowing who you would leave with. A new world every evening, so long as you were brave. That was why she resented Paul, she supposed. After him, the future was rescinded, and she began to accumulate a past. That might also be why she admired those metamorphosing gods, violently alighting in a fresh reality, costumed for the duration in a new form.

Then the music stopped. The pavement was no longer moving beneath her. The crowd, for the moment, had nowhere else to go. She raised her eyes, half expecting that the face she had come out to find would be staring into hers in recognition. Instead she was looking at a shop front, where two skittish window dressers were torturing a pair of dummies, wrenching their arms, transposing their heads, then pausing to take a bow as the loiterers around Kate applauded.

Was this what the city had dealt her today? Abstraction at work: she could have seen that in the museum. Modern art, pledged to revise created nature, concludes by reconstructing the human body. Eyes can't be stopped from overlapping with each other, mouths become indistinguishable from the other orifices. When one of Picasso's sitters complained that she did not look like that, he assured her that she would. Art anticipates the deformations of time. It is always so painless, thought Kate. No cries when limbs are dislocated. No buckets of blood beneath the operating table. No unwanted organs for dogs to gobble. It is only a game, like Paul's arrangements of his building blocks. She left the window dressers to their mincing massacre and turned away.

Which was when she saw the boy: perhaps when he appeared to her. His face at once occupied the empty corner of her imagined painting, as if he had always been there and as if he constituted its centre. Though of course if the mercurial roller-skater was a boy, this face belonged to a child. It had not yet been creased into character. It had no habitual expressions, no set of the jaw or fatigue of the cheeks or lines scraped into the corners of the mouth to silently voice an opinion of the world. It responded to the shocks which assailed it with appalling honesty, not knowing how to tighten the skin or avert the eyes to deny emotion.

He was looking at the charade in the shop window. He seemed to be sick with fear or disgust, on the verge (as a child always is, since the world with its mythical beasts and dark houses has not been tamed by knowledge, or by ignorance and forgetfulness) of crying. Kate, yards away, could feel the breath being forced from him in quick gasps; his skin was blotchy, streaked with a sweat which might have been hot or cold or both at once. But despite his revulsion, his eyes bulged and his mouth was open to ask a question. He hated what he saw, yet insisted on seeing it. In that determination, a childhood was ending. He might be looking, Kate thought, into my underworld.

Gradually she noticed the rest of him, the bits and pieces of an incomplete being. His trousers, woolly and officiously striped, were rolled around his ankles. They had already been worn by several predecessors. His shirt was emblazoned with palm trees, beach balls and the sails of yachts, a remembrance of someone else's used-up holiday. He had no notion of himself: was that what innocence meant? The faceless dummies in the shop window, when their tormenters got round to dressing them up, would do a better job of impersonating persons.

But there was one thing about which the boy felt proprietorial. He had a stick in his hand. He gripped it fiercely. Though he was sitting on a bench, it was as if the stick were supporting him, keeping him from collapse as he gaped at the carnage in the window. Kate wondered what magic he had invested in it, and how long he would be able to continue trusting it.

Her heart went out to him. That, to her surprise, was exactly what she felt: the sensation of a hand gouging a hole beneath her breasts; a sudden venting of energy, which almost dragged her behind it across the few yards between them. She had heard

the phrase often, generally in association with appeals for chari-
table offerings. She was happy to contribute money, but could
never imagine the heart going anywhere. How was it to get out?
Now she knew. It burst from her like a projectile. Emotion
actually meant movement; it entailed being thrown, launched
violently out of yourself. This was the first, irresistible law of
human physics. And if this could happen, your heart was not
your own. Like a bird caged behind your ribs, it was forever
plotting its escape, alert for any opportunity. How many more
such phrases might prove to be physiologically true? When you
fell in love, did you lose your head?

An emotion must have its reasons. Or so Kate reasoned,
remembering how easy it was to understand her fits of irrational
hostility towards Paul. But this baffled her. She clutched her
chest, probing for the site of the damage. What you felt for other
people – she had always assumed – was an extension of your
self-interest. When someone died, you grieved in advance for
your own demise. You gave to the beggars in the street because,
though they were not you, they might have been. Relationships,
self-evidently hers with Paul, were enlightened transactions, cal-
culating risks and awarding bonuses with the statistical exac-
titude of insurance policies. Yet the boy on the bench had
nothing in common with her, and wanted nothing from her.
Why all this spilled, spendthrift feeling? The heart which might
have messily landed, still pumping, at his feet in their dirty boots?

When she consulted her imaginary picture, she found that it
had already been painted over. The boy was no longer peering
down into the gulf at the woman with the blemished mouth. She
was staring up at him, while he looked out of the picture at
something which had not been painted. Kate could read a word
on the woman's vivid lips: a request to be helped, or saved. But
paintings were silent, so the boy had no way of hearing her.

Nor, on the bench with the stick in his hand, had he seen her
yet. All the same, he may have sensed the possessive urgency
with which she stared at him, the hiss of air displaced by the
spirit travelling towards him. Suddenly he glanced around,
though still not at Kate; then he ran.

She followed him, of course. She had to: she was being tugged

III

on a leash. He dodged into the crowd, and she lost sight of him. She blundered through bodies, pressed them apart. When they cleared, he was half a block ahead. He had paused to think things – what things? – over. She sidled on, keeping near to the shop windows, not wanting to startle him. As she went, she considered what she would say. She was going to speak to him: that also she had to do. Excuse me? Yet why was she guiltily asking to be excused?

Having drawn level with him, she crossed the pavement. Let it happen, she thought.

He saw her coming. She had the crazily concentrated gaze of the old woman in the valley, except that it was aimed at him, not at some distant maelstrom in the sky. He had time to run, but not space. The traffic was behind him. The gutter might have been a cliff above rapids or the roof of a tall building, and on the pavement the woman in the raincoat could outflank him. Instead he waited. When she got within range he raised his stick.

It failed him. All at once she knelt down, grabbed the wrist which brandished the stick with one of her hands, put the other on his shoulder, and looked into his stricken face. Though her mouth was open, she had as little idea as the boy of what she would say.

Then she heard a voice, which must have been her own. 'No, no,' it said, 'don't. I only want to know your name.'

10

'IT WASN'T ME,' Wilf said, and allowed her hand to lower his and to disempower the stick.

'What wasn't you?' She tried to smile, and considered which other calming gestures might be appropriate. She could stroke his hair, stiff with knots and tangles: a crown of grubby thorns. But to do that she would have to take away either the hand on his wrist or the one which encircled his shoulder, and to risk losing him.

'I don't', he said, 'know nothing about it'.

His grandfather once advised him on how to behave when dealing with the authorities (and this woman who held him in detention on the street must be one of them). His grandfather's policy was to deny everything and profess drivelling idiocy, which a boy could do as convincingly as an old man. Unfortunately, his grandfather did not tell him that it was imprudent to deny something before you were asked about it.

She unlocked the hand which had clipped like a bracelet around his wrist, and withdrew the other hand from his shoulder, patting him as she did so. He was held there by his fear, by the guilt he denied with his shaking head.

'I only asked your name. You must know that.'

He didn't reply. He had used up all his denials before they were even called for. His grandfather would have clouted him for such poor tactics. Now all he could do was stand there, and hope she would go away. The stick wilted against his leg. His eyes flicked from side to side – not in quest of exits, merely to avoid the interrogation of her gaze.

'So come on, tell me. You do know it after all. Your name.'

He said it voicelessly, with just a gruff expulsion of breath. She would have to lip-read if she wanted to know it.

'Ralph? That's nice . . .'

'No,' he said testily, 'Wilf!' And realised he had been snared again.

'Yes. Wilf. That's what I *thought* you said. Listen, Wilf.' He was listening, though she had not yet decided what she would make him listen to. A shy woodland creature, she thought. Tempt him out of his hiding place with a morsel. But extend the hand slowly, slowly. 'Look, Wilf. Would you like a drink?'

Wilf had never been offered a drink before. 'No thanks,' he said. 'I don't drink.' He had heard Horry's mother say that, grumpily. The grumpiness was probably not appropriate in this case. Anyway, it turned out to be the wrong answer, because she laughed.

'You don't? Never? Then what's that bottle in your pocket?'

'Medicine.'

'Are you sick? What's the matter with you?'

'It's not for me.'

'You came in to collect it? Who for?'

He was helpless. The questions nibbled away at him. 'My grandad,' he eventually said, and bit his lower lip to punish himself for what was surely an indiscretion. That did not prevent him telling her more, even before she asked. 'It's his stomach.'

'Your grandfather lives with you?' The extended family: in the valley, which is where she assumed the boy had come from, people still adhered as in the old times. But she was wrong.

'No, I live with him.' He began to suspect that she was guessing. If he had owned up, that was his own fault.

'Where is it you live?'

'In our house. On the hill. Above the road.'

The fact that he did not mention the valley convinced her that he came from there. Those who lived in the valley had no conception of its singularity or separateness; to them it was neither more nor less than the world. The city was its periphery, an unregarded waste of strangers where the streets needed names in order to be significant and the citizens had numbers on their doors. She was about to say 'Oh yes, I know', then decided against it. Instead she asked 'What do you do in there?'

The boy blinked. In where? He did not recognise the valley

114

when it was pointed to like that. And as for the doing, was this her way of creeping up on the thing he had not done, but had witnessed in imagination? He prepared another denial.

'I mean your grandfather – does he have a job?'

Relieved, he told all. 'He works the signals, down by the tunnel. You know, to stop the cars crashing. We both do it, morning and night. We didn't go this morning, because of his stomach.'

She smiled, this time unfeignedly. Though she had never driven through the valley, she had heard about the signallers. 'So that's how I know you! I was sure you looked familiar. I take that road all the time. I can almost see you from where I live. I'm in one of those buildings right on the edge of the valley.'

Wilf thought of the glass in those walls which smouldered and sparked as the sun set. So there were lives behind those ignited panes. If she lived on those battlements of glass, had she been watching him all the time? Had she been able to see through last night's dark? Perhaps she knew the answers to all those questions before she asked them. For the moment she was asking nothing, but he could not get away. He did not know how to. There were phrases to cover a retreat; he had not learned them. Even for a brief excursion into the city, you needed to acquire the art of lying. He fidgeted, suddenly conscious that his arms and legs needed to be told what to do. Red or green? He was not sure that he remembered the difference. His face seared, as if the sun bouncing back from those windows had struck it.

Kate watched him squirm and flush, and felt suddenly ashamed. She wanted to know why he was afraid; it turned out that he was afraid of her. She had swooped down on him like one of those predatory gods in the paintings. She was unable to explain to him, or to herself, what her motives were. Love was no excuse, if love meant the unannounced invasion of another existence. And to steal his face for her painting was worse. What gave her the right to capture him and then sequester him in her dream? She had seized him on the street: it was almost a case of kidnapping. To make art, did you have to raid life so ruthlessly? Get out of the car, hand over your wallet, surrender your secrets. Oh, and that's not all. I am taking you with me. You belong to me now.

The boy looked at her. She must let him go, but it was no longer easy. Each would continue to worry the other. How could she forget his haunted reverie as he sat on the bench, how could he forget her manacling hands?

She stood up, hoping that he would run. 'I'm sorry,' she said. 'Wilf, I didn't mean to frighten you.'

It was more a plea than an apology: it begged him to release her from responsibility. But the boy stood there. Actions have consequences. This was unlike that earlier life in which you chose a partner for the night and deserted him, after a purgative session in the bathroom, next morning. When you did something, you changed the state of things. A deed was irrevocable, irreparable. She fumbled in her pocket for money to give him, then stopped. To buy him off was insulting. On the other hand, he could probably do with the money. Then again, what use was money to a boy in the valley?

There was no graceful way out of this. In desperation, she was graceless. 'Wilf, I'm really sorry. I made a mistake. I wish. . . . No, I'm going now. Goodbye. You be careful.'

She spun away from him, swivelling on her heels. She would have run, but her thumping heart – having gone out on its adventure, it had come sickeningly home to roost – advised her against it.

A light flared across the painting inside her head. She saw that it had changed since she last consulted it. The woman had climbed out of the crevice; the boy had tumbled in. The woman stood in a field of flowers, her back to the shaft. She tried to smear the colours and obscure the scene. No use: the head is a museum of images; you are always being taken on an illustrated tour of your wrongdoings.

At the corner, she paused. Pull yourself together, she said. That was another of the phrases which meant exactly what it said. Check that you are all there, and in working order. Switch off the light on those images in your head, talk your heart into tapping not banging, find somewhere lower down to breathe from. Adjust your dress (she took off the scarf and pulled her hair loose), find a new aim in life. She would walk, she decided, to Paul's office, and invite him out to lunch. She might even discard the shabby camouflage of her raincoat on the way: donate it to one of the beggars in a doorway. Paul hated it, since wearing it was her declaration of autonomy. It would be her sacrifice.

To get to Paul, she had to turn down a side street. She changed direction decisively – no more trusting to the divinatory chances of the city – and as she did so bumped into something, someone. She looked down. It was the boy. He was following her, dogging her. The hound, she thought, of heaven. She closed her eyes slowly, as if the lids could rub him out like a smudged painting. She kept them shut for a long moment, until they throbbed from the effort. Things were fuzzy when she looked again, losing shape as light strafed them. But not the boy, nor his imploring, accusing stare.

She shook her head, just as he had done when hiding behind his own denials. 'What is it?' she said. He must have wanted the money after all. She dug into her pockets.

He refused it. Confused, buffeted between rage and shame, she almost hurled the handful of coins to the pavement. Then at last he uttered the sentence he had been practising as he followed her up the street. The story was a contagion. He had to transmit it, even though to do so would not give him peace, even if (as he now believed) she already knew it. It must be made common knowledge: after all, it was everyone's story.

'I wanted to tell you,' he said. 'It wasn't true what I said before. I do know about it. But I didn't do it.'

'Yes, yes,' she said, vaguely canvassing the petty crimes he must think she had seen him commit, 'I'm sure you didn't. That's all right.' Now could she go?

No, she could not. He grabbed her sleeve. 'Please. It wasn't my fault. We couldn't help him.'

'Help who?' she said impatiently. The answer did not interest her; she merely wanted to point out the hole in his story. She unfastened his hand from her sleeve. As she did so, she noticed how grubby his fingers were.

Meanwhile he had answered her question. Intent on freeing

her sleeve, she was not sure she heard what he said. 'The man Clem cut up.' Could that be it?

Exasperated, she backed away. 'Whatever it is,' she said, 'I can't be bothered.' His story no longer coincided with hers. She repressed it beneath a mudslide of pigment.

Now, recoiling as from his grandfather's fist or boot, he made his last appeal. It was a quotation. 'Help me,' he said. The words had to force their way through a tightened, aching throat. 'I thought you would help me.'

'Help you how?'

Help me, he meant, to bear it. Not knowing how to explain that, he began to cry. To bawl, as his grandfather would have said: the untuned keening of a siren.

She knew about the tears of childhood, having shed her share of them. She was aware that they functioned as moral blackmail. Children were extortionists wielding water pistols. But tears were also, she remembered, an uncensored commentary on the world as a child saw it. The jungle when the lights go out, the giants with their power to thwart or harm you. These tears, already occasioning glances from the passers-by, announced an emergency. They were a cave-in, an inundation, like the upset in the order of things which created the valley. She no longer saw the grimy skin or the uncombed hair. His face had retreated behind an open mouth, and the mouth was a tunnel, a chute which led directly to despair. He was again the figure in her painting. She found a handkerchief, then realised that more was needed than a mopping up.

She knelt and hugged him. Her body absorbed his cries as she pressed him against her. She felt him gasp; he sucked in another breath, and she tensed herself for a screech. But it did not come. The quake was over. She pushed him gently out from her chest. His face settled back into place now the cavernous mouth had closed, like earth mending the breach in itself once it swallowed the abductor's chariot. He wiped his nose on the back of his hand. He too had been pulled, by an effort, together.

'Come on, Wilf,' she said. 'We'll go for a walk. We'll sit in the park, and you can tell me what happened.' She startled herself by adding 'I'll look after you.' She had never promised that to anyone before.

They walked through the city, away from Paul's office, to the park where she had seen the woman awaiting her time as she wandered between pools of sun. Kate considered what she would say if they met someone who recognised her, how she would explain the boy. Paul's nephew – didn't you know he had relatives in the valley? (Paul would not see the joke.) No, it was unfair to attach him to Paul. But she could hardly say he had stepped out of one of her paintings: out of her head. What if she called him my little consequence, trotting along at her heels? My child, though not by the usual means.

His tears had blown over. His face shone. He was swinging his stick, conducting the air as if with a baton. It hardly seemed the same rough spar of wood which, as he watched the mutilation in the shop window, had propped him up like an old man's crutch.

'Wilf,' she asked, 'what is that stick of yours? What's it *for*?'

He had never had to account for the stick before. In the valley, everyone connected him with it, or attached it to him. They laughed about it at first – it was the emblem of his simplicity; he was a blockhead – and then took it for granted. Wilf frowned, unsure how much she required by way of justification. Could he admit that it was a toy not a tool?

'It's not *for* anything. But it can do everything. I can do everything with it.'

'Including knock me out.'

'I didn't though. I never have. My grandad brained a dog with it once, but that was before he carved it.'

The ant-hill? He didn't mean to destroy it. There was just no other way to find what was happening inside it. Maybe Clem thought the same.

'Do you use it when you're signalling?'

'No. That's work. I leave it home then.'

'But you brought it in with you today.'

'That's different. I don't like coming in here on my own.'

'So it's company. Does it have a name?'

'Don't be silly.' It was his grandfather's most scornful rebuttal, though Wilf left out the blood. He smiled as he said it: why had he never thought of naming the thing?

'Can I have a look at it?'

He was swinging it in such a fury of happiness – sketching alphabets in empty space, drawing numbers which extended to infinitude – that the stick had all but disappeared. Matter was replaced by motion. Wilf steadied it, and it returned jerkily to itself. He gave it to her, using both hands. It lay across his palms like a sceptre, heavy with significance for him alone.

She sat beneath a tree and studied it. It was nothing – a stump the length of her arm, scraped as clean as a bone – but it could become anything. Like her metamorphosing gods, or like a child, it represented a possibility. It might serve as a club. You could end (though not win) an argument with it. Wilf was in a state of preparedness, for war or adult life. Yet he insisted that he only used it to play with. Right now, as he swung and spun it, the stick burned energy and expressed emotion, like the tail of a dog. So far, it only knew how to play the games of the body. Later it might lend itself, with the aid of some surgery, to the grander games of the mind. The music of the spheres resounded inside bits of hollowed wood. Perhaps lurking somewhere in the stick there was a pencil, or a paint brush.

She handed it back, and said 'Now then. What did you want to tell me? About what you did or didn't do?'

'Oh,' he said, 'it wasn't nothing. It doesn't matter'.

The events of last night or of half an hour ago had receded. By taking responsibility for his fear, she had cast it out. Besides, he was sure she already knew what had happened. With her, in the park, he felt safe. The park was itself a denial. Its shaved grass and trees with name plaques showed how nature should behave; it contradicted the overgrown riot of the valley.

You dare, she thought. 'I beg your pardon?' she said. But sarcastic politeness was lost on him. He frowned at her, trying to work out what she was asking to be pardoned for. 'It was certainly something when you were looking at that shop window,' she said. 'It mattered then.'

She meant to upset him. He felt the ground, the pampered grass, shift and split underneath him. So she had seen him. He was dismayed to discover that what you thought and felt was inscribed on your face. A stranger in the street could read you. The sworn secrecy demanded by Horry protected no one; your eyes were blabbermouths.

Out the story spilled, drenching the lawn and gushing between the tame trees, churning the park into a valley of effluvia.

'It was after we finished the signalling last night, on our way back. On the track there's this tap, with water always running. Just before you get to where the Dogs are. You know?' She nodded: imagination could make pictures of things not seen. Wilf took her nod to be a co-conspirator's assent. She also knew, surely, why he called it simply a tap, refusing to mention the drooling faun whose mouth it was. 'Well, he was there. I think he must have been having a drink. I don't know who he was. He wasn't one of ours. He looked ordinary, but his clothes were all ripped. And he asked us to help him.'

So far she had a tap unconnected to the city's water mains, and some ownerless dogs – tethered or not? Now she placed a figure in the scene, adding a request for help as a caption. Ripped clothes: a beggar. She smiled once she had composed the picture. It was her signal to him. He could go ahead into the tunnel.

Instead, he reversed. 'My grandad was in a temper. When we was on our way down, there was some old woman at the same place. She gave my grandad a fright. Her eyes were looking different ways. My grandad asked if she was all right. She said she was on her way to a fire, and her head ached.'

Kate had to find room for this other figure, though she was not sure how to see it, except for the eyes which did not operate in unison. Nor was it clear whether it occupied the indistinct space at the same time as the other figure, the beggar. The humdrum moral, however, was coming into focus.

'Did you help her?'

'No, no, she didn't want help.'

A false move, but easily corrected. Painters called it a pentimento. Repentance was easy and instant in paint: you applied another layer, and were back where you began. She tried again.

'What about the man who was begging? You didn't help him either?'

'You don't under*stand*,' said Wilf, distending the word into a wail. For a moment she was afraid he might start crying again. 'He wasn't begging – not for money, anyway. He wanted us to save his life. And Clem said we were welcome to.'

She now had to incorporate another figure, about whom she had no information, though she thought the boy had mentioned him before.

'He didn't mean it, he only said so. He had a knife, see.'

She saw it, a glacial highlight jabbing the murk, and also saw the direction in which it headed, but there was still no hand to hold it.

'Clem is Horry's uncle. Horry lives where that old farm used to be. He's my friend. Well, no, he's not. I told him he could drop dead this morning. He's killed me enough times. I was fed up with him.'

'Wilf, you've got it all in the wrong order. Go back to the man, and the knife. What happened?'

'Nothing happened. Not then. My grandad said to leave them to it – Clem and the man. But that's what made him sick last night, so I had to come today and get him more medicine. He said we couldn't help him, that we didn't want to know nothing about it.'

Wilf repeated this carefully, because he realised as he did so that pressing up from beneath the words – which his grandfather had spoken as he pushed Wilf up the hill past the growling Dogs – were other words, which Wilf had spoken only to himself. I didn't want to help him either. I only wanted to know what Clem would do to him. I wanted to see it; and I did.

'I can't make out head or tail in this. What's the story?' Would she have to tell it for him, sorting through this muddle of misapprehension and puerile nightmare?

Wilf spelled it out for her as clearly as he could.

'Horry told me the rest this morning. He saw Clem in the middle of the night. And he said Clem took the man up the hill, past the Dogs, and he killed him, and he cut him up. Chopped his head off. Or sawed it, I don't know. Probably gave our Dogs a feed of the longer bits of him. That's what Horry said. So when those men started in the window, it was like it was happening again – still happening. You see what Clem did? Cut. Him. Up.'

But she no longer saw, or wished to see. The light had been switched off the succession of pictures with their impasto of muddy black and clotted red. They were figures from a horror comic, pages soiled by greasy fingers and inky minds. She was reminded of Paul. The gelignite, the jackhammers, the wreckers' ball, the campaign against nature and against whatever already existed, the pulling down and the putting up; the earth with its sedimented bones and sandwiched ruins; the unwinnable war, of which the boy's ridiculous stick seemed suddenly the token. Men frightened themselves with their self-generated violence, and relied on women to assure them that none of it was true.

'Congratulations,' she said to Wilf, who was awaiting her response. 'You've got quite an imagination. A bit over-excitable perhaps. It could get you into trouble, one of these days. I'd like to help you. But I don't believe a word of it. Not. One. Word.'

With which she got up, fussily brushed some dry leaves from her coat, and walked back into the city. Don't run, she whispered, although she could feel herself pursued by his uncomprehending eyes.

11

MONA'S DAYS IN the valley were mostly spent waiting for her nights. By day there were the dull chores of living to be despatched: washing her clothes, combing her hair, searching out new places in which to perform what she called her necessaries, sorting through the litter outside her door. Then when the sun began torching the glass cliff of apartments and resounding in her head as brazenly as trumpets, she got ready for her vigil. Sometimes she spent all night watching the chimneys, and waiting to see whether this paroxysm of flame (or the next, or the next after that) would be the one which finally made the sky twist and curl into tatters.

Of course, there was also the house to attend to, and the garden.

The house Mona had been living in during her month in the valley was built by the most genteel and impractical of the gentleman farmers a century before. It was manorial, two-storeyed, with double doors opening onto the lawns, and on one side a terrace fenced off by a knee-high balustrade, where the owners once sat under awnings and surveyed the valley and the plain of villages and market gardens beyond it which divided them, for the rest of the season, from the city. Now the house looked not unlike Mona: its roof askew, its windows shattered, strips of paper waving from its walls, its protective balustrade kicked away, its foundations foundering. She ignored the resemblance, and installed herself in a dry corner downstairs, once she had cleared away the cobwebs which spun the air into a sticky shroud.

She washed her clothes in a tank she discovered in an outhouse. There was also a brick oven she could use for cooking. Most days, however, she made her way down the hill and awaited a hand-out from Horry's mother. After a week, she came to think of the hand-outs as her right. Horry's mother grumbled (Mona never so much as said thanks) but continued to feed her. Her circumstances, Mona knew, were miserable. But she would not have to put up with them for long. Any day now, she thought, or any night.

While waiting, she worked in the garden. It was not actually a garden, more a rubbish dump. She raked through it assiduously, scavenging for signs. The rubbish had accumulated in windswept piles, in mounds cemented by fermentation, in rugged mountains with valleys between them. Among the number plates which had identified cars in previous incarnations, the dry, dented paint cans, the puffed-out tyres and exhausted exhaust pipes, the mangled bits of mechanical bodies, she did find treasures: things she was certain must have a meaning, though she made her head ache as she tried to decide what that meaning could be.

A mirror, knocked from the side of a car where it once reported on what lay behind – on the past which follows you, keeping its distance so as not to be noticed. It was a mirror for checking on space, though it also reported on time and its laws of sequence and consequence. The mirror had cracked across the middle, one side splintering into shards like silver-grey versions of the veins in a sick eye. Mona could only see half of her face at a time in it, which suited her because the two halves were engaged in different activities. One eye squinted as if through a telescope into the future, abridging distance and anticipating what was to come. The other was her rear guard. It circled the fuzzy hinterland of vision, where the trouble always inconspicuously began; it sometimes seemed to be looking over her shoulder.

In another pile, on another afternoon, she pulled a bundle of keys from the compost of rusted metal, putrid food and disembowelled mattresses. The keys unlocked all the alcoves and compartments of a particular small world. They fitted a car, a house, an office, a desk, a briefcase, a safe in the wall behind a picture; they were the compendium of someone's secrets, the keys to a personal kingdom.

So, thought Mona, I'm not the only one. I am in the right

place all right. She meant that she was not the only one to renounce the world of locked property and business-like conduct. She had left her own key under the doormat on the day she walked out of the suburb. She had also, on purpose, left the door of her house unlocked. Them kids from over the fence, she thought. By now they would have invaded: smashed her crockery, shat in her bed. Or perhaps not, for fear that, living or dead, she might reappear from inside a cupboard.

Still and all, whoever gave the keys away might not have done so, as she did, by choice. She knew about the way the valley robbed people. In any case it hardly mattered how they came to be here: there were no locks in the valley. She prised them off the ring one by one, dispensing them from their duties and picking apart the existence they guarded, then dug them into an unmarked grave in her garden of detritus and forgetfulness.

The newspapers were another of her findings, valueless but precious to Mona. Specially sent, she thought; as clear as if her name had been on them. Tied in bales under one of the mattresses which was shedding its fleece, they must have been dragged out from storage somewhere in the house. The damp paper was growing back into pulp, mashed and mushy grey matter. She untied a bundle and took some specimens back inside to examine. Look in the personals, she thought. There could be a message for you. You might even find your own death notice.

She laid them out on the floor. They were for dog-eared days, superannuated years. They were obituaries for time itself, though they contained no mention of Mona's demise. She looked through them, in no particular order. Merging, the years and days all told the same story of ups and downs, of one more up followed inevitably by another down. The story was called history, and it had passed Mona by. So this is what matters outside: she had adopted the valley's point of view.

She dragged the papers outdoors again. Some the wind distributed, shredding them as they whirled across the valley; the rest were made unreadable by the rain. Mona smiled at the blown litter and the wet mess, like a housewife on the other side of her suburban fence contemplating a tidied room. She had done her bit.

Beyond her plantation of junk lay the outline of an artificial lake, one of those superfluous ponds with scallopy edges on which the swans used to float in the days of the gentleman farmers. It was only a paved, raised outline, with some steps leading down to a mooring post for row boats. Instead of water it contained a sump of sludge; instead of lilies, clumps of rubbish reposed on it and set about taking root. Just offshore on both sides, further away than Mona could reach or poke a stick at, were two tiny islets, also artificial: circles of stone, still keeping their heads above the mud. Seeds had embedded themselves in the stone crevices, and the islets were atolls of weed and flowering grass. Mona could have waded out to them. A few paces would do it. But once she got there what would she do? The islets were hardly big enough for her to stand on.

She contented herself with exploring the margin. It puzzled her because it was full of nicks and bulges, inlets and indentations. Though she could get round it in a few minutes, the trip was like the first circumnavigation of a country, whose profile is being invented by the ship which follows its puckered, ravelled shore. Mona could not make a picture from the doodling line of the margin. Even when she stood on tiptoe and craned across the lake to see it all at once, it looked as shapeless as spilled milk or an egg out of its shell.

If she had climbed high enough — the flayed roof of her house, for instance — the lake would have settled back into meaning. The lake in fact was a head. The margin traced a pair of faces. They were back to back, never able to see each other, though the islets were positioned to represent eyes, of which the faces had one each. It was the conceit of the gentleman farmer, who had modelled the faces on his own and that of his wife. There were triangular extensions around the rim for noses (hers was pointier), ruffled beaches for mouths (hers had a poutier curve), bays for chins (hers was less squarely patrician). They had to be looking away from each other, because otherwise their faces would have merged in the water. The bed of sediment was their comingling brains, as if the contents of their two heads had overlapped into each other and into nature; feathery grass and savage flowers grew from islets that were their eyes.

The farmer and his wife could admire the resemblance from the upper windows. Or, if they walked down the steps inside her slightly open mouth and rowed the boat out into the water, they could navigate the rippling swells and gentle fluxes which were their combined thought-stream.

Past the lake, the farmer had permitted nature to resume. Trees grew there in a thicket, twining together like the strands of a rope. My little jungle, the farmer called it, my early history of the world; this is what we had to contend with. He offered his guests machetes for their afternoon walks, then pointed out a path through the thicket and a rough stone hut he had built among the trees. He had no use in mind for the hut, though he did tell his wife that he intended to meditate in it like a hermit, and would like his meals sent out on a tray.

The hut was a joke, a superfluity, like civilisation. God, he intended to say to visitors in an elaborate mimicry of alarm, look there! Do you see that? There are people *living* in there! Do you think they're the same as us, or what?

He tired in time of his own whimsies, and of the battle with a nature which had no interest in learning to be civilised. He found himself hating the land: its recalcitrance, its readiness — like a seasoned offender — to go to the bad. Frog spawn and slime thickened on the lake. The vines were furry with diseases. Every leaf seemed to swarm with parasites. A concave ant-hill dented the lawn, and dry sifting pools of fine white dust announced woodworm inside the house. The path through the thicket was overgrown; the hut disappeared, even in winter.

You can't win, he said. It's not worth trying to. No one person is ever meant to win, his wife said: others continue on your behalf. (They had children.) But he looked in dismay at the fertility of the place, the feeding of species on each other, the seeds which clung to your trouser legs when you walked through the grass and dug pincers into the cloth. When the farm workers demanded holdings of their own, he left them to it, sourly wished them well, and moved back to the city. Mona, generations later, inherited his earth.

By day, she stayed close to the house. From her ridge she could look down on men tending vegetables, women stringing nappies up to dry, or the ineffectual mission of a police car among the shanties near the highway.

Night put a stop to all these activities, and handed the valley over to Mona. On one of the first nights she got as far as the outer fence of the gas works, only to discover that when you approached the chimneys they retreated, dipping behind the battlements of fanged wire and knotted pipes. She tried other approaches, but the chimneys always eluded her just as she was closing in on them. Perhaps they slid back into the ground, and took the fires with them? Though when she regained her lookout, they reared into view to tantalise her: a combustible cathedral, coming and going in the sky. What she could not work out was why, when the flames railed and lashed, the clouds did not catch alight. They will, she told herself. She was ready. Each night might be the last.

Meanwhile, on nights which turned out to be merely penulti-mate, there were odd bits of witnessing to do on her way up and down the valley. Other people were out on nocturnal errands of their own. Mostly she avoided them, stepping aside into invisibility as the chimneys did when she neared them: gangs of prowling youths, the ferrying of wares to and from the cave which the Dogs guarded. Sometimes she forgot she could still be seen, and was surprised when someone accosted her, or called her a name.

That old man, for instance, whose stomach got a shock at his first sight of her near the water spout. To cover up, he was fawningly polite, but stomachs always speak the truth; as she expected, he soon turned nasty. Sent to mislead her, she was sure of it. The world was an obstacle course of lying signs, signals which pointed the wrong way. She ignored the directions he shouted, and found the lookout despite her blinding head.

The boy he had with him worried her more. He did not point or jeer. He studied her, with his moony face and his eyes which were entries to tunnels. To him she was an almost supernatural novelty. He would have to rearrange his view of the world, now he saw that the world contained someone like her. He might be a Witness too, she thought before she turned away.

And then, just after that, there was another meeting, another

129

incident. Three men from the farm where they fed her, on their way to whatever after-dark work they did. She was at her lookout, listening to the imagined sound of the flames, fuming and sizzling at the end of the valley. Then something thudded into her back and fell to the ground.

She whirled around. One of them glanced at her irritably, keeping count of the time spent baiting her. The second man guffawed. He laughed from the belly, like the old man earlier whose croak of terror resounded from down there; he heaved with hilarity. The third man stared at her, but not in gaping amazement like the boy at the water spout. His eyes were narrowed. He was sizing her up, sectioning her in his head. The stone was no joke. He meant it to hurt, but it was the outcome which interested him. How would she react? Would she fall apart, like a pillar of dust? He waited to see, with eyes which to her looked yellow, ferrety. The corner of his mouth twitched with the beginning of a grin. He was the one. She recognised him, though she had never seen him before; she remembered his names, and she called him all of them.

That was her reaction, for which he had been waiting with such clinical curiosity. It stunned him, and it even surprised her, as the epithets frothed out of her. She wondered afterwards where she had got them from. Hoarded for years, or invented spontaneously there and then? She called him a pig and a swine as well for good measure, and a hyena although she wasn't sure what that was, then a skunk and a weasel and a mongrel thing. 'You snake,' she said, startled by her own lucidity, like the cool blue arrow of the flame before it billowed into orange anger. 'You was seen, you was seen, you rat. Just wait. I'll burn you up.'

He lunged towards her, and as he did so she spat. She flung the words and the spittle in his face like acid, and like acid they corroded the mask of flesh. She had a glimpse of what was behind or beneath: a head of bone. Its eyes were empty, its brain hollow, but its mouth still found mortality funny. 'Don't you laugh at me,' she shrieked.

He looked briefly puzzled, because his face was not laughing. Rage twisted it out of shape. He did not have eyes any longer, and his mouth opened to let out a cry which, like an animal's, could not be translated into words. He reached for something in his pocket. The first man guessed what he was reaching for, and grabbed his wrist; the second man bore down on his shoulder. They led him away.

'There's no profit in her,' said the first man.

'Yeah', said the second, 'that's what I say. No profit.'

Prophet? thought Mona – that's all they know.

She went quietly back to her perch, without pausing for breath. The exchange of threats had no after-effect. She assumed her own impregnability. The world was a cloud of droning flies; she brushed it away with an automatic hand.

All Mona's days in the valley were the same, and all her nights different. The difference depended on the pentecostal chimneys: how many of them were in business, how the flames were treated by the wind and weather. Then, when one by one the nights proved not to be the final night, they became as indistinguishable as the days which followed. So after a while she was not sure whether the next thing she witnessed happened on the same night as the encounter near the water spout and the look-out.

She might have been asleep, though sleep and waking were not so unlike as they used to be. A noise awoke her. Perhaps it was the agitation of the birds on the roof, which made a cawing circuit of the garden. Never afraid, she was always wary. Things in the room – the broken mirror, the pile of leaflets she had brought with her to distribute around the valley like wind-sown seeds, the lame table which needed an artificial limb – were heavy with sleep, entranced by it. But outside was beyond her supervision; she could not keep watch there, and now someone was stumbling through her garden. A man, trailed by a shadow which may or may not have belonged to him.

The man halted when he saw her there. His face was blackened by dirt; rivulets cut grooves through it. And now there was an opening in it: the man had something to say to her.

Save me, she thought it was.

Save him? She didn't do that sort of thing, she couldn't. It was too much to ask. You're on your own (she would have told him, if there had been time), just like I am. I don't watch out for individuals. I don't even see the point of them any more.

But the shadow would not allow her to explain. With a shout, it leapt into independent life and pounced on the man, fastening itself to him, then – as they moved off towards the trees – merging with him.

When the birds stopped flapping on the roof beams and the trees ceased crackling, Mona came out of the house. She stepped through a wall which was no longer there, she glided across the ground without making the rubbish crunch beneath her feet. She had discovered the secret of weightlessness: do not feel attached to the earth. The flames which licked from the chimneys did not believe in gravity; neither would she. Not even the trees betrayed her, though they had creaked around the men. She slid between them like smoke (which, as the proverb said, was the certain prophecy of fire).

By the time she got to the hut, its door had closed. She heard voices inside. There were churches which had boxes like this, where people locked themselves to discuss their sins or crimes. You were not supposed to eavesdrop: this was only permitted to God. But that is another God, she thought. I don't credit that one. She drifted nearer, as smoke unfurls extra tendrils when it needs to, or as flames fork and subdivide.

The two voices were easy to tell apart. One of them talked in a lazy, drawling singsong. The other struggled to get its words out, as if its owner was shivering in the cold, his whole body shuddering. His teeth snapped shut to slice a word in half. She could not understand at first. Neither could the person who owned the other, amused, contemptuously casual voice. He had to repeat his question.

'I don't think I heard you right', he said.

This time the other voice could not manage words. Instead a sob came out, forced up from the pit of his stomach. It was the sound of an entire life reversed, regurgitated, regretted.

Mona remembered the rattle her sister Eileen made. Giving up the ghost they called it, and you could hear the ghost being surrendered. When Mona checked, her sister's face was blue. Soon the body would have to give up its gases.

Inside the hut, the first voice again asked the second what it was called.

He is taking names, thought Mona. The doctor will see you shortly.

The second voice, gasping, said 'What does it matter? Get on with it.'

'In a hurry, are you? I was only being polite – doing it proper.'

He should have told his name, Mona thought. If you don't, they think you don't know it, and out come the notebooks.

'Jesus,' said the second voice. The vowels were a moan, the consonants a hiss. God had become an expletive. No wonder the box was such a privy place.

'Just do it', the same voice added. Mona caught her breath at this. It does not do to rush them. They will get around to you, all in good time. Patients must be patient.

'Do what?' demanded the other voice. Mona recognised the tone. They always asked you to prescribe your own treatment. She always told them, with cunning smarminess, that they knew best.

Now, though there was no reply, the first voice turned vicious. She could hear in it the glint of bared teeth, or of an exposed blade. 'Anyone would think,' it said, 'that you were in charge of this.'

There was a silence. Only the box itself resounded. An engine thumping inside, bellows which opened and closed? Then the rhythm faltered.

'Come on', said the second voice. 'Kill me.'

Mona heard a laugh, and she heard surprise, even alarm, in it. 'I just might do that. I just might. If you ask nicely.'

The second voice panted. It was that of a man at the end of a long race. 'Kill me', it insisted. 'Please'.

'What do you think I'm doing?'

'Now, now, *please. . . .*'

'It's too dark in here. I can't see what I'm doing. What's this I've got my hand on?'

'Chest'.

'So that's your heart making all the racket? Don't worry, I'll put it out of its misery. I'll look after you. Or wait – would you like to do it yourself?'

The answer was only a whimper. Assent, Mona assumed. You had to sign a paper before they would operate.

'Ready,' said the first voice, 'set, go. . . .' It left a pause, a pulsation between the words; it uttered the first two in a whisper, but the third came out as a screech. Or it might have been the other voice, crying in unison.

What Mona heard next was not her sister's polite, gurgling request to be excused from the table, from the room, from the world. Amplified by the walls of the hut, it was a throaty roar, like the flooded creek rushing underground at the bottom of the valley.

Her body suddenly reminded her that she still occupied it. She wrapped her shawl around herself, rubbed the blood back into her hands, coaxed her feet to life.

On the way back through the trees, she heard the howl and the expiring rumble once more inside her head and thought, That wasn't right. Usually they give you something to put you to sleep. It doesn't do to do it while you're awake.

When she woke up, the light was brutal. It glared outside, like an eye dilated in disbelief. The house was no protection against it. It slashed through any crack in the boards. As she staggered across the room, she avoided the diagonal blades of sun: they could cut you. She tried to look at her garden and the drained lake, but a pain branded her forehead. So light could hurt. She left her necessaries undone, and groped her way back to the mattress; she tried to bury her head.

When she next awoke, the light was in remission. She could not be sure that it was still the same day. She risked looking out. This time her garden and the lake were grey, and kinder to her head. From the terrace she scanned the valley. The sun had set without her. The windows on the opposite cliff were already cooling. She checked her head again. It was no longer aching.

Then something crept up behind and tapped her on the shoulder: a memory. No, that can't be mine, she thought.

Dreams didn't count. But dreams were not usually so clear. They faded when you tried to go through them again, whereas this got brighter. And it had voices in it. Her dreams had never talked before, or made sounds like that with which this dream's conversation ended. The voices repeated themselves, reverberating and overlapping. That told her the place. It had happened, if it happened, in the hut. She was hearing the echo from those claustral walls. The voices must be trapped in there, richocheting like trapped birds.

I know, she thought, I'll go and let them out. That should stop them bothering me.

In her garden and among the trees, dusk was gathering. The shadows took up their positions like witnesses, and crammed together. The twigs parted to let her into the thicket, then closed behind her. Everything was denser than she remembered it being. But the clustered trees stood back from the hut, they formed a circle around it. She decided on a challenge.

'Are you there?' she said. The hut, so careless of its secrets before, had nothing to say.

She pushed away the screen of branches, and stepped onto the cleared ground. A feather spiralling through the heavy air grazed her cheek. She tried to hold the hut steady as she moved towards it, but in the half-light things palpitate; objects acquire nerves. She braced herself when she got to the door, expecting the caged voices to rush out and knock her over like a pent-up wind, a dammed torrent.

She pulled the door open slowly, to lessen the impact. She pulled it the rest of the way. No voices escaped. She peered in. The darkness had got there before her. She could not see through it. The darkness was damp and warm; the hut seemed to sweat.

Outside, the air was still the colour of ashes. She looked once more at the black inside the hut, and slammed the door. She was hungry. Time to go down the hill. A body had to eat.

Two weeks later, after Mona had forgotten about the hut and the voices inside it, the head turned up.

She was raking through a mound of rubbish, soggy after rain.

She set aside probable treasures for consideration: a flattened can with a peach on it and the legend EDEN arching above like a rainbow; a single glove, woolly inside and bristling outside, in which her own hand (when she tried it timidly, as if risking it in a dog's mouth) was swallowed up, so she could not even reach into the holes for the fingers – it belonged, she decided, to some enormous hammering fist which must have swung down from the sky and knocked the roof off her house and scattered this wreckage across the garden; a blizzard of feathers, which the same gloved fist might have torn from some fowl which got in its way.

The stick poked at something under the dusting of feathers. Whatever it was would not yield; the stick snagged on it. She separated the feathers and bits of paper which clung to the thing. It rolled down the sloping mound and landed, almost in homage, at her feet. It was a plastic bag, the size of a pudding and fastened with a cord.

The plastic was clear, though fogged by moisture inside the bag. The contents had been wrapped in cloth. Could that be a shirt, its empty arms twisting around the swathed, heavy thing? And then there was the cord, gripping the bottom of the bag in double or treble knots, knots so professional that there were names for them. Yet after being so carefully bound and gagged and tied, the thing had then been lazily discarded in Mona's plantation of refuse. All those layers, and those precautionary tightenings of the cord: they created difficulty, but were also a teasing admission that what was inside would be worth the effort of retrieving. The bag was a puzzle which longed to be solved.

Not here, she thought. She picked it up, gripping it at the end which was gathered by the cord, and took it to the terrace behind the house. She set it down gently – it might be breakable: everything, one way or another, was – and knelt beside it to plan how she should proceed. Undoing it was meant to be a ritual. The knots and the wrappings warned her of that. She should not rush it. She was gratified to find how resistant the cord was. The knots were subtle. Mind and body could not have clung together more inextricably or more ingeniously. Her fingers were baffled by the maze of wet cord. She had a knife inside the house, but she knew that would be cheating. She must work out how it had been done, then it would surrender. The tougher the knots were, the more precious the prize they guarded.

She allowed herself to prod the bag with her finger. More sensitive than the stick or her foot, it distinguished strata, soft and then hard: beneath the plastic and the cloth, something slid aside or quietly receded; beneath that, a sudden wall, a prohibition. She went back to the perplexity of knots. She fiddled at them for the rest of the afternoon, but they were too snarled, interknitting like the converging trails of chance and choice which lead us to the exact spot in which we find ourselves, or like lines on a hand, where every crease is a crossroads.

By the time the sun left the terrace, she accepted defeat. Aware she was breaking the rules, she went to fetch her knife. The blunt blade could saw through neither the cord nor the tough plastic. She threw it aside, and picked the bundle up with both hands. It was then, as her hands extended to clutch it, her fingers spreading like a flower as it opens, that she knew what was inside.

She read it as a blind person does the face of a stranger. First the armoury of bone: a square jaw, an aggressive nose, a forehead unruffled by worries. The helmet we wear into battle. There were also the hollows which had no defences, the caves of sense, the tunnels dug into the interior. She could feel where the ears were, his eyes, his mouth. They were the organs which did the witnessing. Perhaps if she undid the bundle, the mouth would utter the word which was forming inside it, the eyes would reveal the forbidden image reflected in them.

But she now had no desire to undo it. Her fingers had seen it for her. Some things, like the sun, were not meant to be looked at. She sat down on the terrace and nursed it, wrapped the folds of her skirt around it, hugged it with her knees as if her own body could complete it, crooned to it reassuringly and called it by its name.

The sun set; it set in her lap. Though she had gazed at it for so long, she was never able to see it. The glare made a throbbing inside her head, and the disc of gold turned black. When she looked back, there would only be a hole in the sky, like the mark of a burn which a cigarette leaves in your clothes. It was a face, she knew that. They always told her, when she was a girl, that we were under observation all the time, even if the doors were closed, even if we hid under the bed. The sun did the observing. It witnessed everything, but disliked being witnessed itself. She cheated once, with a broken section of a beer bottle. The glass was brown. Maybe through it she would be able to make out some features. Was it a face, beaming, flushed, ruddy – or just a single eye positioned in the middle of the forehead, needing no help from a partner? She wanted it to be the eye. The glass showed her only a blot, and she was punished with a headache for her peeping. Now she knew it was not an eye.

But how come the fire had gone out? The bundle felt as clammy as the moon. Had it lost its power in hurtling down? Could it fail, like light bulbs with their snapped, jangling filaments?

She lifted it out of her lap and put it back on the flagstones. As it bumped to ground, she became aware of its weight: a boulder. How come? Were there thoughts still inside, congealing into density? A puddle slowly formed beneath it. She shuddered at the weeping moisture; the smell, now she noticed it, made her choke. Ferment was happening. The soil was greedy for fertilising blood and bone. If this was nature's way of reabsorbing us, welcoming us home, why should it smell so foul?

She left the bundle where it was. Once the shadows reached it, extending across the terrace, it could quietly decompose. Then the darkness would gobble it up. It was not the sign she expected. It was only a head someone had lost: lopped off, cut short, now busily converting its store of experience into some other creature's food.

That night, Mona did not present herself in the yard of the farm and wait for a plate to be sent out. She marched to the bottom of the valley and searched for a gap in the wire fence which separated her from the chimneys. The fence rebuffed her; she retreated to her lookout, walking backwards so as not to lose sight of that altar and its seething pipes. Once she tripped. She yelped at the boulder which felled her: had the head rolled down the hill to follow her? The view from the lookout calmed her. The balls of fire puffed silently into the air, inflated into flowers, then flicked off, leaving only the scar of their imprint on her brain. There was nothing, surely, which they could not burn up.

At the farm, Mona's absence caused comment. Horry's mother kept something in the stove for her. (Eventually Jacko ate it.) She thought of Mona as a responsibility. Besides, the policy was to keep her sweet, which meant keeping her fed.

'She could have passed on during the night. Had an attack. Horry,' said his mother, 'you go up and see what's happened to her.'

'Aw, ma,' said Horry, stretching both syllables into warbles of anguish. He claimed to hate the old woman. He meant that she scared him.

Horry's mother removed her red, chapped fist from the dish-water, and showed it to him. He went, sulking, and turned the volume on his transistor up to broadcast his protest.

The fountain dribbled through its mocking face. He remembered the stories he had told Wilf about meeting the beast itself in remote outposts of the valley. He missed Wilf, to whom he could conveniently transfer his terrors. At the top of the track, he surprised himself by turning off the radio. Am I that frightened? he wondered. He looked round for Clem, who had vanished in this direction. He even said Clem's name, though only in a whisper. He did not want him to appear: saying the name was insurance against his doing so. To hear himself say it boosted his courage.

Now the silence after he gagged the radio rustled with evidence of the old woman. She must have caused that branch to snap. The bird which propelled itself away in a hurry must have seen her. She might be lurking behind those rubbish heaps. But the house, all its gaps grinning, insisted that it had nothing to hide: with its concussed roof and flayed walls, you could see straight through it; it was a skeleton, not a body.

He crept through a front door which no longer existed. The

hall was carpeted with lumps of plaster and a surf of screwed-up paper: the annals of days which Mona had discounted because they were not the right one.

He heard something wheeze, then faintly rumble. In one of the gutted rooms she sprawled on her mattress. The mirror, the tin stamped with the brand name in luminous, uprisen capital letters, the giant's glove were arranged on the floor in a cordon, a tripwire of totems. Her chest heaved, and her lips seemed to babble.

What if, in her dream, she spoke to me? thought Horry, with a prod of alarm. Though she didn't know his name – or did she? He tiptoed back into the hall, and fled. But he had not bothered to remember the way he came in; he took a different turn behind the stairs and came out on the terrace. She's having a lie-in, he could tell his mother. She snores worse than Jacko. There would be another version to tell Wilf, if he ever saw him again: about how he had swaggered into the room, stood over her as she writhed and snorted in the dream, then tugged back the musty covers . . . .

He got no further with the story because, on the terrace, he saw the bundle. He knew at once what it was. The smell, the puddle around it, and the convoys of ants which laid siege to the plastic told him all.

He had imagined everything Clem might have done to the man, and had tried out the inventions on Wilf; now one of his fantasies had been hurled back at him. Was it dangerous to imagine things? Did it dare them to come true? And yet how cockily he had bragged to Wilf that he was an accomplice.

He ordered himself to stand still. If he ran away, it would somehow or other come after him. But how could he dispose of it? Not by burying. The earth could not be trusted to keep secrets. The valley was forever coughing up fossils, shells left behind when the river silted up, the broken crockery and liquor bottles of the gentleman farmers, scrap from the bankrupt factories, the refuse of the shanty dwellers; you could not expect it to digest a head.

Burning: that was it. The incinerator, where he had stuffed Clem's clothes. A fire was quick and clean. But he could not help making images of what the heat would do: the molten flesh, the shimmering eyes, the licking ignited tongue.

Looking away while holding his breath, Horry picked the bundle up after feeling for the knotted cord. Something tickled his hand. He dropped the thing again, and shrieked as he heard it thud and jar on the terrace. He risked a glimpse of his hands. It was only the ants, which he brushed away. He grabbed the knotted end again and ran with it, the radio tucked under his other arm. He skidded down the slope beside the cave, and wriggled through the phalanx of Dogs, which sniffed and clawed and jumped to reach the bundle. He reached the track to the water spout, gasping, and thought, Not much longer. He could see the farm, and the yard with the incinerator.

Panic glued the sides of his throat together. He set down both the bundle and the radio and doused his head under the spout.

When he stood up, he saw the world through a film, as if from inside a cave behind a waterfall. He shook himself and blinked. The world had altered while he was submerged.

A fence had been built around him. It consisted of spread legs and extended arms. He was encircled by smiling mouths and eyes aimed like rifles. It was a gang of boys from the shanties near the highway: he recognised some of them, having exchanged words and stones with them once. Though they were younger than he was, there were more of them. Within sight, within shouting distance of home, he was lost. One of the boys said, 'Give us what you've got.'

Horry stepped defensively towards the bundle. Then, aware of his error, he picked up the transistor and held it out. 'It's new,' he said like a salesman. His father had stolen it for him only three weeks before. When they accepted it, he pulled his pockets inside out. They were empty anyway.

'What's that?' said one of the boys, nudging the bundle with his foot.

'Nothing,' Horry said. 'I was taking it to the incinerator. Some rubbish.'

'Poo,' said another boy. 'It stinks.'

Horry miscalculated again. 'You don't want that,' he said.

This made up their minds for them. If he did not want them

to have it, then they would certainly take it. The first boy grabbed it by the cord and flung it at the one who had complained about its smell. The second boy caught it, and threw it immediately to someone else. As they ran off towards the road and through the tunnel, whoever held the transistor switched it on so it could report their triumph.

Horry felt strength drain through his feet, as the water had spilled from him. He sat down abruptly in the dust. The fire would have ended everything, sifting evidence and identity into ash. Now, instead of that, there was another beginning. They had run with the ball, like the players of the invisible game which he imagined when he listened to the transistor. Nothing stayed in place for more than a moment. There was no such thing as being safe. Though that was in another game, there was no home base.

Then, as the tunnel muffled the shouts of the boys and the clatter of the music, he felt a sudden lightening inside him. His body knew the reason, ages before his brain worked it out. It was because he no longer needed to worry about it; he was off duty. Let them have it, he thought. They're welcome. That was how the world went round.

Now he understood something his father often said, when trying to convince Horry's mother not to brood if a fox slaughtered their fowls or Jacko not to worry about how their mother was getting on or Clem not to draw up lists of all the people who had looked askance at him since childhood so he could revenge himself on them. 'Turn the page,' his father said. Horry, deprived of other music, began to whistle. Turn the page.

12

A THOL HAD BEEN on a tour of his traps, the coffers where he
kept his earnings. My deposit accounts, he called them: he
had deposited them in the ground. One strongbox he lowered
into a well, another was under the canting floor of Mona's house.
Elsewhere in the valley a stone wall through a field doubled as
a wall safe.

Athol visited them once in a while, taking care to divide what
he had accumulated in equal amounts between the different holes
and gaps and unmarked graves. You should spread your assets
as widely as you could. Banks had been known to fail. The
prospect, however, did not worry him much, and he seldom
bothered to check for illicit withdrawals. The money was useless.
He planted it like seeds, except that it did not sprout; he buried
it like a stiff, except that it did not decay. The pleasure for him
lay not in possessing it or in dreaming of what he might do with
it but in knowing where it was and in denying that knowledge
to the others.

He long ago lost track of how much it amounted to. Counting
it wasted his time. Then he would have to carry the figures in
his head as he tramped from one outdoor depository to the next,
and it was another rule of his never to write things down. It was
easier to turn the page if the page was blank. If the page was
blank, you were sometimes even saved the effort of turning it.
A memory was a nuisance. The inside of your head should be
like the sky, with clouds – pages dismissively crumpled or torn
– dispersing as they crossed it. And if he forgot where his traps
were? He prided himself that he would not mind. What you
didn't remember couldn't hurt you.

On his journey from one hiding-place to another, he often
compared the valley with the city. These prostrate hills and

skulking hollows where everything was under wraps, blanketed beneath rock, dirt, grass; those parading towers, a line-up of hostages. In the late afternoon, tableaux were switched on in the windows of the apartment buildings on the ridge. Each lighted oblong was someone's world, recklessly exhibited between the open curtains. When they looked out, the inhabitants saw only the dark pit of the valley. It did not occur to them that someone might be looking in, laughing at their faith in walls of glass or in locked doors to which he almost certainly possessed a key (and if he happened not to, there was always Jacko's shoulder). Athol owned a pair of binoculars, through which he studied the bright, gleaming boxes. You had to keep up with the technology. They were always inventing new things for him to steal.

The hoard Athol worried about was that inside the cave. Or rather he employed the Dogs to worry about it for him, and Ern to worry about the Dogs. Nor for that matter did the cave really contain a hoard, because nothing remained in it for long. Athol's concern was to keep the merchandise moving. But he loved the cave: the idea of it, not so much the items stockpiled inside. He thought of it as a magician's den, since his light-fingered art could cause commodities, appliances, electrical installations to vanish from rooms in the city and whirl through the air to this vault of limestone. The cave, like the tunnel beneath the railway line, was one of the valley's points of entry to an adjacent world. If the cave had a door, there would have been an occult password to make it open. But the cave's portcullis was the teeth of the Dogs, and the recognisable smell of Athol was the only password they needed.

As the Dogs fell back, fawning, he exchanged the sun for the dim, thin light which trickled from his torch. You turned a corner into the cave, and had to crouch beneath an overhang. It was like a probing venture into the human body: the rock tightened into a gullet; it was a back passage too, squeezing out its contents under cover of night. Once you had wriggled through the retentive canal, the beast had a belly, where it stored the hardware it consumed.

Athol's torch played over television sets and video recorders, video cameras and video display units, cassette players and stereo speakers, calculators and cash registers, microwave ovens and food blenders. On occasion there were even small refridgerators. We keep all major brands, Athol would assure prospective customers. We also take orders. We deliver too (though trusted clients were permitted to visit the cave). Cars were a separate department, housed in barns or factory sheds up and down the valley. The cars were more profitable, but he got his enjoyment from the gadgetry in the cave.

The city could not operate without its toys, its machines which performed their fanatical, specialised tasks when plugged into the sockets. He was punishing it by depriving it of these playthings. People came to him in despair. Their appliances had betrayed them, sullenly withdrawn their labour, and these days no one did repairs; or they had returned home to find the room empty, stripped bare in many cases by the lads themselves.

Athol had no use for any of the items he traded. He despised them all, though he grudgingly exempted cars. Otherwise they created cravings. They were genies who kept their masters enslaved. He liked to think of how disempowered they were here, deprived of the current the city fed into them. Television sets with their faces erased, their heads empty of images, calculators unable to count, famished blenders and microwaves with nothing inside them to irradiate. Stealing these things and selling them and then after a decent interval stealing them once more, he was teaching the users a little lesson. Incorrigible, they refused to learn it, so had to be taught it time and again.

I'm a tax collector, he thought, sort of. Look on it as an extra duty on luxuries, whatever you don't need but can't do without. And I pay my own dues. For what other reason did he bank his money in the ground? Paper was not wealth. Even gold was not wealth. A piece of paper with a serial number and a grain of lines as intricate as a finger print had no more value in the end than the scraps of soggy, obsolete news Mona sorted through; gold was no better than mud. But since the city had decided that everyone should believe in the worth of the paper, Athol went along with the pretence. He refused, however, to forget that it was only a pretence. Hence the plastic bags with their wads of notes which he planted through the valley.

The torch travelled across a stack of grey screens. They had nothing to show for themselves except the reflected beam. He brushed away a spider which was wrapping a calculator in its web. At his feet, cords and plugs were looped like snakes with fangs of copper.

He half expected Clem's face, neatly boxed, to be smirking at him from a screen or his voice, hollowly amplified, to greet him from one of the unplugged speakers. He always smoothed the dirt when he left, to warn him of an intrusion.

He was not afraid of Clem, only apprehensive. Clem was someone whose actions could never be predicted, and therefore never controlled. He did things without a motive or a reason. Killed, for instance, if that what was he had done. When questioned, he would say that he wanted to know what it felt like – to throw a stone at an old woman, to kick a dog which was lapping his hand, to tear the wings from a butterfly. His cruelties always cheated him: they were incapable of making him feel anything. He was curious about pain. He knew all about causing it, but when the victims began to moan or blubber or (in the case of the butterfly) just silently, clumsily throb, they became unknowable, merely laughable.

Athol caught him once, when Clem was younger, tormenting a stray cat. He held it by the tail. It dangled in mid-air, and twisted its body in a buckling curve as it attempted to claw him. Clem was watching its acrobatics like a scientist conducting an experiment. Athol yelled at him, and Clem dropped the cat.

Athol asked why he had done it. 'I don't know,' said Clem. 'Why not?'

He addressed the question to the vacant sky, not to the baffled face of his uncle. Where were the repercussions to come from? Actions happened in a world which absorbed them and forgot them. Each thing you did was a pebble thrown into a pool. The surface smashed for a moment, then settled down to show you still your own expectant, unanswered stare.

'I'll show you why', said Athol, and struck Clem's head with his fist.

He winced as he drew back his stinging hand; Clem paused until the blood stopped booming in his ears and then quietly said 'It didn't hurt.' Athol lurched towards Clem, but found himself turning away instead. Clem, judging the distance exactly, waited until he was far enough off to rule out pursuit yet still within earshot and shouted after him again 'It didn't hurt.'

There was an appeal in the phrase as much as a challenge. Athol glanced around at the valley: it had happened behind the barn in their yard. The world sluggishly went about its business. He heard the cough of a scooter somewhere and the banging of pans inside the house. The valley had already laid on its earthquake, or its clumsy, accidental landslip. No gash was going to open to swallow Clem up. No mallet-shaped fist, tougher than Athol's, was likely to swing down from a cloud to smite him. This world had no fences, no areas which were out of bounds, no red lights. Why not indeed?

An admiration grew up beside Athol's dislike of Clem. Athol himself took pride in not caring. He was free because he disbelieved. But he had to admit, at the cost of a pang, that Clem's refusal to care was greater and somehow grander than his own. He did not care about the business. 'You should open a shop,' he would say to Athol: it was his most considered insult, aimed as precisely as a knife. He also did not much care about himself. 'It's my apprenticeship,' he said when he was sent to prison. Released, he came back to the valley and announced, 'I've finished my schooling.'

But petty theft bored him. Even stealing cars seemed trivial. It all went round in circles (which for Athol was the charm, the beauty of it). He even had his doubts about crime. Since its motive was profit, it merely copied the getting and spending and mean-minded grafting of the city. Even when Athol recruited him for some act of violence, just as he employed Jacko to do the lifting and all other dumb chores, he treated Clem as an unofficial policeman. It was force not right which sustained the law, and when Clem was asked to show his knife it was as if he had produced a badge or pedantically unfolded a warrant. The display of credentials generally did the trick, though Clem had once or twice grazed some skin or made a neat sleek incision while putting the knife away. 'You can say you cut yourself shaving,' he would tell his victim. 'It happens every day.' Athol found himself having to apologise.

Clem, frustrated, dreamed of doing something on his own initiative: an ultimate provocation, which would once and for all test the limits of his freedom. He made no specific plans. He wanted the occasion to surprise him, just as he wanted to surprise himself by what he did. He knew, however, that what he did would be more than a crime. It would be an investigation, an inquiry, addressed both to the body it took apart and to a world which had made no protest when he dismantled its taboos.

Apparently he had done it at last, thought Athol. And found that it was much the same as picking a pocket or teasing a cat. All he could say was that it was hard work, and dirty too. But the world did not end. He discovered where all the joins were, the ligatures you had to hack through, though not where the hook was which connected matter and mind, the shuddering body and the disinterested, migrant spirit. The man gave up too soon, willing it to be over. He made it too easy. Or he was not telling Clem all of the truth. It was like sex: you could not find out what it felt like by watching someone else do it. Which was why Clem, in spite of his casualness, was so angry when he came back down the hill.

They had agreed between themselves not to speak of him after he left. But their silence could not banish him. Athol watched for him everywhere. It was easy to believe he was there in the cave: his face, the shadow or the image of him, drained of colour by the grey-green tube, smiling from one of the screens, mouthing words Athol could not hear, unreachable behind the glass where he could never be hurt. . . .

Athol sent the torch on a last inspection, making it run all the shadows to ground. Then he switched it off: he always left it on a ledge just inside the cave. Although he expected it, the darkness was a blow to the head, a lunge into unconsciousness. While he was still struggling to see, clearing a way through a blitz of red flashes, he heard the Dogs outside. He always knew what they meant. They had one chorus for recognition (sniffling, whining, whimpering with joy) and another to signal hunger (then they howled, or let off single indignant barks like exclamation marks).

What they were doing at present was raising the alarm, strangling themselves with their chains as they threatened a stranger. Athol pushed his way to the entrance. He did not notice until later that he had grazed his forehead on the overhang; his brow was furrowed with blood.

The cave disgorged him into daylight. The small world he guarded inside, the den which immured his secrets, suddenly had to confront a world owned and ruled by others. He had visitors, who had driven their car with the silent siren of blue light up the track. They carried guns.

He walked towards them, which was the only thing he could do. There were no more pages to turn. Why didn't I notice before? he asked himself as he pushed the Dogs aside. It was the end of the book.

Ern was in a temper.

He stumped round the hut, mumbling complaints at the empty air and cuffing the innocent furniture. He had several gripes.

In the first place, he was sick. His stomach was playing up. He had humoured it for a week, dosing it with the brown medicine and hoping it would settle back to sleep like a fractious baby. But it refused to be chivvied. Now it hurt him all day, it kicked at him from inside. An embryo of pain was growing there. He poured the medicine down himself, and it promptly gushed up again. After a while, when the nausea retreated like a wave lumbering down the beach and back out to sea, the pain announced itself again with a series of taps, then a thump. He swore at it. The bottle was empty. He needed Wilf to go for a refill, much sooner than usual.

Wilf, however, was the second of his grievances. Wilf had taken to malingering. He brooded in the corner, or doodled in the dirt with his stick. Sent to the chemist with the empty bottle, he returned twice at the end of the day with excuses. The chemist was closed, maybe he was sick too. Or he got lost in the city. On the third day, he came back without the empty bottle. 'It broke', he said, and would not enter into a discussion of who had broken it, or how. Ern pulled himself out of the chair, since he could not hit Wilf while sitting down, but found that he needed both hands to grasp the place where the pain was.

Wilf's next refusal was to go to work at the tunnel. 'I don't feel like it', he first said. Then 'I don't want to'. Finally, flatly, 'I won't'. Ern noticed, as he said this, that his hand tightened round his stick.

Ern, vowing that he would engage a replacement, went on his own, got confused while attempting to use both bats at once, caused a crash, and came home having torn branches off as many saplings and trampled as many flowers as he could manage. Wilf had made no meal for him. When he made one for himself, his stomach rejected it. Wilf just watched, as if there were worse things happening behind his eyes than in front of them – as if, thought Ern, there could be.

The next night, Ern excused himself from the signalling, and let the valley revert to lawlessness. Wilf looked anxious, but said nothing. 'I'm on sick leave', grunted Ern, 'not on strike like you'. He could afford to do without his earnings from the drivers, because the lads employed him to feed the Dogs. They could have fed the Dogs just as easily themselves, but Ern was one of their charities.

This became the third grievance, an aggravation of the other two. Because the lads had not sent up the week's food for the Dogs, or the extras they always included for Ern. Wilf, ordered to investigate, reported that there was no one at home at the farm. Ern assumed he was lying, and had not been down the hill at all. So he decided to go himself. 'To demand my rights,' he said. He went to bed early to recruit his forces, and rehearsed all night the speech he intended to make to Athol, with inserted hints about what should be done with Wilf, or to him; his stomach would not lie down.

In the morning, he got ready for the journey. The valley was elastic, its distances bewilderingly relative: in prospect it seemed a long way, though he used to do it daily. His absence from the tunnel had changed, without his noticing it, from sick leave to retirement. Now he was housebound, his world had contracted. I should have a good breakfast before I go, he thought. Then a qualm warned him against eating. He cursed the pain as if it did not belong to him, then took it down the hill. Belching would have helped, except that he had lost the knack. The discomfort did not gather itself into little bullets and explode upwards. It stayed there, battering at him. He began to concentrate his fury on his stomach, to blame it and threaten reprisals. It was being bloody-minded, like Wilf. Yet how could you deal with an enemy gone to ground inside you?

Pulling his hat on, he tugged at the brim, wishing he could make it squeak. Pain was something that could not be shared: if only he could inflict it on someone or something else. Plants were supposed to shriek on a frequency we could not hear when you cut them or rooted them out. He promised himself to lay waste to the bushes along the track.

But the track reduced him to hobbling. He used to be able to rotate on his stiff leg, using it as a fulcrum. Now it felt splintery, like dried-out timber, and every step sent a twinge clambering up it to collude with the pain in his stomach. He took to breathing in discreet, hurried gulps: did he hope to outwit the pain, persuading it he was no longer alive? It jolted him, annoyed at his evasions. Winded, he leaned against the low wall beside the track overlooking the farm. I'll just consider my position, he thought. He had not been there for long when he realised that there was no need to continue.

Wilf had been telling the truth, even though he was probably making it up. There was no one at home. No shouting in the yard, no cars behind the barn, no fires alight. The lads had moved on overnight, and without telling him. The realisation went straight to his stomach.

The lads were unofficial lords of the manor. He did jobs for them, attending to the Dogs, diverting or halting traffic to assist their robberies; they were therefore, he reasoned, obliged to him. Especially because of what he knew: he remembered the last time he had seen them, on the night which began with the frazzled woman who had lost her way and ended with Clem standing over the sobbing man at the water spout. There was a story in that, if only he could devise how to tell it, and find the proper authority to listen.

He would first have to work out when it was. His days were

all alike, without names or numbers. He relied on Wilf to tell him when the week had ended, so they did not have to do their signalling. Otherwise he saw no point in keeping count. Everything that happened had happened before, and the cars which went through the tunnel in one direction sooner or later came back in the other. His stomach was his only time-keeper. He dated events according to the attacks the events had brought on. That night was a medicine bottle ago.

I wanted to tell, he would say; to do my duty. But I'm an old man. And Clem had a knife. Then he would take to whimpering so piteously that someone would look after him. He might even request protection, and of course rehousing. He had done his time in the valley. Now he deserved ease, comfort, honour as an elder. He would tell the story of the truant Thelma and the child she left with him like a parcel. As for Wilf, there were surely institutions.

Having sorted out the prospects and organised the future, he stood up. His powers of recovery amazed him. The pain buried its head in shame. His legs got their springiness back. He decided to go down the hill. Who knows what might have been left behind as a keepsake? Once he was rehoused outside the valley, he would be connected to the electricity: all those appliances could be made to work for him. He positively bounded to the cave.

The Dogs, not having been fed, flung themselves at him. He parted their ranks, and left them to their concerted tantrum. He could not hear it in any case, since his heart was thumping.

The overhang butted him, and knocked his hat off. His pain looked up, with a grin which tore at his stomach. He found the hat, but did not put it back on his head. It hung respectfully from his hand: he might have been going through a church door.

He grappled forwards, using both hands to see with. When he ran out of contours to grope, he supposed he had arrived. But the light, grey and filmy by the overhang, was black in here, as thick and viscous as oil. Batting his eyelids as if to disperse the dark, he told himself to wait. All would be revealed. The things he had dreamed of would materialise before him. He even, while he was waiting, brushed at the dark with his hat as if bailing it out. He counted minutes by timing the little eddies of nausea in his stomach. Soon the darkness would untie his blindfold.

Eventually it dawned. The sun popped up, though only inside his head. He still saw nothing. Then he realised that there was nothing to see. They had cleaned the cave out.

He wanted to believe that the shadows were a blur on the surface of his weak eyes; he stumbled in a circle, swiping the air with his hat, punching it with his fist, hoping he might meet some obstruction. But the cave contained only the sound of his breathing, and then the curses which accompanied the flailing of his hat. 'Oh my godfathers,' he wailed. 'Christ almighty. Damn you all to bloody hell.' Blasphemy was as inefficient as prayer. He stamped his foot, and at last felt something yield underneath. It crackled, like a snail shell when you crushed it. A killing, no matter how small, would be some consolation. He reached down to see what it was: only the ground glass of a screen damaged during the removal, and the remains of a tube in which pictures could have glowed into life. His pain laughed out loud.

'You can go to blazes', he said, meaning the lads and the broken glass and the agony inside him, 'the whole flaming lot of you'. Nothing caught fire.

He battled out into the day. The sun hurt his eyes. He would have to get along without heavens or hells. What he had were the Dogs, cheering him as a hero in the hope of food. 'I'll fix you lot,' he said. 'This is the end of you.'

He had no intention of feeding them. Instead he would free them. That would be his revenge, unleashing them onto the world. He foresaw what would happen: a dozen wolves, maddened by hunger, marauding their way across the valley to feast on sheep, goats and hysterical chickens, snatching food from the hands of children, maybe even snatching the chubby hands as well, leaping over walls and rampaging on until they got to the city. They were his personal furies, sent out on a mission whose finale he also foresaw: stand-offs in the streets of the city, blocked traffic, fleeing pedestrians, and a cordon of Dog-catchers with guns taking aim as they foamed forwards.

He passed along the line, unhooking them. It ought to have been more solemn and ceremonial, he thought. He was sending them off to wreak havoc on his behalf, and then to face the guns. But they were confused, not knowing what was required of them. They were usually let off only to die, like the Alsatian. Freedom meant nothing to them, since they could not retrace the invisible trails of odour which connected them to the homes they were stolen from. Why even begin the journey of detection, following tenuous clues through the labyrinth of the city? If they were ever by accident to arrive back where they came from, the house might be gone or the people might have moved or might have found themselves another object of affection or might not recognise this matted, mucky, foul-smelling traveller . . . .

One or two of the Dogs raced down the track towards the fountain, just to try out their rusted legs. They splashed under the spout, then shook themselves. What next? No dogs ran from the yard to engage them in a border dispute; the lads had loaded up their animals when they marched on. The Dogs returned up the hill faster than they had careered down it, fearful that they would find no one left to belong to. They jumped up at Ern in gratitude, lapping the hands with which he tried to beat them off.

'Go on,' he said, 'git.' He pointed at the wall of windows where the city began. 'Off you go.' The Dogs danced round him in a circle, enjoying the game.

Eventually he tired of ordering them. As they grovelled, his pain bit him. He limped back towards the hut, ready to weep with frustration; and the Dogs, forming themselves into a gambolling line, followed him. He kicked at them, but they bounced back playfully from his boots, as resilient as rubber.

He remembered the incident with the mongrel which defied him among the shanties by the highway, and the cudgel he bashed it with, which he whittled for Wilf. And then he remembered that it had not actually happened; it was only a story, and after many repetitions he had come to believe in it. There had been a dog, and it was bad-tempered. He did carry a stick, just in case. Once he even showed it to the dog, which in return showed him every tooth in its mouth. Both deterrents worked:

that was as far as it went. The blood and fur belonged to a rabbit, already dead when he found it in a ditch and therefore no good for the pot.

Having struggled to the top of the hill with his escort, he looked back at the lie, which mocked him now like his pain, and at the valley. There had been other lies. He had passed them on to Wilf like an inheritance. Stories about how he and his ancestors had owned the valley until they were evicted by the gentleman farmers; about the mile-long pile-ups and cymbal-clashing head-ons he had organised at the tunnel in his heyday; about how one day the earth would shift again and give the perched apartment towers on the cliff a fright. The lies were heroic so long as Wilf trusted him. But Wilf had already withdrawn his obedience; next he would withdraw his belief. The lies, the legends, the belligerent sagas and myths of entitlement had filled the valley like flood water. Now, draining away, they left a muddy hollow.

He looked across the valley. It was the size of his life. He had been tethered here along with the Dogs, which nuzzled his face and tugged at his trouser legs. With every yelp and yap they called a bluff. The empty cave contemptuously yawned at him; his pain crowed.

He made a last spurt, chased by the Dogs. He managed to squeeze through the door of his hut and then − debarring them with both legs, pushing back eager snouts − to slam it. Outside, the Dogs whined and entreated, wheeled and grieved, demanding to be looked after.

13

B Y THEN, it had already been in the newspapers, which neither
Athol nor Ern ever read: the battered football inside the
plastic, the swaddling made from a torn shirt, the boys who
were playing with it on the other side of the tunnel when the
bag split open, and the shocked local residents.

The head made headlines in the more excitable papers, but
the serious ones relegated it to a paragraph on an inside page.
After all, there was no story attached to it. No one had reported
it missing, and the rest of whoever it had belonged to was still
lost.

The police had the teeth examined, and went through the
motions of reconstructing a plot. They worked backwards from
the end for a few steps, but got nowhere near the beginning.
The boys who had used it for a football were rounded up, and
they told on Horry. Horry was questioned, and said he had
found the thing on the track above the cave. Of course he was
on his way to surrender it to the police: it smelled suspicious.
Athol was questioned too, and knew nothing about it. The police
impounded the contents of his cave, just to make their journey
worthwhile. They also detained Athol; Jacko took charge and
moved the family back to his mother's place in the suburbs.

The police next paid a call on Ern, who complained about
being ill but had no other information for them. They spent the
rest of the afternoon rounding up the famished Dogs. They
trampled Ern's cabbages in the process, and several of the Dogs
escaped; the rest, muzzled and roped, were led away. 'When all's
said and done,' remarked one of the policemen as the Dogs
protested their innocence in the back of the van, 'we made a few
arrests.' None of this got into the newspapers.

Paul's newspaper was a serious one. The head was allocated

a paragraph, which encapsulated it as neatly as a hat box. He read it, as his eye slid down a ladder of paragraphs packaging similar fragments of human interest, in the morning while he waited for Kate to appear.

The paragraphs reminded him of those narrow compartments in which they collected the ashes of your loved ones after the flames had simplified everything: a life could be fitted into this black-bordered square. Small print was what it all came down to, black spots on grey paper which, if you looked at them closely enough, decomposed into particles of dust. The head was a speck. It may have been a planet to whoever had owned it, but now it was just the dot left off an i and it had rolled, a mile or so from the room where he was reading about it, to a full stop.

He was glad Kate was still in bed, that she had not been in the room when he noticed the paragraph about the head. He would have read it out to her, and then would have produced his own paragraph anathematising the people who lived down there, those savages she liked to admire from a safe distance above. A head. What next? We could look forward – he supposed he would go on – to the outlying bits of him (it was a man's head, didn't the paper say so?) turning up piecemeal. A fist thrusting through the soil like a spring shoot, a leg which had fallen by the wayside, a torso quite unlike those blood-less classical amputees in the museum.

He was glad that the situation had not required him to say all this, because it had begun to sound false. He saw through his own disgust, which was no more than an iterated effort of denial. I know whose head it is, he thought. I removed it myself: a clean incision. But they should not have carried it off to be analysed while they searched for the rest of him. It was a sacrifice. It was supposed to stay there.

He put the paper aside, went to the window, and gazed at the valley. He knew exactly where they had found it. The road to the tunnel lay off to one side, blocked by the towers along the ridge; but he could see through them: they were one more flimsy denial. The paragraph had not surprised him. He seemed already to know what had happened, to remember it. Did that make him responsible? The valley was the uninhibited arena of dreams. It was his own head when the lights were dimmed and the fears and desires came out to play, entwining in a dance, a copulation, so that you could no longer tell them apart from each other.

He recalled his scheme for a platform across the valley, with a city on top of it. What his dream showed him was the cracks in the cantilevered floor. Building, like flying, was an escape from the earth. Nothing could be founded on the mud and shifting sands beneath. All the same, that was our element. It was where the imagination, quitting the lofty perches of the city, sloped off to after dark.

The body leaves its head behind: it has a better time that way. But the unseated head still knows what the body intends to do, and won't stop dreaming. We build upwards against our natures. So there have to be sacrifices, to thicken the floors and stiffen the walls. Without them, the mortar will not set.

Wasn't there some prophetess who had been closed alive inside a wall, her mouth stopped by the stones? And in New York they told stories about the victim of gangsters dropped into those trenches they gouged from the granite, then buried under slopping concrete. Beneath the skyscrapers, holding them up, sprawled human fossils, preserved from decay by the second skin which coated them. The rituals had to be performed. A spot of ground only became significant or sacred if it marked where someone was interred; a city could only rise if it had a bedrock of bones.

But in the valley the ritual had not been completed. No piles or slabs or floorboards or layers of carpet trod down the evidence of what we were like before we decided to scale the sky. The ground had been left unsealed. Dreams lasted into the day, which meant that there was no reality any more. A head used for a football – why not? Was there anything which was not allowed?

He looked down from the window. The angle today seemed more abrupt; the valley was like a continental shelf. He knew how rubbly and pitted the road was, yet it could have been a chute of polished metal to speed you into the gulf.

He turned away from it. Kate had come in. She smiled at him, and he felt a reviving glow in his chest. The heart had a job of

158

its own to do and surely could not be bothered with his love life; still, it was there he felt this sudden tender fullness. Best not to ask which organ was responsible.

He put his arms round her. Since she was already browsing in the paper, this meant that he crushed it between them like a tangling bed sheet. Inside it, she was warm. He kissed her and said goodbye. When he released her, he saw a numbed, startled look on her face, and thought it must be because she had not woken up. He left. And she pressed her arms out from her body and unfolded the paper.

At first she could not find it again: the paragraph which her eye had homed in on by instinct, magnifying the words until the type exploded into black shrapnel and the terse, silent sentence brayed out loud; the paragraph about the valley, and the head.

Where was it hiding, in the grey nondescript stripes of print? It had slid out of sight like a face in a crowd. Or perhaps it was the remnant of a dream. She spread the page on the table and smoothed it, flattening the wrinkles with her fist.

By now she was so agitated that her eyes could not read. They bounced off the letters, which jabbered at them separately and refused to add up into words. She made herself breathe slowly; she closed her eyes. When I look back, she thought, I'll know there was nothing, just a blank space in which I saw my own reflection; the page will be like a filthy window wiped clean.

So she looked, and saw it again after all. Her thumb was even gripping the corner of it, as if able to read the indentations of print while her eyes were shut. It had happened. She had not dreamed it; nor had the boy, whose story she laughed at when they sat in the park. There was a head as proof, and this laconic obituary in black and white. It had been starkly printed into fact. Such things did occur. She would have to revise her notion of what kind of place the world was. The frontier between reality and danger was nearer than she thought, and was already being redrawn.

She read the paragraph through again. It told her nothing new. She realised that she knew much more than the paper or the police. She knew when it happened, and how. She also knew who did it. The boy had told her that. But the name eluded her.

She had been trying so hard to forget her seizure of the boy in the street, and then her flight from the park. Who did he say had done it? Someone's uncle. Cliff, Clive? The name had submerged. Yet nothing could ever be forgotten. The mind, like the swampy floor of the valley, preserves all mementoes, caked in mud or filed away in stone. The name would bob up again; she would hear it being whispered in her ear.

Meanwhile, she was responsible for what she knew. A story had to be told, to be passed along. It was like a chain letter, which threatened you with retribution if you did not help it to increase and multiply. Now she understood the boy's urgency: fear craved company.

But who was she responsible to? Her civic duty was to tell the police. They would type her story out and ask her to sign it, attesting its truth. They would also probably ask why she had not told it to them sooner. The lame, embarrassed answer was that she had considered it to be only a story. Next she would have to explain how she met the boy, singling him out for a part in her fantasy, then refusing to participate when it turned out that he had a fantasy of his own. How would she tell that story, inside which the other one, about the head, was set? She surprised herself when she realised that the problem did not arise, because she had no intention of narrating any of it to the police.

The responsibility she acknowledged was to the boy. She had sent him back to the valley with his burden. He had told no one else, otherwise there would have been more than the paragraph with its abrupt dead end in the paper. Was he still relying on his length of wood to defend him, tilting at phantoms?

Her guilt bit into her. Then she remembered what she had said to Paul, intending to puzzle or (even better) alarm him, that morning as he left: that she was going out to look for faces, heads. Or was it a head? And she had found the one she wanted, taken possession, and hurried home with her prize. Life, she assumed, made these donations to you. There was never a charge. Oh no, it was an honour to be in her painting, to be recreated by her.

Actually, she was running from life in panic, extricating herself as she once did from the grip of the old woman. She always thought of those tight arms and that sucking mouth as death. But they belonged to a live, needy creature, who wanted something more than to be made the subject of a painting.

The guilt now gave way to shame. Guilt was a pang, the sudden and specific ache of a nerve; shame shook her like an ague, and left her feeling weak at the knees. She had amends to make. She would start with Wilf. She had no idea what she would say to him, or persuade him to do. She would think about that while she looked for him. And looking for him (she heard again his appeal to be looked after) would mean going into the valley.

That reminded her of another overdue atonement: the valley. She had spent years looking down at it, but had never been into it. Imagining was a softer option. It was not that she had been afraid; she dismissed the city's hostility to the valley. Societies required outlaws, they invented them and set aside an out-of-bounds area for them to live in. The city tolerated the valley (she used to think) because the valley was the city's alibi. Its deprivation made the city possible. That was why she had never given Paul's scheme to build on top of it a chance. The valley was too precious for the city to consider abolishing it. She had always thought of the valley-dwellers as victims. But it turned out that they were capable of hacking a man's head off and kicking the head along a gutter.

Now she saw that the valley was a precipice, a sheer drop into unpredictability. That was where she was bound, with only the protection of her old raincoat, to be used today – she promised herself – for the last time.

What followed was a ritual, a sequence of ordinary actions made extraordinary by her awareness that today they were a preparation for something quite unknown. Today, she hoped, there would be magic in them. She did the same things she did every morning, but she did them differently. She washed her face but not her hair. She did not even comb it, just raked through it with her fingers. Rituals usually involved a purifying. For this one, she thought it better to stay unclean. For rituals you also were supposed to choose your best clothes, those sacred, lacey or starchy garments you were baptised or married or laid out in. She hunted through a wardrobe for whatever was oldest and tattiest: a shirt and trousers spattered with paint, shoes with a hole (she knew she would suffer on the unmade, uneven tracks in the valley, but suffering was the purpose of the exercise), and the raincoat. My vestments, she thought. In the streets, she trusted the raincoat to make her inconspicuous. In the valley it would need to make her impregnable. She buckled it around her as tightly as she could.

Doing so, she noticed that there was one more renunciation she had to make. She had put her watch on automatically, in the sleepwalking way she did when assembling herself for a normal day; she took it off again. It was not so much a pre-caution against theft as a gesture to placate the valley, which did not live by the clock. It was also an instruction to herself, a warning that she must allow the search as much time as it required, that her own life could not resume until she made this small peace.

Finally, she tore the paragraph from the newspaper.

The action puzzled her even as she performed it. The paragraph told her nothing to help her on her journey. She already knew the way, if she recalled the boy's circumspect scene-setting – through the tunnel and up the hill, past a tap. She had nodded in collaboration when he described the place. She was bluffing then, humouring him. Now she heard another meaning in the laggard details she had tried to hurry him past. He had drawn a verbal map for her, and in handing it over was making a plea to be rescued.

She had that map, so why the scrap of newspaper? Its very brevity and inconclusiveness were its appeal. It reduced a tragedy – no, more than one, because the boy was a victim too, and so might she be – to a telegram. Working backwards, climbing uphill from these few facts littered in the bottom of the valley, she would reconstruct all the lives which had crossed there and reach a climax or conclusion. The paragraph also let slip another truth. It showed what came after tragedy: the haphazard comedy of continuation. The bulb in the head might have failed, but it still had a use. You could play a game with it.

The paper ripped, and the tear she made veered off in the wrong direction. She started again, and pulled the page apart along a frilled border around the paragraph. The little story, separated from everything else in the world, had a fissure through its middle where the paper's hidden seam lay.

She studied the shape, as random and portentous as an ink blot; she pondered its colour, as grey as the matter which heads contain; she folded it as carefully as if it had been money, and put it in her pocket. Then she threw away the rest of the newspaper, with its digest of all the day's other lives and deaths.

She decided that she was ready. Usually, going out involved an effort to remember what she should take with her. Today, the imperative was to leave things behind. Her last decision was about the key. She hid it in a drawer. Paul could let her in, which meant – at the very least – that she was sentencing herself to expulsion until he came home at night. She paused as she entered the hall. This was already the edge, the dividing line. Then she pulled the door shut behind her gently, to soften the shock of irrevocability.

She waited for the lift to take her down. She stepped into it: a humming, lighted coffin, with steel doors in which she could see her own face. Down it delivered her. She noticed that she was biting her lower lip, and let it go. Then she noticed that it hurt. She thought about the painting she had begun after that last ramble through the city. Persephone with her smirched mouth, hesitating between the valley of shadows and the sane, shining world upstairs. She claimed that he carried her off against her will, that she did not understand what the fruit was. Someone or something else always had to take the blame: an abductor, an enchantment. Why not her own desire, her curiosity? Or the need to be rid of a lie and forgiven for a denial?

The doors of the lift slid open, splitting her face and her body in half. Ahead were glass doors, which also swung aside. Had the building released or expelled her?

The towers of apartments joined in a wall along the top of the cliff, as solid as a formation of fighting men. She walked along in front of them, waiting for the lane which was her exit from the city.

She turned into it. Huts leaned against each other on both sides of the track; at the end of the lane, they seemed to tumble into a heap of dented tin and splintered wood, barring the way. She walked into the perspective, towards the vanishing point.

It was like a walk into a painting: she had to believe that, once she had penetrated the ridges of colour, there would be other views, glimpses beyond the frame, not available to someone who stayed outside; scraping away at the surface, she might find other scenes painted beneath it, suppressed by the opaque outer layers. Another denial: why was she always so anxious to cover up the canvas, muddying its blankness with the images of things which did not exist? The clutter and crowding of the huts, out of which poured heat, smells, noises, lives, reminded her of the doodling games she had played when she was a child, scratching lines and circles and streaks on a page until the paper disappeared behind her obsessive scribble. Crushed together, growing in crevices, cramming people in, the huts were like that. There was a comfort in this congestion. No vacancy anywhere, no estranging spaces, no singleness.

A car squeezing through the lane skidded in a puddle and splashed her. Mud hardened on her shoes and the hem of her coat. The driver of the car smirked, but Kate was grateful for the mess. It was her disguise. It was also painting. The art she practised was about dabbling in dirt. Its materials were seeping soil and sticky ochre, as bright and fluent as blood or as the juice on the mouth of Persephone, not the clean hard blocks of stone and spines of metal Paul manipulated into place. The next time she came to a puddle, she took care to step in it. She could feel it happening: her vanishing act.

She was wrong. A dog had seen her. It barked to summon assistance, then snarled to detain her. She stopped. She couldn't tell whether the fear which shook her was hot or cold, fire or ice. She swivelled slowly, wanting to run back towards the highway and the city. But the dog would not allow that. It darted round her in a circle. She heard herself saying to it 'Please, let me past,' and even stretched out a trembling hand. The dog pounced at the bait; she shrieked.

A woman waddled from one of the huts, kicked the dog in its

belly, and sent it moaning away. Then she took stock of Kate. 'What do you want?' she said.

'Nothing,' said Kate, shiftily aware that it was the wrong answer. She tried again. 'Looking for a friend.'

'What name?' said the woman. She was fat. Her body had swollen to fill up the hut she lived in. Bulk was her source of authority in the informal, ungovernable street; she worked at it. She was chewing now. She allowed a pause for a reply and then, as Kate tentatively opened her mouth, she snapped 'You don't know no one down here.'

'I do, I do,' Kate said. The flustered repetition only seemed to make it less plausible. 'But he lives further on. In the valley. This leads there, doesn't it?'

'If I was you,' said the woman, and snorted at the idea of it, 'I'd go back where I belonged,' with which she poked a thumb upwards.

Kate ordered herself not to argue. But why can't I belong here? she thought. And why shouldn't you be me, or I you? Why should any life be off limits to me? Yet this one was. The woman, hands proprietorially on hips, stood guard over her street, her space, herself. She scoffed at the raincoat. The flecks of colour on it did not qualify as dirt.

'You think we're a curiosity, don't you? Good for a quick look on the sly. Heads rolling round in the gutter. Is that what you're after?'

No, no, gasped Kate, only able to mouth the words: her voice would not lend itself to the lie. 'I do know someone,' she finally managed to say. 'A boy. He needs some help.'

The woman rolled her eyes. 'All right, off you go. Who's stopping you? I wish you luck. Why don't you call in and see me on your way home? You could tell me how it went. I might make you a cup of tea. If you get back, that is.' She bellowed at her own joke.

Flustered and blushing, Kate aimed ahead. Collect yourself, she said. The problem was exactly that. Where were her legs? She felt in her pockets for them. And how did they walk? They had a stiff, awkward memory of it. She talked them along, flinching from scrutiny on all sides.

It was as she expected: the lane bent. She walked off at an angle into a recess of the picture which was hidden from her when she entered the lane. She was in undiscovered country. The huts thinned out. Here there was no level ground for them to be founded on. Fields tilted into the valley's basement. She stood at the top of the road leading down. Steepness foreshortened it, abridging distance and instantly fulfilling a wish. But she was not sure that she wanted to get there, to where the road twisted again and spilled into the tunnel, so quickly.

Why fight it? she thought. Gravity knows best. Show the body a drop, any sheer fall, and it will long to plunge. Only the mind cringes, gripping the guard rail. It was like her painting, her version of the wanderer bestriding the mountains. Perhaps it was not a picture of Paul after all.

Half way down she stopped herself and looked back: the road above her, like a rope ladder dangling tenuously in the air; above that, the range of apartment towers, sleek, glazed, unclimbable. She tried to pick out her own building, the windows marking the niche she lived in. She counted up, down and across, but kept on losing track, finding that the tiny squares blurred into each other and glinted as innumerably as stars. She walked further, and when she next looked the towers had retracted into the cliff. How could she go home to them, since they no longer existed?

The road twisted past a ledge, which jutted out from the rock like a pulpit. Grateful for any reason to delay the descent, she stepped onto the lookout and saw the valley rip apart beneath her feet.

Where the valley narrowed, decanting its contents into the river, the gas works closed off the view. She remembered Paul's schemes for screening them: one more denial. But they were, in their bizarre way, beautiful, like dragons intermittently puffing fire into the sky. Above the river, the clouds were inky; the spurts of gas came and went against them like brief blossoms. Each burst, once a pipe exhaled it, spread into its own form – a blue rose, an orange orchid, a white-hot lily – and then was stifled. Kate thought of how she had been frightened, when she was a child, by the condensing breath which escaped from her on cold mornings. Whenever she spoke, ghosts materialised outside her mouth. Am I sick? she had asked. Although they reassured her – the purpose of parents was to demystify the world – the idea of it still made her uneasy: she was expelling life into the frosty air, which gripped her throat and chest as if strangling her. The earth, however, had energy to spare. Its combustible panting never tired it. The gusts of gas scorched the frigid sky before it snuffed them out.

So I have seen the lights, she thought. Now for the darkness. The tunnel was below.

She climbed back from the lookout and returned to the road, staggering down the incline. Her legs stopped of their own accord when the slope flattened. It was just as Wilf described it. The dream, bit by tenuous bit, was becoming solid, extending into reality. There was the hutch, where Wilf or his grandfather sheltered from the rain. She touched it to make sure, and was pleased when the unshaven planks pricked her fingers. There was no pain, after all, in dreams. Above the hutch ran the railway line, raised on an embankment to protect it from the flooded creek and the soaking valley floor. Now there was no avoiding the tunnel.

She stood away from the opening. Like the hole where an eye has been, she thought; a blind, black hollow. To go in was no simple matter, since it meant agreeing to emerge wherever the tunnel chose to take her, in some place she did not know but was bound to recognise.

For a moment she thought she could outwit the tunnel, by scrambling up the bank, crossing the railway line and rejoining the road on the other side. But brambles like barbed wire pushed her back. Then she thought, What if I waited for a car, and asked just to go through the tunnel? I could say – what exactly? That I'm allergic to tunnels? Would I also have to explain what I'm doing down here, all for a ride lasting a few seconds? Improvising the lies would take longer than the ride. No, it is a test. It is all a test. It was a test before, two weeks ago, which I failed. So now I have to go through there on my own.

She hung back as nervously as if it were vertical, a shaft she could topple into; she even held onto the brick arch. Surely she would be able to see through to the other side? There must be some promise of daylight. A dot of it, seen through the wrong end of a telescope, would do. But the tunnel twisted as it dug beneath the railway line, so only when you got to the middle — by which time it was too late to go back — could you see if the way was clear, or if indeed it ever intended to keep faith with you and return you to the world. You began without any guarantee of an ending.

She took herself in hand like a refractory child. Off you go. Quick march. Now. Was it the rational mind which walked the dumb body into the opening, or the brute force of the body which dragged the mind, engrossed in the invention of nightmares, along behind it? Either way, she pushed or pulled herself into the tunnel, ignoring her own protests.

The tunnel instantly shut her eyes. Except that they were not shut, they were simply useless. Daylight leaked in for a few feet, then was doused. She could not see the walls. Her hands groped, longing for something to clutch. Her feet shuffled in the dust, prepared to take only one unadventurous pace at a time. Outside there had been sounds: wind making the shrubs rustle, the cackle of birds, a motor coughing, the scream of an aeroplane above — signs of life. In here there was only a smell, as sickly as fungus; the smell of things crushed and squirming under stones. She held a hand to her mouth. Meanwhile she nudged herself forward, though her legs would only move from the knees down, as jerkily as the lower limbs of a marionette.

She knew without looking back that the entry had receded, that there was darkness behind as well as ahead. It closed around her, and since she had no way of measuring space it confounded time too and slowed her down. She had to check that her legs were not just pretending to walk.

Then she saw the end: a circular sample of the world, framed in the black exit. She ran towards it.

Details came alive as she jolted closer. The scene bounced and jarred, threatening to break apart before she could race into it. Finally it settled down. It contained most of the items she had had to surrender on the other side, though now they were differently assorted. Another hutch, more birds, the sound of an engine. She dashed into this world which contained things, which perhaps even contained people, as if catapulting herself through a barrier, through glass, into another dimension.

After the darkness, whatever she saw pulsed with light as violently as the exhalations of gas. A bird flaunted a yellow wing; it had been pecking at a berry like a drop of jewelled blood. The planks of the hutch were striped with blue paint left over from when they belonged to some other structure. The car bumping towards her was as white as a snowstorm. The driver waved as he passed on his way into the tunnel. You see, she said to herself. It is only a continuation of the road, burrowing under the railway line.

The boy's voice whispering in her ear prompted her. A path beckoned. This was where she must leave the road. He had talked about living on the hill above. First would be the tap where he saw the man begging, then the dogs, then the house.

She had images prepared for each place, to be revised as she went along. The path trodden into the bank was precisely where she expected it. She pulled herself up, gripping the bushes. At once a revision was necessary. The tap, if this was it, was not a tap at all. This was one of the earth's mouths, into which a pipe had been plugged. Water splashed and sprayed from it unstoppably, gurgling down a stone drain to start the cycle over again. She could see the man there, pleading as the water chortled. On his knees: did Wilf tell her that?

Thirsty, she bent over with a cupped hand. That was when she saw the face cemented into the tiles. She jumped, and the water ran away through her shaking fingers. She recognised the face, which peered from the undergrowth in so many paintings at the museum. It belonged to a satyr, a horned demon of the classical woods. The pipe poked between the satyr's lips, which aimed the water at her like venom. She should not have been surprised. The valley was the cellar where the city stowed unregarded lives, obsolete machines, discredited gods; like the unconscious mind, it never forgot. She walked on watching for the dogs Wilf mentioned. Bit by bit, she was proving his story true. To walk through it was to enter his existence. It was like an experiment in reincarnating herself; and the motive, she suspected, was expiation. She began to regret her mental assaults on strangers in the streets. Like a pickpocket, she purloined faces and ransacked them for their secrets. She never asked herself whether they noticed the theft, or minded it. Only the boy had demanded something in return, which she refused him. Why should she give these robberies the name of art?

She postponed answering because she had arrived at the place where the dogs were. No, where they had been. All that remained were spikes driven into the rock, with lengths of chain between them. She had not been permitted to stroll into another life. She inherited only left-overs, like the unattached head in the bag.

She frowned at the cave, another tunnel to elsewhere; like the extra mouth which a wound makes, a gateway to pain. She was still staring at it when the shadows inside it began to stir. She stepped back. 'Wilf?' she whispered to herself.

The shadows bent and buckled. Getting out of the cave was as complicated as getting yourself born. There was an overhang, like a muscle of stone, to be squeezed past. A pair of legs were followed by a twisting body, with hands which gripped the rock and launched it into the light. The body straightened itself, stood up, faced her. If this had been a birth, it would have made a cry, its objection to the life it had been delivered into. There was a cry, but Kate herself made it. Had she caused this to happen? Had she lured the man out into the air? For she recognised him: the unsunned face, the suspicious eyes, the lank hair; even the jacket of polished skin with the hedge of red bristles. It was the man she had seen while waiting to cross the highway that day, who had seen her looking at him and smiled, puckering his lips to say something, like the satyr lazily salivating.

The advantage was hers. He was stunned by the light, and when he saw her he registered surprise, not recognition. She could not have been more to him than a random face, swirled away by the current; it had happened months ago. He merely thought it odd to find her there outside the cave. A customer who did not know what he had only just discovered: that the shop was closed? Kate was braced, holding herself ready for a collision. It was that which warned him.

She jerked herself as if to dispel a dream. 'Hey,' he said, puzzled. She ran.

She ran uphill, which she then realised was the wrong thing to do. Safety lay in the opposite direction, but so did the tunnel. She made frantic bargains with whoever was in charge of these coincidences, these fated repetitions: If you let me survive this, I will never . . . . What offer would be slavish enough? Never look out of the window at the valley, never look inside myself, never paint again, lock all those treacherous images in the spare room for ever?

Before the terms were agreed, she expected to feel his hand on her shoulder, tugging her back into the dream. Waiting to feel it was intolerable. She needed to know when it would descend. She swung around. She expected to see his face closing in on hers, fusing with it as faces do when they kiss. But she was running from nothing. The man stood at the bottom of the hill, so far away that he no longer had a face. He was watching her, shading his eyes with a hand; when he saw her stop, he turned and walked away. He was walking too quickly, she thought, as if anxious to be out of her sight and her mind.

He disappeared, and she noticed how her limbs ached and her body steamed. Where would she find the strength to continue this laughable, alarming quest of hers? She turned wearily to see how far she was from the top of the hill.

And he was there on the path above her, gripping his stick and getting ready to transform it into a cudgel again: Wilf. I must reach him, she thought, before he vanishes too.

She flung herself across the distance between them, extending her arms to encircle him. She called his name. He raised the stick, but one of the things it had no power over was this projectile of emotion, its coat tails flying. She fell on him. He toppled over, and she slumped on top of him.

'Help me,' she heard herself saying. So that was what it was all about; it was not — she had to admit — about helping him at all.

He was ready with an accusation. As soon as he could disentangle himself, he sat up and demanded, 'What were you doing with him down there?'

'Oh, that was a mistake. I came to find you.'

'What for?'

'To help you. I didn't believe you before, that's why I walked away. And now I know you were telling me the truth. So I felt sorry.' She grabbed his hand, and felt him try to pull it away.

'If you came for me, why were you with him?'

'Who? That man? I wasn't. I just got frightened when he popped out. But he didn't mean me any harm. He's no one.'

'He's not no one,' said Wilf. 'He's Clem.'

A chill singed her skin, as if Clem had touched her. Of course, she thought. It had to be. So I knew about him even before Wilf told me. Now they both needed help. 'Wilf, where's your grandfather?'

'Gone,' he said.

'Gone where?'

'I don't know, just gone.' He was trying to be casual, but his voice trembled. 'He got sick. He wanders off at all hours. Today I haven't seen him at all.' His face let its guard down. He could not keep the urgency out of his voice. 'Where do you think he *is*?'

'Don't worry,' she said, aware that it was no answer. At present it was more important to get out of Clem's way. 'Wilf, where's your house?'

He led her along the wall from where he watched the sunsets, and on through the mutilated cabbages. The door of the hut was open. She followed him in, and tried to stop herself studying the room: the hearth with its blizzard of white ashes, the iron bedstead, the table on which a fly was probing for crumbs. Don't look, she told herself. It's not fair.

'Can I sit down?' she said.

He was startled by the notion that she should ask permission, that she should consider him to be in charge. He did not answer, but when she sat in the one chair she saw, a creaking rocker, he said with a yelp of alarm, 'No, not there. That's his. He doesn't like you to,' and pointed to a stool by the hearth. 'That one's all right. It's only mine.'

She lowered herself onto it, and saw the world as Wilf did: the jutting table, a kerosene lamp impending from a beam. She still felt uneasy. 'Wilf, could you close the door?' The request seemed odd to him – what would it prove? – but he pulled it shut, and even bolted it as an extra concession. Then he waited for her to look after him.

She wanted to ask him to sit down, but it was not her place to do so, and he edgily avoided the rocker which was the old man's throne. Anyway, why was she dithering over preliminaries?

She had no choice, and therefore no reason for delaying. There would be consequences, which she could think about later: abandoning the old man wherever he was, inventing an explanation for Paul, and of course keeping clear both of Clem and the police. Meanwhile, she had to take him home with her.

'Wilf,' she said, 'I'm going to take you home with me.'

At once she realised that these were the wrong words. It sounded as if she considered him to be a purchase. Or, even worse, a stray dog she had taken pity on. She should at least have asked, as she did about the chair and the door.

He objected to more than the way she phrased it. 'Why?' he wanted to know.

'To be safe. Can you stay here by yourself? Aren't you frightened? Did you know Clem was back?'

He shook his head. It was an answer only to her last question. She stretched her hand out, in a hurry to conclude. 'You will come, won't you?'

'Where is it?' he asked. How could he go somewhere he had not imagined?

'It's in those buildings over on the other side. You can see it from out there. And you'd be able to see back here. Besides, it wouldn't have to be for always. Just until this is over.' She was not sure whether this was a clause suddenly inserted to reassure him or to provide her with a let-out. 'So', she said, 'what do you think?'

He said nothing. I have misunderstood again, she thought. I'm waiting for him to decide, while he assumes I've decided for him. He wants it to be like that. 'Now then, what do you need to take?' She instantly regretted the question. He was not held here by possessions. It was a life easy to walk out of.

'Only this,' he said. He meant the stick.

'You won't need it.'

'Then I'm not going.'

173

'No, no. I didn't mean you couldn't bring it. What else?'

He shook his head one more time. He was not accustomed to brooding over the past, or fretting about the future. He unbolted the door and held it open. She walked through. He followed, swinging the stick.

'Wilf, didn't you forget? Are you going to leave the door like that?'

He shrugged, but dragged the door shut anyway.

'There's no key?'

A look, more pitying than offended, said it for him. Then she laughed. He scowled, unable to work her out.

'Don't worry,' she said, taking his hand and fastening it inside her own, 'I'm laughing at myself. I just remembered I don't have a key either.'

They were waiting for Paul when he came home, camped in the corridor outside the front door. The lobby of the building would have been more comfortable, and Wilf could have entertained himself by studying the traffic, but Kate did not want to subject him – or herself – to the comments of her neighbours.

Wilf, she saw, felt trapped. First she made him travel in that upright crate, telling him something about pulleys: his feet had never left the earth before, and when it jolted into motion his stomach felt the homesick tug of gravity. Now she claimed that, just inside the door, she had her private realm of tamed water, servile gas, and tubes which made pictures when plugged into the wall, all of which – she insisted – would be his. He believed none of it. She was as mad as the other one with the flustered hair and the unsynchronised eyes. Besides, he wanted to wee.

He had led her out of the valley, explaining it to her as they went. He found her another ant-hill among the cabbages, and wanted to demonstrate how it worked by slicing its top off; she would not allow that. On the way down the hill, he described their routine with the Dogs. He wished they could look inside the cave, but by prior arrangement they ran past it, not stopping until they got to the tap. He told her that the animal through whose mouth the pipe drooled had been sighted in the valley. 'I believe you,' she said, though he was hoping she would scorn the idea. Adults were supposed to cast out your fears, not elect to share them. It seemed, however, that it was Wilf's job to persuade her not to be afraid.

He talked her through the tunnel, and on the other side showed her his sentry post. His grandfather's used to contain a chair; they stole it, and he replaced it with a shelf nailed to the walls, low enough to sit down on. One day, his grandfather prophesied, they would steal the boxes too.

After that, Wilf backed away from her into silence. He was remembering the last time he had climbed this slope towards the city, with Horry. The ditches, the puddles, the sagging walls and crooked trees all marked stages in Horry's story; knowledge clung to them like a stain or stench. It might have been why the tunnel alarmed her. She asked what he was thinking about. Did people have a right to know? He guessed that she knew already: wasn't she thinking about the same thing?

Currently, squatting outside the door which she had promised would open on wonders, she was telling him about her husband. It was he who would open the door. He was an architect, she said. Wilf blinked. He built buildings, she explained. He understood that, Jacko used to do the same. She tried to define the difference. He didn't build them exactly, he just had the ideas for them. He drew them, and left the pouring of cement and piling of bricks to others.

Then the lift arrived, and he walked into the corridor, into reality. 'That's him', Kate said. 'This is Paul.'

Wilf checked and discovered he was short of preconceptions against which to measure the man. And what he saw he would not have been able to imagine, since city people belonged to none of the familiar categories. Kate scrambled to her feet, leaning on his shoulder. He looked up, but could not see a face, only a glare of interrogation.

'What's this? I mean who is this?' Paul was saying. 'And what are you doing out here? Forgot your key?'

'Not exactly', Kate said, and introduced them to each other.

Paul waited to hear more. Instead she asked him to open the door. He glanced at Wilf, waiting for him to leave. Kate ushered the boy through the door, then said to Paul, 'Come in.' He came in, crossing the threshold as hesitantly as if he too were now stepping into another dimension. Where did this tunnel lead? His eyes entreated her.

'I want to go,' said Wilf in an urgent whisper, tugging her hand. Paul reached for the door. 'No,' she said. 'He means he wants to go to the bathroom.' She hustled him off.

When he came back, he could tell they were talking about him. Kate was saying 'I just did it. You could say I lost my head.' Paul's eyes widened. 'I didn't think – but he's got no one. And he saved my life, he protected me on the way back home. Haven't you seen his stick? Wilf, tell him about it.'

She put her arms around Wilf and pressed him to her, daring Paul to hurt the boy by rejecting him. Paul stared in bewilderment at a situation he would have to accept, at least until the two of them were alone.

Wilf, with her arms slotted around him like armour, felt he had a safe place from which to observe Paul. The man's eyes were tired, his forehead and the corners of his mouth ruffled by fault lines of uncertainty. He held his head in his hands. It seemed as fragile as an egg, its shell barely equal to the pressure of its contents. What made those rifts in the surface – the worming vein in the temple, the furrows which were graphs of disturbance? Only me, Wilf realised.

Paul took stock of him: a child whose hair had not been combed, whose face had not been washed, whose sweater had not been darned, who menaced the world with a bit of hacked wood, and who in a few minutes had succeeded in dislodging him from the centre of his life. His keys on the table, his jacket over a chair, his briefcase on the floor were like the disintegrated bits of him left behind after an explosion.

Kate proposed a diversion, a drink for Wilf, and persuaded him to give his stick a rest. He followed her to the window to see the view of the valley.

'How do you like it?' she asked. But the sight dismayed him. Height diminished it. His world, with its unexplored frontiers stalked by that mythological animal, its caves of booty and its fields which it took him hours to hike across, had shrunk to a trench. The glass silenced it, censored its smells, and excluded him from it: the valley had become a picture.

'I can't see our place,' he complained. 'You told me I'd be able to.'

'Don't worry, it's still there, it's just around the corner. You don't want to go back – do you?'

Rather than give him a chance to answer, she sat him down on a sofa (he sank into it as if falling asleep, tumbling into softness) and put a cold grey thin thing covered with numbers into his hand. 'To replace the stick', she said. 'You'll see.' She showed him how to aim it, to press with his thumb, and a screen in the corner coincidentally filled with life. 'You made that happen, you know.'

She came back later, while he was discovering how many other lives the wand could summon up, to ask him what he liked to eat. He nominated sausages. She did not have any. 'Tomorrow,' she said. 'All right?' He nodded, which she took to be an agreement to stay.

She fed him, and watched him eat. Paul, in a corner, soothed himself with a drink. They would eat, she explained to Wilf, when he went to bed.

Before that there was the business of the bath, or rather shower. She took him to a room she said was his, though she used it for her painting. Canvases were stacked against the wall; she would clear them out tomorrow. Paul, sullenly conscripted, turned on the shower for him, collected his dirty clothes, and gave him a white robe to wear when he was dry. He yelped when he felt the water bombarding him with arrows, leaving red blotches on his flesh. Grit from a previous life flowed away between his legs.

He clambered into the robe and padded off to find them. They were eating, with the lights turned down. It was dark outside. They were also arguing, as best they could with voices lowered like the lights.

Kate hooted when the robe with the head protruding out of it wavered into the room: 'Wilf, you look like a spook.' Her laughter was meant to be infectious, but Paul remained immune. Only when he saw Wilf retreat in shock did he relent and beckon him nearer. He even pushed out a chair for him to sit in, the robe spilling on the floor below his feet like melted snow.

The chair, however, was a trap. As soon as he had settled in it, Paul said, 'Wilf, we've been trying to decide who you belong to.'

Wilf felt he had been strapped in the chair to undergo questioning. Their lunar faces, whitely lit by a shaded lamp above the table, seemed to hover there, separated from the rest of them. The arms and hands they were eating with had been drawn back into the covering darkness. There were only those suspended heads: his sharpened to a point at the nose and chin, hers softer, yielding, like a pillow.

'I told you that,' she said, and repeated it to stop Paul talking. 'His mum dumped him with his grandfather, and now his grandfather has taken sick and wandered off. That's how it was when I ran into him this afternoon.' She looked at Wilf as she spoke. He knew why: to align their stories, to agree on what was omitted. 'He doesn't have anyone. He was hungry, that's why he asked me to help him. So I'd say he belongs to us.'

She realised after she said it that she had corrected herself. What she meant to say was 'to me'. She was treating him as he treated his stick, as the playmate children invent to share their solitude. She withdrew a little, to appease Paul and to absolve herself. 'At least until we can find out where his grandfather is. I bet he'll turn up.'

'In the meantime, though,' said Paul, 'he does not belong to us. Wilf, do you know you've been kidnapped? It's a crime.'

Wilf grabbed the arms of the chair. So after all he was to be accused. She had betrayed the secrets which flooded out of him that day as involuntarily as his tears.

'No, no, don't get upset, it's not your fault. You're the victim. But tomorrow we'll have to take you back where you belong.'

And where's that? thought Wilf. Because he belonged nowhere and to no one. Only, perhaps to himself. Had adult life arrived so prematurely, before it could even be announced – as Horry told him it would be – by the hair that pushed through the skin in unexpected places and ejected you from childhood?

'We'll sort it out,' Kate said, reaching over to rub his shoulder as if assuaging an ache.

He flinched. It was his rescinding of faith in her, and in anyone else's capacity to manage his life. A man would have, as his grandfather might say, to look after himself.

'Can I go to bed now?' he asked her. It meant, she knew, something different. He was asking if she had finished with him, for the time being.

She fussed over him, wanting to make up for a failure. Was hot milk appropriate? Was he too old to be tucked in? Did he read in bed? How cloyingly could she risk saying good night? When she asked whether he wanted her to turn off the light, she worried that it would sound as if she did not want him to do so for himself.

Wilf lay there, imprisoned by the bed. The starchy sheets expected him to be rigid, the mattress did not know his shape. He punched the pillow until it made a hollow for his head, and thrashed about so that the sheets relaxed. Eventually he leaned out, picked up the stick and smuggled it beneath the covers. Then he slept.

He awoke in darkness, terrified. A reincarnation had happened. He was somebody else. It was the wrong bed. The silence alarmed him: no snorts or wheezing from his grandfather, no branch scratching the side of the hut.

Then he remembered. But he could not remember what the room was like, where things were in it. He fumbled for bedside light. The room reared at him, blindingly bright. A wall was papered with postcards: paintings of nailed Christs, of angels on errands, of naked women lolling on couches, of golden land-scapes, of melting cathedrals, of blue guitars and heads with extra eyes and displaced mouths and massacred facets – images of everything Wilf didn't know that the world contained. And in a corner the shrouded canvases turned to the wall like children in disgrace.

Wilf went to the connecting bathroom. 'It's yours,' she had told him. He checked that the water, the torrent in the bowl and the scalding jet in the basin, would still come when called. He checked on his own face in a mirror surrounded by bulbs. Of course it might have been a trick, a window not a mirror; that might be a stranger peeping in at him from outside. He opened his mouth and stuck his tongue out. The other one did the same. He switched off the bathroom lights and extinguished the replica of himself.

On his way back to bed, he bumped into the canvases. One of them flopped backwards onto the floor, pulling away the sheet thrown over them. It lay face up, a square of dry mud and muddle, brown and black, white and red, meaning nothing.

Then he saw that it was upside down. He walked around it and tried again. He squatted to see it closer. One by one he read the colours. Brown was the wet, loamy earth, black a gap slashed through it as if by an axe. White was skin, bodies; red stood for a mouth. He pieced together two bodies bit by bit, making sure they each had the right number of parts. One was a woman's. She was kneeling in the dirty field. She was apparently naked. The mouth was hers, attached askew as by a child making messes with lipstick. The woman was looking down into the pit, just as Wilf was looking down into the painting. She was looking at the other figure, lost below: boney, ragged, with pleading arms and a face pulled elastically out of shape by some emotion which paint could not account for.

Wilf felt suddenly dizzy. The painting might have been a trapdoor which opened into an underworld, or into someone's mind. The second figure was himself.

He jumped to his feet. As he did so, he knew that his own face had been startled into a likeness of the one in the picture, holes drilled in it where his eyes and mouth should be, his chin sagging unsupported.

He found the door. I won't stay in here, he was thinking. Not with that. Even if I put it back against the wall and cover it up again. It could leap out at me. Why would she do that?

He grabbed the door handle and twisted it. It slipped in his hand; his palm was moist. He gripped it tighter and jerked sideways. It budged a little, then swung back. He doubled his hands on it. Still it resisted. Oh, he thought (and the thought was accompanied by a wrenching sensation, as if his heart had toppled from its shelf behind his ribs and tumbled through the floor), so they have locked it. They have locked me in.

14

ERN SAT IN the hut, on the immobilised rocker, and watched the door. The past was besieging him. It had taken advantage of his pain, and then of Wilf's desertion. He did not dare to nod off, or let the rocker rhythmically cradle him. Then the past would sneak in, smashing the windows, stealing like smoke through cracks in the wall. He kept his feet on the floor as anchors. He remembered the Dogs on the day he unleashed them: the past was like that, bivouacked on his doorstep.

Once he stopped thinking about the threat for a moment in order to concentrate on his pain, which was jealous and tended to play up if he ignored it. After he felt it pulse inside him like a lower, alternative heart, organising his body around a new centre, he realised he had briefly forgotten about the rest, like an old woman who miscounts stitches and drops her knitting. He shook himself and reassumed his guarded position in the chair. Don't you slacken now, he told himself. You've got to spend all your time making sure you forget. Otherwise you'll remember, whether you like it or not.

There were a lot of things to regret. New ones kept arriving all the time. He imagined them forming a queue outside the door, with their wounded faces and piteous voices and clutching hands. Did they want retribution? Would they bite and gobble and end up eating him alive, as the starving Dogs might have done if they had not been rounded up? No, they just wanted to tell their stories. Ern had tried blocking his ears, but that was no remedy against thinking.

First came his mother, meekly expiring just when she said she would and bequeathing him the ulcer in the bottle. He went for walks when left to take care of her, always hoping that it would conclude before he returned. She of course obliged him, and did it on her own, unassisted, like any other household job. He had his tears ready to shed by the time his father came home. 'I was holding her hand when she went', he remembered saying. 'She was very peaceful, like.' His father looked at him askance, but since the only witness was dead he could not make an issue of it.

Next there was his wife, stalking off to the shop in the suburbs, alleging a broken promise. When that happened he discharged a curse like a belch and loudly insisted that she was no loss. There was no one left, however, to hear his avowal and encourage him to believe it. Cowardice had kept him in the valley. It did not do to expect too much from life, or to venture too far from your place of safety. Left behind, he began to preach the valley's virtues and to pride himself on his own hardihood (and, once he fell in with the lads, on his cunning). He became a partisan. As the towers advanced along the cliff, he came to think of the valley as nature's revenge on the city. But despite the hold-ups, despite Clem's singling out of someone at random to be sacrificed, the scores remained unequal. His wife was probably still alive, living a few miles away, still married to him perhaps – so far as the law was concerned – and not to the grocer. The past hurt, even when you succeeded in forgetting it.

After this, skipping a generation since he had decided to have no regrets about Thelma, Ern arrived at the case of Wilf. He could have killed the brat when he realised, very late in the day, that the high-heeled Thelma had no intention of returning to reclaim him. The child by this time was screaming with hunger. The consensus in the valley, when word got around, was that Ern had done the right thing, and the credit fondly went to human nature.

Ern sneered in private at that idea. Nature he knew about: the Dogs climbing on top of each other and drily grinding, the Dogs wolfing lumps of raw meat or unplucked chickens, the Dogs let off individually to die in the undergrowth. Human nature seemed too soft and milky an amendment of the process. For the family, the holy bloody family, distributing guilt like portions dished out evenly around the dinner table, he reserved a special contempt. All it meant was that your errors came back

like indigestion, or like Thelma when she left him a little snivel-
ling souvenir.

Lately, when Wilf first withdrew his labour and then took to
disappearing all day to sulk, Ern had come to change his mind.
He's mine, he thought, at the exact moment when the boy had
decided he no longer was. Me at two removes, me mixed up
with God knows what others (when he asked Thelma where her
husband and then who the father was, she laughed and said she
didn't keep a diary), me gone wrong (as the boy's misuse of the
stick went to show), but still me: all there is. And if he walks
away, who'll look after me? The family was a way of insuring
yourself against the future. Dogs didn't know there would be a
future, so had no worries about it. But Ern knew there was going
to be one. Its definition was this: a world that did not contain
him.

Now that the present was suspended, since the daily routine
at the tunnel was in abeyance, the past encroached and the future
inched closer. He would need a hand, crossing over. He should
have been better to the boy. No one was to blame, after all, for
happening to exist.

This led, by a subterranean route of association, to something
which Ern could not see that he had any business regretting. He
tried to ignore it, but it kept rattling the door of the hut or
spying on him through the window. It was the man whose lights
had flashed in his eyes at the tunnel, who was pulled from his
car and taken off by Clem. He too wanted help. He had asked
twice. The first time was more of a demand, the second a plea.
Ern could hear his voice. He also heard his own silence. Best,
he remembered thinking, to leave them to it: to whatever truth
the knife was about to reveal. It was between them. That was
his mistake, because whatever it was had turned out to include
him. Though there were intermediary stages he could only guess
at, it had trailed him, tracked him down. The clearing-out of the
cave, the evacuation of the farm, the visit from the police (who
when Ern gave a display of dithering idiocy satisfied themselves
with carting off the Dogs), these were all results. And Wilf's
drift into sullen hostility, that too.

But even if none of this had happened, there was another

reason why the man had not been easy to forget. Who was he? Ern wondered on the way back to the hut that night, and his answer was, Nobody. He's nobody. Yet when he harked back to the incident, his memory sketched a picture he did not want to see. He could not remember what the man looked like. His face had faded; the frightened voice spoke out of a cloud. Why was it then that each time the picture recurred, the cloud got thinner until he could once more glimpse a face behind it? And why did the face have to be his own? My head, on the wrong shoulders. A bad joke, Ern thought it, unable to understand why he had played it on himself. Unless the transplant meant that we are members of each other, that lives and deaths are interchangeable.

All this nagged at him as he sat morosely in the hut, nipping his flesh in a succession of pains. There was the other, underlying pain to worry about as well; it chewed at his stomach. While he sat still, he allowed it all to gain on him. I'll go and have a scout around, he thought. Perhaps the ghostly retrospective griefs would stay behind. Perhaps he could shed the ache on the way. He was prepared for an outing, he already had his hat on. Wilf's was hanging from a nail inside the door. Wherever he was, he had no need for it. The sight caused Ern a minor pang, while he amassed the energy or the courage to open the door. Outside there was only vacant daylight, which saw through ghosts but also made his eyes smart.

Now what? he thought. Or where? He had to give himself a goal, a purpose. Then he could prise his mind free of the past and concentrate it on a modest, approximate future.

Therefore he would not go downhill. It was the route through his losses. So he plodded lopsidedly uphill. He had not been that way for years, though when he was a boy he used to do odd jobs for the would-be farmer in the fancy house. He even helped to pave the outline of the lake, without knowing or caring what it was supposed to represent.

Having scrambled onto the plateau, he trudged around the sites of his ruined childhood. The lake stagnated under humps of refuse. Scraps of paper stuck to the trees. A rat prospected.

The lawn he used to cut was a jungle of shaggy grass and thorns, which tripped his ankles and scratched his knees.

Serve him right, he thought, recalling the farmer who wanted the place to match the landscapes he hung inside the house. Ern kicked his way through the knotted weeds towards the house. Half the roof was off, one wing had burned, the walls looked at if moths had made a meal of them.

We had to wait outside, Ern remembered, and only at the back door. He used to stand on tiptoe to see through the windows. That was how he knew about the paintings, with their fields as smooth as green baize table cloths and their trees as well-behaved as potted plants and their syrupy varnish of sun. And what had the paintings been good for? Only, in their smiling perfection, to make the silly man unhappy.

Ern had been called in to help shift the furniture when the farmer moved back to the city; left alone in a room, he studied one of the paintings close up, then carefully scratched a diagonal line across it with his finger nail. He broke his nail in the process, but it was worth it. The scar ravaged the landscape like the seam through the hills which once had marked where the valley would be. Soon afterwards the doors and windows were boarded up.

Now the house had no way of excluding Ern. In he hobbled. He would have strutted, if there had not been shocks jolting up his legs like electricity, and if his pain had not advised him against bragging.

At once, although it was an effect with no apparent cause, he slumped over. A cave-in underfoot? Would he be swallowed by the cellar? No, it was his pain that did it. A convulsion in his stomach, followed by what felt like a blow on the head, though there was no one to administer it.

His legs folded neatly up, and the floor knocked his hat off.

He came to with a grunt, confronted by a miniature world of grainy wood and a dune of dust. As consciousness returned, so did his pains, which had multiplied in the interim. He growled at them, rolled over, and made his hand look for his hat. Before he could reach it, he noticed a white shape fluctuating above him. His eyes took their time to interpret it. A fog – a person –

a woman – the woman he ran into on that particular night, with the billowing hair, the unsymmetrical gaze, and the vigil to keep.

She wavered in and out of focus, and he grabbed the hem of her dress to make sure she existed. She did, though he was not sure that he could say the same for himself. When he tried to speak, his throat made a noise like a shutter on a rusted hinge.

'What are you doing?' said the woman. 'What's your business? Keep your hands off.' She had a weapon: a dinner plate, none too clean. It was the first thing that came to hand.

Ern groaned, which gave him his voice back. 'I don't have no business', he said. 'I was just having a look around. Was it you that hit me?'

'I never hit you. You was already down when I came out to see. But I will. I will. Charging into my house with never even a knock!' She raised the plate, not sure whether it would do more damage flat or sideways. He cowered, and she recognised the fear on his face. She knew him. 'Up here to lead me astray again, are you? Is that boy with you?'

'No,' said Ern. 'That's just it. He's run off, I don't know where, I came looking for him. He's my grandson, all I've got. And I'm not a well man. You wouldn't have seen him about?'

'I don't see no one. I don't concern myself. But he might have been here. Someone stole something of mine, from out the back. A while ago, I don't know when.'

'Ah, that would have been him. He's been had up before for stealing. He's a worry to me. I had to raise him on me own. His mother died, see. She was killed.'

Then he saw that it was not worth the bother of inventing more. Neither of her eyes moistened in response to his small, spurious tragedy. As she said, she was not concerned with events at ground level. She took the long view, down as far as the funnel-like end of the valley where her chimneys blazed.

Ern raised himself on his knees. He might have been a child setting out on the dangerous adventure of standing upright. 'Listen,' he said. 'I don't mean you no harm. I'm feeling bad. It must have been that giddy turn I had. Could you give me a hand, do you think?'

Not lowering the plate, she allowed him the use of her other hand. He took it with both of his. He noticed how chilly it was. He squeezed bones beneath the crinkled skin. But he could have kissed the hand. It was his only hope. I must have got feeble, he thought: the single hand held steady while he attached himself to it and pulled his body off the floor. Dead things seem to weigh more, as he knew from his disposal jobs with poisoned cats and used-up Dogs. Why is that? His legs were not sure about resuming the burden. He wobbled, and lapsed into her arms. She stiffened. Her fingers let the plate go. Ern heard it bounce and shatter a long way below.

'I'm still not right,' he moaned. 'I'm sorry. Have you got a chair anywhere?'

She must have had one because he sensed it beneath him, though there was another interruption and he had no idea how it came to be there. He was now in a room. That must be her bed, with a border of battered charms around it. He wanted water. She had that too; he heard it glug from a bottle. When he took the glass from her, it banged against his face. The water dribbled down his chin.

'Thanks,' he said as he gave the glass back, ashamed of the gratitude in his voice. 'You're a good sort after all.'

If he expected her to simper or blush, he miscalculated. She glowered at him. 'I'll go and call that boy of yours,' she said. 'You can't stay here. What's his name?'

'Never mind about him. I wasn't even after him. I made that up. I'll be off home when I've had a spell.'

'So what are you doing up here, if you're not looking for the boy?'

'I had to go somewhere, just to see if I could. I was sat at home, and I couldn't stop thinking.'

'What about?'

'Everything. It wouldn't let me alone. It ganged up on me. The older you get, the more there is of it. You run out of new things, you've just got your memories. A whole load of them, enough to bend you double.'

'I don't hold with it,' she said. 'Remembering. You don't look too well on it. It's like those newspapers, better to chuck the lot. Who cares what happened then? You've got to get yourself ready for the future.'

187

Her refusal to sympathise irritated Ern, and irritation revived him. He sized her up: a woman with an eye loose in its socket, with her head not screwed on tight, camped in this tumbledown house. 'Excuse me for asking,' he said, 'but just what is it you've got to look forward to?'

She heard the sarcasm in his voice, but overlooked it. 'The fires,' she said. 'That's why I'm here.'

'The gas works? What's the gas works to you?'

He could see her considering whether he deserved an answer. He had sent her off on the wrong path that night, he was mocking her now, he would not understand even if she told him. Still she decided not to give him the satisfaction.

'I'm a Witness,' she said. 'I started witnessing back where I lived in my other house. I used to go to the church there, but then the witnessing started to happen at all hours, not just during church. In the street when I was shopping, in my back yard, mostly in the afternoon when the sun was going down. Every day I was sure it would be the last time, though it never was. At least not yet. Then they started talking about me, over the fence, as if I chose the witnessing! One day I walked out on it all, didn't even lock the door behind me. They're welcome to the house. It won't be there for long anyway. It was an afternoon, all clouded over, no sun. I got on a bus, and went as far as I could. It finished its run over on the highway. It was dark by then, but I wandered in here, I knew I wouldn't go wrong. And after a while I saw the fires, blue and orange and white, blazing up all night long, and I was sure this was the place to wait — the place where the end would begin.'

'The end? What of?'

She stared. Of course he knew the answer already; he was daring her to spell it out. So she did. 'Of all this, of everything.'

He laughed, because he was clammily frightened, not of the end but of her belief in it.

She was accustomed to laughter like this, and to dealing with it, which she did briskly. 'What do you think — that it will go on forever?' And she made a gesture that included the decrepitude of the valley and of the house, his pain and her own raggedness.

She raised her arms, as if casting it all into the air where it would burn; she let out an angry breath like the sibilant chimneys.

Ern's response was a lie. 'I don't think about it.' She knew it was a lie, not worth reacting to. He tried again. 'I wouldn't get my hopes up, if I was you. All they're doing down at the gas works is burning off. That's the waste coming out. I don't know when you came in here to live; I've always been here. I can remember before there was any gas works, I can even remember when this was a fancy house. It changes, but it goes on. I guarantee you it will outlast the pair of us.'

'If you've been around so long, you ought to know that there wasn't always a valley. One day there were hills, next day there was a valley in between them. The ground came apart, did you know that?' Ern looked down at the floor boards, as irregular as an ocean. 'It's no more here to stay than us. You'll see. You might see before me.'

'I'll let you know if I do,' smirked Ern, and set about getting to his feet, not sure he could rely on them or on the floor boards or the dislodged, skidding rocks beneath.

But she would not allow it. 'You stop there,' she said. 'I've got something I want from you.'

Ern dropped back into the chair, aghast at his inability to resist. Time was when he would have shoved her aside. That time evidently was no longer.

It took her a while to get ready. She had to be careful how she put it. 'I want to know something,' she finally said. 'That head – was it yours?' She frowned at her error. 'I mean, did it belong to you?' This was also wrong. She grimaced in frustration. 'Did that boy of yours steal it from me?'

Ern, relieved, watched her wrestle with the idea. He could have left there and then, while she silently experimented with other ways of asking the question. But he lingered. To taunt her, he said, 'I don't follow you'.

She struggled to get it all into sequence and into sentences. 'One night, it was a while ago, I saw two men up here. Wait a minute, it was the same night I ran into you, when I was lost.' Ern wished he had not prompted her; she was beginning to make sense. 'There were two of them, and they went into the trees over there. I didn't see any faces, but I heard them inside that shed. I listened to what they were saying, and I ran away when the noise started. The next day I went back to look inside. There was nothing there. I was sure I dreamed it. Then I found the head. I didn't open the bag. I couldn't, but I knew what it was. Only whose was it? And why was I the one who had to find it? I couldn't work any of it out. So I left the thing on my porch. I had my fires to see to, and when I got home it was pitch black. I must have gone to bed. In the morning, it all came back to me. Not the head though. It was gone. Where could it go to on its own? Someone was here and took it. That boy you had with you, I bet. But why?'

'It wasn't him,' said Ern. 'You can be sure of that. Forget what I said about him thieving. He's too simple for that.' He was thinking, If you and me put our heads together. . . . But the combination of what she had seen and what Ern could tell her was too much. He preferred not to know, or not to believe. It must be a matter of dreams crossing and compounding, until they made your faith in reality falter. That was what being mad meant: not knowing the difference. He remembered his vain attempts to teach that difference to Wilf.

'Did I dream it then?' Her voice was sharp, urgent.

'You must have done,' said Ern, feigning commiseration.

'No,' she said. 'I don't think I did.'

Ern felt the need to say something conclusive. 'I wouldn't worry about it. Just so long as it wasn't yours. The head, I mean. Eh?' She did not find it funny. Nor did Ern, because as he got up his pain roused itself too and walloped him. He staggered, then straightened himself. He wanted to make a dignified exit.

'What's wrong with you?' she asked.

It was her first concession to him. He basked in it, though he took care not to let on. 'Stomach trouble. Something I ate.'

'Give us a look at you,' she said. He was heading for the door. He turned back with a woebegone grin, which clung to his face as her eyes appraised him. What he thought was the good one travelled up and down him like an X-ray; the other picked, scraped, made peripheral enquiries. He stood there suffering it, behind his aching grin. He noticed that his hands had closed into fists. It was not aggression; they were trying to squeeze and strangle the pain. He thrust them, embarrassed, in his pockets.

By this time she was ready to pronounce. She did so without switching her voice into a euphemistic key. No one had warned her that you should adulterate the truth, or – better yet – not say it at all. She announced her discovery almost gleefully.

She said 'It's not what you ate. Don't you know what's going on? You're dying. That's it.'

She retreated down the corridor into her room. She seemed to be humming, unless it was a buzz or whine in his ears. His first thought was, How could she tell?

Only then did he remember to deny it: No, no, I'm not. He wanted to shout after her, but decided against it. She might tell him more – when, for instance.

His legs found the way outside without his needing to direct them. The sun too was an unwelcome truth, chilly but somehow scorching. The cold could burn you. Then he noticed, with a rush of the blood resembling happiness, that his pain had gone quiet. Afraid also, dismayed by the news of its imminent end? I'll gain a march on it, he thought. I'll show her. He scurried through her matted garden, nearly up to his old speed; he negotiated the slope with a goat's agility. A little shortness of breath made him pause. It was the excitement.

Glancing across the valley, he saw that the shadows had lengthened behind things. A bush had another life in retrospect as a tapering tree, and it grew as he watched like the swag of memories he carried over his shoulder. At least the shadows were behind, not ahead. This made him think of Wilf, who in the days before he had the stick used to enlist his shadow – when it preceded him down the road – as an older, taller brother. Sometimes that shadow annoyed him, and he jumped on it to stamp it out. It imitated his agitation, then when he gave up unfolded into life again. That was one of the differences Ern tried to explain, without success. Now he walked on into the sun, glad his own shadow was where it belonged, where he could not see it, hugging his heels like a well-trained Dog. He had to keep going. The problem was where. Since it was that time of day, he would go to work.

He stopped at the hut first, to collect his equipment. He took out his own bat, and decided to take Wilf's as well. He had not thought about how he would do the job alone. The pile-up last time had brought on his retirement. He was sure he could work it out. Puffing, he permitted himself a brief sit-down. While he breathed, he looked around the hut, as attentively as if he were counting possessions or blessings. All I've got, he thought: he had said that to the old woman, about Wilf. It wasn't true of Wilf. Anything alive could and would run out on you. All he actually had was the objects in the room. The rocker, the lantern, the kit of knives, the extra pair of boots behind the door. Then even those quavered, melted, ran away. He could not see them any more. It must be because he was crying. Not quite: his eyes were watering. He had no reason for tears. But his body had moods and fluxes these days, with a peace of its own to make. He got up. There was the pain to keep in front of.

He stumped down the hill. There were no more individual shadows, strange elongated sequels to the ordinary existence of the hut, the tree clawing its side, the knobbly cabbages, the stone wall. The shadows merged and mixed like pigment, and were taking over the world. Below on the road, the lights of the cars prodded the dark, then were absorbed. The valley had become an extension of the tunnel. Ern began to tread carefully, nudging the night aside with his boots. It was something he used to rely on Wilf for: to clear the way. His pace slowed. He took life a step, a breath at a time, with pauses in between. The darkness had no features.

He passed the cave without knowing it, because the Dogs were not there to greet him. But he heard the fountain talking to itself up ahead. I might make a stop there, he thought. I deserve another sit-down.

He found that the sit-down had to be carefully planned, one arm and leg at a time, so as not to alert his pain. He deposited himself on the stone rim surrounding the spout. At the risk of a crick, he twisted his head towards the water. He was sweating, despite the cold. The animal with the copper gullet laughed at him. The water was no unction; it spat in his face.

Behind him, a voice said 'Hallo, Ern.'

His neck jerked back automatically, with a wrench that made

him yelp. He knew the voice – its lilt of derision, its snaky undulation – even though all he could see, until his neck allowed him to look up, was the lower half of a figure whose hands dangled into his field of vision.

'Clem,' he said.

'Hope I didn't surprise you.'

'No, of course not. We haven't seen you for a while though.'

'Yes,' said Clem. 'I was just thinking, when would the last time have been?'

Ern was sure it would hurt, but he had to see Clem's face. He forced his neck to make the manoeuvre. At the price of a rupture somewhere inside, he saw that Clem was smiling. It was not much help.

'I can't rightly remember the last time, Clem. I'm a bit vague about things like that.'

'You don't look too good, I must say.'

'It's my old trouble, Clem. Can't let it interfere. I'm off to work, same as usual.'

'Where's that kid of yours?'

'I don't know, Clem, he's been a bit wayward lately. If you see him . . .'

'And what's become of your Dogs? Pensioned them off?'

'Yes, there's been a few changes, while you've been away.'

'But I haven't been away. I've been around. Where would you expect me to go?'

'Nowhere, Clem, nowhere, suit yourself.'

'Well, I don't want to keep you.'

Ern could tell, from the way the smile faded, what this meant. It was not an announcement that Clem was leaving but an order that Ern should leave. Still, Clem would have to give him time. Getting up required thought. He tried using one of his arms as a lever. It refused the weight. He flopped back onto the stone rim like a beached fish.

'Clem,' he said, hating the way his voice quaked.

'Yeah?' said Clem, with an abstracted look. He was smiling again.

'Could I ask you for a hand? To help me up? I'm that stiff.'

One of the hands which had hung in front of Ern's eyes shot

towards him, too quickly. It jabbed the air. And its fingers were rigid, stretched as far part as they would go. The hand was four splayed mouths, with darkness inside each of them. It's no use to me like that, thought Ern. I can't get hold of that. The fingers were like pincers.

Very slowly, the fingers closed. The hand relaxed. The fingers curled towards Ern, who remained suspicious. 'Come on then,' said Clem. 'What are you waiting for?'

Ern gave his hand — warty and calloused, with all his years written into it — to Clem. A few knuckles was all he would venture. Clem's hand tightened at once around those tentative fingers. Ern was expecting to scramble up Clem's arm like a climber on a rope. But the hand took control, and tugged him instantly to his feet. It was as if Clem were pulling a plant up by the roots.

'All right then?' he asked.

'Yes,' said Ern, gasping, 'thanks'. It's a good thing I can't run, he thought; he would not have been able to stop himself.

'Wrong way,' Clem called after him. 'It's down there. You're a bit confused.'

Ern reversed, humiliated. I'll creep past him, he thought. And hope I never set eyes on him again. But to be prudent he said 'See you later then, Clem.'

'Yeah,' said Clem, who may or may not have believed it.

As it happened, it was a man on his way to the airport who stopped. He regretted it as soon as he did so. Now he was bound to be delayed. However, traffic was light, there was no one else around — Ern, losing count of the days, had forgotten that it was a weekend — so the man jumped back in his car, drove off, and within an hour had left the country.

Ern was sitting in his sentry box, on the bench which had been installed to replace the stolen chair. The bats were on either side of him, green and red, cancelling each other out. He did not speak when the man hailed him, or blink either. His eyes were open, still keeping watch. But there was now no telling what he was looking at.

15

PAUL SHOULD HAVE been thinking about his solution to the problem of the valley: the skyline he wanted to raise on top of it, which would suppress the valley forever. He stared at the white paper until he was almost hypnotised by it. But thoughts were reluctant to come. He could not see his own scheme because two other cities got in the way. Babylon was one, with its plastery pomp and those elephants which he used to imagine himself battering to powder. The other was Rome.

Not an actual Rome; the Rome he was thinking about was a place you could not see, a metaphorical city. He found the description of it in a book. He had not read the rest of the book, only the description of Rome, for fear that it would be made to mean something different from what it immediately meant to him. 'Let us suppose,' the description began. The words invited him to collaborate in a dream. He was eager to do any amount of supposing. The description went on to sketch its suppositional Rome, after specifying 'that Rome is not a human habitation but a psychical entity with a similarly long and copious past.' Paul accepted the qualification. What then?

What followed was a vision of the city as an epochal memory, where 'nothing which has come into existence will have passed away.' Outside, in the real Rome, things had to be knocked down so that others could be built. Each generation trod on the bones of the generation before it until, like the Babylonian elephants, only rubble was left. But the mind did not occupy space. Memories required no attics or basements as storage areas. The writer gave details in his tour of Rome: the site of the Coliseum contained also Nero's Golden House, Hadrian's Pantheon stood beside or perhaps on top of Agrippa's. It must have been crowded, Paul thought.

Still, the idea was beautiful in proportion to its absurdity. How did the mind acquire its skill at preserving experience? And why did its preservative power grow as the body decayed? Old age gave your earliest years back to you; this suggested that minds outlasted bodies, that all the accumulated savings of our lives – the towers and columns and teetering skyscrapers of it – might be capable of reconstruction inside someone else. They said that nothing in the world could ever be destroyed, despite the savagery with which Paul had set about demolishing Babylon. There was always some residue, some dust so fine that it escaped detection. If this was true of physical substance, might it not also be true of mental events, knots and nodules of emotion, harder to hunt down and stamp out because they had no shape or solidity?

The more he thought of that all-inclusive Rome, the more he felt ashamed of his own crushed, brutalised Babylon, and the more he understood his own antagonism to the valley. Architecture set itself to periodically remake the world. It was the visible sign of our triumphant evolution. The valley obtusely, unteachably signalled the opposite: instead of changing, things only repeated themselves. Whenever he looked out of his window, someone was always marching up the hill in hope, and someone else – or the same person, meeting himself half way? – was trudging wearily down. And it seemed that he was always at the window looking.

So when he returned to the paper on which he was meant to be designing the valley's future, it remained blank. Of course, he thought, demoralised, the valley had no notion of a future. Perhaps it had no notion of the past either. In it, the present arduously performed the same tasks over and over again: digging, eating, living, dying. The sun crossed it every day on the same track, and at night the gas works tried to set fire to the sky, without ever succeeding. It punctually flooded every winter. There was no solution to any of it.

Wilf had turned out to be equally insoluble. He was still with them. Paul on the first night made Kate agree that she would hand him over in the morning; they were unable to decide to whom, or to what. That was Kate's responsibility, he told her.

Then, on his way to bed, he paused outside the spare room and quietly, almost guiltily, turned the key in the lock. They're all thieves, he thought in nervy self-justification. They cut heads off, don't they, and play football with them? He could clean us out overnight while we're asleep.

In the morning he regretted it and, before Kate was awake, unlocked the door. The moment he did so, it opened from inside, as if Wilf had been standing there — all night long perhaps — waiting for them to release him. He said nothing. He did not even look reproachful. He had the suffering patience and passivity of an animal. Was I ever like that? thought Paul. Or am I still?

He asked the boy if he was all right, if he was hungry. Animals and children could always be bought off with food. It was the way you purchased trust, and atoned for wrongs done. But Wilf, who probably understood this kind of transaction, shook his head. Paul wondered whether you had to apologise to children, who were not able to retaliate. He was about to invent something about the door jamming or the lock being faulty and to ask why Wilf had not knocked or called out. Then he noticed the painting, still lying on the floor where it had toppled.

'What's that?' he said, though he saw at once who the figures were.

'I didn't do it,' said Wilf. 'I mean I couldn't help it.'

That's as may be, thought Paul as he picked the canvas up and draped a cloth over it. But you're in it, and so is she; and it was here before you were, which means that she didn't just bump into you yesterday.

He lifted the corner and looked again at the painting. 'Wilf,' he said, 'close the door. Please.' He did not want Kate to see him. The reason, he suddenly understood, was to spare her — to protect her from the knowledge he had stumbled on. And also, he reluctantly admitted, to protect himself from discovering why she had done this.

Wilf sat on the bed, his stick beside him, waiting now for a verdict. But Paul, inspecting the painting, was not concerned to blame him. Was it his fault that he had blundered into her fantasy, only to find that he was held there in detention? They had both abused him. Kate first entrapped his image, then lured him here to confront it; Paul locked the door, so he had spent the night imprisoned with his own appearance in someone else's bad dream.

The painting alarmed Paul, because it was unable to tell a story, to explain how the two figures in it got where they were or to reveal whether that was where they had to stay, the woman on the muddy edge, the child in the crevasse below. Shouldn't she rescue him? But if so, why was he staring at her with such terror? Had she pushed him in, was she gloating over him with that besmirched mouth? Had any of this happened in what people called the real world? This question at least he could answer. It must have happened, because she had painted it. Whether it happened as act or as wish did not matter.

'Is this you?' Paul asked. No, that was too much of an accusation. 'I mean, it looks a bit like you.'

Wilf shook his head once more. It was safer than risking a denial out loud.

'My mistake,' said Paul. 'Did you ever see her before yesterday though? The lady?' He was referring to her as a stranger, he noticed. But she is, he thought.

Wilf looked carefully left and right, seeking exits from the impasse. He could not be sure what they had talked about last night, or how far they were in alliance. This might be a test. He nodded.

'I thought you must have. When was it? Was it at your place, in the valley?'

Wilf's only way of dating it was as the day after the night before which Horry narrated. Before it, all days were the same. Since then, days had turned dangerously unpredictable. One of them, yesterday, had altered his life.

'It was in the street,' he said, 'a while ago. The last time I had to go for his medicine. Just after the bottle ran out. It was for his stomach.'

'I see,' said Paul. The ease with which he accepted it made Wilf suspicious. 'And what happened? Did she tell you she wanted to put you in a painting? Did she ask you if she could?'

Paul saw him frowning as he tried to work it out. Of course it made no sense to him. Being stolen by the imagination, smuggled away, hoarded in private beneath that dust cover: he did not know that this was one of the things you had to be prepared for. He understood, surely, all the other kinds of robbery. The valley had transformed them into fine arts. But no one had told him about love.

Finally Wilf was ready to say something. 'No,' he said. 'She just asked me what my name was.'

Paul's heart sank. It was a confirmation. It began that way. The name was a charm. Knowing it gave you power. No one had told him about the sorcery we practise. It won't be me, thought Paul.

He took coffee to Kate, who was still in bed, the sheets twisted around her. She enquired about Wilf. Paul said 'He's still here, he's all right,' and readied himself to ask the question. But it stayed inside, reiterating itself silently. Turned away, she did not see his mouth open, then close again.

He left her secret intact, out of dread. He had never opened letters or even held them up to the light; if she had kept a diary, he would never have snooped in it. What alarmed him was that he might find some reference to himself, seen from outside, with no allowances made. She had the capacity to tell him the truth, but he shrank from it when she did so. There were two kinds of love: one was a collusion of fictions, the mutual comforting and sustaining of weakness; the other was sterner, tolerating no falsity. He suspected that the second kind was not meant for human use. It should be reserved for whatever god contemplated the creation. Nevertheless, he and Kate had promised this severity to each other, and agreed that without it there could be no trust. She had kept the promise, while he soon repented ever having made it. At least he thought she had kept it, until he saw the painting of Wilf. Wasn't this love of the other, prohibited kind – the shared lie, induced by saying 'Let us suppose . . . ?'

Her head lay on the pillow in a nest of hair. Her eyes were not yet unglued, the hair curled and tangled across her brow. He sat on the edge of the bed, handed her the cup, and when she sat up he kissed her brow. It was still warm from sleep, tepid with dreams. Her head was a strongbox. Safe as houses, he thought; actually, much safer.

When he returned from his office that night, there was no one home. It happened as in his dream, almost. The difference was that he had the key, it opened the door, and he walked through the rooms calling names – yes, both of them. On his second tour of the apartment, he checked the paintings under their cover in the corner. The one of Wilf had gone. Destroyed, or only hidden? He began to search for a note, although dreams did not explain themselves. He was still searching when they came back.

'We've been for a walk', Kate said. Wilf still had the stick, and of course the guarded contents of his head. Otherwise he had undergone re-invention since yesterday. Paul, looking closer, noticed the new clothes and the haircut. The painting had gone, but Wilf was still here. Paul considered the fairness of the exchange. Sooner the boy, perhaps, than the painting. He had forfeited his chance to discuss the matter in the morning. She took that to mean acceptance. When I don't protest, she assumes I am avoiding an encounter with the truth. She is probably right.

Now, a week later, he was worrying about his solution to the valley while puzzling over the insoluble Wilf. Irresistibly, the two problems merged. The valley was no longer outside the window, slumped compliantly below. It had invaded the apartment in the person of Wilf, who moped through the rooms trailing his stick as if scratching grooves in the dirt or sat on the floor for an hour at a time watching through the porthole as clothes frothed and revolved in the washer or listened as voices murmured messages into the answering machine. Paul asked Kate whether Wilf should not be going to school, and flushed – it was fortunately dark at the time, they were in bed – to hear himself sound so like a parent. She agreed at once, but said that the school he went to before, on the other side of the valley, was out of the question. She was glad he had it in mind; she hugged him. Inside her arms, he was welcomed into partnership.

When the daylight returned, he made a bid to start a rational discussion of it. He began with the school. Whatever was wrong with the old one?

'If he goes back there, he'll just fall in with all the delinquents from the valley. Don't you think he should have a chance to start again?'

'Perhaps he should, but you can't be the one to decree that. You can't just take a child off the street, away from his family, and make him the subject of a experiment.'

'He doesn't have a family. His mother dumped him with his grandfather and was never seen again, and now his grandfather has walked out – or probably sloped off into the bushes to die, like an animal. It's gruesome down there, Paul.'

'Come on, you're believing everything he tells you. Perhaps he knows what an imagination you've got, and he's playing to it. Children are shrewd. And since when have you had such a low opinion of life in the valley?'

This was his mistake. She saw her chance to make a concession to him and express repentance, thus winning the argument. 'I was wrong about that. I'm sorry. I should have listened to you.' She smiled with infuriating sweetness, aware that – for the moment – she had blocked him, and asked how his plans for the new city across the way were going: she now approved of it.

That was her mistake. 'Oh I don't know,' he said, 'not too well. I'm beginning to have my doubts. I was just thinking that you might have been right all along. I can't build my folly on top without knowing what's underneath. I don't mean geologically. I've never been in there to have a proper look at how things are on the ground.'

'Don't go. You might lose your head. It's been known to happen.'

So she had seen the paragraph in the paper, though she never mentioned it. She mentioned it now, he thought, half as a joke and half as a threat. He seemed to remember that it appeared in the paper on the day she brought Wilf home. That evening, they had another topic of conversation. No wonder it had been forgotten.

Wilf was waiting for them, seated at the kitchen table with his stick in front of him. He snatched it up when they came. He knew they did not approve. Kate had first tried to wean him by persuading him to abandon it in exchange for that electronic wand with the buttons. He shook his head. Then she proposed cleaning it – hypocritically, she realised, since the childish pleasure of her own painting was dabbling in mire and gore. The stick was grimy, and greasy from his palm. Perhaps, somewhere underneath, was the blood of the dog his grandfather claimed to have clubbed, on the day of the stick's initiation. Wilf was wary of saying no to her, but hid the stick behind his back. She gave up the idea of scrubbing its magic from it.

Paul saw Wilf grab the stick and smuggle it to safety under the table, and was surprised at his own reaction. Something pierced his chest like a dart. Feelings were an attack from outside on the slumbering, complacent body. They all left different scars and had different names. This one was called compassion, or sympathy. He could suddenly see what it was like to be Wilf, clinging to the sole thing that was his.

Had he resented the boy as a usurper? But Wilf had not settled into this new world. He behaved like an intruder, who might be expelled at any moment. The whole episode, he must have suspected, would turn out to be a practical joke. Perhaps today the woman with the impulses would take him out and leave him on the street, or wherever else she had found him. She had captured his image; the original could be discarded. Love was as terrifyingly arbitrary when it ended as when it began. Those swans and eagles which swooped down from the air in the classical fables, plucked their prizes and whisked them off to transcendence: they could easily drop you again.

The feeling dictated its own terms. Paul wanted to say or do something to cancel his initial hostility. But all he could think of to say was 'Hungry?', which Wilf vigorously denied, and all he was able to do was ruffle the boy's hair with his hand, which Wilf mistook for castigation. When Paul let him go, he scraped it back into place with his finger nails.

Paul tried to recall the time of games, when he must have known instinctively how to resolve stand-offs like this. Did you ask for a truce? He had forgotten the rules. But he understood all of Wilf's sensations as he sat there clenched and tense, studying some neutral spot on the table while locating the stick with his feet: bafflement, frustration, an abiding grievance. The world contained a multitude of strangers, avoiding each other's eyes, imagining themselves unique even while they were assailed and injured by exactly the same feelings. Our interchangeability offends us, Paul thought. We're prepared to make single exceptions, one at a time, though reciprocation is never guaranteed. That is what we call love. Otherwise there is only story-telling, which lets you inhabit someone else's skin, wear their head on your shoulders for the duration. But what stories do I have, he wondered, to tell Wilf?

Later – too late, since he was on his way to work – he realised that they had the stick in common. He had one sometimes in his dream about the pasteboard Babylon. He remembered braining an elephant with it. But Paul's stick laid waste to a city; Wilf's seemed to serve only as a crutch. Perhaps it had powers in the valley. Down there it might have twanged and tingled in his hands like a diviner's rod. Up here it dragged along behind him, malingering like a wooden leg. Unless, Paul thought, he raises it against me. Let us suppose that I too could be broken down like the elephant, into a drift of white powder. To suppose it was only too easy. He could see Wilf purusing him through the mouldy arcades, across terraces reclaimed by grass. When he was caught, would it be enough to say 'No, don't, it's yourself you're doing it to. Other people are only the projection of ourselves'?

If he turned aside from Babylon to Rome, Wilf was waiting for him there, but this time not armed. In Rome, nothing needed to be knocked over and trampled underfoot. All periods of time, all the ages of man, coexisted companionably. You never outgrew what you were. Wilf had not shed the valley, despite the clothes and the estranging haircut. Nor had Paul ceased to be Wilf, though the child was cooped up somewhere inside him. This time there was no chase. When Paul thought about it, what he saw was the two of them walking together through the reef of buildings with their old and new and newer versions of themselves. Paul was telling Wilf about the buildings, what they had been, were, would be. That was how it worked: you passed on all the stories you knew. In the process you regained your entire life, then gave it away. You made a résumé of that life, and consigned it to the memory of whoever came next. The child would at first refuse to believe the stories. Then, as his own life proved them true, he would look around for someone else to recite them to. For safety's sake, the stories were written down, the surfaces of the city papered with them. They walked along between walls made of words. In order to keep yourself from passing away, you did not have to clear a space and erect your own monument, like the men of stone striking poses on columns. It was perhaps enough that one person thought of you, or spoke about you.

That night, at home, he laid a bait for Wilf. It was merely a door left ajar, but he thought of it as a tactic for coaxing some wild, mistrustful creature out of its cover. Paul went to his study, spread plans and blank pages across his desk, and waited. Though he had his back to the door, he could hear Wilf pass in the hall.

'Wilf', he called, 'is that you? Come in.'

The boy wanted to bolt, but there was no more valley to absorb him into anonymity. He ventured in: it had been a summons, not an invitation. The room had no window, and was stacked with books to the ceiling. A lamp bounced light from papers on the desk. Beyond it, the room was a cave, a cranium.

'Come over here, there's something I want to ask you about. Something you could help me with.'

Wilf moved a step backwards, away from the lamp.

'No, no, it's not about you. It's my geography I want some help with. Look, I've been making a map of the valley, and I want you to tell me if I've got it right. I've only ever seen it from up here, or when I was driving through. And you know it – well, like the palm of your hand.'

Paul looked down at his own hands. The lamp examined the folds of skin, the puncture marks of pores. On the palms, maps were imprinted. But of what country?

'Sit down,' he said. 'Take the books off that chair.'

All Wilf said was 'Why?'

Paul ran through the list of possible questions Wilf could have been asking, which went back to the primal one: Why is this happening to me?

'Why am I drawing a map of the valley?'

That was evidently not the question, but it would do.

'Well, it's a long story.' What story wasn't? Stories criss-crossed like the lines on his hand or the tracks through the valley. 'I want to build something over there, and I need to see how it fits in.'

'Can you just go and do that?'

With children, Paul perceived, everything went back to first principles. They took nothing for granted. Each step had to be justified. But which assumption was Wilf challenging this time? Was he asking whether Paul was able to build something, or demanding how he dared to do so? Paul chose to answer the easier question, by showing Wilf a sketch of the building which looked like an iceberg.

'That's mine,' he said. 'I mean I had the idea for it.'

'Is it real though?'

'Yes, yes, it is – it will be, it's almost finished. I've got a photograph.' He ransacked a drawer, astonished at how much he wanted to prove it to Wilf.

The photograph was taken months ago, when all that existed was scaffolding, girders, and workers with heads for heights behaving as if there were floors beneath them. Wilf frowned at it, determined not to be tricked.

Paul, defeated, put the photograph away. It was like expecting him to identify someone by showing him a skeleton. He laid out the map, which he had copied from a geological survey, taking care to confuse its point of view and muddle it with vague, conjectural lines of his own to make it look personal.

'See,' he said. 'This is the best I can do from up here. What do you think?'

Wilf thought nothing. It meant nothing to him. 'Where is it?' he asked.

'It's the valley, where you live – lived. Don't you recognise any of it?'

'No,' said Wilf.

He is shamming, Paul thought. But Wilf had never learned the language. 'What's that?' He pointed at a line which wormed down the centre of the page. It was the creek, Paul explained, draining towards the river. And the looping line which crossed it, hatched with little bars: that was the railway, those were its trestles.

'It's not like that,' Wilf said. 'They've pulled it out. They sell it for scrap.' Paul obediently erased the railway, but Wilf made him restore the trestles. Now we're in business, Paul said to himself.

Wilf next wanted to know about the shaded line a quarter of an inch thick, coloured with the side of a pencil, which twisted horizontally over the page. 'The road,' Paul told him. Wilf raised his eyebrows. And those consecutive dots, speckling the paper like rabbit droppings? 'Footpaths,' Paul said. 'I mean tracks to walk on, through the fields. Aren't there any?'

Wilf glanced sideways at him, long-sufferingly. He had learned the expression from Horry. It was exactly what Paul hoped for. Then he had to account for the frill down the edge of the page, with other lines sprouting from it like a dog's hair. That represented the cliff. He began to tell the story, as if he had seen it happen, about the valley splitting open.

'I know,' said Wilf. 'We live on top of there.' To Paul, the remark sounded proprietorial. Did Wilf sense that the making of maps was a first step towards invasion?

'You haven't put in the cave.' He said it jubilantly. 'And where's our tunnel?'

Paul indicated the intersection of those lines, the curling creek, the railway with its hackles, the grey stripe of road.

Wilf was unconvinced. 'I can't *see* it'.

'I tell you what,' said Paul, as if he had just thought of it. 'Why don't you make your own map? You know it all from the inside, I can only show what I see from up here. And then we could compare notes.' Wilf hesitated. 'Have you ever drawn things?'

'Yes,' said Wilf, remembering his scratches in the dust. 'Not on paper though.'

'Here you are, use as many sheets as you want. And there are pencils, colours and all. Can I leave you to it? I'll be back in a while. Do you want the door closed? No, I'll leave it open.'

He ate without being hungry, drank without being thirsty, flicked through the rota of television channels without looking, and was pleased that Kate, taking a bath, could not see his agitation. Fifteen minutes, he decided, was the minimum. After fourteen minutes he concluded that his watch was slow. In the hall he coughed to announce himself.

Wilf was slumped in the chair, swinging his legs. The pencils were upright in their mug. Hadn't he started? 'Have you finished?' asked Paul.

'Hours ago.'

Wilf sighed, and Paul rejoiced at his impatience. Annoyance was the inception of a relationship.

'Can I see?' He leaned over the boy's shoulder and looked down at his view of the world. It was a mess of scrawls and whirls, as inarticulate as graffiti. 'That's how you practised, is it? – trying out the pencils?'

'No,' said Wilf indignantly, 'this is it.'

It must come from sleeping in the same room as those paintings of Kate's, thought Paul. The style is catching. Then he understood that he was wrong, or at least unfair. He had asked Wilf to describe the place from the inside. That meant recording how it felt, not what it looked like. The boy still lived in a mental era before art and its cheating artifice began. He did not know how to represent things – which meant returning them to the present, as memory did – because the activity implied that they were somehow absent, retrievable only as imitations of themselves, like Kate's antiquated gods or Paul's own allusive towers. Wilf drew sensations, garishly immediate: the neural shocks caused by things he saw, which he continued to see even in this room without a window.

'I'm sorry,' Paul said, and looked again at the paper.

There were four marks on it, four blotches of colour and centres of energy. At the top was an angry vortex of red, at the bottom a fitful patch of blue. In the middle were two black scribbles. One was an obsessive asterisk, made from too many converging strokes. It had been drawn over and over again, until the lines acquired a contour like the forming of a cicatrice. The other was a circle, bordered in black but shaded grey inside the margin.

Paul decided it would be best not to guess. 'Give me a guided tour,' he said.

'What of?'

'The valley, your valley. I told you I needed some help. Let's start here. What does the red mean?'

'It's the sun.'

'Why did you put that in?'

'I watch it in the afternoon, as it's going down. That's it shining back from the buildings – from these here buildings we're in.'

'And the blue thing?'

'It's the gas, down by the river.'

'I think I know what this is, the star with all the criss-crosses coming and going. That's your tunnel, right? But how about this bit of grey? Some kind of lake?'

'No, the cave I told you about, where our Dogs used to be. We weren't supposed to go in. There's something else I haven't put.' He rubbed the page, smudging the area between the tunnel and the cave. 'The tap, and that animal. But I don't know how to draw it. I've never really seen it. My grandfather used to say it didn't exist. But then she said the other day that she believed me. So now I'm not sure.'

'Who said? Kate? When did she say that? I mean where?'

'When we went past it, on the way out.'

'So she was in there with you? You didn't meet in the street?'

'No, that was only the first time.'

'Ah,' said Paul, and tightened his hands on the back of Wilf's chair.

He gazed down again at the page. The coils and fits of colour pulsed on the paper like a galaxy. The black star and the grey hollow were points of entry to a depth beneath the white sky or behind it. This is not the valley, he thought; it is a universe of outer and inner spaces, where we are all bound to lose ourselves.

'Wilf,' he said, moving his hands from the back of the chair and settling them on the boy's shoulders, 'I think I want to see it all for myself. Could I? Would you take me?'

Drifting around the valley to revisit the sites and stations of his life – the leaking barn with the doused brazier, the evacuated cave, the shed among the trees which had memories brightly painted on its floor and walls – Clem puzzled over the mystery of an act without consequences.

Nothing had happened, except the disappearance of Athol and the rest, and the clearing-out of the cave. That he took to be their revenge on him, depriving him of his share in the spoils. But since he did not care about their warehouse of appliances, he ignored the judgment. He saw it anyway as a tribute to their awe of him, and laughed at the idea of their packing up goods and chattels, Dogs and all, out of fear.

It's a disappointment to me, he thought. Really it is. You can get away with it. If I was to run into God, I'd have to tell him I was disappointed in him. Nothing happens.

Except that he now had the world to himself. Of course there was the woman in the raincoat, who seemed to recognise him, then raced away up the hill. Once he would have given chase, aroused and amused by her terror. But what more was there, in that line, for him to prove?

There was also Ern. Or there had been. He could now be deducted. After meeting him at the water spout, Clem went off to eat from the provisions left behind at the farm, then came back to look for him. He missed the sound of his own voice, particularly if he could use it to scare someone. Besides, he had passed up his earlier opportunity to find out what Ern meant about the changes. I'll just pay him a call at the tunnel, he thought, and see if I can make him jump.

Between cars, Ern was resting. Clem slithered towards him and stood outside the box. 'Hallo again,' he said.

Ern, annoyingly, did not jump. Instead he stared. The stare made Clem uncomfortable. Ern was always shifty, cringing. Now his gaze was aggressive. The eyes accused him, like index fingers in an identification parade.

'Come on Ern,' he said. 'What are you playing at?' He then saw that Ern was playing at being dead.

He prodded the old man's chest to make sure. He did so with superstitious speed, as if testing the temperature of water, but

the force of the gesture was enough to make Ern lean sideways.
A car passed, a horn blew at them. They were paralysed in a
circle of light. Clem waved to the car, then settled the body
upright again. He even, in case anyone could still see, patted its
shoulder. After that, he ran.

His reaction baffled him. When he stopped near the cave, he
was shaking. Why? he wondered. Why, by contrast with the
other time when he had been so calm through it all? And this
time there was no mess. Not a mark on him. Perhaps that was
what made the difference.

The other time it had been an operation, showing how a
person came apart. Fear disassembled the man before Clem
thought of dismembering him. But Ern had managed to wriggle
out of his body on the quiet, leaving it behind him so Clem
could be enticed into talking to it.

And the eyes were open. That was the worst of it. Clem now
knew why closing them, weighting the lids with coins, was part
of the ritual: to save us from looking into them and to keep
them from looking at us; to protect us from that knowledge.
The other one had refused to look at him, even when Clem
grabbed his chin and thrust his own face forward so that he
could feel the man's pumping breath on him. Ern's stare was
triumphant. It announced, in substituting this unsteady dummy
for the live thing, that he had sneaked off with his secret. Spirit
had changed back into matter.

Last time it had been tougher to bring about, but easier to
understand. His knife analysed the body. The discoveries it made
amazed him. First that a life was so tenuous. You yanked the
driver from the car, the ghost fled from the machine. Next
came the inventory of contents, the useless possessions we lug
around with us: the cementing bones, the gadgetry of organs,
the irrigation system in its tangled pipes. People made sure
they disposed of all their other, outer belongings, but what
could be done with all this internal equipment, good for nothing,
of no value second hand? It lay there, supine and stupid.

Then he discovered that it was indestructible. There was no
such thing as killing someone. The spirit, which you could not
see, escaped, and no doubt began looking for another vehicle.

Meanwhile something had to be done with the abandoned matter. But whatever you did merely helped its transformation into something else. On the way down to the farm for utensils, the plastic bag and the twine, he considered sowing it around the valley, planting it the way Athol did his bundles of money. He gave up the idea. The surgery would be hard work, it would take too many trips, and the result would be the wrong one, dissemination not disposal. Afterwards it might worry him. That sudden unaccountable flowering over there: had it happened thanks to him?

Removing the head, however, was essential. Bodies are as exchangeable as suits of clothes. Only the sex makes them different, and that difference is standard. But a head is yours alone. The rest could be anyone's, any body's, like a suit which comes ready to wear. A head is also a convenient size for getting rid of.

Even so, it amazed him to find how hard it was to break the connection. Breath evacuated effortlessly. When then did the body cling to an obsolete head? He expected it to be like twisting a flower off its stalk. But flowers are merely pudenda; the plant, better designed than we are, keeps its head embedded in the ground. This was more like grubbing out a tree. There were so many lines, fibres, filaments to sever. As for clothes, he thought, I'll have to change mine after this.

It was tiring. Otherwise he felt nothing in particular. One by one, ever since his first lie and his first theft, he had worked his way through the register of unthinkable things and defied successive taboos, which were never more than shoddy magic. The sky had not fallen in on him, the earth had not opened. This particular taboo was as much of a bluff as the others. Morality made a coward of you by insisting that you imagine this being done to you; not doing it to someone else was supposed to be your own insurance. It depended on your willingness to change places with the other person. Clem was not willing. That set him free.

He wrapped the head in the man's own shirt and vest. As he did so, he noticed the stitching on the shirt pocket. Initials: the man did have a name, even though he wouldn't or couldn't say it. But it was too dark for Clem to read the letters so finely written in thread. He looped the sleeves of the shirt around the bundle and tied them in a knot, as if the man were burying his own head in his hands. Then he wrapped it in the vest, which was still damp with panic, and slid it into the bag. Why the buffering layers? It was his trophy, after all; it deserved special treatment. There might have been another reason. Perhaps he wanted to shut its eyes, to stop its mouth. He fastened the bag with string, tying recondite knots. Although he knew they could be sliced through in a moment, it was another necessary precaution. Try and get out of that, he was saying. I dare you.

He inserted it under a cairn of rubbish, and put the rest into the drained lake, covering it with a counterpane of papers. Of course he had been careless, leaving the parcel and the lumber-like bulk where he did. But his carelessness expressed his contempt. If they were found, all the better. He deserved credit for doing something so motiveless, so profitless. He did not know the man's name, did not even dislike him. The choice was random. So much for the need to pretend that we have fated, appropriate endings.

He washed, changed his clothes, gave Horry the discarded ones to burn. Good as new, he thought; almost a reincarnation. Once his hands were clean and his wet hair slicked back on his scalp, once he buttoned himself into a shirt he had never worn before, he was ready for anything. Love, for instance, or an activity that went by the name. Someone else's death had made him feel jubilantly alive. The proof of it was the itch in his groin.

He hiked across the valley to one of his current women, who lived in a concrete tower on the western edge. She was indignant about being woken up. He thought she was probably not alone.

'I missed you,' he said. The itch, irritable at first, was by now an ache. It radiated pain. I must get rid of it, he thought.

'Yeah,' she said, 'I bet you did,' and let him in.

During it, the similarity occurred to him. The incision, the access to a wet and warm interior, the noises she made. But at the end it was he who made the sound which the man had made earlier that night: the exhalation, like a spirit breaking free. 'Jesus,' said the woman. He didn't hear her say it, because it was as if he had been cudgelled. He slumped onto her, unconscious. Straddled, she thought, by a corpse.

He was frightened when he woke up. He thought, for a long moment, that he was in the shed. A disembowelled doll leered at him from a chair. Sun torched the room. He hesitated before he checked to see what the bulk was lying beside him. Then he lay back and reassembled his life in reverse order. How much of it was true? Did the memories belong to him, or had they just strayed through his head while he was asleep?

'Still here?' she said when she woke up. He did not usually spend the night.

'I thought I might stay for a while,' said Clem. 'How about a feed?'

He stayed for a week, reading two papers every day in the hope of discovering whose life it was he had put a stop to. There was no news. The man might never have existed. Or else Clem did not do it after all. He even thought of telling her about it. But what if she didn't believe him?

Instead of telling, he went on with his recreation of what he was sure had happened. He pieced together the dialogue, filling in phrases as if completing a crossword. Then he recited it to himself, to make sure it sounded right. He did so in the bathroom while she was out. The bathroom had the same acoustics as the shed. His whispers rebounded from the walls. He noticed, as he worked through the things they had said to each other, that the other one seemed – once the door of the shed had closed – to have taken control. First there was his refusal to give his name, then that last order, abrupt and insistent. When Clem did the dialogue, he found himself lending his own voice to the other man. After a while there had been nothing for Clem to say. He just did as he was told. Had he ever been in control, or was he only acting out the other man's bad dream?

The thought made him angry, but he knew how to wipe clear his consciousness. When she came back, he discharged it into her. He began by fastening her shoulders, then noticed that he was gripping the sides of her face, tugging the skin until it showed the angular bones beneath. An enraptured skull looked up at him.

Afterwards, he left. He said he was going out for the paper, but he did not return. She threw away the meal she had cooked for him. It wasn't, she reflected, the first time. She scraped the plate as if she wanted to do it harm.

Down in the street, Clem wished he had stayed long enough to have a wash. His hands smelled of the scent which his fingers dug into on her neck and behind her ears. So that particular oblivion had failed him. It turned out to be the same act as the other one, though he was no longer sure who was killing whom. It could be mutual. Certainly it left him feeling brained. He looked down at his body and wondered at the force and fury it had expended.

Then he surveyed the street. He could, he supposed, go anywhere, call himself anything. But he did not have the imagination for all the lies, and you could not disown your memory. He pulled his collar up around his ears, raised his shoulders as if hoping his head would retract, and walked back to the valley.

For a few days he holed up in the bankrupt factories and waited for the memory, like a pain, to pass. One day he woke up and only half an hour later remembered who he was. The memory was supplanted by other, more pressing matters: cold, hunger, discomfort, the scratching of his whiskers. After a while, he decided to risk a return to the farm. Just for a change of clothes, he would say. He calculated that they would behave as if it never happened, and since nothing seemed to be happening as a consequence of it, why should he insist that it did happen?

When he got to the farm, no one was there. He shouted their names, one by one. The cars had gone also. At the cave, no Dogs greeted him. The cave itself had been cleaned out.

At the fountain, he smeared water on his scalp. The animal gave him its usual smirk of recognition. It was still there, but then it was not alive, or at least not in the world outside him, where all existences had been suddenly rescinded. And what about me then? he thought. How can I be sure? You're not alive unless other people can testify to the fact. Then he noticed he was dripping in the dust. That too could be evidence. Only beings still inside bodies felt thirst and hunger. Back at the farm, he attacked a can. He wolfed the food gratefully. It proved he was somebody.

By the time another day passed, he had decided on a view of it. It was a joke, he concluded. They thought it was their joke on him – shipping out, deserting him. But he saw it differently. The joke was on them. They had run away from a story he told them. If he ever saw them again, his first words would be 'You didn't believe me, did you? Surely you didn't?' As for the blood, he could explain that away as a rabbit's. The joke was also on society, not to mention the universe. Nothing happened, he repeated to himself; nothing ever happens.

Then, disconcertingly, Ern's death happened.

Of course, Clem thought when he got his breathing under control, there was no connection. It didn't happen because of anything. Or else its reasons were internal, private: some agreement between the knot of disease in his stomach and his labouring heart that they would call it quits. He was looking sick, said Clem to himself. He wanted to think he had seen it coming. An end must not come without warning. But he knew it had taken Ern by surprise. The old man did not even have time to close his eyes, lower the shades, turn the lights off. Could it be called death if you didn't know it was happening, if words in capitals did not announce THE END?

Paul insisted on keeping it a secret from Kate. He had no need to bother, because Wilf had grown wary about saying anything to anyone. He went along with whatever was proposed, assuming he had no choice. Paul left a note for Kate, which said 'Gone for a walk – both of us'. Actually they drove. 'It's easier,' Paul said to Wilf, meaning that it was safer. Wilf made no comment, but took his stick. There was no certainty, after all, that he would be allowed to come back for it. Paul might be intending to dump him.

The world looked different from inside the car. Paul was wrong, thought Wilf, if he fancied it was any protection. Walking, he could sidle down the alley without being noticed. But the car was conspicuous; it was too early in the afternoon for anyone to be using the short cut. A child Wilf thought he knew pressed his face to the window, squashing his nose, pushing his fingers against the glass, and poked his tongue out. Paul slowed the car. Wilf shrank in his seat. Then, relieved, he remembered his camouflage: the haircut and the new clothes. Yet rather than disguising him, these marked him out. He now officially belonged to the enemy. Eventually the boy reclaimed his tongue, unglued his fingers, let his nose spring back into shape, and ran off laughing. Paul accelerated.

After the alley, there were no more obstacles. They had used up their share of warnings, with the face flattened against the window and a stone which had struck the bonnet and the woman who threw a bucket of slops at the wheels. They plunged down the hill as if on a sled. Gravity made everything inevitable.

Then Wilf called out 'Stop, stop,' and grabbed Paul's arm. The car swerved. They were at the tunnel. Before the car halted, Wilf jumped out. He must have gone into the tunnel. Otherwise Paul would have seen him on the slope to where the railway line used to run, before he ordered it rubbed out.

Paul started into the tunnel, then stopped. He did not know how long it was, or what he might find inside it. A blow to the head as he rounded the bend? The tunnel could be a passage to nowhere, or to the next world. He thought he heard steps inside it, resounding like clapped hands, but he was not sure whether they were travelling towards or away from him. Banged back from the walls, they multiplied, and ran now in both directions at once. Then they gave up. The exhausted feet, running back and forth but unable to escape, dropped dead.

I have to go through, Paul thought. I'll make the car do it for me. He climbed in, locked all the doors, strapped himself to his seat, and turned on the lights, though above the valley there was still a pale sun. He had a choice – to speed through, as if crashing one of those invisible barricades of possibility in the sky which planes shattered, or to coax the car slowly along, idling it to escape observation. He was afraid of speeding, because the darkness of the tunnel could suddenly turn solid: there was a twist in there, though he did not know where. But how could he hope to sneak through slowly, since his lights would awaken the shadows?

He switched them off, and drove the car into the tunnel.

Afterwards, he realised he had no idea of the length of it, or how long it took him. It was as immeasurable as one of those naps when you wake up convinced you have been asleep for hours and find that the clock has moved only a minute; it could have been an interim between lives, which you are forbidden to remember. Now he was on the other side. And there, waiting for him in the middle of the road, was Wilf, crying.

Wilf leapt at the door of the car. When it wouldn't open, he banged on the window. Paul unlocked it for him and pushed it open. But he didn't want to get in.

'What's happened?' he said. 'They've taken them.'

He meant the hutches. Both were gone, his own at the entry to the tunnel and his grandfather's here at the exit. He showed Paul where they had been, and wanted to know why. Children always assume, Paul thought, that we know the reasons. All he could say was that it had happened recently: the earth was moist, black and crawling where the planks had been prised up. The floor of the box had been a roof to worms, ants and spiders, which scattered in search of another darkness.

With his stick, Wilf picked at the imprint of the planks, and the piles dug as the box's foundations. Whether or not he came back, he expected everything still to be here. You'll see, thought Paul. A past life did not wait around in the hope that you might visit.

'I want to go and find him,' said Wilf.

'Who?'

'My grandpa.'

It was not that he missed him. Since leaving the valley, he had scarcely mentioned him. But now it was important to see him. Paul guessed the reason: there had to be a point you started from, which you could return to; there had to be a story in it, and there was not one without a beginning. 'Lead the way,' he said.

He abandoned his itinerary. His own map, with its diagram of places he had not seen, had been replaced by Wilf's. The story would take him to whatever end it pleased. He only hoped it would not leave him there: dump him. He locked the car – there had to be some means of safe conduct back to the beginning – and followed Wilf up the bank.

'Where are we?' he said when he reached the top. 'Wait a minute. You've got to explain it to me.'

'This? It's just where we get the water.'

'But you mentioned it before. You said you'd left it off the map.'

'It was because of the animal. I didn't know if it was real or not.'

Paul looked at the face of the beast, pushing through the plated rock and furry moss. Its eyes were lidded, open only as slits, drawing shutters down on the images that flickered within. Its horns poked directly from its brain. Its lips curled around the salivating pipe. The water spilled in the sink and splashed Paul's legs. Swilling away, it made a noise like laughter. He sat on the edge of the sink. He was in the faun's province, its underworld, the place he had such grandiose plans for abolishing; he had been led here by curiosity, or by something more insidious – despair, the enticing ease of self-destruction. Wilf was his guide, but it was someone else's traces he was following. Had she come for the same reason?

'Were you here with Kate?'

'Yes, on the way out. It's the only way. And when I told her about it the time before, she said she knew where it was.'

'The time before?'

'In the park, the first day.'

'Why were you telling her about it?'

'Because I saw the man here, there where you are.'

'What man?'

'Didn't she tell you?'

'I suppose so. Maybe I've forgotten.'

Wilf frowned. Was forgetting possible?

'So what about the man? Who was he?'

'I don't know who he was, only what Clem did after we saw them.'

'Clem?'

'The one she ran away from.'

'And he did what to the man you saw?'

'Killed him. She must have told you. Cut him up.'

Paul had to ask him to repeat it, because his mind was stalled at the first of the secrets. One secret, he thought, is all it takes. After that, there is nowhere firm to plant your feet. Another valley inside the valley might rip open at any moment.

Wilf repeated his last words uneasily. The look on Paul's face alarmed him. It had caved in. It reminded Wilf of his own face in the painting. He felt he had to take charge. 'Come on then,' he said, and pulled at Paul's sleeve. Paul staggered behind him. Wilf worried that there were no more questions. He occupied the silence with the story of the Dogs.

'Stop,' said Paul, who did not recognise the dent in the cliff as the grey fuzzy pool of shade on Wilf's map. 'Where are we going? Where are you taking me?' Some quest of Wilf's had superseded his own. He had already come too far.

'I want to see my grandpa. When she took me away, she said I could come back if I wanted to.'

Paul had to follow. With each lurching step ahead he travelled one pace further into the past. So she had taken him from his grandfather, abducted him from his own life. It was not necessary to ask more questions. If he kept moving forward, he would arrive at the meaning. But the path was steep. He panted, his heart thumped. Wilf reached back and helped him up the last few feet.

'Wait, wait,' Paul said, and slumped onto the remains of a low wall, a parapet looking over the valley. Behind him, on the other side of the gulf, the windows were beginning to play with fire.

Wilf was restless. I must ask him something, Paul thought, to slow him down. Something I am not frightened of hearing the answer to; something to which I already know the answer.

'What's that?' he said, pointing.

It was a funnel of winnowed dust, tapering at a dangerous angle, which clung to a weed and used it as a skeleton.

'The ants make those,' Wilf said. 'Want to see what's inside?' He got ready to swing the stick.

'No, don't.' The edginess of his voice surprised Paul. It was one of his own buildings.

'Come on then. It's over there. His name is Ern, you can call him that. See what the Dogs did to his cabbages. He was wild! But he's not as bad as he makes out. You tell him what happened. He must be worried.'

Wilf ran through the wrecked garden to the hut. By the time Paul caught up, he had opened the door and gone in.

Inside the hut, all was present and correct: the lamp, the table, the bedstead, the rocking chair, the precious impedimenta of an interrupted life. But something else was present, and not correct. In the rocking chair, with legs sprawled, sat a child who might have been a younger and grubbier version of Wilf.

'Get out,' said Wilf to the child.

'Get out yourself,' said the child to Wilf.

'I live here,' said Wilf, squaring up with the stick.

'Ma!' yelled the child.

The door to Ern's bedroom opened and the child's mother came out. Another child, even younger, adhered to her chest. She looked over Wilf's head at Paul, with the sullen expression of someone accustomed to being challenged. 'Who do you think you are?' she said to him.

'Are you his mother?' said Paul. 'Isn't this where he lives?'

'She's not my mother,' said Wilf, although since he had no memory of his mother he could not be sure.

'No, I'm not, thanks a lot,' said the woman. 'Is that what you wanted?'

'But he says he lives here . . .'

'I don't just say it, I do. With my grandpa. That's his chair. These are all our things.'

'Maybe he did live here,' said the woman, shifting the child to her hip, 'once upon a time. But he don't now, we do. We've been here a week. It was empty when we come. My husband should be home soon, if you want to have it out with him. He'll put you right. What do you care anyhow? You don't look like one of the locals to me.'

The child in the chair rocked it to assert ownership.

'Make them go,' said Wilf to Paul. He waved the stick in front of his face, as if it had the power to expunge them.

'I can't,' Paul said. 'How can I?'

'No, you can't,' said the woman, and advanced across the room towards him. Paul backed away and Wilf did too. Was he no longer confident of his claim, or of the ground where he made his stand? She slammed the door on them. Outside, they heard a bolt slide into the lock.

Wilf trembled with rage and misery. Paul recognised the grievance in his white, stunned face. He should have been spared these truths about the world and his own impermanence in it, at least for a while longer.

It was Paul's dream they were living through, or a version of it – without the enigmatic driver, or the bell echoing inside the house. In a way, it was worse than his dream, because it was about usurpation. In Paul's dream, he had no place in the world. Wilf's was about having a place and then losing it. If, that is, this ever was his place. Because the reason he could not help Wilf was that he did not know whether to believe him.

He coaxed the boy into retreating as far as the wall, then said 'Wilf, are you sure?'

'What of?'

'That this is the place. Everything and everyone you tell me about seems to vanish just before we arrive. Can't you prove any of it to me?'

'How?' wailed Wilf. His face was burning. A guilty flush, Paul thought – but no, it was the glare of the afternoon sun, refracted from the windows. 'You've *got* to believe me,' he said. 'That's all.'

Paul understood the terms of the contract. It was like faith and like love. You hazarded yourself without reason. There was never anything more to rely on than the look, which you interpreted to suit yourself, in another person's eyes. In the case of faith, there was not even the eyes, only a vacuous sky.

Wilf's eyes, however, were shining in his red face. Suddenly he jumped onto the wall and swayed above the drop into the valley. He raised his arm and swung the stick. Paul, confused, cowered. 'I'm not going to hit you,' Wilf said. 'I'm going to throw it away. Would you believe me then?' His arm sliced a circle in the air with the stick, picking up speed.

It could be the supreme sacrifice, thought Paul, or it could be blackmail. Either way, I'll never know. Either way, there is never anything more than trust.

'All right,' he said. 'Get down.'

Wilf hopped back to earth, too nimbly perhaps, and waited for Paul to restore his past or organise his future.

'Perhaps they moved in one day when he was out. Squatters' rights, we call it. I suppose we all do it, one way or another. But where would he have gone to?'

Wilf shrugged. It was now up to Paul to answer that question.

'We know he's not down there, where we came from. What's up that way?'

'A house.'

'What kind of house? Would he have gone there? Who lives in it?'

'I don't know,' said Wilf in answer to one or all of the questions.

'Let's go and see.' Paul proposed it without enthusiasm, expecting another dead end. 'Then we've got to go home. Do you know the way?'

'The way up?'

'Yes, even I know the way home.'

'No, I'm not sure.'

It was over the edge of Wilf's world. He had been there once or twice, but without treading it into familiarity. His grandfather refused to talk about it, because he wanted to eliminate his memories of working for the gentleman farmer. For a while, Wilf made it the habitat of the animal Horry said he had sighted. It was like the part of your mind to which you banished the things you did not want to think about, or the things over which your thinking had no power. As they walked, dusk shadowed them, rising from the bottom of the valley.

Paul knew when they had arrived, although he had never seen the place before: not, at least, while awake. There were scuffles and scavengings in the bushes. Paper blew from the mounds, as dispensable as people. The house had a roof of folded wings.

222

'He isn't here,' Wilf said. 'He wouldn't be here. Can we go? You said we had to go home.' But a woman came out to greet them. They were expected. And Wilf, apparently, expected her. 'That's her,' he said to Paul, 'she's the one I saw before. Didn't I tell you that bit of it?'

She had an eye for each of them. The one that looked straight ahead kept Paul skewered; the other, rolling sideways, took note of Wilf more glancingly, since she had seen him before. Paul shivered. Stared at like that, he felt as transparent as a leaf. What could she see inside him – the panicking scenes behind his own eyes, the clenched throat, the percussive heart, the gnawing of nerves around his stomach, the muscles which threatened to let his legs down?

He could once have disposed of her by classifying her. She was one of those women who had renounced ordinary life to pursue a vision through the streets. He saw them all the time, wrestling with their demons on park benches. Now, away from the city, there was no business-like definition of normality to judge her by. Here he was the oddity, the intruder. He could not tear himself free from the transfixing eye, because she had something to tell him.

First, however, she had something to tell Wilf.

'So you decided to come back?' she said. Paul assumed it was Wilf she meant, though her eyes still addressed each of them separately. Her voice was dry, cracked with age and disuse. 'Well you've left it a bit late.' She seemed angry with Wilf, or was it that she did not know how to control the volume of her voice, which suddenly screamed? Paul imagined an arrow on a dial, quivering into the red zone. Then it returned to the black, and she mumbled that she really could not be bothered with things like this.

I should take charge, Paul thought.

'Late for what?' he said.

'Is he your grandfather too?' said the woman.

'No,' said Paul, and wondered a second later how he could pretend to such certainty, here in this area of dreams where lives were rewritten. If she asked me my name, would I have the courage to say it? Would I still believe that it meant something?

And how would I prove it anyway? He had left his driving licence behind: you should not tempt the valley to rob you of yourself. 'But it's his grandfather we're looking for. Have you seen him?'

'Yes, of course I have, and I've seen you too.'

Paul did not stop to deny it.

'Is he here? Do you know where he's gone?'

'He was here, but he went. He didn't wait for the end. He's dead by now, surely. I told him it wouldn't be long.'

Without knowing why, Paul took the news personally. It was the casualness of the way she said it: the lethal honesty. He looked down at Wilf, thinking with an effort, This is his story; I am only a spectator of it, maybe an interpreter. Wilf said nothing, which must have meant acceptance. But Paul noticed that his own hand had been taken away from him. Wilf clutched it.

He tried – he felt obliged at least to try – to make it not be true.

'How do you know?'

'Every day is one day less. I've started counting. You have to count backwards.'

'I don't mean that.' It was another surrender to her: he claimed to understand her meaning, and so was willing it into truth. 'I mean how do you know about his grandfather? What was the matter with him?'

'I'm not the doctor,' she said. 'He was just finished, used up. I had to tell him, then off he went.'

'When was this?'

'Before I started counting.'

'I see,' said Paul, now agreeing to recognise her timetable. He was attempting to conclude it as easily as possible. When they got away from here he could think about what came next. And they must get away. The dusk was overtaking them, like a tide.

She had been standing at the door of the house, on her border. But now, as he turned away, she came down the broken stairs. She might have been stepping out of a frame. Paul could not move, though he felt Wilf pulling him. There were chills down his back and his shaking legs.

She walked up to him, reached out and covered his face with

her hands. Her fingers scuttled up and down his features. She traced the line of his brow, the sockets of his eyes, the angle of his nose. She pressed at his lips, then the hands hurried to his neck. Wilf, frightened, let him go; abandoned him, Paul thought. He managed to push her away.

She stood back, considering him. He wanted to run, but stayed because he had to be told the reason.

'I knew I'd seen you before,' she said, more to herself than to him.

Now he denied it, though the time for doing so had passed. In any case she raised her hand, refusing him the chance to speak. Listen, he ordered himself, and then it will be over. Why argue with her? In a minute you can start forgetting.

'It was your head. I know it was. I felt it, even though I couldn't get it out. Don't say it wasn't. I saw you before it happened, and I was listening too. Then when the head went missing, I got worried. The old man made out it didn't happen. But what are you doing back here? Isn't once enough?'

She was right about the uselessness of denials. He looked to Wilf for reassurance, but Wilf corroborated the wrong story. He knew what he had seen and what Horry told him. She filled in the events between, and afterwards. It all made sense, except that it involved another adjustment of his ideas about how the world worked, and where the limits of possibility were set. The limits had moved back, as if the valley were extending its dominion into the city, gobbling streets and swallowing sky-scrapers whole. He looked at Paul, and at his nightmare.

Paul could not deny what she said, because he saw in a flash that she was right. Why shouldn't he be the one? He remembered what he thought when he saw the paragraph in the newspaper: the thrill of self-congratulation with which you automatically greet the death of another. Your body rejoices and cries out, It's not me. But all it means is, It's not me now, or not yet. Fates are not singular, nor are the identities guarded – no, invented – by the bits of paper in our wallets. What happened to one of us had happened or would happen to the rest. Even if it did not, we knew in our bones and our flesh what it felt like. Why was he here in the valley, if not to rehearse death or repeat it?

Wilf rescued him. He had to in order to save himself, to re-establish the limits and decide on what, secure inside them, would be reality. He pulled Paul out of the thought, as if he were drowning in the dark which gathered on the ground and inched upwards.

'She's mad. My grandpa said so. It wasn't *you*. I saw who it was. He asked us to help him.'

Paul was dazed. The words worked too slowly on him. Wilf said it again to the woman. 'You're mad. It wasn't him.'

She did not shriek in protest, as she did when the stone was thrown at her. She was accustomed to being misunderstood. They called you mad if you defied their definitions of where things began and ended. But she remembered the boy's bemused, witnessing gaze from the time before, and decided to explain it to him.

'I saw him too, and he asked me to save him. But I can't do that. The sooner it happens the better, if you ask me. Ask him, he looks like he agrees. They went over there to do it, and I went too. He wouldn't say his name.'

Wilf paused over the details, which gave it substance again. He had no way of contradicting them. He did not dare to, in case that provoked her to supply more. Meanwhile Paul asked a question, not sceptically, more to seek confirmation for a memory of his own.

The question was 'Where did we go?'

'As if you didn't know,' she said, and gave him a moment in which to hope that she was bluffing, or would say something incoherent. After the moment passed, she said, 'Over there,' and pointed. The distance was blurred: white humps like dunes, black trees behind. 'Through the trees. There's a box, a shed, whatever you call it. That's where you ended up.'

Paul made a noise in the back of his throat: a humming sound, the vibration of a taut string. It was the compression of many words.

'Happy with that?' asked the woman. She seemed genuinely concerned that he had found what he came for. 'I'm going then. I've got other things to look out for.' She went back into the house.

'Can we go home?' said Wilf.

Paul was already walking.

'It's this way,' said Wilf, tweaking his cuff.

'No, she said it was over there.'

Wilf tried to steer him on to the path which led down the hill to the car, to the city. But Paul, so feeble when Wilf helped him over the wall, had regained the advantage. An adult was a thing with weight, force, purpose. Wilf could not stop him.

Paul paused. He had to cope with the hindrance. Wilf was slowing him down, holding him back. 'I have to do what she said.' He explained it coolly, as if he were running an errand not walking towards an unavoidable destination, a destiny. 'I have to see the place. You all know more about this than I do, though I'm the one it concerns. I have to see what's there, otherwise how will I ever know anything? And if there's nothing there, then we'll go home.' He started walking again. Wilf could only follow.

They edged around the lake. The branches opened to admit them. The box or shed or whatever it should be called – chapel occurred to Paul, and so did crypt – was where she promised it would be. Paul recognised it: it was any and every building in the world, his own included. A dark place to crawl into. It was wrong to die in the open air; you needed a door to close behind you. After which, perhaps, another door opened.

A circle had been cleared around the crouched structure. Paul stepped into the circle. Wilf hung back among the bushes. This, he decided, was his limit. Paul did not notice. He reached for the door.

It was then that Clem, quickly and softly covering space, started into life. He had been standing on the other side of the circle; had been standing there for a long time, waiting as the dark rose around him. His knife was in one hand. With the other he grabbed the back of Paul's neck and thrust him into the little cell. Paul, his arms thrashing and his legs skidding, banged his head and plunged into a feather bed of blackness.

Clem fell too. He crumpled in the door, knocked over by a stroke of the stick which Wilf brought down on his head. The stick bit through flesh and cracked on bone. Wilf struck again before Clem reached the ground. The strength he had, which changed the stick from a wand to a club, was not his own. He wielded it with an unholy joy, yelling. The cry came from a gash of pain in his throat. He knew the pain: it went with tears. He was not so much bludgeoning Clem into unconsciousness as blotting out his own consciousness of fear and loss, his anger at having been born.

Clem sprawled face down. Wilf concentrated on the back of his neck, as you did with rabbits. After a while, Clem's head lolled sideways. Wilf stopped. Had the stick been holding him up? Now that there was nothing to support him, his legs gave way.

As he slumped, he noticed the silence. Time agonisingly held its breath. He missed the noise he had made, and the singing of the stick through the air. The trees stood still, like Clem when he was pretending to be one of them. Then Wilf heard a moan. He raised the stick again. But it was Paul, who had knocked himself out when he tumbled through the low door.

Numb, Wilf looked at the figure stretched out beneath him. How had the change happened? You could kill someone and still discover nothing about death. He searched for clues. Clem's face was beaten into the dust, his arms thrown wide. He might have been a swimmer struggling in the wrong element, who found water thickening into dirt. But his fingers, bunched up, seemed to be clawing the ground, as if he had been digging a refuge for himself. The knife had done its best to help, stabbing and gouging the soil.

Then there was the wound, which should have shown Wilf what a head contained. Wounds were like keyholes, letting you glimpse the interior. Here there was just the blood like a dried-up lake, the torn flesh beneath it, and after that the impenetrable bone. Did the head still hold its secrets? Was there no way for the thoughts to get out? Wilf remembered the ants decamping with their eggs.

Paul had climbed back to his feet, back into life. He stood in the door. He had his own drying lake of blood, entangling his hair and bruising his forehead.

'Wilf,' he said, 'you saved me.'

Oh, thought Wilf, did I? It was not what he meant to do at all.

16

THE NEXT DAY, Mona had visitors again, who persecuted her with questions. Their questions were the wrong ones. She laughed at them at first. That irritated the visitors, so she endeavoured – when they went through the quiz again – to see it their way. They were trying, they said, to ascertain who he was. 'I'm not interested in that,' she said. 'He was no one to me.'

'But you did see his face?'

'He didn't have much of a face, not to speak of, not at that stage.'

'But you said you didn't open the bag.'

'I don't mean then. I mean that night. I didn't see features, any more than when you look at the sun. His face was all twisted. It could have been inside out. Why don't you ask him who he is? He was here again yesterday.'

'That was someone else.'

'How can you tell?'

'Because he's still alive.'

Mona merely sniffed.

'What about the other man, the one who killed him?'

'Are you sure there were two of them?'

'You said you overheard them talking.'

'He could have been talking to himself.'

'A man can't cut his own head off.'

'But the other one wasn't to blame. He was only doing what the first one asked. He even said please. I heard that.'

'Yes, yes, so you said. Had you ever seen the other one before?'

'He threw a stone at me. I knew he wouldn't get away with that. I told him he was seen. I'm a Witness.'

'We know that'.

'How could you? Who told you?'

229

'You just are. Now what did the man who threw the stone look like?'

'The same as the other one. His face was twisted too, when he came at me. Does it matter, if they're both dead?'

'We're only trying to work out what happened.'

'You'll never know.'

'Why not?'

'Because you haven't understood anything so far.'

They began to commiserate with her. Looking around the carcase of the house, they asked whether she thought that this was the right place for her to live.

'I wouldn't worry,' she said. 'I won't be here for long.'

After that they carted away her garden of refuse. It took an entire day. She protested, but they had already ploughed up the bed of the lake to recover the body, and they decided to clear the hillocks of disintegrated matter round its margin at the same time. It was infested, they told her. It was hallowed, she told them. One of them took her by the elbow and propelled her inside. In the evening she looked out on a world wiped clean, good as new, but useless to her since its mystic signals and enigmatic meanings had been shovelled into containers and carried off. All she had left were her chimneys with their timed, inexhaustible spasms of fire.

The next day, it seemed that the end had begun. She stood on her terrace and studied the weather. The bare trees were throwing a fit. Their upper branches thrashed in circuits. Since the cause of the agitation was invisible, it looked as if the trees were committing suicide. Gravity provides everything with a hook connecting it to the earth, but today all the links were breaking. Sheets of paper and the number plates of cars, overlooked in the bushes when they abolished her garden, aimed themselves at Mona. Don't blame me, she cried into the gale. A slate from the roof crashed at her feet. Down in the valley, a cart did a somersault in the middle of a field. Her hair flew around her head, as if the wind wanted to pluck it out.

Mona was elated. So it was not just the fire. Another element had lost its temper.

During the afternoon, the wind retired to its cave, to the

corner of the sky where it stored its force. White light smote the apartment towers. The glare was acid in Mona's eyes. In the city, there must have been rain. Above the northern suburbs half a rainbow shuddered, not quite managing to write out the covenant before the sky changed its mind again. Then clouds, massed and thick like an avalanche of boulders, rolled across towards her.

The next element to misbehave was water. As night fell, the rain began. Will this be it? thought Mona.

She intended to go on her usual expedition, to check that the wind had not blown out the flames or the water quenched them, but the rain forced her back. It surrounded her ramshackle house with four new impregnable walls. Inside, it seeped through from the floor above and staked her out in bed, muddying the print in her stacks of papers. She lay there looking up at the infirm ceiling and felt something stab her between the eyes, then on the forehead. Having jabbed her skin, the drops coursed down her cheeks like mocking, counterfeit tears. It was the wrong emotion; this was not the way it was meant to happen. She spent the rest of the night in a watertight cupboard under the stairs.

In the morning, the world had been simplified to a cloud of grey moisture. She stumbled out into it, but the vague, veiling cloud baffled her. There was no way of piercing it. With every step it became harder to repossess her feet. The mud slurped around and over them. Had she wandered into the lake? When she tried to find the house again, it too had been consumed by the cloud. Then she saw that she was actually inside. Behind a layer of mist she bumped into the partition between two of her rooms. The cloud had moved indoors. She wrung out her soaking hair and sat down inside the capsule of vapour.

By the afternoon, a sun which she did not recognise – sickly, jaundiced – mopped up the mist. The cliffs on either side of the valley sprouted waterfalls. The creek overflowed. An embankment drunkenly collapsed onto the road: earth too had loosened its grip. Soon the downpour began again.

That night the rain discovered her hiding place under the staircase. Drops needled her through the crevices. The totems and trinkets around her bed circulated in puddles. She would have left the house, even at night, but the rain clamped gates of steel around it. She listened to it thud onto the ground and grumble as it searched for somewhere to run away.

At first she was merely downcast, sure it would rain itself out, like a child histrionically sobbing until it can produce no more tears. Then, when it did not relent for twenty-four hours, she began to panic. It invaded the food donated to her by the last set of visitors. The bread was sodden. Fungus grew on the cheese. The air was too dense to breathe. When she walked, her shoes squeezed trickles through the toes.

She hated the rain. It was the wrong ending: instead of purgative fire, this deluge in which things became clogged, bloated, heavier than they had any right to be. Fire reduced bodies, refined them. In water they swelled. She knew the place where the creek dived underground on its way to the river. She could imagine it choked, sending a backlog of branches, bubbling scum and stiff floating animals to rise up the valley. There was a limit to what the river could drink.

Her predictions were going wrong. Had she made one mistake, or had every action been an error? She struggled, as the house sprang new leaks, to get events in the proper order and decide when and how she provoked this liquefying of the sky.

Nothing, she was sure, was accidental. But causes were difficult to construe. Anything at all could be said to cause everything else. You could draw so many criss-crossing lines that your life would be unreadable beneath the scrawled, scratched fretwork of possible connections.

Perhaps she made it happen with a string of words she did not know she knew until she heard herself uttering them: the names she called the man who threw the stone at her. It was her he first aimed the knife at. She goaded him into a rage which then he had to pass along. He could only relieve himself by hurting someone else. So the man had been selected to take her place. Perhaps she could have undone it when the two of them appeared outside the house. Were they looking for her then? She recalled the cry the first man gave when the second asked her to save him. Since it was too dark to see faces, it could have been the first one who was pleading with her. If she had stepped forward then, he might have dropped his knife, grateful she had woken him from this shared dream. She could have saved both of them, and stopped the rain before it started. She was given another chance with the head; she failed then too. Why did she assume it was hers, a gift to her? It belonged to whoever had once worn it; he lost it because of her, and it was stolen from her to remind her of that.

Then she sent the old man off to die. He no doubt promptly did as he was told. But he too could have been lied to, consoled, and – for the time being – saved.

She also thought she was doing a favour to the next one who came, sending him off on the same path he had trodden before, though this time he was doing it voluntarily: through the trees and into the stone box where he would hear the echoes of that earlier dialogue, or of his conversation with himself, damply adhering to the walls. At least this time – if she understood what the men who asked her the questions had said – it turned out differently. But, on second thoughts, not really. You could not be saved from the sequence of repetitions. You just found a replacement for yourself. The first man might have intended the knife for her, though he killed someone else with it. He was killed in his turn, but the second man handed over the job to a substitute: the boy.

All my fault, she thought. She had given the wrong answers to those questions the other day. It was me, she should have said. 'I'm sorry,' she said now, out loud – but to whom, and for exactly what? The rain, in any case, paid no attention to her.

It continued throughout a soggy, submarine morning. The sky sagged under the weight of water. Up here she was safe, she thought, from the flooding of the creek, but the lowering clouds might drown her. Her garden was a delta of streams, competing with each other to gnaw away the world. 'Make it stop', she said. Then, correcting herself, she said 'Please stop', as you might address a pain. It continued.

As it continued, she began to suspect that she was wrong about everything. She had been counting backwards, and had no more numbers left. On the day she arrived at nought, she held her breath and awaited nullity. But her lungs would not give up their old habit. Her body, along with the rest of the obstinate world, insisted on living. Should she start counting again, from a higher number this time? There was no point, she decided. The days merged in the rain; they were no different from each other, or from the nights. How could she keep track?

And without sunsets, there were no conclusions. Time was as sloppy and as stupidly continuous as water. The creek poured into the river, the river into the sea, the sea was sucked up into the sky and the sky collapsed again into rain. Even the sun, when she had been able to see it, only teased her by pretending to set while the earth rolled over in its sleep. Ends did not come when called. Even when they did come, like the deaths in her garden or that which the old man trudged off to meet, they were not a terminus, merely a transference. Others continued on your behalf or you continued inside them; and time continued to pour down on Mona in the form of rain.

Now she saw why the men who asked the questions had agreed so readily when she said she was a Witness. To them, she was only a witness: a by-stander, a passer-by. She might have seen things but she was not a seer, and the things she saw would have happened whether she had been in the vicinity observing them or not. She was not a participant in the story. When they thanked her, they said they would not need to trouble her again. Worse than that, there was really no story, only a succession of accidents, as unpredictable as weather. It was the same with the causes, despite her attempt to draw straight lines between her own motives and the movements of other people. There was no shortage of causes. Every explosion of burning gas qualified as a cause. But there were never any effects.

Then, too late in the day for her to claim any credit, the rain stopped. It was a while before she noticed: the sound went on pounding in her head, like the wet shoes your feet still feel long after you take them off.

There was even a sunset. She saw it at second hand, in the windows across the valley, while she bailed out the house. Her mattress was soaked. She threw away the mildewed food. But the dusk tricked her, sneaking things out of sight. By now the fires sparking on the windows had gone out, replaced by the dull soft domestic glow of electricity inside.

Dusk was a dubious time, an interval of doubts. She paced about in the fading house and thought, I might have been wrong about being wrong. It could mean something; it must. She decided to make a last trip to the chimneys.

She found that she needed to map the valley again. The rain had rearranged it. A path down from her ledge was now a cascade, a field she was used to traversing had sunk beneath the water. Everywhere she slithered in mud. That's a sign, she thought: a good one. Water like fire could melt things down, make the world raw and runny again.

She began to enjoy the difficulties of the trip, since her perseverance would surely earn her a reward. Hitching her skirt up, she negotiated the mud on tiptoes, as if she were dancing. Soon she began to see clues, short cuts obligingly marked out for her. An uprooted tree had scattered the loose stones of a wall down the slope to make a ladder for her. It lowered her into another swamp, but she splashed off in a direction which she was sure must be the right one. She smiled when she came out by the fountain. The road was submerged, the tunnel throttled. The creek, now a torrent, roared. But the pipe piercing the animal's lips dispensed the same dribble as always. That also signified something. The chimneys like the copper pipe were a vent for pressures beneath; the fires concocted between grating rocks would be more than equal to the blubbering sky.

How could she go forward from here? Usually she followed the creek, but the creek tonight had no bank. She wandered about uncertainly, then reached a thorny fence of bushes and trees. A dead end? No, it would not dare to be. She pushed her way through and strode up another slope.

I told you so, she admonished herself. She was standing on the trestles of the railway line. All she had to do now was follow it to where, skirting the gas works, it ran out. She marched forward triumphantly: a way had been cleared for her. She smartened her pace, and put the planks behind her two at a time.

As she bounced along, the chimneys lifted into view above the trees, breathing blue and orange flowers. She looked down across the silver city of coils, tubes and cauldrons. Each burst of fire gathered within her and gushed to her mouth, searing her throat. When the next spasm came, she would start counting.

Then there was a crash above her head, a hammer blow which dinned from one side of the sky to the other: thunder. The flames showed the metallic underside of clouds. Rain slapped her, as stingingly as an open hand striking her cheek. In a moment she was drenched. Her clothes hung from her leadenly. She could not hear herself howl.

They've got to take me in, she thought. Even though I was wrong again. I've come this far, I'll never get back to the house, I've given up everything.

She reeled down from the railway line, tripped by vines. A wire fence knocked her backwards. She tried to tear apart its links; she jangled it with both her hands; battered it with her head. Behind it, the silver apparatus seethed. If she followed the fence, there must be an opening. She clung to it as she went. It held her up, sustained her while the rain flung itself in her face and her feet skidded through mud. Still gripping it, her eyes screwed closed to keep out the rain, she arrived in a circle of white light. The lamps, glaring at her from high on poles, forced her eyes open. The fence had run out. Here was the gate, with the blue fires erupting ahead. She picked up her soggy hems and walked in.

Again there was an obstacle, which her dazzled eyes overlooked: an elongated arm with a red sign ordering her to stop. She walked straight into the barrier. Its blow threw her off balance, and she fell into slippery mud. 'Oh God,' she groaned. It was less of an appeal than a curse.

Then her life was taken out of her control, confiscated. It was perhaps what she was waiting for. A pair of hands inserted themselves beneath her arms and pulled her into somewhere dry and coldly, accusingly bright.

'Where,' she was asked, 'do you think you're going?'

'In,' she said. 'Can't I?'

'No,' said the guard in whose sentry box she was sitting. 'It's closed. You don't have business in there.'

She wanted to explain the business she had, but energy had drained from her like that dripping water. Besides, he surely knew, and was choosing not to admit her. She sat quietly until she had summoned strength for a plea.

'Listen,' she said to him. 'You've got to help me. Save me.'

He was already dialling the number from which help and salvation would be despatched. 'Don't you worry,' he said. 'They'll look after you.'

Is this the end? she wondered. She didn't like to ask it out loud, for fear of seeming dissatisfied. But then she realised that it could not be the end. She was still aware, experiencing, forced to witness things. Her sopping clothes, inside which she shuddered. Her noisy teeth. The lacerating light in the ceiling. The mug of tea he – of all things! – offered her.

She decided to give it a few more minutes. There was a clock on the wall for her to time it by. Out the windows she could see, through the rain, the bluster of the chimneys expelling sulphur. He smiled at her: encouragingly, she thought.

Finally she had to ask. 'Why didn't it end?' she said. Her teeth were chattering, and she had to repeat it.

Even so, he did not understand. She sounded annoyed, though only with herself. He smiled again, this time guardedly. He was a guard after all.

Why didn't it end? It never does, he might have told her. Only in stories.

17

Afterwards —after the killing of Clem, after the stories in the papers, after allowing an interval in which Wilf's mother could claim him, after the flood – they compared notes, like marital partners who agree to whisper in one another's ears the name of the other person each had been concentrating on while the lights were out. They had both been to the valley, but separately. They saw it differently; it meant different things to them. Shy at first, they settled on a procedure. They would take it stage by stage.

'So,' said Kate, 'you start.'

'Why me?' said Paul.

'You were the one it happened to.'

'As if nothing happened to you! Anyway, you went in before me. And as we used to say, "Ladies first".' He stretched out his hand, as if opening a door for her and waiting for her to walk through. 'You can start at the tunnel,' he said.

She was grateful that he allowed her to leave out the dog which blocked her way in the lane, and the woman who jeered at her quest. It meant that she was still keeping secrets. But what else is a mind for?

He gave her a push. 'Go on,' he said. 'In you go.'

Sitting at the round table beneath the shaded lamp, she walked into the tunnel.

'Well?'

She shrugged. 'No one jumped out at me, if that's what you mean. Not then anyway.'

'But what was it like?'

'Don't you know?'

'No, I drove through.'

'Trust you! It's quite short, but it closes around you –

implodes. There's no space because there's no light to measure it by. And time stops too. It's hard to convince yourself that you're still alive, that there's still a world behind you or up in front.'

'I know.' It was the way he felt during those night flights. Above and below ground, the sensation of not being was the same. Then he remembered the landslip during the days of flooding. There were no more short cuts through the valley. 'But we don't need to worry about that any more. The tunnel has been put out of business.'

She looked sceptical. Did he really believe it? It was all bound to happen again, at least once. This had only been a rehearsal. She should have known better than to become so intrigued by Persephone. A myth was a story which compulsively went on telling itself, and came out differently every time. All roads led through the tunnel.

'What's next? That water spout. Did you tell Wilf you'd been there before?'

'No. He asked me if I knew it, and I must have pretended to, to make it easier for him. It's one of the rules of the game, isn't it? When someone tells you a story, they need your help. You have to show you believe in it, that gives whoever is telling the story the courage to go on.' Here she manoeuvred around another omission: her disbelief, which made her walk away from him in the park. She had told Paul that Wilf ran away from her. This, she said, gave her grounds for dismissing the story until she saw the paragraph in the paper. 'Anyway, I was right. I hadn't been there before, but I had seen it.'

'How?' He was expecting her to introduce a dream into evidence.

'You mean where: in the museum, of course. Don't you remember the faun? The valley and the museum aren't all that different. We go there to see the past; fauns go there when people stop believing in them, to save themselves from becoming extinct.'

'I hated it. I mean it frightened me. That cynical leering. And it was there that I found out about everything: that you'd been there, then about the man, whoever he was, and all the time with that animal drooling. If it's an endangered species, so much the better. I never saw Clem. He came from behind, and afterwards he was lying face down. But that was the face I gave him.'

'He wasn't like the faun at all.'

'How do you know?'

She had tripped over some more omissions. She had not told him about her two glimpses of Clem. After all, she could not be sure about the first, and the second time she did not know it was him. Now she wished that she had looked at him for longer, and that Paul had seen him just once. As it was, he had a blank face with features they each filled in differently; and having created him, how could they rid themselves of him?

'I mean what you say about why he did it. Animals kill to eat. He wasn't hungry. It's as if he was trying to show that he could do it, that it could be done, that he could get away with it.'

'But he didn't.'

'I was thinking about the time before. With you it wasn't the same thing.'

'Wasn't it? Only because he didn't finish.'

'Stand back from it a bit. Doesn't it puzzle you? The bravado of dumping the body – both parts of it – just a few yards from where it happened. It seems so disinterested, doing something obscene on principle. Not for profit, maybe not even for pleasure. And something that obscene is a way of going past the bounds, of extending the limits. It must have been terrifying.'

'It was.'

'No. I mean for Clem: I mean doing it.'

'I know we said we'd tell the truth, but if your truth is that you admire him . . .'

'Ever since men have started crawling on the earth, they've been trying to offend God. The first skyscraper was a blasphemy. But as time goes on, God gets harder to shock. There's always a need for new outrages. You read about them every week; this one isn't unique. Why would a boy of sixteen rape a woman of eighty? Remember when that happened, in those towers on the other side of the valley? Do you think he did it because he fancied her?'

'That's not what we're supposed to be discussing. You've jumped ahead. It's not time for him to try to kill me yet. We're still at the fountain. Then what?'

'I went up the hill. It was easy to find the way, because he mentioned all the places when he first told me the story. Children are so circumstantial. It must be a way of making believe you belong. For me, the next place was the worst.'

He was watching her as intently as Clem, in the instant before she ran away. But after what she had already said, she could not tell him this. She forced Clem back into the cave, and waited until the shadows absorbed him.

'It was that cave, behind where the dogs used to be.'

'I didn't notice it. I must have been beyond caring by then. What happened?'

'Nothing. It was just the place itself. It upset me more than the tunnel, even though I didn't go in. The sight of that opening, and not knowing what it led to. There might have been a whole system of caves with tunnels in between, a whole other world past the overhang of rock and round the corner.'

'What was so bad? Why did you say it was the worst?'

'Because I wanted to go in. Why should I want to lose myself like that? It's the imagination that leads us astray. If we do what it suggests, we destroy ourselves. That's what it's hoping for.'

He remembered her painting of Wilf. She did not know he had seen it; he did not know what she had done with it. She might have destroyed it, but she could not destroy the fact that she had painted it. A thought was the real betrayal. The action or the image were not necessary. To conceive it was to accomplish it; that was incriminating enough.

'You don't need to worry,' he said. 'Not about the cave. All you would have found was stolen television sets. And they've concreted over the entrance. Just like I wanted to do with the whole valley.'

'Wanted to? You no longer do?'

'Not after seeing it. And it would take more than concrete! You're not sorry, are you?'

'I think I am.'

She fell silent. The silence seemed dangerous to him, as if she were slipping back regretfully into the hollow filled with flickering, delusive half-light. If she did not hurry, she would be trapped behind the wall of concrete. He pulled her back.

'On you go,' he said. 'What's next?'

'Wilf is. He was at the top of the hill.'

'Did he take you back to the hut where they lived?'

'I asked him to. I felt ashamed of my curiosity, I tried not to look around. It was all so sad and shoddy, and so important to him. He wouldn't let me sit in the rocking chair. I've worried about it a lot since then. Why should I dream about other lives when I ought to be grateful for my own? Anything else is scary. But who decides which life you get? Ours with everything, or theirs with nothing at all? Justice doesn't come into it.'

'You should have seen it when I did. The moment his grandfather was dead, that other family moved in. It was a good deal for them: the place came furnished, and the rocking chair wasn't reserved any longer. You say we have it all and they have nothing, but I don't see such a difference. Chairs and tables and all those gadgets you showed Wilf how to use — we only have them on loan, and there's always someone waiting to snatch them away. So much for architecture, and all my immortal monuments.'

Now it was he who fell silent. She came to his rescue, urging him ahead.

'So we've done their house. Where to now?'

'We go home.'

'But it's not finished.'

'Your part of it is, and I don't want to go through the rest of my part again. Once is enough.'

'You've already been through it more times than that. This time I'll go through it with you.'

'You don't want to help. You're just curious.'

'Then you help me. If I see the place, perhaps I'll be able to stop imagining it.'

'I doubt that. I bet you'll want to bring your sketching pad. Won't you?'

She smiled, and reached across the table to pull his hand into the circle of lamp light.

'Come on. Can we adjourn?'

'All right. To the scene of the crime.'

They had to go – when they went a few days later, after Kate reminded Paul that it was a promise – by the back way. The tunnel was blocked, and the city was in no hurry to unblock it; besides, the road beyond it had been partly washed away. They crept up on the valley from behind.

They drove to the western suburbs, left the car in a side street, and walked through the towers of cracking concrete until the fields began. Wilf, who was with them, did not know the track, but they found it easily: Paul unfolded an aerial survey map. It had always been in a drawer of his desk; it was there when he made his own cunningly inaccurate chart and got Wilf to draw that diagram of the valley as a small world of sacred sites, skulking monsters and exploding suns. Kate of course had her sketch book. Wilf did not have his stick, even though it had been returned to him wrapped in plastic, tagged with his name and the number which the police assigned to the episode. He had not unwrapped it.

When they reached the house, Paul called out for the old woman. He wanted to show her to Kate, who had not believed his description of the askew eye and the tangled hair. He also wanted to show himself to her, to make her accept that he was not the revenant she had declared him to be.

They walked between the rooms, picking their way through her cordon of ineffectual charms. They even climbed the stairs, avoiding collapsed treads. The floor above was white with the droppings of birds. Kate tried not to breathe. The air was a soup of dust and sweet decay. She held her mouth shut, her nostrils clamped against it, and thought about the embrace of the elderly relative: the suction of dry lips.

When they were outside again, she sat on the doorstep, in the spot where Mona stood the time before. She said, 'Are you sure there was such a person?'

'Ask Wilf if you don't believe me. He knew her all along.' But Wilf had wandered off on his own. Paul beckoned her to get up. 'Don't you want to see the rest?'

'I don't know. I feel sick. Will the rest of it smell as bad?'

'I can't promise you anything.'

'I thought it would be so different. Remember that painting I did of the valley, with the Breughel figures dancing? I thought it would be the world before we ruined it. Now it seems we don't need to ruin the world. It falls part on its own. Just look.' She glanced up at the decomposing house. 'Did you mean it when you said you'd given up your plan for all this?'

'Yes. I don't see the point. I could bury it under concrete, but it would still be there — I mean here. I wouldn't have eliminated it. I'd only be denying it.'

'There's something else . . .'

She did not go on. It was a signal that she needed encouragement, the assurance of sympathy.

'You can tell me,' he said.

'Then you mustn't laugh. Or get angry either. It's about what I used to think the place meant, why it was always pulling me in. I had an idea for a painting. Persephone with Hades, the forbidden fruit smeared all over her mouth. I went out looking for faces, but the one I found was Wilf's. It didn't seem the right one at the time, it belonged in another painting. He had his story and I had mine. I tried to keep them separate. What I wanted to show was a girl in this lair of pleasure under the earth. What he wanted to tell me about was how violent and terrifying and murderous it was: how grateful we ought to be that we're only on the edge of it, or the surface. I had to struggle to keep the stories apart. I thought I'd succeeded, but when I started painting I couldn't help myself. It was his face I painted. And I felt so ashamed, as if I'd been the Hades who spirited him away.'

'You did the painting?'

'No, not really. Well, I destroyed it. But as you said, that's only a denial. Just imagining it all was bad enough. And once I'd imagined it, of course it happened. In a way, it already had. I don't mean the painting. I mean the way I walked into the painting, and then – without knowing anything about it – you followed.'

'But we walked out again. One of us a bit worse for wear, I admit.'

'And now here we are inside it once more. Hadn't you noticed? Do we have to keep on doing the same things over and over, like the myths being retold?'

'How can we stop ourselves? We can't help imagining what's beyond the border. What dying is like, what it will be like when we're dead, whether we have to go on repeating it until we get it right. . . . That's what the myths are about. Up you get. There's something more for you to see.'

'I don't want to see anything more.'

'I want it though. You said you'd go through it with me. Come along.'

She did as he demanded. She only asked 'Where?'

'This way.' He led her into the trees.

'What about Wilf?'

'He'll be all right. He won't want to see this.'

'To see what?'

'This. This is where it happened.'

They were in front of the stone shed. It was padlocked now: an absurd precaution, since whatever could it contain except darkness? But Paul had his hands on the padlock and was shaking it in fury and frustration.

'What are you doing? Leave it alone!'

'I didn't see what was inside it before. I was in there, but I knocked my head and I couldn't see anything. Now how will I ever know?'

He turned back to her imploringly.

'Leave it,' she said again.

She said it softly, which was what made him realise how frightened she was and how irrationally he was behaving. He took his hands away from the door. 'I'm sorry,' he said.

As they were walking back through the trees, he said, 'I seem to remember there's a myth about this too. Not about what happened to me, or what didn't happen. About the other man, whoever he was. About the head. It's to do with Orpheus, long after he got back from the underworld. The Dionysian women set upon him and tore him to pieces. They pulled his head off. But that wasn't the end of him. The head floated down the river all on its own, and it was singing.'

'The head was singing?'

'I didn't make the story up, I'm only retelling it.'

'Singing *what?*'

'Don't ask me,' he said, almost indignantly. 'I mean I don't remember.'

Out of the trees, he looked around. 'Wait a minute. This is all different.' He was looking at a damp, flattened waste. But if he closed his eyes he could see himself walking through a ruined city of pulped paper and broken glass. When he opened his eyes he saw only the cleared earth, ready to support – for a while – another civilisation. Something else had happened since the time before. There was a lake, filled by the recent rain. 'Where did that come from?' he asked.

'It must have been here.'

'I'm sure it was a rubbish dump. I had no idea there was a lake underneath. And look at the shape of it. Who would lay out something like that and leave it so messy? You see, the margin is just a doodle. And what are those two clumps of rock sticking up from the water?'

They walked around the paved rim. It made no more sense than a piece from a jigsaw puzzle, cut out at random in order to confuse. Why all the inlets and indentations, the swollen curves and finicky narrows? It was a labyrinth in the open air. They passed two sets of crumbled steps, one on either side. You must have once been able to row a boat to the outcrops of rock, though when you got there, where had you arrived? Paul, who was walking in front of Kate, stopped. 'We've been all the way round, I'm positive we passed this bit before.' He stepped back from the margin and frowned at the blob of insignificant water.

Kate, however, went on walking. He watched her pace out another trip around the rim. When she got back to where he stood, he asked what she was doing.

'Wait over there,' she said. 'I have an idea.'

He returned to the house and sat on the doorstep. The birds were gathering on the roof with angry flurries of wings; in the abandoned rooms, wind scratched at a strip of paper on the wall or plucked a shawl which Mona had left behind, inflating it for a moment as if it were wrapped around a body made of air. Once or twice he looked over his shoulder when the timbers groaned.

In the distance Kate trod in the same warped, pointless circle. On every circuit she vanished behind the trees which concealed one end of the lake. He watched for her to reappear and found he was holding his breath if she took longer than she should have. And the more anxiously he watched, the less he trusted what his eyes were claiming to see. When the figure walked out from behind the trees and continued around the lake, he thought, How do I know it's her? Am I only seeing it because I want to? The light faded between them; the lake receded. The figure when it reappeared was out of focus. He thought she waved to him, but without turning back, a farewell rather than a greeting. There was no point in going to her. The figure would dissolve into grey air or drown in the lake.

He closed his eyes and thought, When I open them again it will all be clear. He covered his face with his hands and tried not to see the images which flickered behind his eyes: Kate's face in its cocoon of hair when he came back that morning from his trip, Wilf's face looking out from the prison of the painting, Clem's face bedded in the ground and staring into the earth, the face belonging to the head and the face of the old woman who told him it was his face.

When he opened his eyes, she was standing in front of him. 'Kate,' he said.

'Who else?' She held out a page from her sketch book. 'Look, I've worked it out. I've drawn it, the same way they mapped new countries, by following the outline of the coast. Look at it.'

He gazed at the page, unseeing.

'Not like that. It's the wrong way up. Don't you get it?'

All he saw was a blot, liquid and elapsing.

She sat down beside him and led him through it with a finger. 'First look at this side. You see what all those bumps and little bays add up to? A forehead, a nose, a mouth, a chin. It's a face. A woman's profile. Then look at the other side. The same thing, only it's obviously a man. See the jaw? And those silly islands, which don't make any sense since they're so close to the edge – they're eyes. The faces are in profile, so they've got one eye each. The lake is a double portrait, a man and a woman. They probably lived here once. Of course they're back to back, not looking each other in the eye, but that doesn't matter because their heads overlap in the middle. The water is their thoughts. One head, two faces. Isn't it strange? Don't you think it's beautiful?'

His brain made an adjustment, which enabled him to see it. The same emotions and experiences merged in the pool, until they were drawn to the edge by eyes seeing the world from particular angles, profiles as unrepeatable as finger prints or signatures, noses and chins jutting out aggressively, mouths which if they spoke would utter names no one else possessed. The lake, as Kate had drawn it, was the ocean we swam in, before we clambered onto the stranded rock – an island like the eyes – which we occupied alone. Did she also know the rest of it? That a third head, joined to nothing, had been thrown away there among other refuse? That a body it could be matched with had been dredged up from a lake which was no more than mud, ooze, waste?

He gave her back the paper, kissed her cheek, and rested his head for a moment on her shoulder, letting her hair deliciously tickle him.

Then he stood up, separating himself from her. 'It's a beautiful idea,' he said. 'You really are kind. I know you're trying to cheer me up, I appreciate that, but it's too good to be true. Thanks all the same. You have an amazing imagination. A pity, I can't believe it. And now that's it, for this time at least. We ought to go home. Whatever has happened to Wilf? Wilf,' he called, 'Wilf!'

The roof of black wings which had settled on the house flew apart at the noise, and flapped through the air until it was safe to land: until the bits and pieces which made up the world could be slotted together again.

Wilf was on the terrace, on the other side of the house, looking over the valley. The view was different from the one he was used to, on the wall at the end of his grandfather's vegetable patch. Here he was higher up, detached. He could see the same things as always — a motor scooter on an errand, a rowdy gang of unknown children in the yard where Horry lived — but the sounds they made did not reach him. It was as estranging as the view from the apartment, where his former world resembled a diorama in one of the museums Kate had taken him to. This muted, glassed-over valley contained no one he knew. People crossed it, and left no more of a mark on it than a bird whose shadow travels across the ground.

The wall of windows on the opposite cliff began to smoulder. Of course he was beyond expecting that the towers would catch fire, any more than the chimneys of the gas works would singe the sky. He understood how everything worked, what all the switches in the apartment meant, how they were causes reliably producing the same effects. There was less to marvel at, and supposedly less to be afraid of.

In this new life, he would have no need for the stick, which is why — when it was returned to him — he pushed it out of sight under his bed. It was not so much that he had outgrown it, he had lost faith in it. After battering Clem with it, he saw that it could not be relied on. No one understood what the incident was about. Paul regarded Wilf as his saviour, though that was not what Wilf intended to be. He wanted to save himself, not Paul; and he wanted to save himself not from Clem's knife but from his own dreams. The stick had only battered the consciousness out of Clem. It had no power over what was inside Wilf's head. Clem and the others left no remains behind them in the valley. But when Wilf turned all the switches off and shut his eyes, they promptly came alive again. He now also understood about the animal at the fountain: it both was and was not true.

As he gazed across the gulf of his brief past at the wall where his future began, he felt an itch on his hand. Ants had decided that he was a fixture in the landscape. They were laying a road over his body. He brushed them off. They altered their ideas, re-grouped, and set out on a detour around him. He remembered toppling their dusty city, and watching the evacuation of their eggs. All you could be sure of carrying with you – all you needed – was what you stored inside your head. You unpacked your world from there and crammed it in again to be ready for the next move.

The time would come, though he did not know that yet, when it was too heavy a load to lift, when you could not balance the memories of your stooping shoulders. Then what? It would tumble off. Perhaps it would shatter when it hit the ground. Perhaps it would roll away and wait to be picked up by someone else. But a life lasted a long while. There were many removals, many repetitions to go through. His small load was still not heavy enough.

He heard them calling his name. Hands on his shoulders claimed him.

There was a home, they said, to go to. For them, apparently, it was over. For them, he was where it ended.

18

THEY FOUND OUT who the man was, or whose his teeth had been. Paul, as it happened, had met him once at a party; at least he had seen him across the room. It was before his name became a patent, a byword. Kate said nothing when Paul told her about the party. He could easily have asked her to go home with him, she thought. She could easily have gone.

And what were the consequences? A skyscraper collapsed. Or rather a few of its floors emptied. His business depended on the wizardry in his head and the allure of his name, which he no longer possessed. Soon enough, the floors were rented to someone else. A friend of Paul's redesigned them, to erase their history.

Knowing who he was did not help me much. He could have been anyone. It was just that in the middle of his journey he strayed, as everyone does, into a dark wood.

Early on, I thought of ringing to offer the police an identification. It's my head, I intended to say. You'll see: it fits. I ought to ask for it back. They returned Wilf's stick, after all. But actually I always wanted to lose it.

Yet why should I have pretended to be the victim? What I fancied being, as my dreams began to second-guess the facts, was the executioner. Who put the stick into Wilf's hand, and lent him the force to deal the blow? Demolishing the ant-hill took only a tap. To finish off Clem required more strength than the boy would have on his own. Why eliminate Clem anyway, except as a guilty atonement for having thought of him in the first place?

I know why I did not make the foolish phone call. Who would

want their head back, if it meant accounting for what is inside it?

I made sure I kept the cutting from the newspaper. I did not rip it out in haste like Kate, and I filed it in an envelope, the way parents keep the first lock of a child's hair. It came from the same paper Paul read, though I bought the tabloids later in quest of details. I even filched a day-old copy from a waste basket, in case it had anything the others missed, or scrupled to make up.

It was the idea of the bodiless head which appealed to me. The headless body interested me less (and by the time it was recovered from the lake the newspapers had tired of the story, since a war had fortuitously broken out somewhere). But the head with no owner, up for grabs, seemed a logical notion.

The body, of course, is aghast at the thought. The head is our headquarters, our head office, the boss of the corporation beneath: the sole, proud evidence of individuality. Yet why should heads, like the receivers they are, not be plugged into other bodies? A mind is a room we rent ready furnished, and our predecessors leave teasing traces of themselves. A stain on the curtain; a burn in the woodwork; the bright empty oblong on the wallpaper, hidden from the sun, where a picture once hung – but a picture of what? Forgotten in the backs of cupboards, there are memories that cannot possibly belong to us.

Why do we spend so much time imagining ourselves to be someone else? Because we are or were or will be. Consciousness is not private property. A head, like Athol's cars or Ern's hut, can have serial owners or occupiers.

Even so, I am still waiting for the end. Having sent all those others to explore the valley on my behalf, I suppose I should go and see it for myself. Though if I wait for long enough, the valley will come to me. One of these days. All in good time.